"We can't be lovers, Kade!"

"We can be anything [...] replied. "But for now, [...] try to be friends first, figure out how we're going to be parents together without complicating it with sex?"

He confused and bedazzled her, Brodie admitted. She couldn't keep up with him. She felt like she was being maneuvered into a corner, pushed there by the force of his will. "I don't know! I need to think."

Kade smiled, stepped back and placed his hands into the pockets of his khaki shorts. "You can think all you want, Brodie, but it isn't going to change a damn thing. I'm going to be around whether you like it or not." He ducked his head and dropped a kiss on her temple.

"You might as well get used to it," he murmured into her ear.

* * *

Pregnant by the Maverick Millionaire
is part of the series
From Mavericks to Married—
Three superfine hockey players

9112000029 1253

PREGNANT BY THE MAVERICK MILLIONAIRE

BY
JOSS WOOD

MILLS & BOON

First Published in Great Britain 2016
By Mills & Boon, an imprint of HarperCollins*Publishers*
1 London Bridge Street, London, SE1 9GF

© 2016 Joss Wood

ISBN: 978-0-263-91873-1

51-0816

Our policy is to use papers that are natural, renewable and recyclable products and made from wood grown in sustainable forests. The logging and manufacturing processes conform to the legal environmental regulations of the country of origin.

Printed and bound in Spain
by CPI, Barcelona

Joss Wood's passion for putting black letters on a white screen is matched only by her love of books and travelling (especially to the wild places of southern Africa) and, possibly, by her hatred of ironing and making school lunches.

Joss has written over sixteen books for the Mills & Boon KISS, Mills & Boon Presents and, most recently, Mills & Boon Desire lines.

After a career in business lobbying and local economic development, Joss now writes full-time. She lives in KwaZulu-Natal, South Africa, with her husband and two teenage children, surrounded by family, friends, animals and a ridiculous amount of books.

Joss is a member of the RWA (Romance Writers of America) and ROSA (Romance Writers of South Africa).

One

Funny.

Built.

Sexy.

Smart. So, so, smart.

Courteous, hot, confident.

He was the entire package, a gorgeous combination of everything any woman would ever want or need for a flash-in-the-pan encounter. That being said, Brodie Stewart knew there were at least a billion women in the world who would slap her senseless for what she was about to do and she didn't blame them.

"Brodie? Did you hear me? I asked if you want to come upstairs," Kade whispered into her ear, his hand on her rib cage, his thumb rubbing the underside of her right breast.

She licked her lips and tasted him on her tongue, inhaled the citrus and spice of his soap-scented skin and tipped her head sideways to allow his lips to explore the cords of her neck. Man, he was good at this, Brodie thought.

She should step away, she *should stop this…*

She'd been saying the same thing for three weeks. She shouldn't have waited for Kade every early morning on the running trail, shouldn't have felt the butterflies in her stomach when he loped toward her, a six-foot-plus slab of celebrity muscle. She shouldn't have laughed at his jokes, responded to his gentle flirting. And she certainly shouldn't have accepted his offer to return to his place for a lazy cup of Saturday morning coffee/sex after their seven-mile loop around Stanley Park.

As much as she wanted to know what that cocky, mobile mouth could do, she definitely should *not* have kissed him.

She'd thought she had it all worked out, had convinced herself she could handle this, him. It wasn't like she hadn't had sex since Jay. There had been a few guys—okay, two—since the accident a decade ago. On paper, Kade was perfect. The ex-professional ice hockey player, now second in charge of the Vancouver Mavericks, was resolutely single. Proudly unavailable and, unlike most females of a certain age, Brodie had no desire to change him. In fact, one of the reasons she'd said yes to his offer for coffee was because she knew exactly what he wanted and it wasn't a happily-ever-after with her.

Okay, it had been a while and she was out of practice, but why, oh, dear Lord why, couldn't she get past her hang-ups and have a quick tumble with the gorgeous, very practiced Kade Webb?

Maybe it was because something about him resonated with her, because he was more than a pretty package. Because his kisses were deep and compelling and made her quiver with more than a quick physical connection. He reminded her of love, of intimacy, of emotional connections.

She really didn't want the reminder.

Brodie peeled herself off Kade's wide chest and dropped a quick so-sorry kiss on his chin, her lips brushing the golden stubble on his jaw. She rolled off the leather couch, stood up and walked over to the floor-to-ceiling folding doors leading to an expansive balcony. Brodie placed her hand on the cool glass. From this penthouse loft downtown he had the most amazing view of False Creek and the Granville and Burrard bridges. It was a big-bucks view and absolutely fabulous. She took it in…and gave herself time to form a response to his question.

Reluctantly Brodie turned and placed her hands behind her butt, leaning against the glass. Her heart and libido wanted to return to his embrace, trace those long, hard muscles, taste his naturally olive-shaded skin, shove her hands into his loose, surfer-boy blond hair, watch those brown eyes deepen to black as passion swept him away. But her brain was firmly in charge and it was telling her to run, as far and as fast as she could, before she found herself in a situation that was out of her control.

God, he was going to think she was a tease, that she was playing him. She wasn't, not really. She was just protecting herself.

Emotionally. Psychically. In all the ways she could.

Brodie felt his eyes on her but stared down at her sneakers, wishing she was wearing more than a tight hoodie and running tights. She knew he was waiting for an explanation for her blowing hot and cold, for kissing him senseless and then backing away. She couldn't tell him—this man she'd jogged with, who knew nothing more about her than her name and that she liked to run—that even though she was crazy horny, the idea of sex, *with him*, reminded her of intimacy and intimacy scared the skin off her.

He was supposed to be a fun time, a quick thing but, dammit, Kade Webb had stirred up emotions she thought were long dead. Of all the men in Vancouver, why him? He was such a cliché—handsome, wealthy, charming, successful. In Jane Austen's world he would've been called a rake and three hundred years later the moniker still suited him well.

Brodie sighed, wishing she'd played this differently. Everyone knew what a fitness fanatic he was, how fast he ran, and it was common knowledge that he ran most mornings in Stanley Park. She'd wanted to see if she could, in any way, keep up with him. Instead of keeping pace with him at the crack of dawn, she should've hung back and kept her distance. At first he'd been amused with her idea that she could match his long-legged stride, but she'd run track in college. She had speed and stamina on her side. When he realized he couldn't shake her he started bantering with her. Many runs and many conversations led to this morning's invitation for coffee/sex.

She'd enjoyed those random conversations so much she'd frequently forgotten she was jogging with the city's most elusive bachelor. To her, he was just a guy with a wicked sense of humor, a sharp brain and, admittedly, a very sexy body. Running alongside him had certainly not been a hardship. She'd actually taken pleasure in his appreciation of her.

So much so that she'd thought she was strong enough, brave enough, to have a casual encounter on a Saturday morning as any other confident, sophisticated, modern woman would. Yeah. Right.

"You've changed your mind, haven't you?" His voice was as rich as the sunbeams dancing across the wooden floor. Her eyes flew up to meet his and, to her relief, she didn't see any anger in his expression, just regret.

"I'm so sorry. I thought I could." Brodie lifted her hands in an I-don't-know-what-happened gesture.

"Was it me? Did I do something you didn't like?" Aw…

Brodie blushed. "No, you're fabulous. God, you must know you kiss really well and I'm sure…" Her blush deepened. "I'm sure you do everything well."

Kade pushed himself into a sitting position on the couch and placed his ankle on his knee. He leaned back and the muscles in his big arms flexed as he linked his hands behind his head, his expensive running shirt pulling tight across his broad chest. She could see the ridges of his stomach and knew the fabric covered a perfect six-pack of sexy-as-sin muscles.

Stop thinking about his body, his stomach, about those hard thighs…

"Maybe you'd feel more at ease if I tell you you're in control here. You say no—to anything, at any point—and I'll back off," Kade quietly stated.

This was a prime example of why she was attracted to him. Beyond the charm, beneath the sexy face and the scorching body, was the man she suspected the public never saw; someone who was thoughtful enough to put her at ease. Someone who could quiet her fears, who could make her consider casting off a protective layer or two.

Thoughtful Kade reminded her of Jay, which reminded her of the person she'd been before her life had been turned inside out. The open, happy, sunny girl who'd loved life with a vengeance. A young woman who had the world at her feet.

That was what scared her most about being with him. He made her remember who she'd been before she wasn't that person anymore.

Sex she could handle, but she was terrified of feeling good, contented. She couldn't deal with happiness.

Not when she knew how quickly it could be ripped away.

Brodie bit her lip and lifted her hands in the air. She saw a hint of frustration pass across Kade's face.

"Okay, then I really don't understand. You seemed to be as into me as I am into you."

Brodie scratched the back of her neck. "Yeah, I'm a mess. It's difficult to explain but trust me when I tell you it's all me and not you."

Kade nodded. "Oh, I know it's all you 'cause if I had anything to do with it then you'd be naked and panting right now."

Well, there wasn't a hell of a lot to say to that. She should just go. "This was a very bad decision on my part." Brodie moved away from the window and clasped her hands behind her back. "I'm really sorry to blow hot and cold."

Kade stood up and raked his fingers through his hair. "No worries. It's not the end of the world."

She was sure it wasn't, not for him. He'd had a variety of woman hanging off his arm since he was eighteen years old and new to the Mavericks. In sixteen years, that was a lot of women and a lot of hanging. With one call, one text message, he could have Brodie's replacement here in ten minutes.

So, there was an upside to this stupid scenario; she would never be one of "Webb's Women."

As she walked toward the door, Kade's phone buzzed and he picked it up off the coffee table. He swiped the screen with his thumb and frowned as he read the text message.

"Quinn and Mac are on their way up," he said.

Quinn Rayne and Mac McCaskill, Kade's best friends, his ex-teammates and current business partners. Yeah, she wasn't proud to admit that, like every other obsessed Mavericks fan, she read about their exploits in the papers and online. The women, although Kade wasn't quite as much a player as Quinn and Mac, the crazy stunts—mostly Quinn—the scandals... Quinn again. Actually, these days, it was mostly Quinn who gave the press grist for the mill.

Brodie glanced at her wristwatch. It was 7:36 a.m. on a Saturday morning. "So early?"

"Yeah, weird." Kade stood up and walked across the expansive loft to the kitchen area. He opened a huge fridge and pulled out two bottles of water. He waved one in her direction. "Want one?"

Brodie nodded and easily caught the bottle he lobbed in her direction. "Thanks." She gestured to the door. "So, I think I should go."

Kade nodded his agreement, saw she was struggling to crack the top and walked toward her. He took the bottle, opened the lid and handed it back to her. "There you go."

"Thanks," Brodie said and gestured to the couch. "Sorry, you know...about that."

Kade's expression was pure speculation. "Maybe one day you'll tell me why." They heard a clatter of footsteps outside the door. "My boys are here."

"I'll get out of your way."

Kade moved past her and opened the door to his friends. Brodie opened her mouth to say a quick hello, but her words died at the looks on their faces. They pushed past her to flank Kade, looking pale. Their eyes were rimmed with red.

"What's wrong?" Kade demanded, his voice harsh.

Brodie watched as they each put a hand on Kade's shoulders. Her stomach plummeted to the floor at their expressions; she recognized them instantly. They were the bearers of bad news, the harbingers of doom. They were going to tell him his life was about to do a 180.

She'd seen the same expression on her aunt's face when Poppy had told her that her parents, her best friend, Chelsea, and her old friend but new boyfriend Jay were dead, along with six other people, in a nightmarish accident. They'd been on their way to a dinner to celebrate her twentieth birthday and apparently life had thought being the lone survivor of a multivehicle crash was a suitable gift.

Why was I left behind?

"Tell. Me." Kade's snap brought her back to his hall, to the three men looking like the ground was shifting under their feet.

"Kade, Vernon had a heart attack this morning," Quinn said, his words stilted. "He didn't make it, bud."

She saw the flash of denial on Kade's face, the disbelief, and she quietly slipped out the door. Grief was an intensely personal and private emotion and the last thing he needed was a stranger in his space, in his home. Besides, she was still dealing with her own sorrow, still working through losing her own family, her closest friend and the man whom she'd thought she'd marry.

Sorry, Kade, she thought. *So, so sorry*. A long time

ago she'd had a brave heart and a free spirit and she hoped the news of his friend's death wouldn't change the core of who he was, like the same kind of news had changed her.

But life *had* changed her and she wasn't that free-spirited girl anymore. She walked back into her real life knowing she certainly wasn't the type of woman who could handle sexy, bachelor millionaires tempting her to walk on the wild side.

Six months later

Brodie typed her client's answer into her tablet, hit Enter and looked up. Dammit, she thought, instantly recognizing the interest in his eyes. This appointment was already running overtime and she really didn't want to fend off his advances.

This was one downside to dealing with male clients in her matchmaking business. Because she was reasonably attractive they thought they would skip the sometimes tedious process of finding a mate and go straight for her.

"What type of woman are you looking for?" she asked, deliberately playing with the massive-but-fake emerald-and-diamond monstrosity on the ring finger of her left hand.

"Actually, I was going to say a tiny blonde with a nice figure but I'm open to other possibilities. Maybe someone who looks like you…who *is* you. I have tickets for the opera. Do you like opera?"

Ack. She hated opera and she didn't date her clients. Ever. She didn't date at all. Brodie sent him a tight smile and lifted her hand to show him her ring. "I'm flattered but I'm engaged. Tom is a special ops soldier, currently overseas."

Last week Tom had been Mike and he'd been an ace detective. The week before he'd been Jace and a white-water adventurer. What could she say? She liked variety in her fake fiancés.

Brodie took down the rest of his information, ignored his smooth attempts to flirt with her despite her engagement to Tom and insisted on paying for coffee. She watched as he left the café and climbed into a low-slung Japanese sports car. When she was certain he was out of view, she dropped her head to the table and gently banged her forehead.

"Another one asking for a date?" Jan, the owner of the coffee shop, dropped into the chair across from Brodie and patted her head. Despite Brodie trying to keep her distance from the ebullient older woman, Jan had, somehow, become her friend. She rarely confided in anybody—talking about stuff and discussing the past changed nothing, so what was the point?—but Jan didn't let it bother her. Like her great-aunt Poppy, Jan nagged Brodie to open up on a fairly regular basis.

Funny, Brodie had talked more to Kade in three weeks than she had to anybody—Jan and Poppy included—for the last decade.

Well, that thought had barreled in from nowhere. Brodie rarely, if ever, thought about Kade Webb during daylight hours. Memories of him, his kiss, his hard body under her hands, were little gifts she gave to herself at night, in the comfort of the dark.

"Being asked out on dates is an occupational hazard." Brodie stretched out her spine and rolled her head on her shoulders in an effort to work out the kinks.

Jan pushed a pretty pink plate holding a chocolate chip cookie across the table. "Maybe this will make you feel better."

It would, but Brodie knew there was something other than sympathy behind Jan's fat-and-sugar-laden gesture. "What do you want?"

"My cousin is in her thirties and is open to using a matchmaker. I suggested you."

Brodie scowled at her friend, but she couldn't stop herself from breaking off the corner of the cookie and lifting it to her mouth. Flavors exploded on her tongue and she closed her eyes in ecstasy. "Better than sex, I swear."

"Honey, if my cookies are better than sex, then you ain't doing it right," Jan replied, her voice tart. She leaned forward, her bright blue eyes inquisitive. "You having sex you haven't told me about, Brodie?"

She wished. The closest she'd come to sex was Kade Webb's hot kiss six months ago, but sex itself? She thought back. Three or so years?

She was pathetic.

After taking another bite of the cookie, Brodie pulled her thoughts from her brief encounter with the CEO of the Mavericks professional ice hockey team and narrowed her eyes at her friend. "You know I only take men as my clients, Jan."

"Which is a stupid idea. You are halving your market," Jan said, her business sense offended. But Brodie's business model worked; Brodie dealt with men, while her associate Colin only had women clients. They pooled their databases and office resources. As a result, they were doing okay. In the hectic twenty-first century—the age of the internet, icky diseases and idiots—singles wanted help wading through the dating cesspool.

"Women are too emotional, too picky and too needy. Too much drama," Brodie told Jan. Again.

Brodie snapped off another piece of cookie and wrinkled her nose when she realized she'd eaten most of it. She was a sucker for chocolate. And cookies. Thank the Lord she had a fast metabolism. She still ran every day, but never in the morning.

"The men don't really want to date me. They just like the attention I pay them. They tend to forget they are paying *me* to pay attention. And I know far too much about them too soon."

An alert on her tablet told her she'd received a new email. Jan pushed herself to her feet. "I'll let you get back to work. Do you want another cup of coffee?"

Brodie already had caffeine-filled veins but why should that matter? "Please."

She swiped her finger across her tablet and accessed her inbox. She'd received quite a few messages when she'd been dealing with Mr. Suave but only one made her pulse accelerate.

Your donation to the auction at the Mavericks' Charity Ball filled the subject line and all the moisture in her mouth disappeared. Jeez, she'd had a brief encounter with Kade months ago, shouldn't she have forgotten about him by now?

Unfortunately Kade wasn't the type of man who was easily forgotten. And, if she had to be truthful, she still missed those early-morning runs when it seemed like they had the park to themselves. She missed the way her heart kicked up when she saw him, missed the way he pushed her to run faster, train harder. She'd enjoyed him, enjoyed that time with him, more than she should have.

Brodie rubbed her hands over her face and gave herself a mental slap. She was almost thirty, a successful business owner and matchmaker to some of the sharpest, richest, most successful bachelors in the city. She should not be thinking about *the* sharpest, richest, best-looking bachelor in the city.

Pathetic squared. Brodie shook her head at her ridiculousness and opened the email.

Dear Ms. Stewart,
On behalf of the Chief Executive Officer of the Vancouver Mavericks, Kade Webb, may I extend our heartfelt gratitude for your donation to the Mavericks' auction to be held on June 19.

Attached is your invitation to a luncheon my department is hosting for our valued sponsors earlier on the day. You are most welcome to attend the ball and charity auction; the cost and details are attached.

We look forward to your presence at lunch on the 19 of June. Please see the attached document for the venue and time.
Yours,
Wren Bayliss
Public Relations Director
Vancouver Mavericks

Thanks but, no thanks. She wouldn't be attending. Donating to the charity auction had been Colin's idea and he could attend the luncheon and ball on their behalf. She wasn't even sure donating their services to the charity auction would raise any money... What bachelor or bachelorette would admit to wanting to use a matchmaker in a room full of their friends and colleagues? Their business was based on discretion and her clients came to her, mostly, via word of mouth. But Wren, and Colin, had dismissed Brodie's concerns. They seemed to think sisters, brothers and friends would bid on their siblings' or friends' behalf. Besides, the guest could bid silently via cell phone as well, so anonymity, if it was required, would be assured.

Thanks to the competition of online matchmaking Colin was convinced they needed to cement their position as matchmakers to the elite of Vancouver society and they needed to network more and foster relationships. Being part of the Mavericks' silent auction was a huge coup and would be excellent direct advertising to their target group. Since marketing and PR was Colin's forte, she'd told him he could represent them at the luncheon.

Yes, a part of her reluctance was the fact there was a chance Kade would be at the function. Months might've passed but she was still embarrassed down to her two-inch designer heels. She'd acted like a ditzy virgin who said yes but meant no. God! How could she be in the same room with him without wanting to jump him—the man still fueled her sexual fantasies—but also wanting to hide under the table?

Her computer dinged again and she looked at the new message that popped into her inbox.

Hey, Brodes,
I presume you received an invite to attend the sponsor's lunch hosted by the Mavericks? I can't attend. Kay and I are seeing a fertility specialist that day. Can you go and do the thing for us both?
Thanks,
Col

Brodie groaned.
Please let Kade not be there, she prayed.

Two

"Whose stupid idea was this?"

Kade Webb scowled at his two best friends and rolled his shoulders under his suit jacket, wishing he was anywhere but in the crowded, over-perfumed bar area of Taste, one of the best restaurants in Vancouver. He'd spent most of last night reading P&L statements and had spent a long, tedious morning with Josh Logan's hardass agent negotiating a deal to buy the hotshot wing, and all he wanted was to plant himself behind his messy desk and make a dent in his paperwork. He was trying to finalize their—his, Mac's and Quinn's—partnership with old man Bayliss, Wren's grandfather, so the four of them could make a solid counteroffer to buy the Mavericks franchise before Vernon's widow sold it to Boris Chenko, a Russian billionaire who owned a string of now generic sports franchises.

Kade didn't have the time to socialize. To play nice.

What he really wanted, despite it only being noon, was a cold beer, a long shower and some hot sex. Or, to save time, some long, hot sex in a shower. Since he hadn't had time to date lately the hot sex would have to be a solo act later—how sad, too bad—but really, he'd give it all up, sex included, for a solid eight hours of sleep.

He was burning the candle at both ends and somewhere in the middle, as well.

"Will you please take that scowl off your face?"

Kade looked down into the face of his newly appointed director of public relations and wondered, for the hundredth time, why there was no sexual attraction between him and Wren. She was gorgeous, slim, vivacious and smart, but she didn't rock his boat. He didn't rock hers, either. They were friends, just like he was with Mac's new fiancée, Rory, and for the first time in Kade's life he was enjoying uncomplicated female relationships.

That being said, he still wouldn't say no to some uncomplicated sex.

"Kade, concentrate!" Wren slammed her elbow into his side and he pulled his attention back to business.

"Your guests of honor, the main sponsors, should be arriving any minute and you need to pay them some special attention," Wren insisted, a tiny foot tapping her only indication of nervousness.

"Who are they again?"

Frustration flashed in Wren's blue eyes and Kade held up his hands in apology. "Wren, I've been dealing with player negotiations and your grandfather as our new partner, and fending off Myra's demands for us to make a counteroffer. Sponsors for this ball haven't been high on my priority list."

"Did you read *any* of the memos I sent you?"

Kade shrugged. "Sorry, no. But you can tell me now and I'll remember."

He had a phenomenal memory. It was a skill he acquired as a child hopping from town to town and school to school following the whims of his artist father. Within a day of arriving in a new place, he'd find a map and memorize the street names so he'd know exactly where he was at all times. He'd felt emotionally lost so often that being physically lost was going a step too far. His memory helped him catch up with schoolwork and remember the names of teachers and potential friends, so he could ease his way through another set of new experiences.

Wren ran through the list of the bigger donations and then said, "The Forde Gallery donated one of your father's paintings, a small watercolor but pretty."

Jeez, he remembered when his father had to swap paintings for food or gas or rent money. Even his small paintings now went for ten grand or more… It was a hell of a donation.

"We have dinners on yachts, holidays, jewelry, the usual bits and pieces businesses donate. The item that will be the most fun and will get the crowd buzzing is the matchmaking service…"

"The what?"

"Brodie Stewart and Colin Jones are providing their matchmaking services. The winners, one girl and one guy, will be matched up and sent on three dates to find a potential mate. Sounds like fun, doesn't it?"

Brodie Stewart? His Brodie? The girl who'd kissed like a dream but who'd bailed on him before they got to the bedroom?

"It sounds like hell." Kade managed to utter the response even though his mind was filled with memories of Brodie, dark hair spilling over her shoulders as she lay against his chest, bright green eyes languid and dreamy after one spectacular hot, wet kiss. He dimly recalled her saying something about her having her own business but why did he think she was in consulting?

"Is she attending this lunch?" Kade asked and hoped Wren, or his friends, didn't hear the note of excitement in his voice.

"You know this Brodie person?" Quinn demanded. And there was the problem with being friends with someone for so damn long. There was little you could get past them.

"Not really," Kade replied, sounding bored.

"Let me give you a hint about your boss, Wren," Mac stated, his arm around Rory's waist. "When he lies he always sounds disinterested, faraway, detached."

Unfortunately, being in love hadn't affected Mac's observational skills and he was as sharp as ever. "Shut the hell up, McCaskill, you have no idea what you are talking about. I met Brodie once, a while ago."

"Why didn't you tell us about her?" Quinn demanded, unsatisfied.

"Do you tell me about the women you meet?" Kade responded.

Quinn thought for a moment before grinning. "Pretty much, yeah. And if I don't tell you, then the press will."

Kade pulled a face. The society pages of their local papers and many internet sites devoted far too much time speculating about their love lives. Mac had provided a break for Kade and Quinn as the media devoured the news that he was settling down with the lovely Rory, but recently they'd restarted their probing inquiries about the state of his and Quinn's love lives. Many of the papers hinted, or outright demanded, it was time the other two "Maverick-teers" followed Mac's example.

Kade felt that he would rather kiss an Amazonian dart frog.

Only Mac and Quinn knew his past, knew about his unconventional upbringing as the son of a mostly itinerant artist who dragged him from place to place and town to town on a whim. They understood his need to feel financially secure and because they worked together, invested together and always stuck together, the three of them, along with Wren's grandfather, were in the position to buy their beloved hockey team, the Vancouver Mavericks.

Yeah, he might be, along with Quinn, a wealthy, eligible and elusive bachelor, but he had every intention of staying that way. Legalities and partnership agreements and a million miles of red tape—and his belief in the loyalty of his friends—had allowed him to commit to his career with the Mavericks, formerly as a player and now as the CEO and, hopefully, as a future co-owner. But a personal commitment? Hell no.

He'd learned that hard lesson as a child. As soon as he found someone to love—a dog, a friend, a teacher, a coach—his father would rip it away by packing up their lives and moving them along. Emotional involvement sent Kade backward to his powerless childhood.

He'd hated that feeling then and he loathed it now. His theory was if you didn't play in a rainstorm, then you wouldn't get hit by lightning. He made damn sure the women he dated had no expectations, that they thoroughly understood he was a here-now-gone-tomorrow type of guy. That they shouldn't expect anything from him.

Despite his up-front attitude, there were always women who thought they could change his mind so he'd still had to ease himself out of situations. Sometimes he managed it with charm, sometimes he had to be blunt, but when he sensed his lovers were becoming emotionally invested, he backed off. Way, way off.

Brodie Stewart was the only woman who'd ever turned the tables on him, who'd backed away before he could. Backed away before he'd even gotten her into bed.

"...she had all the emotional depth of a puddle!"

Kade pulled his attention back to the conversation and caught the tail end of Rory's comment. She was scowling at Quinn and he looked unrepentant, being his bad-boy self.

"Honey, I wasn't dating her for her conversational skills," Quinn stated.

Rory shook her head and rested her chin on Mac's shoulder. "One day you are going to meet someone who you can't resist and I hope she gives you hell," Rory said, her tone and expression fierce.

"Rorks, unfortunately butt-face here claimed you before I did so I am destined to be a free spirit." Quinn put his hand on his heart, his eyes laughing.

Rory, smart girl that she was, didn't fall for Quinn's BS. Instead, she poked Quinn's stomach. "You will meet her and I will not only laugh while I watch you run around her like a headless chicken, I will encourage her to give you as much trouble as possible." She stretched past Quinn to jab Kade in the stomach. "That goes for you, too, Kade. The female population of Vancouver has spoiled you two rotten."

"I'm not complaining." Kade smiled, taking a sip of his lime-flavored water.

"Me neither," Quinn quickly agreed. He stuck his tongue in his cheek as he continued to tease Rory. "And I don't think we've been spoiled—we've been treated as per our elevated status as hockey gods."

"That just shows how moronic some women can be," Rory muttered. She looked up at Mac and narrowed her eyes. "You're very quiet, McCaskill. Got anything to say?"

Mac dropped a kiss on her forehead and another on her mouth. "Hell no! This is your argument with my friends. But, since I am taking you home and hoping to get lucky, I'll just agree with everything you say."

Quinn made the sound of a cracking whip and Kade rolled his eyes before he said, "Wimp."

"You might wear the trousers but Rory picks them out," Quinn added and immediately stepped back to lessen the impact of Mac's big fist smacking his shoulder. "May I point out that before Rory snagged you, you were—"

"No, you absolutely may not." Wren's cool voice interrupted their smack talk. "Can you three please act like the responsible, smart businessmen that people—mistakenly I might add—think you are and behave yourselves? The first sponsor has arrived."

Kade didn't need Wren's nod toward the ballroom to tell him Brodie had arrived. He'd felt the prickle of anticipation between his shoulder blades, felt the energy in the room change. He was super aware of her. As he slowly turned, he felt the world fade away.

She hadn't changed, yet...she had. It had only been six months, but somehow she was a great deal more attractive than he remembered. Her dress hugged a toned body and her long black hair was now a short, feathery cap against her head. What definitely hadn't changed was her ability to send all his blood rocketing south to a very obvious and inconvenient place.

"Well, well, well…isn't this interesting?" Mac drawled in Kade's ear.

"First time I've seen our boy gobsmacked, dude," Quinn added. "Shut your mouth, boyo, you're drooling."

Kade ignored his friends. Life had unexpectedly dropped Brodie back into his realm again and he wanted what he'd always wanted every time he'd laid eyes on her: Brodie in his bed, under him, naked and legs around him…eyes begging for him to come on in.

Her perfume reached him before she did and he realized it was the same scent he remembered. It took him straight back to those early-morning runs in the park, to crisp air and the hesitant smile of the black-haired girl who waited for him by the running store and kept up with his fast pace along the seawall. He hadn't run in the park since the morning he'd heard about Vernon's death.

And kissed Brodie.

It had been an incredible kiss and the one highlight of a couple of really tough, horrible months. If only he had the memory of taking her to bed, too…

So it turned out he didn't want long, hot sex with any random woman. He wanted to make love to Brodie. Interesting.

Crazy.

And pretty damn dangerous. He wouldn't—couldn't—allow her to know the effect she had on him, how he instantly craved her and the crazy chemical reaction he was experiencing. It wasn't clever to admit she was the only woman he'd ever encountered who could thoroughly disconcert him, who could wipe every rational thought from his brain.

Okay, he was officially losing it. Maybe it was time, as Wren had suggested, he started acting like the CEO he was supposed to be.

With anyone else, he could do it with his eyes closed. Around Brodie, he might have to put his back into it.

So here goes...

Brodie held out her hand to Kade and hoped her smile wasn't as shaky as she felt. "Kade, it's been a while."

"Brodie." Kade took her hand and she held his eyes even though her pulse skittered up her arm and straight to her belly. She met his eyes and felt her heart roll over, as it always did. She knew his eyes were a deep brown but today, against his olive complexion and dark blond hair, they glinted black.

Oh, this wasn't good. He was a sexy man. They'd kissed but that wasn't enough of a reason for her hormones to start doing their crazy dance. She looked down at their intertwined hands and could easily remember what his tanned fingers felt like on her back, his wide hand sliding over her butt, his lips on hers...

Dammit, Brodie!

Kade touched her elbow and gestured to his friends. Hot, hot and *steamin'*. Brodie wanted to fan herself. Quinn Rayne was the ultimate sexy bad boy, Mac McCaskill was even better looking—if that was possible—after falling in love with the attractive woman tucked into his side, and Kade...? Why, with him looking as fantastic as he did, the urge to jump him and do him on the nearest table was nearly overwhelming.

This was the problem with Kade Webb, Brodie reminded herself. He had the ability to turn her from a woman who considered all the angles into a wild child who acted first and regretted later. She hadn't made an impulsive decision for nearly a decade and yet, around him, that was all she seemed to do! For weeks she'd met him in the park as the sun rose. Then she'd accompanied him home, kissed him senseless and been so tempted to make love to him. Around him, *impulsive* was her new middle name.

Stewart, start acting like the adult you are! Immediately!

Pulling herself together, Brodie greeted Kade's friends, kissed Wren hello and looked, and sounded, like the professional she normally was.

Quinn smiled at her. Whoo boy, it was a potent grin and she could easily imagine girls falling like flies at his feet. That smile should be registered as a weapon of mass destruction, but Brodie caught the wariness in his eyes and the intelligence he hid behind his charm. "So, you're Brodie."

"I am."

"And you're a matchmaker."

"I am." Brodie tipped her head, assessing him. "Would you like me to find you someone?"

She had to smile when Quinn flushed and sent a help-me look at his friends. Since Quinn's exploits, mostly in love, kept Vancouver entertained on a weekly basis, she knew he had no problem finding a date. Finding a *partner* was a very different story.

"You know, most of my clients don't have any problems meeting women and they often date a variety of women."

Quinn frowned. "So why do they need you?"

"Because they are dating the wrong type of women. They want to be in a relationship," Brodie patiently explained. "Do you want to be in a relationship, Mr. Rayne?"

She was taking the circuitous route to find out what she desperately wanted to know: would Kade be bidding for her matchmaking services? The thought of matching him to any of Colin's clients made her stomach roil. Colin's clients were wonderful women, but Brodie thought the *ick* factor was a bit too high to match her fantasy man with a flesh-and-bone woman.

She'd rather pick her eyes out with a cake fork.

"Hell no! And why am I the focus of attention?" Quinn complained. "Kade is as much of a lone wolf as me!"

Brodie lifted an eyebrow in Kade's direction, as if to say "Are you?" He immediately read her question and responded with an inscrutable smile.

Brodie looked around, her eyes falling on the honey blonde surgically attached to Mac's side. Rory's look was speculative, bouncing from Quinn to Kade and back again. Brodie recognized her assessing, mischievous look. This was a woman wanting to cause trouble...

Mac's deep voice broke her train of thought. "Your hands are empty, Brodie. What would you like to drink? Wine? A soda?"

A small glass of wine couldn't hurt, could it? "I'd love a glass of Tangled Vine Chardonnay."

Rory tipped her head and looked at Quinn. "Is that the wine you brought over the other night? It was seriously yummy."

Quinn nodded. "I'll bring a case over tonight. What's for supper?"

"Risotto. Troy is joining us tonight," Rory replied.

Mac looked appalled. "We're having them for supper again? Troy I don't mind, but these two? Babe, they are like rats, if you keep feeding them, we are never going to get rid of them."

"Kade and I are the rats," Quinn told Brodie, smiling. He lifted a huge shoulder. "What can I say? She's a good cook."

Brodie looked into Mac's eyes and noticed the amusement under his fake scowl. Yeah, he looked hard-ass and a bit scary—they all did—but she could see these men shared a bond that went beyond love. It was too easy to say they loved each other, but it was more than that; there was loyalty here and support, a deep and profound desire to make sure their "brothers" were happy. She couldn't help feeling envious of their bond despite knowing she'd chosen her solitary state. She'd had friendships like that; bonds with Jay and Chels that couldn't be broken by anything except death.

She still missed them, every day. She missed the people who could finish her sentences, who got her jokes. She missed the I-know-it's-after-midnight-but-I-brought-you-pizza conversations. She missed Chelsea, missed those crazy antics—"I'm outside your window and I have a date. Toss down your lucky belt/new shoes/red lipstick/flirty dress."

She missed Jay, the boy who knew her inside out, the man she'd just been getting to know. His sweet kisses, his endless support, his newly acquired fascination with her body. She still missed the man she thought she'd spend the rest of her life with…

She hadn't been able to reconnect with people on that level again. She wasn't prepared to risk heartbreak. Having her heart dented by loss and being left behind without any emotional support sucked. It stung. It burned. It made her cautious and wary. Scared.

She was very okay with being scared. "And I'm sending you a bill for the food we buy," Mac grumbled. "Spongers."

"Rory's a great cook and she likes having us around. Maybe she needs a break from you," Quinn told Mac as he took the glass of wine Kade had ordered for her off the waiter's tray and handed it to Brodie, ignoring Kade's scowl. "I'll bring the wine."

Rory grinned. "Excellent. I love that wine."

"Might I remind you that you won't be able to drink it for a year or so?" Mac muttered.

Rory frowned and then her expression cleared and a small, tender smile drifted across her face. She touched her stomach and Brodie immediately caught on. It took Mac's friends seconds longer to catch up. And, judging by Quinn's and Kade's stunned faces, that wasn't news they'd been expecting. But once they realized what Mac had revealed, they swept Rory into their arms for a long, emotional hug. Kade hugged Mac, as did Quinn, and Brodie felt tears prick her eyes at their joy for their friend. She stepped back, feeling she shouldn't be here, sharing this precious, intimate moment. She half smiled when she noticed Wren doing the same thing.

Weird that Brodie seemed to be present for some of the big, personal Maverick moments. Vernon's death, Mac's baby... She was an outsider, on the wrong side of this magical circle, so it didn't make sense that she was again in the position to hear something deeply personal. This time, at least, it was good news.

"This wasn't how we planned on telling you," Rory said, jamming her elbow into Mac's side.

Brodie looked at Rory, who had her back to Mac's chest, his big hands on her still very flat stomach. "Congratulations," she murmured.

"Yeah, huge congratulations," Kade said, before slanting a sly look at Mac. "Now you're going to have two children under your feet, Rorks."

"Ha-ha." Mac scowled.

"I know, right?" Rory replied, her voice wobbly. "I'm going to be a mommy, Kade."

"You'll be great at it," Kade assured her and tipped his head at Mac. "But he'll need some training."

"I'm not old enough to have friends who are about to be parents." Quinn clapped Mac on the shoulder and nodded to the bar. "We definitely need champagne. I'll get some."

Wren shook her head and stepped forward. "As much as I hate to break up the party we have work to do and a lunch to host."

Quinn wrinkled his nose. "Our head girl has spoken."

Wren threaded a hand through his arm and pulled him toward the dining area. "C'mon, brat. I've put you at a table where you can't misbehave."

Brodie felt Kade's hand on her back and she immediately, subconsciously moved closer to him, her fingers accidentally brushing the outside of his hard thigh.

Kade tipped his head and dropped his voice so only she could hear his words. "It hasn't gone away, has it?"

Brodie wished she could deny it, dismiss his comment, but she couldn't lie to him. Or herself. She forced herself to look him in the eye. "No."

His fingers pushed into her back at her reluctant admission. "So, just to be clear, we're saying this crazy attraction is still happening?"

"Yep." One-syllable answers were all she could manage.

"So are we going to do anything about it this time?"

Wren's efficient voice interrupted their low, intense conversation. "Kade, you're at the main table up front. Brodie, I'll show you to your seat."

Brodie gave Kade a little shrug and followed Wren into the private dining room of Taste. When she tossed a look over her shoulder, she flushed when she noticed Kade was still watching her.

And he didn't stop looking at her for the next ninety minutes.

He wanted her. The heated looks they'd exchanged over the three tables that separated them left her in no doubt of that. Jeez, it was a minor miracle the room hadn't spontaneously combusted from the sparks they were throwing at each other.

He wanted her as much as he had six months ago, possibly more. It was insane; it was exciting.

What *was* she going to do about it?

She knew what he wanted, to take up where they'd left off in his loft. In the ladies' room Brodie pulled a face at her reflection in the mirror above the bathroom sink and ran her wet fingers over the back of her neck, hoping to cool herself down but knowing it was a futile gesture. She was hot from the inside out and it was all Kade Webb's fault.

Every look he'd sent her, every small smile, had told her he wanted her in the most basic, biblical way possible.

She was pretty sure she'd returned his message. With interest.

Brodie sighed. Having a fling with Kade wouldn't hurt anyone. Unlike an affair with a married man it wasn't icky, immoral or dishonest. It wouldn't be embarrassing or hurtful. It wouldn't—unless she did something really stupid, like fall for the guy—be painful.

She hadn't had an affair, or sex, for a long, long time; she hadn't been naked with a man since Jared the IT guy and he was around three, or was it four, years ago? She was nearly thirty and she was tired of dating herself.

Could she do it? Could she have a one-night stand with Kade? Was she okay with being another puck he shot into his sexual net? Brodie grimaced at her bad analogy. But could she be another of Webb's Women?

If she was looking for a relationship, and she wasn't because she was relationship-phobic, Kade would be the last person she'd be interested in. Brodie gripped the vanity and stared at the basin, thinking hard.

He was famous and she'd matched enough semifamous guys to know how much time and effort it took to date a celebrity. She couldn't think of anything worse than having your life dissected on social media platforms or in the society columns, but some women got off on it.

She hadn't considered any of this that long-ago morning when she'd agreed to coffee. Everything had moved so quickly and she'd only been thinking in terms of a couple of hours spent with him. But she had noticed that over the last six months the spotlight on Kade had become even bigger and brighter. His life was routinely dissected; his dates scrutinized. The press was relentless and easily turned a movie into a marriage proposal, a dinner into destiny.

Brodie shuddered. Yuck.

That being said, she still wanted him.

If she could go through with it this time—and that was a big if—she couldn't ignore the fact that a quick fling with Vancouver's most eligible, slippery bachelor could have consequences. If they did do the deed and it became public knowledge, as these things tended to do with the Mavericks, it would affect her business. She had a database of clients who trusted her, who confided in her. Quite a few of them thought she was engaged, and a liaison with Kade would not inspire her clients to trust her judgment.

Men, she'd realized, were frequently a lot more romantic—or traditional—than most woman gave them credit for. They could have affairs, play the field and have one-night stands, but they wouldn't appreciate their matchmaker doing the same.

No, it was smarter and so much more sensible to ignore Kade's suggestion that they continue what they'd started. Sleeping with him probably wouldn't be as good as she imagined; she'd probably romanticized exactly how good Webb's kissing was to excuse her crazy, uninhibited behaviour when she was alone with him. No, best to keep her distance…

Good decision, Brodie thought, eyeing her reflection in the mirror. Sensible decision.

Adult decision.

Safe decision.

So why did it feel so damn *wrong*?

Three

The ladies' room was on a short flight of stairs above the men's restroom and when she stepped into the passage, she looked down and saw the blond head and muscular shoulders that could only belong to Kade.

She flicked off a piece of fluff from her shocking pink blouson dress, belted at the waist and ending midthigh. Nude heels, scalpel-thin, made her legs look like they went on for miles. Back in her apartment it had seemed very suitable for a business lunch, but when Kade looked up and his eyes darkened from a deep brown to a shade just off black, she knew he wanted to rip off her clothing with his teeth. Keeping her hand on the banister, biting the inside of her lip, her heart galloping, she walked down the three steps to the marble floor, a scant couple of inches from his broad chest.

He didn't give her any warning or ask for her permission, his mouth simply slammed into hers. Brodie had to grab his biceps to keep from falling off her shoes. Those amazing hands covered a great deal of her back and she was sure her dress would sport scorch marks from the heat. She was intensely aware of him and could feel the ridges of his fingers, the strength in his wrists.

Brodie wound her arms around his neck and pressed her mouth against his. He tasted like coffee and Kade and breath mints and his lips seemed to feel like old friends. Warm, firm, dry. Confident. That word again. His hands bumped up her spine, kneading as he worked his way to her shoulders, moving around to catch her face. His thumbs skated over her cheekbones as he deepened the kiss, his tongue sliding into her mouth.

Loneliness—the slight dissatisfaction that hovered like a fine mist around her, the ever-present sorrow— dissipated as he took command of the kiss, pushing her back against the wall and pushing his knee between her thighs. This was kissing—raw, raunchy, flat-out sexy. Brodie felt heat and warmth and moisture gather and felt an unfamiliar pull of fulfillment, a desire to lose herself in the heat and strength and sexiness of this man.

Kade's hand skimmed the side of her chest, down her waist and around to her butt, his fingers strong and sure, experienced. He cupped a cheek, pulled her up and into him, and she sighed as his erection pushed into her stomach. He yanked his mouth off hers and she tumbled into his sinfully dark eyes. "Same old, same old."

Brodie placed her hands on his pecs and tried to regulate her breathing. Where was an oxygen tank when she needed one? She felt Kade's fingers on her cheekbone, tracing her jaw. "Brodie? You okay?"

Fine. Just trying to get my brain to restart. Brodie placed her forehead on his sternum and pulled in some much needed air.

"Dammit, Kade," she eventually muttered.

"Yep, we're a fire hazard," Kade agreed, resting his chin on the top of her head. "What are we going to do about it?"

"Nothing?" Brodie suggested.

"Yeah…not an option." She heard the determination in his voice. She knew he would do what it took to get what he wanted.

What *she* wanted. He wouldn't need to do much persuading—she was halfway to following him to hell and back for an orgasm or two.

She was allowed to share some amazing sex with someone who knew what he was doing, her usually quiet wild child insisted. She was twenty-nine, mostly normal but terribly sexually frustrated.

You had this argument with yourself earlier. He's single. You're single. You don't need anyone's permission…

Kade didn't need to use charm, or to say anything at all. She was doing a fine job of talking herself into his bed all on her own.

"Brodie?" Kade stepped back and bent his knees so he could look her in the eye. "What do you say? Do you want to take this to its very natural conclusion?"

Brodie gripped his big biceps, or as much of it as she could get into her hand. He felt harder, more muscular than she remembered. How was that possible? She wanted to undo the buttons on his shirt, push aside the fabric and see what other wonders lay under his expensive clothes. Was his chest bigger? His shoulders broader? His thighs stronger?

"Are you going to put me out of my misery sometime soon?" Kade asked. He sounded like sleeping with her was neither here nor there. Then she took another look at his expression, read the emotion in his eyes.

There was frustration, a whole lot of desire and a hint of panic. Because he thought she might say no? He looked a little off-kilter and not as suave and as confident as she'd first suspected. His hint of insecurity made her feel steadier. That their chemistry had rocked him allowed her to regain her mental and emotional balance.

"God, woman, you're killing me."

She knew if she said yes, there would be no going back. She couldn't get cold feet, couldn't retreat this time.

She was a little scared—and she should be. She'd laid out all the arguments in the ladies' room. But she could no more stop a freight train than miss this second chance to find out if he was as good as her imagination insisted.

Time to put them both out of their misery. Brodie slowly nodded. "Yeah, let's revisit the past. One night, not a big deal?"

"You sure?"

She knew he was asking for some reassurance she wouldn't change her mind midway through, so she placed her hand on his cheek and nodded. "Very sure. On the understanding this is a one-time thing and it stays between us."

Relief flashed across Kade's face and she felt his fingers flexing on her back. "I never kiss and tell. But are you sure we'll be able to stop after one night?"

Brodie shrugged. Probably not. "We can give it our best shot."

Kade stepped back and ran a hand around the back of his neck. "Interesting," he said.

Brodie frowned. "What is?"

"You have a very…businesslike approach to life. And sex."

She supposed she did, but life had taught her to put emotion away from daily life. If she allowed emotion to rule, she would've crawled into a cave after the accident and never come out. She turned her back on her feelings because they were so big, so overwhelming. Before the tragedy, she'd loved hard...wildly, uninhibitedly. She'd engaged every one of her senses and she'd been the most emotional creature imaginable.

A car accident had taken her family, but emotion had hung around and nearly killed her, too. To survive she'd had to box it up and push it away...because she couldn't feel happy without feeling sad. No joy without pain. No love without heartbreak.

It was easier just to skate.

Brodie lifted her chin and sent Kade a cool smile. Time to get the conversation back on track. "So, when and where?"

Kade lifted his eyebrows in surprise and Brodie sent him a look, daring him to make another comment about her frankness. He looked like he wanted to and Brodie prayed he wouldn't. Kade seemed to have the ability to look beyond her shell to the mess inside...

She didn't need anyone upsetting her mental apple cart.

Kade looked at his watch and thought for a minute. "I have meetings this afternoon or else I'd whisk you back to my place right now."

That was something her old self would've done, Brodie mused. Breakfast at midnight, dancing in the rain, unplanned road trips and afternoon sex. The Brodie she was today didn't do wild anymore.

"And tonight is the ball. Are you coming?" Kade placed his hand flat on the wall behind her head and she had to resist the urge to rest her temple on his forearm.

Brodie shook her head. "No. Besides the tickets are sold out."

The corners of Kade's mouth tipped up. "I'm sure I know someone who can slip you inside."

It was tempting, Brodie thought, but no. Attending the ball with Kade would make it seem like a date and she didn't *date*.

"Why don't you give me a call in a day or two?" she suggested.

"I don't know if I can last that long," Kade said, his tone rueful. He jammed his hands into his suit pockets and Brodie couldn't help her urge to straighten his tie. "But…okay."

"Lipstick on my face?" he asked.

"No, you're fine."

Kade nodded. "Give me your cell number. And your address."

Brodie put the info in his phone. Kade nodded his thanks.

Kade's eyes warmed to the color of rough cocoa. "Do you work from home?"

"No, I share an office with my friend and associate downtown. He's also a matchmaker."

Kade scratched his chin. "I am still wrapping my head around the fact you set people up and they pay you for it. It's…weird."

She couldn't take offense. Frequently she thought it was a very odd way to earn money—especially for someone who'd once specialized in international banking and who intended to remain single for the rest of her life. But she was curious as to why he thought her business was weird so she asked him.

Kade rubbed the back of his neck. "I guess it's because I've never had a problem finding dates.'

It was such a common misconception. "Neither do most of my clients. They aren't looking to date, they are looking to settle down." She saw him wince and she had to smile. "So I guess you're not going to be a client anytime soon?"

"Or ever."

Kade pushed all thoughts of her career out of her head when he lifted his hands to cradle her face. She shivered with a mixture of lust and longing. Her hands drifted across his chest and skimmed his flat, ridged belly.

"I can't wait to spend some time with you." He bent to kiss the sensitive spot between her shoulder and neck. He lifted his head and gave her a hard stare. "Soon, I promise."

Brodie swallowed in an attempt to put some saliva back into her mouth.

Keeping his hands on her face, Kade twisted his wrist to check the time and softly cursed. "I've got to get back to the office, I am so late." The pad of his thumb brushed her bottom lip. "Please don't talk yourself out of this, Brodie."

She wanted to protest, wanted to reassure him, but she didn't. "See you."

Kade nodded abruptly, dropped a hard, openmouthed kiss on her lips, then whipped around and headed back to the restaurant.

"You'd better make it very soon, Kade Webb."

She'd run ten kilometers and had a cold shower, and despite it being four hours later, she could still taste Kade on her lips. Her lady parts were buzzing; her heart was still thumping. Her heart rate had actually *dropped* when she'd all but sprinted around Stanley Park. How was she going to function for the next couple of days if this heightened state of awareness didn't dissipate?

It had to dissipate—she couldn't live like this.

God, this was why she ran from entanglements. It was so much easier to slide on the surface of life. She didn't like feeling this way. It felt too much like she was...

Well, *living*. Living meant anticipation, excitement, lust, passion. She wasn't good at any of it anymore and she didn't deserve to feel all that, not when her entire family, practically everyone she had ever loved, was no longer around to do the same.

Why didn't I get hurt?

Why did I live when other people died?

Survivor's guilt. She was the poster child for the condition. Brodie walked across her living room, hands on her hips, her brow furrowed. She'd seen the psychologists, read the literature. She knew guilt was common and part of the healing process. Her healing process was taking a damn long time. She knew she isolated herself. Living a half life wasn't healthy—it certainly couldn't bring her loved ones back. But she couldn't stop thinking she didn't deserve to be happy.

Love was impossible.

The sound of her intercom buzzing broke into her thoughts. Brodie pushed back her hair, frowning. She wasn't expecting anybody—her great-aunt Poppy, who lived on the floor below, was out of town—so she couldn't imagine who could be leaning on her doorbell.

Brodie walked to her front door and pressed the switch. "Can I help you?"

"I have ninety minutes, can I come up?"

Kade. Holy freakin'... Because her mouth was instantly bone-dry, she found it difficult to form words.

"C'mon, babe, don't make me beg," Kade cajoled.

This was madness. This was crazy. She should tell him to leave, tell him that she didn't want him to come up. But that would be a big, fat lie… She did want to see him, preferably naked.

So Brodie pressed the button to open the door downstairs and wrenched open her apartment door to watch him run up. He was still dressed in his suit from earlier. His tie was pulled down and he carried a small gym bag and a tuxedo covered in plastic over his shoulder.

Hunky, sexy, determined man, Brodie thought, leaning against the door frame. Kade reached her and flashed a quick smile but didn't say a word. He just grabbed her hand, yanked her inside, kicked her door closed and threw his stuff on the nearest chair. Then two strong hands gripped her hips and swept her up and into him, her feet leaving the floor. Then his mouth was on hers, warm and demanding, and his tongue swept inside, allowing her to taste his frustration-coated passion.

Whoo-boy!

After a minute had passed—or a millennium, who could tell?—Kade gently lowered Brodie to her feet, but he kept his lips on hers, his tongue delving and dancing. She responded, awed by the pent-up longing she felt in the intensity of his kiss. Her response must have seemed just as demanding, as urgent. Brodie moved her hands to his shirt, tugging it out of his pants. Desperate to feel his skin on hers, she moaned her frustration and then resented the brief separation from Kade's body as he stepped away to unbutton and remove his shirt.

Brodie moved forward and ran her lips across his bare chest, stopping to flicker her tongue over his nipple, to rub her cheek on his chest hair. He was such a man. From the hardness of his muscles to the slightly rough texture of his skin and the smell that called to her senses, he awakened every cell in her body. She could no more stop this than she could stop a freight train. Neither did she want to, she realized.

She needed him, right now. She had to have him— in her, around her, sharing this with her.

"Bed," Kade muttered against her jawline.

"Too far." Brodie managed to lift a hand and wave to the right. "Desk, over there."

"That'll work."

Running his hands over her bottom, Kade lifted Brodie onto the edge of the desk and pushed the files and papers off the table. They slid and tumbled to the floor. She didn't care. Part of her knew this was a mistake, but she didn't care about that, either. Nothing mattered but having him in her arms, allowing him to make indescribably delicious love to her.

Kade quickly stripped her of her clothing, while Brodie watched him through heavy, half-closed eyes. Keeping one hand on her breast, he reached into his suit pants and yanked his wallet out of a pocket. Scattering cards and cash, he found a condom and ripped it open with his teeth. He shed the rest of his clothes, and slipped the condom on. Brodie was not shocked when Kade grabbed the flimsy material of her panties and ripped them off her. His erection was hard and proud as he rubbed himself against her most secret places, seeking her permission to enter.

His lips followed his erection, and Brodie thought she would turn to liquid. Just when she could tolerate no more, Kade lifted his head to worship her breasts with his mouth, tongue and lips. Brodie closed her fingers around him and relished the sound of his breathing, heavy in the quiet of the early evening. Brown eyes met green as she tugged him toward her. Kade's one hand slid under her hip and the other cradled her head, both encouraging her to ride with him.

The desk felt like a soft bed. The cold coffee she'd left there earlier could have been the finest champagne, the mixed-up papers rose petals. They were locked together. Finally. Kade moved within her and Brodie followed. Kade demanded and she replied. Deeper, longer, higher, faster. She met him stroke for stroke, matching his passion, uninhibited, free.

On that thought Brodie fractured on a yell and a sob. Then Kade bucked and arched and collapsed against her, his body hot.

"Brodie?" he muttered against her shoulder. "You alive?"

"Uh-huh."

"Desk survived?"

Brodie's mouth curved into a smile. She patted the wood next to her hip. "Looks like it. You?"

Kade kissed her neck before reluctantly pulling out of her. He straightened and turned away. "Yeah, I'm fine—"

Brodie sat up and frowned at his stream of curses. "What on earth…?"

Kade grimaced at the condom in his hand and then back to her. "The condom split. Dammit, it was brand-new."

Brodie hopped down from the desk and looked around for her shirt, which had landed on the back of her couch. Well, that was a big bucket of freezing water. Dressing quickly, she thought about what to say, how to act. Expressing anger or disappointment was sort of like bolting the stable door after the horse had fled. It wouldn't help. So she decided to be practical.

"If you want to, uh…clean up, my bedroom has an en suite bathroom, second door on the right."

Kade, utterly unconcerned with his nudity, stalked away. Brodie folded his suit pants, hung his shirt over the back of a chair and tucked his socks into his shoes. Picking up her ruined panties, she balled them in her hands before walking into her kitchen and throwing them into the trash can.

Putting her hands on her hips, she considered the angles. What were the chances of her becoming pregnant? She was on a contraceptive, which she took religiously. Was it even the right time of the month for her to be ovulating? Walking toward the calendar she kept on the side of her fridge, she tried to remember when last she'd had her period. Brodie counted back and pursed her lips. She'd be okay, she decided. There was no need to panic.

"And?"

Brodie turned to look at Kade standing in the square doorway, still naked, still hot. "It'll be fine. No need to stress, I'm on the pill."

Relief, hot and sure, flooded Kade's face, his eyes. "Good."

Brodie bit her lip, wondering how to phrase her next question. She didn't want to offend him, but… "Do I need to get myself tested for anything, well, yucky?"

Kade shook his head. "I had a medical three weeks ago and I always use a condom. This is the first time one has broken, I promise."

Well, that was a relief and a less awkward conversation than she'd thought it would be. When Kade grabbed her shirt and pulled her toward him all thoughts of pregnancy and STDs evaporated. He kissed her, long and slow. "You have too many clothes on."

Man, how was she supposed to resist when he made her feel all squirmy and hot? "You don't have any condoms left."

"You do. I saw some in your bathroom cabinet."

Brodie pulled a face. She'd bought them years ago, during her sleeping-with-the-IT-guy phase. "They've been in there for years."

"I checked the expiration date, we're good to go." Kade's lips nibbled her jaw. "You good to go?"

"Bed this time?" Brodie asked.

"And in the shower the next."

Brodie glanced at the clock on her kitchen wall. Twice more in an hour and fifteen minutes?

Well, she'd heard about Kade Webb's ambition, but she'd never thought she'd see it in action.

Kade walked out of her bathroom dressed in his tuxedo pants, his white dress shirt hanging loose. While he was showering she'd run a brush through her hair, pulled on a loose cotton sweater and a pair of yoga pants and was now sitting cross-legged on her bed, trying to act like it was an everyday occurrence for Kade to be in her apartment, showering in her bathroom.

"Why aren't you going to the ball? Surely it's a good place to promote your business?" Kade asked as he sat down next to her to pull on his black socks. "After all, you came to the lunch."

"I came as a sponsor, not to tout for business." Brodie placed her elbows on her knees and her face in her hands. "I've got to be careful how I network. It's not like I can work the room, handing out business cards. My business is based on discretion and most of my clients come to me via word of mouth. Our website and contact numbers are on the program—if someone wants to

talk to us they'll call. I only match guys and I can practically guarantee no man there will talk business to me
at the ball, not when they can be overheard."

"Would I know any of your clients?"

"More than a couple." Brodie held up her hand. "And
no, I'll never tell so don't bother asking."

Kade sent her a quick, assessing look. "I bet a lot of
the guys hit on you."

Brodie cocked her head at him. "Why would you
think that?"

"So they do, I can see it in your eyes. As for how I
know...?" He shrugged. "Say I'm a guy and I'm looking for someone. Then I meet you and think, hey, she's
gorgeous and nice, I don't need to look any further.
Men are lazy."

"It happens," Brodie admitted.

"How do you deal with them?" Kade pulled on his
dress shoes—hand-tooled black leather, Brodie noticed
as she scooted off the bed and walked over to her dressing table. She picked up her diamond-and-emerald ring
and threw it in his direction.

"Nice ring," he commented and threw it back at her.
"Except it's fake."

"As fake as the fiancés I invent every week so I have
a good excuse not to date," Brodie replied.

"Ah." Kade bent over to tie his laces and turned his
head to look at her. "You've never been tempted?"

Brodie took a moment to consider his question. She
was surprised when Kade's eyes narrowed. With jealousy? Not possible.

"My clients are successful, frequently really nice,
quite rich men. They drive expensive cars, have gorgeous homes and are intelligent. All very eligible."

Kade scowled.

"But they are also men who are looking to settle down and I am not." Brodie placed her ring back in the shallow bowl holding the jewelry she most often wore. "Besides, becoming involved with a client, in any way, is very unprofessional."

"Good thing I'm not your client, nor will I ever be." Kade sat up and reached for the two sides of his shirt. "I'd rather shoot myself than allow a matchmaker, you or anyone else, to set me up."

Brodie silently admitted she'd rather walk on molten lava than have him as a client.

Kade cocked his head. "So why don't you date?"

Brodie flushed. "Because there are two types of dating. People either date for sex or date for a relationship. I don't do relationships, as a rule. And I very rarely do—" she waved her hand at her bed "—this. I'm as virulently anticommitment as you think you are."

"As I *think* I am?"

Brodie shrugged. She'd seen him with his friends, seen how much he enjoyed his connection with them. He'd be a great husband, a stunning father—if he ever moved out of his party-hearty lifestyle.

Kade held her eyes for a long moment before making a production of looking at his watch. He sent her a crooked grin. "I'm only in it for the hot sex, thanks."

Brodie smiled back. "Then don't win the bid on my auction."

Kade reached into his bag for his bow tie and draped it around his neck, quickly tying it without the use of a mirror. "I very definitely won't," he promised her. "I've got to move or else Wren will have my head."

"Have fun."

Kade picked up his bag and jacket and walked over

to her. He dropped a kiss on her temple, then her mouth. "I'd much rather be having fun with you."

Brodie made herself smile. She was pretty sure he said that to all the girls. "'Bye. See you."

"See you," Kade said, walking out of her bedroom. Within seconds she heard her front door open and close and two minutes later, heard the roar of his sports car.

So that was that. She'd had the fantastic sex she'd been craving. But she'd forgotten how much she enjoyed talking to Kade, how easily they slid into intimate conversation. It was as if there were no barriers and it felt way more intimate than post-sex conversation should be. So why on earth was she craving more?

Four

Kade reached for his glass and took a long sip of whiskey. How much longer could this damn ball last?

It was eleven now. If Quinn would move the auction along, Kade could be out of here by midnight. Was it too late to phone Brodie? Was she exhausted? Would he come across as desperate if he called her again so soon? If she was in bed, what was she wearing? A slinky negligee or a tank top and boxer shorts or just her golden skin?

He loved her skin. He loved everything about her body and when he'd held her earlier he'd felt… How had he felt?

Kade cursed the action in his pants. He needed more than a whiskey on ice, he needed a plunge into an ice-fishing hole. At this rate, when he got Brodie where he wanted her—under him—he'd last about two seconds. His reaction to her was ridiculous, insane… There had to be some sort of scientific explanation for why they wanted to rip each other's clothes off at the drop of a hat. Shouldn't the amazing sex they'd shared earlier have taken the edge off? Was it pheromones? Biological instinct? But why her and not one of the many, many good-looking women—many of them Mavericks groupies—scattered throughout the ballroom? None of this made sense.

All he was certain of was that he wanted Brodie again. Urgently. Immediately. Tonight.

Move the hell on, Rayne!

"And now, one of our more interesting donations," Quinn announced. Kade turned his attention back to the stage. "Ms. Brodie Stewart, one of the city's best matchmakers, is offering the opportunity to bid on her matchmaking services. So if you are a guy and are looking for a good woman, Brodie can find one for you." Quinn looked at the Mavericks who occupied the back tables and nodded. "I know one or two, or ten, of my men who should bid."

"I'll bid on a date with Ms. Stewart!" someone shouted from the back. Kade looked down at the photograph of Brodie on the program and couldn't blame the guy for trying his luck. She was gorgeous...

But, for the immediate future, she was *his.*

"She's too smart to date you, Higgins," Quinn warned. "A reminder, this is a matchmaking service for men looking for their perfect woman. So, who is going to give me a hundred dollars?"

Immediately a couple of hands shot up and Kade watched, astounded, as the bids flew up to a thousand dollars, then two. Bids were still bouncing around the room when a cool female voice cut across the hubbub. "Three thousand dollars."

Quinn spun around and his genial smile turned to a scowl. Rory had her paddle raised and was holding his intense stare.

"On whose behalf are you bidding, Rory?" Quinn asked, his frown clearly stating her bidding had better not have anything to do with him.

Kade leaned back in his chair and grinned. Oh, this was going to be fun. Rory had been nagging Quinn about his ability to jump from woman to woman and hobby to hobby—skydiving, white-water rafting, and his obsession with superfast motorcycles—and was determined to nag him into settling down with a wife and two-point-four kids.

She didn't have a hope in hell of changing Quinn. He was even more entrenched in his bachelor lifestyle than Kade. But Kade would enjoy watching her try. He was also damn grateful she was nagging Quinn and not him…

He liked Rory, loved her even, but he wouldn't tolerate her interfering in his life.

Rory's smile was stolen straight from an imp. "Are you taking my bid or not, Rayne?"

Quinn held up two fingers, turned them to his eyes and flipped them around in her direction. "I'm watching you. McCaskill, make sure your woman behaves."

"Yeah, right." Mac leaned back and folded his arms against his chest. "This has nothing to do with me."

"Three-five." A voice from the back got the auction back on track.

"Three-seven," Rory countered.

"Three-eight," Wren calmly stated. She was bidding on behalf of the silent bidders, those who didn't want the room to know they wanted to use a matchmaker.

"Four." Rory waved her paddle in the air.

Four grand? Wow, not bad. The audience obviously loved the notion of being professionally set up.

The bids climbed and Rory matched every one. As the bids went higher, Quinn's face darkened. Oh, yeah, he knew exactly what she was up to. She was buying Brodie's services to find Quinn a woman who would stick around for more than a nanosecond. She was playing with fire, Kade thought, but he couldn't help admiring her moxie.

"Rory," Quinn warned after her bid topped five thousand dollars.

"Quinn," Rory drawled and added another hundred dollars onto her bid.

"You can't bid against yourself," Quinn snapped.

"I just did." Rory's face was alight with laughter. "Oh, I am so going to enjoy this, Rayne. And so will you. So, be a darling. Bang your gavel and tell me I've won."

Quinn looked at Mac. "Doesn't she drive you crazy?"

Mac dropped a kiss on Rory's temple and smiled. "All the time."

Quinn smacked the gavel and told her she'd won the bid before pointing the gavel in her direction. "I won't use it. You can't blackmail me into doing this, Rory."

Rory placed her hand on her heart and batted her eyelashes in his direction. "Quinn, you wound me. I would never dare to set you up." Kade, along with the rest of the guests, leaned forward in their chairs, eager to hear more. "You keep telling me you're not ready for a relationship and I respect that. I do. Besides, wait your turn."

Huh? If this wasn't for Quinn who was she setting up?

"It won't be my turn. *Ever*." Quinn looked relieved

and perplexed at the same time. "So then, pray tell, who is the sacrificial lamb to be led to slaughter?"

Kade smiled at his description as Rory stood up and walked around the table to his side. Oh, crap, oh double crap, he thought as she placed a hand on his shoulder. Kade felt his teeth slam together.

She wouldn't dare. She wasn't that brave.

"Why, who else but one of my favorite people in the whole world? I bought this for my very good friend, Kade Webb." Rory sent Kade a huge smile. As if she could charm him into changing his mind about tossing her from the nearest balcony.

"I just know Brodie will find Kade a stunning woman. I'm counting on her to find someone who'll make him supremely happy."

Dammit, hell, crap.

The room erupted into hoots of laughter and excited chatter. Dammit, hell, crap multiplied.

Kade met Mac's eyes and scowled when his friend raised his glass in a mocking toast. "Welcome to my crazy world, dude."

Kade really liked his best friend's fiancée and thought it wonderful they were having a baby, but his anger over her stunt hadn't disappeared.

What the hell was she thinking? Had she been think-ing at all? He didn't need anyone to find him a woman! And he certainly didn't need his current lover to find him a new love!

If he could get past Mac, he had very strong words for Rory. He didn't allow anyone to play fast and loose with his life and he allowed no interference when it came to his sex life. Rory hadn't just stepped over the line, she'd eradicated it.

From his seat in his low-slung German sports car Kade stared at the still dark windows of Brodie's apartment and ran a hand over his jaw. It had taken all his acting skills to breeze through the rest of the evening, to bat away the wisecracks, to laugh at the admittedly good-hearted banter. Well, everyone's banter except his partners' had been good-natured. Mac and Quinn had teased him mercilessly.

For that they would pay...

Kade was perfectly capable of finding his own woman and he didn't want to be in a relationship. Damned women and their meddling. He refused to have anything to do with Rory's scheme and he refused to feel guilty about her wasting her money. She shouldn't have pulled such an asinine trick in the first place!

And if he found out Mac had anything to do with this, then he and McCaskill would go a couple of rounds in the ring, no holds barred.

Kade massaged his temples. It was past 6:00 a.m. He'd had no sleep. He hadn't changed out of his tux. His head was pounding and he wanted nothing more than to climb into bed with Brodie and lose himself in her. He'd done that last night, he remembered. With Brodie the world had disappeared, and for the few hours they were together, he'd relaxed and forgotten. Forgotten about his responsibilities, his past. He'd stopped worrying about his future. With her he'd lived in the moment, something he usually couldn't do.

He wouldn't start to rely on her to feel like that, wouldn't enjoy what they had more than he should. He'd keep it light, he promised himself. This was a one-time, short-term thing. He wasn't looking for long term and neither was she.

All well and good, he thought, but how was he going

to handle this stupid situation Rory had placed him in? He had to tell Brodie. That was why he was sitting in front of her apartment complex at the butt crack of dawn.

Brodie had said this—whatever it was between them—would probably be just be one night. And she'd also said something about sleeping with clients being unprofessional.

But if he didn't take up Rory's offer and didn't allow Brodie to set him up, then he wouldn't be her client. He knew their chemistry was combustible enough for more than one night. So everything would be fine. Either way, he had to tell her.

Rory Kydd, if you weren't a woman and if my best friend didn't love you so much, I would kick your very nice ass all over Vancouver.

Maybe he was overthinking this. Brodie was sensible. Kade felt a bit of his panic recede. There was no way she'd accept the challenge to match him. She'd just laugh off Rory's bid and the money would go to charity…no harm, no foul.

He'd call Brodie later, he thought, when he was rested and clearheaded. He lifted his hand to touch the ignition button. His finger hovered there but instead of allowing the powerful engine to roar to life, he instructed his onboard computer to call Brodie.

What are you doing, idiot?

Yet he allowed the cell to ring and eventually he heard Brodie's sleep roughened, sexy voice. "'Lo."

"I'm outside. Let me come up."

"Kade? What time is it?"

"Early." Kade opened the door and climbed out of his expensive car.

He started walking to the front door and his heart

jumped when a light snapped on in a corner room on the top floor. She was awake.

Kade flew up the stairs. As he reached her apartment the door opened and Brodie stood in the dark hall, her hair mussed, wearing nothing more than a hockey jersey. His number. Lust and warmth and relief pumped through him. Rory and her machinations were instantly forgotten; his world was comprised of this woman and how desperately he wanted her.

"What's wron—"

Kade cut off Brodie's words by covering her mouth with his. Without ending the kiss, he picked her up, kicked the door shut with his foot and carried her to her bedroom.

They were being perfectly adult about this, Brodie decided as she poured coffee into two mugs. Civilized. So far they'd managed to avoid the awkwardness that normally accompanied the morning after the night before.

He hadn't faked any emotion he didn't feel and she hadn't felt like she was being used. They'd made love, slept a little, made love again and then Kade asked if he could use her shower. She offered to make him breakfast. He declined but said he'd take a cup of coffee.

As extended one-night stands went, it was practically perfect. Then why did she feel like she didn't want it to end?

She was just being silly; she was tired and not thinking straight. After she'd had a solid eight hours of sleep, she'd be grateful Kade was so good at this. Brodie frowned. He'd obviously had a lot of practice.

"Are you going to drink it or just stare at it?"

Brodie turned slowly and sucked in her breath. Kade

naked was a revelation, but Kade in a wrinkled tuxedo wasn't too shabby, either. Too shabby as in freakin' damn hot. "Uh…"

Kade walked over to her, lifted the cup to her mouth and tipped it. "Coffee, a magical substance that turns 'uh' into 'good morning, honey.'"

Brodie rolled her eyes as he took her cup and sipped from it. "I'd forgotten you were a morning person. It's okay to kill happy, cheerful morning people, I checked."

Kade handed her cup back and walked over to the pot and poured his own. He leaned his butt against her counter and sipped. "You need a shower and six hours of sleep."

"Eight." Brodie pulled out a wooden chair from the table and dropped into it. "And you're the one who woke me up so early so it's your fault."

Kade grinned. "I didn't see you fighting me off. Sorry about your panties, by the way."

"You owe me a new pair," Brodie told him, both hands wrapped around her cup. Such a nice tuxedo… and it fitted him beautifully. The bow tie was gone and his face was shaded with blond stubble. Then she sat up straighter, remembering why Kade was wearing a tuxedo. "The ball! I'd forgotten… How did it go? Did you manage to raise any money from my donation?"

"Uh, yeah. It sold."

"You don't sound too enthusiastic." Brodie cocked her head. "Didn't it make any money at all? I'm *so* sorry."

"It made quite a bit of money. That's not the problem."

"There's a problem? How can there be a problem with my gift? The guy comes to me, I set him up on three dates and hopefully there's a happily-ever-after."

"It all depends on who the guy is."

Right, now she was confused. "So who is the guy?"

"Me."

She knew it was early and she wasn't a 100 percent awake, but she thought, maybe, Kade had said *he* was the one she would be working with.

"Please tell me you are joking?" Brodie begged. She knew instinctively that Kade hadn't had anything to do with her donation. So whose stupid idea was this? "Mac? Quinn?"

"Rory."

So Brodie hadn't misinterpreted Rory's mischievous look after all. Rory was very brave, or very stupid, and obviously very determined to get Kade hitched. Pity she hadn't a clue that Brodie and Kade could spark a wildfire from one kiss.

Damn. She'd just had earth-scorching sex with her client. She'd unwittingly and unknowingly broken her number-one rule. Brodie took a sip of coffee and pushed past the surge of jealousy to work out how, exactly, she was going to do this. Unfortunately there wasn't a manual dealing with the pesky problem of how to match your one-night stand.

God, this was far too confusing for someone whose blood didn't start to circulate until she'd had three cups of coffee. Think this through… Sex, ball for him and sleep for her, sex, client.

Brodie lifted her head to glare at him. Kade had come over to her house and seduced her again, knowing her views about dating her clients. Brodie stood up, anger obliterating the last of her sleepiness.

"How dare you! Why didn't you tell me right away that Rory had bid on my services for you! What the hell,

Kade? Did you not think that might have had an impact on my decision to sleep with you again?"

"Whoa, hold on…" Kade lifted his hands.

"You should've told me! I had a right to know, you manipulative jerk!"

"That's not fair."

Brodie brushed past him and tossed her coffee into the sink. "The hell it's not. You knew about this and you knew I'd back off from sleeping with you if you told me. So you didn't say a damn word!"

"I thought about telling you." Kade jammed his hands into the pockets of his pants and scowled.

"*Thought* about it?"

"Yeah! I was going to explain what she'd done, tell you I wasn't going to do it. I was hoping we'd have a laugh about it."

"I'm not finding anything vaguely funny in this."

Kade shoved his hands into his hair, linked his fingers behind his head and stared at her with hot eyes. "I didn't mean to make you feel used, or bad. The truth is that when you opened the door the only thing I could think about was the fact you were nearly naked. I had to have you. Again. Being set up was the last thing on my mind."

She wanted to tell him she didn't believe him, but she saw the truth in his eyes. He'd wanted her like she'd wanted him. Impulsively. Wildly. Crazily. Their need for each other didn't stop to, well, *think*. And, damn, it was hot.

And deeply, utterly problematic. She couldn't control her attraction to him and it seemed Kade was having a similar problem. Such need wasn't healthy, nor was it easy to resist. She needed to step back, to create some distance between them, but every time they were in the same room all they wanted to do was rip off each other's clothes.

They had to stop the madness—this was supposed to be a one-night fling. They were already on day two—sort of—and Kade was like any other man: he wasn't going to walk away from fabulous sex.

She didn't want to walk away from it, either, but for her, being with him felt like it was about more than just the sex. With him she felt alive and vibrant and animated and she couldn't afford to feel like that, even if it only happened in the bedroom. She might come to like it and, worse, get used to it. How would she get that genie back in its bottle?

So this had to stop now. She liked her life exactly as it was. Bland, safe, predictable.

She needed to walk away, far, far away. But Kade just needed to kiss her and she'd be all *yes, please, take me now.*

So she was going to match him.

"You're making too big a deal of this, Brodie," Kade stated. "Just tell Rory we are seeing each other, that there's a conflict of interest. Tell her to let you match Quinn."

Ha! Right. Kade would get out of the matchmaking, keep sleeping with Brodie and annoy Quinn in the process. For Kade, it would be a trifecta win.

But that wasn't going to happen. Brodie shoved aside the heat and the lust and ordered herself to use her brain.

"That would be rude and disrespectful. No, Rory's bid was for you so I will match you."

If she hadn't been feeling so miserable she would've laughed at his horrified face. "What? No!"

Her thinking hat firmly in place, Brodie paced the free area in her small kitchen. "Wren is a smart cookie and I bet she's already thinking of ways to spin this to generate PR for you. Mavericks fans will lap it up. They need a feel-good story, what with the owner's recent death and the future of the team still up in the air. And you released one of their favorite players last month. They are not happy with *you*."

"You seem to know a lot about my business."

Brodie waved away his comment, not feeling the need to tell him that after he left last night she jumped online to read about him and the Mavericks.

"I had solid reasons for releasing him," Kade argued. "It didn't matter that he was the best rookie in the league, a BC native and one of the first graduates from the Mavericks Ice Hockey Academy. He was photographed snorting coke, he was underperforming as a player and he was undisciplined. He had more chances than most, not that the fans care about that." Kade's tone was flat, his eyes bleak.

It had been a joint decision to boot the player, but as CEO, Kade took the flak. He led from the front, Brodie realized, and she had to admire him for that.

Quickly, she returned to the topic at hand. She couldn't afford to get sidetracked *admiring* him. "Matching you would be good publicity, for the Mavericks and for me."

"Not happening."

"Go to the office, see what Wren's working on. I guarantee it's something similar to what I've been thinking."

A muscle jumped in Kade's jaw and he tipped his head back to look at the ceiling. "I'm going to kill Rory, I really am. Want to help me bury her body?"

At his rueful words the rest of Brodie's anger dissipated. "I'll dig the grave."

Brodie raked her hair back from her face, then grabbed her mug from the sink and poured coffee back into the cup. She took a couple of sips. "I'm sure this is the most interesting conversation after a one-night stand in the history of one-night stands."

Kade rolled his head and Brodie assumed he was trying to work out the tension in his neck. "It's not exactly the conversation I planned on having."

Brodie's heart bounced off her ribs. She shouldn't voice the words on her lips but she had to—it would drive her nuts if she didn't. "What would you have said?"

Kade stepped closer and curled his hand around her neck. "I would've said that I had a great time and I would've asked if we could do this again."

Yeah, that's what she'd thought and that's exactly what she couldn't do. She'd liked it too much, liked having him around. She needed distance and a lot of it. Matching him would give her that.

"We can't," Brodie whispered. "It's too complicated. And, if I'm going to be setting you up...too weird."

"That's not confirmed yet. I'll try my damnedest to get out of it."

He'd come around, Brodie realized. It was too good a story to pass up, too good an opportunity to give the fans something to smile about. And Kade always, always put the Mavericks first.

Kade pulled her forward so her cheek lay against his chest. "If I do this, and I'm not saying I will, when it's done, can we...?"

Brodie knew she should just kill this...thing between them but she simply couldn't. "Let's just play it by ear." She pulled back and looked up at him, forcing her lips to curve into a smile. "You never know, one of those women might be the love of your life and another one-night stand with me will be the last thing on your mind."

"Not freakin' likely," Kade retorted.

Brodie stepped away and folded her arms, trying to remove herself from him mentally and physically. She had to stop *feeling* and keep *thinking*. "We will have to meet professionally, though. I need information from you to find out what you are looking for."

Kade glared at her. "You're talking like this is a done deal! If this happens, be very clear, I'm not looking for *anything*, with anybody! Find me three women who are marginally intelligent, someone who I can talk to for two hours over dinner."

"This is my business, Kade. If we do this, we will do it properly…"

Kade swore and started to roll back his sleeves, revealing the muscles and raised veins in his forearms. Brodie imagined those hands on another woman's skin and felt sick. Now she was adding jealousy to her messy heap of tangled emotions? Wasn't there enough crazy on that pile?

She took a breath. Seeing him with someone else would be good for her. It would put even more distance between them. And that was what she was trying to do here.

"That's the way I work, Kade. It's not up for negotiation."

"Dammit, crap, hell," Kade muttered another string of swearwords under his breath as he finished rolling up his other sleeve. When he was done, he placed his hands on either side of Brodie's face, gave her a hard kiss and picked up his jacket. "We'll talk about this again."

Brodie touched her lips as he walked out of her kitchen, leaving as quickly as he'd arrived.

So that was that. Well, then.

She was now Kade's matchmaker.

Five

Three weeks later Brodie sat in her usual seat at Jan's
waiting for Kade, her trusty tablet on the table in front
of her. How was she supposed to ask Kade all these intensely personal questions knowing he'd touched, caressed and kissed every inch of her body?

What had she done to piss off the karma fairy?

Brodie placed her cheek in her hand and swallowed
down her nausea. Her stomach roiled and she tasted bile
in the back of her throat every time she thought about
this upcoming interview. She'd had twenty-one days,
thanks to Kade's insane schedule and Wren wanting
maximum publicity, to feel this way. Three weeks of
restless sleep, of feeling on edge, miserable.

Angry.

*Once you've done this interview and you've entered
the relevant data into the program, you can find his
three dates and get on with your life.*

Her donation to the auction only included three matches. She wouldn't have to set him up again if none of those woman suited. One batch, she decided, was enough.

And then, when it was done, she'd walk away for good and Kade Webb would be a memory of the best sex she'd ever experienced.

As she'd predicted, Wren had made a charming PR story of Rory's matchmaking gift. Every few weeks, depending on Kade's schedule, a new "date" for Kade would be introduced to the public. Their likes and dislikes would be posted on the Mavericks' website with their photos. Pictures and short video clips of their date would be uploaded and the public could comment. Once all three women had been on a date with Kade, the public would vote on their favorite match.

Such fun and games, Brodie thought. Brodie slipped out of her lightweight cardigan and draped it over her bag. It was hot in the coffee shop, something she'd never experienced before. Usually the air-conditioning made her feel chilly. She also had a headache; damn, she hoped she wasn't getting sick again. That was all she needed.

Brodie heard the tinkle of the chimes announcing a new arrival into the coffee shop. She looked toward the door and immediately sighed. Kade embodied business casual in his dark gold chinos, steel-gray jacket and checked shirt under a sweater the color of berries. Successful and urbane. Too sexy for words.

And she wasn't the only one reacting to his arrival. She felt the collective intake of female breath and knew many sets of ovaries were shivering in delight. Kade pushed his sunglasses onto the top of his head and looked around. He smiled when he saw her and her heart stumbled. Stupid organ.

Kade bent down and brushed his lips across her cheek, and she inhaled his cologne. Sandalwood and spice and something all Kade. She felt her nipples prickle and cursed. Yep, the attraction hadn't lessened one damn bit.

Annoyed she couldn't control her reaction to this man, she frowned at him. "You're late."

"Two minutes and hello to you, too," Kade replied as he sat down. He leaned forward and gripped her chin. "Why are you looking tired? And pale?"

So nice to know she was looking her best, Brodie thought. "I'm fine."

"You sure?"

"I had a chest infection shortly before the auction, maybe it's coming back."

"Are you coughing? Short of breath? Should you see a doctor?"

"I'm fine, Webb. Jeez, stop fussing." She pulled her tablet toward her, hitting the power button. "Shall we get started?"

"Tired and pale and *grumpy*. Can I order some coffee first?" Kade tapped her hand with his finger and waited until she met his eyes. "This situation is crazy enough without us snapping at each other."

She heard the rebuke in his voice and blushed. She was acting like a child. Okay, it wasn't the ideal situation, but she shouldn't be taking her bad mood out on him. He didn't want to be set up any more than she wanted to set him up and he was right, it would be a lot easier if she acted like an adult, even better if she could be friendly.

Pull yourself together, Stewart.

Brodie straightened her shoulders and sent him an apologetic smile. "Sorry. Hi…how are you?"

Kade nodded. "Good. Sorry we haven't been able to meet before this but I've been swamped."

Brodie had realized that. If the papers weren't talking about his upcoming dates, then they were discussing the Mavericks' purchase of Josh Logan, superstar wing, the negotiations to buy the franchise and the legal action against the Mavericks for unfair dismissal by the former star rookie. "What do your lawyers say?"

"About the dismissal?" Kade asked to clarify. He shrugged. "He's wasting his time, and mine, but we all know that. He doesn't have a leg to stand on. It's just a pain in my ass, to be frank." Kade scowled at her tablet. "As are these stupid dates. Seriously, Brodie, I don't want to answer your questions…just choose three women and let's get it over with. Nobody will know but us."

She wished she could but it went against her nature to cut corners. Besides, her questionnaire revealed a lot about her clients and she was curious about Kade.

Not professional, but what the hell? They'd never date and this was the only way she'd be able to assuage her curiosity. "I can't enter the data until I have the answers and I can't match you until I have the data."

"How long does it take?" Kade demanded as Jan approached their table.

"An hour for the long version, half hour if you only answer the compulsory questions." Brodie looked at Jan. "Kade, this is my friend Jan. Jan, Kade Webb."

"I figured." Jan shook his hand. "What can I get you, Kade? Brodie here usually has a coffee milk shake."

Brodie shuddered. She couldn't stomach it today. Too rich…

"Not today, Jan. I'll just have a glass of water."

Jan frowned at her. "You okay?"

"I'm feeling a little flu-ey," Brodie reluctantly admitted. "Hot, a little dizzy and I have a headache." Jan put her hand on her forehead and Brodie slapped it away. "I don't have a temperature and I'll see a doctor if I start coughing, okay?"

"When did you last eat?" Jan demanded.

Maybe that was what was wrong with her. She'd had soup for supper last night and she'd skipped breakfast. She was, she realized, starving. A hamburger would chase away her malaise. "I am hungry." She turned to Kade. "Jan's hamburgers can cure anything from depression to smallpox. Do you want one?"

Kade nodded. "I can eat."

Brodie ordered two cheeseburgers with everything and when Jan left, Brodie smiled at Kade. "Her burgers are really good." She reached into her bag, pulled out her reading glasses and slid them onto her face. "Shall we get started?"

Kade had never considered glasses to be sexy but Brodie's black-rimmed frames turned her green eyes, already mesmerizing, to a deep emerald. He loved her eyes, he thought as he answered questions about his date of birth, his height, his weight. Then again, he also loved her high cheekbones, her stubborn chin, her small but very firm breasts and those long, slim legs.

He liked everything about her and he wished he could blow off lunch and take her to bed. When this stupidity was over, he promised himself. When it was done, he'd kidnap Brodie for the weekend, take her somewhere private and keep her naked in his bed until he'd burned this craving for her out of his system.

He was hardly sleeping and when he did, his dreams were erotic, with Brodie taking the starring role. He thought about her at the most inappropriate times. Memories from the night they shared obliterated his concentration. It was torture trying to negotiate when he recalled the way Brodie fell apart under his touch.

Brodie pinching his wrist pulled him back to their conversation. "What?"

"I asked…siblings?"

"None." He'd always wanted a brother, someone to take the edge off the loneliness growing up. Someone to stand by his side as he entered the hallway of a new school or joined a new team. Someone who could help him recall the towns they'd lived in and in what order.

"Parents?"

"My father lives in the city, my mother died when I was ten." He snapped the words out. He rubbed a hand over his jaw. God, he didn't want to do this. He never discussed his childhood, his past, his on-off relationship with his socially inept, now reclusive father. "You don't need information about my past so move along."

He saw the furrow appear between Brodie's eyebrows. Well, tough. His childhood was over. He finally had his brothers in Mac and Quinn and he was content. Sometimes he was even happy.

Kade leaned back in his seat. If he had to answer personal questions, then so did she. "And your parents? Where are they?"

"Dead." Brodie didn't lift her head. "I was twenty."

"I'm sorry, Brodes."

"Thanks. Moving on…what characteristic in a woman is most important to you? Looks, empathy, humor, intelligence?"

"All of them," Kade flippantly answered, wishing

he could ask how her parents died, but he could tell the subject was firmly off-limits. "Do you have siblings?"

"No." Brodie tapped her fingernail against the screen of her tablet. "I'm asking the questions, Webb, not you."

"Quid pro quo," Kade replied. "Were you close to your parents?"

He saw the answer in her eyes. Sadness, regret, sheer, unrelenting pain. A glimmer suggesting tears was ruthlessly blinked away. Oh, yeah…they might've passed many years ago, but Brodie was still dealing with losing them.

He was fascinated by this softer, emotional Brodie. She was fiercely intelligent, sexy and independent, but beneath her tough shell she made his protective instincts stand up and pay attention. He wanted to dig deeper, uncover more of those hidden depths.

"Tell me about them, Brodie."

"Where is our food?" Brodie demanded, looking around. "I could eat a horse."

"Why won't you talk about them?" Kade persisted. And why couldn't he move off the topic? He never pushed this hard, was normally not this interested. Maybe he was getting sick? He was definitely sick of this matchmaking crap and he hadn't even started with the dates yet. He just wanted to take Brodie home and make love to her again. Was that too much to ask?

Apparently it was.

Brodie finally, finally looked at him and when she did, her face was pale and bleak. "Because it hurts too damn much! Satisfied?"

Dammit, he hadn't meant to hurt her. Brodie flung herself backward and stared out the window to watch the busy traffic.

"Sorry, sweetheart," he murmured.

"Me, too." Brodie, reluctantly, met his eyes. "Please don't pry, Kade. I don't talk about my past."

Maybe she should. Someone, he realized, needed to hear her story and she definitely needed to tell it. It was a shock to realize he wanted to be the one to hear her tale. He wanted to be her friend, to offer comfort. To find out what made her tick.

Jan approached them with two loaded plates. She set the first one down on the table in front of Brodie and then put a plate in front of him. If the burger tasted as good as it smelled, then he was in for a treat, he thought, as he snagged a crispy fry and shoved it into his mouth.

He reached for the salt and frowned when he saw Brodie's now white face. She stared at her plate and, using one finger, pushed it away.

"What's wrong?" he demanded. "I thought you said you were hungry?"

"I was, not anymore." Brodie swallowed and reached for her water. "I think I am definitely getting sick. I'm hot and feeling light-headed."

Jan narrowed her eyes at her, then silently, and without argument, picked up Brodie's plate. Kade didn't understand the long, knowing look Jan sent Brodie and he didn't give her another thought after she walked away.

He frowned when Brodie picked up her tablet and swiped her finger across the screen. "Just choose three women, Brodie, I'm begging you. Any three."

Brodie, who, he was discovering, could give lessons in stubbornness to mules, just shook her head. "Not happening. So here we go…"

Do you base your life decisions more on feelings or rational thinking?

Are you more extroverted or introverted?

Is your bedroom, right now, messy or neat?

Are you more driven or laid-back in your approach to life?

After twenty-five minutes, Kade had a headache to match hers.

A week later Brodie tucked her wallet back into her tote bag and stuffed her phone into the back pocket of her oldest, most comfortable Levi's. Slinging her tote over her shoulder, she took a long sip of the bottled water she'd just purchased and ignored the craziness of the airport. Brodie looked up at the arrivals board, thankful Poppy's flight had landed fifteen minutes ago. Brodie really didn't want to spend her Saturday morning hanging around waiting.

As per usual, there were no empty seats.

Brodie shook her head and headed for a small piece of wall next to a bank of phone booths. Propping her tote behind her back, she placed her booted foot up on the wall, leaned her head back and closed her eyes. God, she couldn't remember when last she'd felt this overwhelming tiredness.

She was overworked, run-down, stressed out. Maybe she was flirting with burnout. She'd been working fourteen-and sixteen-hour days for the last few weeks, partly to keep up with her ever increasing client list. The publicity around Kade had resulted in a surge of business. Work was also an excellent way to stop thinking—obsessing—about Kade.

She really didn't like the amount of space he was renting in her brain. And she wished she could just make a decision on who was going to be his first date. She knew she was being ultra picky but she couldn't help it. She wanted pretty but not blow-your-socks-off attractive. She wanted a good conversationalist but not someone who was intriguing. She wanted smart but not too smart.

She didn't want him to date anyone at all.

Which was ludicrous—she had no claim on the man and hadn't she decided they needed some distance? God, maybe she was the source of her own exhaustion. Donating to the charity auction had not been one of her smarter ideas. Sure, it was a good cause, but following up her one-night stand with finding her said ONS someone else to have a one-night stand with left a sour taste in her mouth.

Brodie silently urged her great-aunt to hurry up. Poppy had the energy and enthusiasm of a ten-year-old with a tendency to talk to everyone she encountered. Brodie wondered how long Poppy would be staying in town before the travel bug bit again. She'd visited more countries in three years than most people did in a lifetime and Brodie couldn't help but admire her great-aunt's sense of adventure. It took courage to travel on her own and to make friends along the way.

Just hurry yourself up, Poppy. I really am feeling, well, like hell. And the sooner we get out of here, the happier I'll be.

A cramping stomach accompanied Brodie's nausea. She clenched her jaw and clutched her stomach, frantically thinking about what she had recently eaten that could have given her food poisoning. Cornflakes? Last night's boiled egg?

Brodie took a series of deep breaths, sucked on some more water and felt the nausea recede. When she opened her eyes again she saw Poppy, one hand on her travel case and the other on her hip, a speculative look on her face.

Brodie managed a wan smile. "Hey, you're here. That

was quick." She kissed Poppy's cheek and gave her a long hug. "How was Bali?"

"Loved it," Poppy replied. "I was considering staying another month but then I was invited to join a cruise to Alaska leaving in the next month."

"You're leaving again?"

Poppy dropped into a recently vacated empty seat. "You look dreadful. Are you sick?"

"Yeah, so nauseous. I must've eaten something bad last night.

Poppy grinned. "Unless you've discovered sex in the last six weeks and someone has dropped a bun in your oven. But that's not likely since you have the world's most boring sex life."

Brodie stared at her great-aunt while Poppy's words sank in.

No, no… God, *no*!

"I'm not pregnant." Brodie ground out the words, pushing back her hair. She wasn't even going to consider such a ridiculous scenario. She was on the pill! Brodie scrabbled in her bag for another bottle of water and after trying to open it with a shaking hand, passed it over to Poppy for help twisting off the cap. Brodie felt her body ice up with every drop she swallowed.

"Pregnancy would explain how you are feeling and is a result of sex. So, have you had any lately?"

Admitting to sex made the possibility of her being pregnant terribly real. "One time, weeks ago. The condom split."

"Ah, that would explain it."

"It explains nothing! I'm on the pill!"

"Even the pill can fail sometimes."

Brodie lowered the bottle and started to shake. Could she possibly be pregnant with Kade's baby?

From a universe far away Brodie felt Poppy's hand on her back. "Come on, Mata Hari, let's find you a pregnancy test and you can tell me who, what, where and when."

Three pregnancy tests could not be wrong. Unfortunately.

It had taken a week of Poppy's nagging for Brodie to find her courage to do a pregnancy test and now she desperately wished she hadn't.

Brodie stared at the three sticks lined up on the edge of her bathroom counter and hoped her Jedi mind trick would turn the positive signs to negative. After five minutes her brain felt like it was about to explode so she sat down on the toilet seat and placed her head in her hands.

She was pregnant. Tears ran down her face as she admitted that Poppy had called it—the girl who had the sex life of a nun was pregnant because Kade Webb carried around a faulty condom.

Jerk. Dipstick. Moron.

Brodie bit her lip. What was the moron/jerk/dipstick doing tonight? It was Saturday. He might be on a date with one of her suggestions for his first date. Which one? The redhead with the engineering degree? The blonde teacher? The Brazilian doctor? Brodie pulled her hair. If she thought about Kade dating, she'd go crazy.

Maybe, instead of feeling jealous of those women, it would be sensible to consider the much bigger problem growing inside her. The exploding bundle of cells that would, in a couple of weeks, become a fetus and then a little human, a perfect mixture of Kade and her.

She wasn't ready to be a mommy. Hell, she wasn't ready—possibly wouldn't ever be ready—for a relationship. And motherhood was the biggest relationship of them all. It never ended. Until death…

Brodie felt the room spin and knew she was close to panicking. She couldn't be responsible for another life. She couldn't even emotionally connect to anyone else. How would she raise a well-balanced, well-adjusted kid with all her trust and loss and abandonment issues?

How could she raise a kid at all? She couldn't do this. She didn't have to do this. It was the twenty-first century and if she wanted, she could un-pregnant herself. Her life could go back to what it was before… She could be back in control. She wouldn't have to confront Kade. She wouldn't have to change her life. By tomorrow, or the day after, she'd be back to normal.

Brodie stood up and looked at her pale face in the mirror. Back to normal. She wanted normal… Didn't she? She wanted smooth, unemotional, uncluttered. She wasn't the type who wanted to sail her ship through stormy seas. She'd experienced the tempests and vagaries and sheer brutality of life and she didn't want to be on another rocking boat.

Right. Sorted. She had a plan. So why wasn't she feeling at peace with the decision? Why did she feel at odds with herself and the universe?

"You can't hide in there forever." Poppy's voice drifted under the door. Brodie reached over and flipped the lock. Within ten seconds Poppy's keen eyes saw the tests and the results. Poppy, being Poppy, just raised her eyebrows. "What are you going to do?"

Brodie lifted her shoulders and let them hover somewhere around her ears. It would help to talk this through with someone and since Poppy was here Brodie figured she was a good candidate. "I'm thinking about—" she couldn't articulate the process,"—becoming un-pregnant."

If she couldn't *say* it, how was she going to *do* it?

Poppy, unmarried by choice, didn't react to that statement. "That's one option," she stated, crossing her arms over her chest, her bright blue eyes shrewd.

"Raising a child by myself is not much of an option," Brodie snapped.

"Depends on your point of view," Poppy replied, her voice easy. "Your parents thought you were the best thing to hit this planet and they had you in far more difficult circumstances than you are in now."

Brodie frowned. "I'll be a single mother, Poppy. My parents were together."

"They were married, yes, but your father was in the army, stationed overseas. Your mom was alone for six, eight months at a time and she coped. Money was tight for them." Poppy looked at Brodie's designer jeans and pointed to her expensive toiletries. "Money is not an object for you. You are your own boss and you can juggle your time. You could take your child to work or you could start working more from home. This is not the disaster you think it is."

Brodie tried to find an argument to counter Poppy's, but she came up blank. Before she could speak, Poppy continued. "Your parents were practically broke and always apart and yet they never once regretted having you. They were so excited when you came along."

Brodie's mom had loved kids and had wanted a houseful but, because she'd had complications while she was pregnant with Brodie, she'd had to forgo that dream. "I can't wait until you have kids," she'd tell Brodie. "I hope you have lots and I'll help you look after them."

Except you are not here when I need you most. You won't be here to help and I'll have to do it...alone.

Poppy wouldn't give up her traveling to become a nanny. Besides, knowing Poppy, she'd probably leave the baby at the supermarket or something.

"What about the man who impregnated you?"

"You make me sound like a broodmare, Pops," Brodie complained, pushing her hand into her hair. She looked around and noticed they were having this life-changing discussion in her too-small bathroom. "And why are we talking in here?"

"Because I'm standing in the doorway and you can't run away when the topic gets heated."

"I don't run away!" Brodie protested. Though, in her heart, she knew she did.

Poppy rolled her eyes at the blatant lie. "So, about the father."

"What about him?" Brodie demanded.

"Are you going to tell him?"

Brodie groaned. "I don't know what the hell I am going to do, Poppy!"

Poppy crossed one ankle over the other and Brodie saw she'd acquired a new tattoo in Bali, this one on her wrist. "I think you should talk to him. The decision lies with you but he was there. He helped create the situation and he has a right to be part of the solution."

"He doesn't have to know, either way."

"Legally? No. Morally? You sure?" Poppy asked.

Brodie tipped her head up to look at the ceiling. "I was at the point of making a decision," Brodie complained. "Thank you for complicating the situation for me, Great-aunt."

"Someone needs to," Poppy muttered, looking exasperated. She pointed a long finger at Brodie's face.

"Your problem is that since your parents and friends died, you always take the easy route, Brodie."

"I do not!"

"Pfft. Of course you do! Not having this baby is the easy way. Not telling the father is the easy way. Living in this house and burying yourself in your work—finding other people love but not yourself!—is taking the easy route. You need to be braver!"

"I survived a multicar pileup that wiped out my parents and best friends!" Brodie shouted.

"But it didn't kill *you*!" Poppy responded, her voice rising, too. "You are so damn scared to risk being hurt that you don't live! You satisfy your need for love by setting up other people. You keep busy to stop yourself from feeling lonely, and you don't do anything exciting or fun. Do you know how thrilled I am to find out that you've had a one-night stand? I think it's brilliant because someone finally jolted you out of your safety bubble. And, dammit, I hope you are brave enough to talk to the father, to have this kid, because I think it will be the making of you."

Through Brodie's shock and anger she saw Poppy blink back tears. Poppy was the strongest person she knew and not given to showing emotion. "I want you to be brave, Brodie. I want you to start living."

Brodie felt her anger fade. "I don't know how," she whispered. "I've forgotten."

Poppy walked toward her and pulled her to her slight frame. "You start by taking one step at a time, my darling. Go talk to the father…" Poppy pulled back to frown at Brodie. "Who is the father?"

"Kade Webb."

"My baby has taste." Poppy grinned. "Well, at the risk of sounding shallow, at the very least the baby will be one good-looking little human." Poppy grabbed Brodie's hand and pulled her from the bathroom. "Now come and tell me how you met and, crucially, how you ended up in bed."

Six

Date one of three and he was officially off the publicity wagon until he had to do this again next month.

Well, he would be done as soon as she left his apartment. He wouldn't offer her any more wine, Kade decided. He wasn't going to extend the date any longer than he absolutely had to. He'd wanted to have supper at a restaurant but Wren had insisted he cook Rachel dinner in his expansive loft apartment. Cooking her dinner would show the public his caring, domestic side.

The public, thanks to the photographers who'd hovered around, would also see his residence in downtown Vancouver and Simon, his mutt. Kade stroked his hand over Si's head, which lay heavy on his thigh. Simon, whom he'd found in an alley on one of his early-morning runs, considered Kade his personal property and any woman would have to fight his dog for a place in his life.

Kade stifled his sigh and resisted the urge to look at his watch. When he'd received the portfolios of his potential dates from Brodie, he'd flipped through the three candidates and opted to eat with the doctor. Then he'd contacted Wren and instructed her to arrange his first date for as soon as possible. Breakfast, lunch and supper…whenever, she just had to get it done. Wren, efficient as always, had done exactly that. One down, two to go.

"And then I spent three months working in the Sudan with Médecins Sans Frontières."

His buzzer signaled someone was downstairs wanting to come up. Kade smiled at his guest, hoping Wren had read his mind and come to rescue him.

You're a big boy, he heard Wren's amused voice in his head. *If you can talk them into bed, then you sure as hell don't need my help to talk them out of your apartment.*

Or maybe it was Quinn downstairs. The doctor was his type—brainy and built. Quinn would, if Kade asked him, take Rachel off his hands. Kade stood up and walked across the open space to his front door and intercom. He pressed the button, called out a greeting and shrugged when no one answered.

It had to be Mac or Quinn. They both usually hit the buzzer to signal they were on their way up.

Kade turned to walk back to his guest. It was definitely time to maneuver her out the door. Please let Quinn be thundering up the steps, he thought. *Please.*

A tentative knock told him it wasn't Quinn, or Mac, and Kade frowned. Who else would be visiting him at 9:45 p.m. on a Saturday night? Then again, whoever it was would be a distraction and he'd take what he could get.

Sending a fake smile of apology in Rachel's direction, he walked back to the door and opened it. As per usual when he saw Brodie, his mouth dried up and his heart flipped once, then twice.

What was it about this woman that turned his brain to mush? If he compared her to Rachel, Brodie came up short. She was wearing ratty jeans and a tight T-shirt in pale gray, a perfect match to her complexion. Pale gray tinged with green. Her eyes were a flat, dark, mossy green and accessorized by huge black rings. Her hair was raked off her face and she looked like a spring ready to explode.

"We need to talk… Can I come in?"

Kade tossed a look over his shoulder and sighed when he saw Rachel walking in their direction, a puzzled look on her face. "Hi, there." Rachel appeared at his shoulder and he watched Brodie's eyes widen as she gave the buxom doctor a good up-and-down look.

"Doctor Martinez." Brodie's voice cooled.

Brodie stepped to the side and looked across his apartment to the small dining table at the far end of the room. Kade sighed. Fat candles, muted light, wineglasses, her heels next to her chair. It looked like everything it really wasn't, a romantic dinner for two.

Kade heard the click of Si's nails against the wooden floor and waited for the dog to take his customary place at Kade's side. Si, to Kade's surprise, walked straight past him and up to Brodie. Kade waited for the growl and cocked his head when Simon nuzzled his snout into Brodie's hand. Brodie immediately, and instinctively, dropped to her haunches and rubbed her hands over Si's ears and down his neck.

Delight flickered in her tired eyes. "Oh, he's gorgeous, Kade. I didn't know you had a dog."

"We haven't exactly had a lot of time to talk," Kade

pointed out and Brodie flushed. "Meet Simon, part Alsatian, part malamute, all sappy. I've had him about two months."

"He's a lovely dog," Rachel said, her tone bright and chirpy. Oh, hell, he'd forgotten she was there.

Kade watched as Brodie stood up slowly, a blush creeping up her neck. Kade could see she was ready to bolt. He wanted to hustle Rachel out, pull Brodie in, pick her up and cradle her in his arms and find out, in between kisses, what was making her so very miserable.

Because she was—he knew it like his own name.

Brodie darted a look at Rachel and he saw her suck in a breath. He watched how she added two and two and somehow ended up with sixty-five.

Brodie lifted her hands and stepped back. "I am being inexcusably rude, I'm so sorry." She gave them a smile as fake as this date.

"But you said you needed to talk," Kade reminded her. "I'm sure Rachel will excuse us."

"Please… It's really not important," Brodie insisted and jammed her hands into the back pockets of her jeans. "I'm so sorry to have disturbed your evening. Good night."

"Brodie." Kade didn't want her to leave.

"Good night!" Rachel called, turning and walking back to the table. He watched, irritated, as she picked up his full glass of wine to take a healthy sip. She cradled the glass between her ample breasts and sent him a speculative look.

Kade stopped by the coatrack and pulled her bag and jacket from a hook and held them out to her.

Rachel put down her wine and cocked her head. A small, regretful smile tilted her wide mouth upward.

"Well, that sucks," she cheerfully stated, suddenly

looking a lot warmer. Kade scratched his forehead in confusion. But before he could ask for an explanation, Rachel spoke again. "Want to tell me why you are doing the dating thing when you are completely besotted with your matchmaker?"

"I am not besotted with her!" Kade responded, thoroughly disconcerted by the observation.

"Well, something is happening between you two." Rachel slipped into her shoes, then walked over to him and took her jacket and purse from his hands. "Pity, because I rather like you."

Kade rubbed his hand across his forehead. "Look, I enjoyed our evening…"

Rachel laughed. "Oh, you big, fat liar! I've never worked so hard in all my life to impress someone and most men are easily impressed!"

He had to smile and was so damn thankful he wasn't dealing with the drama queen he'd expected her to be. "I'm so sorry. I'm really not besotted with her but it *is* complicated. And these dates are…" Could he trust her not to spill the beans?

"A publicity stunt?" Rachel had guessed before he could say more. "I figured that out as soon as I saw the look on your face when you opened the door. Don't worry, I won't say anything."

Kade let out a relieved sigh. "Thank you." He bent down and placed a kiss on her cheek. "I really appreciate it. I'll take you home."

Rachel patted his biceps. "I'll call a cab and you can go and find your girl so that you can sort out your complications."

Kade watched her walk out of his loft, resisting the urge to deny there was anything between him and Brodie besides some great sex and a couple of laughs.

There was nothing to sort out, nothing to worry about. If that was the case, then he shouldn't be desperate to find out exactly what it was Brodie wanted to say.

He was just curious, he told himself. It didn't mean he had feelings for her. He wasn't besotted with her.

Besotted? What a ridiculous word! He wasn't... He couldn't be. He didn't *do* besotted. But he would admit to being curious, that wasn't a crime.

Brodie left the rain forest and the Willowbrae Trail and walked onto one of the vast, sandy beaches characterizing this part of the west coast of Vancouver Island. She stared at the huge waves rolling in from Japan and slipped out of her sneakers, digging her toes into the cool sand.

This place—Poppy's cabin—with its magnificent sea views, was her hideout, the place she ran to every time her life fell apart. She and her family had spent many holidays here, in winter and summer and the seasons in between. This was where she felt closest to them. After the accident, she'd spent six weeks up here, to recuperate. Her body healed quickly but her heart never had.

Despite the memories, she still wanted to run up here when life threw her curveballs. Here, if she didn't think too much, her soul felt occasionally satisfied. This was her special place, her thinking place.

Two days had passed since she'd left Vancouver and she'd spent all that time thinking of Kade, and trying *not* to obsess about what happened between him and Doctor Delicious after Brodie left.

The thought of him and another woman so soon— was six weeks soon?

And she still had to tell him about the pregnancy. Brodie placed her hands on her stomach and sucked in a breath. She also needed to tell him she intended to keep this child, to raise it on her own.

Poppy was right. Keeping the baby would take courage and sacrifice and…well, balls. Brodie also knew her parents would have wanted her to keep the child, to care for the next generation of Stewarts as they'd planned to do.

So she'd decided to be a mommy. She needed to tell Kade he was going to be a daddy. There was no rush, Brodie thought, as she picked up a piece of driftwood and tossed it toward a bubbling wave. She had eight or so months.

Or, hell, maybe not.

Brodie recognized his stride first, long and loose. His blond hair and most of his face was covered by a black cap. Simon, Kade's huge, sloppy mutt, galloped between him and the waves, barking with joy. Then Simon recognized her and let out a yelp of elated welcome. Brodie was glad that he, at least, looked happy to see her.

Kade did not. He stopped in front of her, tipped back the rim of his cap and scowled. "Sixteen missed calls. Six messages, Stewart. Seriously?"

"I needed some time alone," Brodie replied, rubbing Simon's ears. She looked up into Kade's frustrated eyes. "Why are you here?"

The wind blew Kade's cotton shirt up and revealed the ridges of his stomach. Brodie had to stop herself from whimpering. "I'm here because you came to my loft, looking like hell on wheels, saying we needed to talk. I've spent the last two days looking for you."

Brodie picked up a small stick and threw it for Simon, who ran straight past it into a wave. "I suppose Poppy told you where I was."

"When I managed to find her," Kade muttered.

Brodie frowned. "She's not difficult to find. She lives below me."

"Not for the last two nights. She finally came home, on a Harley, with a guy who was at least fifteen years younger than her."

Brodie grinned. "Good for Poppy." At least one of them was having fun.

Brodie felt her throat tighten. She had to tell him, now.

"Kade…" Brodie met his eyes, dug deep and found a little bit of courage. "The night we were together… Do you remember how we brushed off the issue of the split condom?"

Kade frowned and his face darkened. She didn't need to say any more, she could see he'd immediately connected the dots. "You're…?" He rubbed his hands over his face.

"Pregnant," Brodie confirmed.

"But you said you were on the pill," Kade stuttered and the color drained from his face.

"I was on the pill, but apparently it fails sometimes."

Kade linked his hands behind his head. He looked shaken and, understandably, mad as hell. Brodie couldn't blame him; she'd experienced those emotions herself.

"Might I remind you," she added, "the condom *you brought* was faulty."

"So you're saying this is my fault?" Kade shouted, dropping his hands. Simon whined and Kade patted his head to reassure him everything was okay. Brodie wished he'd reassure her, too.

Brodie made an effort to hold on to her own slipping temper. "I'm not blaming you, I'm explaining what happened."

Kade dropped a couple of F-bombs. "I'm not ready to be a father. I don't want to be a father!"

"Being a mother wasn't in my five-year plan, either, Webb."

Kade folded his arms across his chest and glared at her. "You don't seem particularly upset about this."

Where was he the last couple of nights when she'd cried herself to sleep? The same nights she'd paced the floor? "I'm pregnant and it's not something that's going away. I have to deal with it. You, however, do not."

"What the *hell* do you mean?"

Brodie tucked a strand of hair behind her ear and shrugged. "If you want I'll sign a release absolving you of all responsibility for this child."

Kade stared down at the sand and Brodie noticed his hands, in the pockets of his khakis shorts, were now fists. He was hanging on to his temper by a thread. "Is that my only option?"

"What else do you want? You just said you don't want to be this baby's father. Have you changed your mind? That would mean paying child support and sorting out custody arrangements. Is that what you want?"

"For crap's sake, I don't know! I'm still trying to deal with the idea you're saying you're pregnant!" Kade yelled.

"I'm *saying* I am pregnant?" Brodie frowned. Did he think she was making this up for kicks and giggles? "Do you doubt me?" she asked, her voice low and bitter.

"We slept together several weeks ago, how can you be sure?" Kade retorted. "Have you done a blood test? How can I be sure you're not jerking my chain?"

Brodie's mouth fell open. How could he, for one moment, think she would lie about this? Didn't he know her at all? Actually, he didn't, Brodie admitted. They'd shared their bodies but nothing of their thoughts or feelings. And now they were going to have a baby together... No, judging by his lack of enthusiasm, she was going to be walking this road solo.

Brodie slapped her hand on his chest and pushed. He didn't shift a millimeter and her temper bubbled. "I am not lying, exaggerating or jerking your chain! This isn't fun for me, either, Webb, but I'm going to be an adult and deal with it!" Her chest felt tight and her face was on fire. "I've done my part. I've informed you. I'll get my lawyer to draw up a document releasing you from your parental rights."

Brodie spun around and started toward the path leading back to the cabin. God, she was tired. Tired of stressing, tired of arguing. Just plain exhausted. Tired of dealing with the emotions Webb yanked to the surface whenever she was around him. She just wanted some peace, to retreat, to shut down.

"I don't know what I want!" Kade hurled the words and Brodie felt them bounce off the back of her head.

Brodie slowly turned and shrugged. "I can't help you with that. But accusing me of lying certainly doesn't help make sense of the situation."

Embarrassment flashed across Kade's face. He stared at the sand and then out to sea. She could see the tension on his face. "It's happened before...with two other women. They said I made them pregnant."

Brodie tipped her head. "Did you?"

His look was hot and tight and supremely pissed off. "Hell no! When my lawyers asked for DNA proof they backed down."

Of course they did. Brodie sighed and tried to ignore the growing hurt enveloping her heart. "So, naturally, I'm just another one-night stand, another woman you slept with who wants to trap you." She released a small, bitter laugh and lifted her hands in a what-was-I-thinking? gesture. "That's an example of how extraordinarily stupid I can be on occasion. Goodbye, Kade."

Brodie took a couple of steps before turning around once more. "My lawyer will contact yours. I really don't think we have much more to say to one another."

Brodie walked away and Kade didn't call her back, didn't say another word. When she hit the trail to the cottage, Brodie patted her stomach.

So it'll be you and me, babe. We'll be fine.

Of course she would. She always was.

So that wasn't what he'd been expecting, Kade thought as he sank to the sand and stared at the wild waves slapping the beach.

Brodie was pregnant? With *his* child? What the hell…? He scrubbed his face with his hands. What were the chances? And why was fate screwing with him?

Kade stroked Si's head and rubbed his ears. With his busy schedule, just remembering to feed and walk Si was problematic. And life was expecting him to deal with a child?

This was karma, Kade thought. Life coming back to bite him in the ass because he'd been so rude about Mac becoming a father. But Mac had Rory—patient, calm and thinking—to guide him through the process.

Kade didn't have Brodie and, judging by the final sentence she'd flung at him, he didn't need to worry about her or his child. She was prepared to go it alone.

He shouldn't have accused her of lying. Brodie wasn't another bimbo trying to drag a commitment out of him. Brodie didn't want a relationship. She didn't need a man in her life. She was independent and self-sufficient and she was strong enough to raise her child—their child—on her own.

If he wanted to he could walk away, forget about this conversation and forget he had a baby on the way. According to Brodie all he needed to do was sign a piece of paper and his life would go back to normal.

No child.

No Brodie.

Pain bloomed in the area below his sternum and he pushed his fist into the spot to relieve the burn. Could he do it? Could he walk away and not think about her, them, anymore?

Probably.

Definitely.

Not.

He couldn't keep Brodie off his mind as it was. There was something about her that was different from any other woman he'd ever known. He was, on a cellular level, attracted to her, but despite her I-can-handle-whatever-life-throws-at-me attitude, he sensed a vulnerability in her that jerked his protective instincts to life. She also had more secrets than the CIA, secrets he wanted to discover. Oh, he wasn't thinking of her with respect to the long term or a commitment. He hadn't turned *that* mushy and sentimental, but he couldn't dismiss her.

It would be easier if he could.

As for her carrying his child...

He'd always been ambivalent about having children. As a child, his family situation had been dysfunctional at best, screwed up at worst. He'd been an afterthought to his parents and when his mom died, he'd been nothing more than a burden to his head-in-the-clouds father. Practicality had never been his dad's strong suit and, teamed with a wildly impulsive nature, having a ten-year-old was a drag. A kid required food, clothes and schooling, and sometimes his dad hadn't managed any of those. To his father, Kade had been a distraction from his art, a responsibility he'd never signed on for.

Kade felt his jaw lock as the realization smacked him in the face: his child would be a distraction from his own career and a responsibility he'd never signed on for.

Like father, like son.

Except he wasn't his father and he refused to follow in the man's footsteps. It was *his* condom that broke; Kade was as responsible for the pregnancy as Brodie. He took responsibility for his actions, both in his business and in his personal life. He faced life like a man, not like the spoiled child he'd frequently thought his father to be.

And, for some reason, he couldn't get the image of Brodie, soft and round with pregnancy, out of his head. He could see a child sleeping on her chest; he wanted to watch her nursing. Dammit, he could even imagine himself changing a diaper, running after his toddler on a beach, teaching the boy to skate.

For the first time ever, Kade could imagine being part of a family, working for and protecting *his* family. Having his own little tribe.

It wouldn't be like that, really. Of course it wouldn't. Nothing ever worked out like a fairy tale, but it was a nice daydream. He and Brodie weren't going to have the dream but they could have something…different.

He could share the responsibility of raising their child. Taking responsibility meant paying all the bills their child incurred. From pregnancy to college and beyond, he'd supply the cash. Kade hauled in some much-needed air. Cash was the easy part. He had enough to financially support hundreds of kids. The notion of being a *father* had him gasping for air. Being a dad. Because there was a difference; he knew that as well as he knew his own body.

He couldn't be like his father...

Kade never half-assed anything. He didn't cut corners or skimp on the details. He worked. And then he worked some more. He worked at his friendships; he worked at his career. He gave 110 percent, every time.

And he'd give being a dad 110 percent, as well. His child would not grow up feeling like a failure, like an afterthought, like a burden. He wasn't going to perpetuate that stupid cycle.

And if Brodie didn't like that, then she'd better get with the program because that was the way it was going to be. He wasn't going to be a husband or a long-term lover, but he'd be a damn good father and, more importantly, he'd be there every step of the way...

Seven

Brodie placed her heels on the edge of the Adirondack chair and rested her chin on her knees, the expansive view of the Florencia Bay blurry from the tears she refused to let fall. She was used to being alone. She'd made a point of it. But for the first time in nearly a decade she felt like she could do with some help. Just a shoulder to lean on, someone to tell her she could do this, that she was strong enough, brave enough.

She wanted a pair of arms to hold her, someone else's strength to lift her, a little encouragement. This was the downside of being alone, Brodie realized. When you'd consistently kept yourself apart there was no one you could call on. She'd made this bed and now she had to sleep in it.

Alone.

Well, this sucked. Brodie shoved the heels of her hands into her eye sockets and pushed, hoping the pressure would stop the burning in her eyes. That she wanted to cry was utter madness. She was pregnant, not dying. She was financially able to raise this child and give it everything it needed—she had to stop calling it an *it*!—and this situation didn't warrant tears. If memories didn't make her cry, then her pregnancy had no right to. She was stronger than that.

Brodie straightened her shoulders. So she was going to be a single mother, big deal. Millions of women all over the world did it on a daily basis, a lot of them with fewer resources than she had. *Stop being a wuss and get on with it. Rework those plans; write a list. Do something instead of just moping!*

She needed to see a doctor and she needed to contact her lawyer. She needed to stop thinking about stupid Kade Webb and the fact he'd accused her of scamming him.

The jerk! Oh, she so wasn't going to think about him again. From this moment on he was her baby's sperm donor and nothing else.

She simply wasn't going to think about him again.

"Brodie."

Brodie looked up at the clear blue sky and shook her head. "Seriously?"

No one, not God, the universe or that bitch karma, answered her. Brodie reluctantly turned her head and watched Kade walk across the patio toward the other Adirondack chair. Without saying a word, he sat down, rested his forearms on his thighs and dropped his hands between his knees. Simon sat near the edge of the stairs and barked at a seagull flying over his head.

Kade had come straight from the beach, Brodie realized. Sand clung to his feet, which were shoved into expensive flips-flops, and clung to the hair on his bare calves. He had nice feet. Big feet. He was a big guy, *everywhere*.

And it was his *everywhere* that had put her into this situation. She scowled. "What now, Kade?"

Kade turned and looked at her. "I don't want to fight."

"That's fine." Brodie dropped her legs and pointed to the stairs. "So just leave."

"That's not happening, either." Kade calmly leaned back and put one ankle onto his opposite knee. He rolled his shoulders and looked around, taking in the wood, steel and glass cabin and the incredible view. "This place is amazing. Do you own it?"

She had some money but not enough to own a property like this. "Poppy's."

Why was he here? Why was he back? Was he going to take more shots at her? She didn't think she could tolerate any more this morning. She felt nauseous and slightly dizzy and, dammit, she wanted to crawl into his arms and rest awhile.

Huh. So she hadn't wanted just anyone to hold her, she'd wanted Kade's arms around her. And she'd called *him* a moron? She took the prize.

"What do you want, Kade?" she asked, weary.

"Are you okay?" Kade waved in the direction of her stomach, his brown eyes dark with—dare she think it?—concern. "I mean, apart from the whole being-pregnant issue?"

"Why?"

"You just look, well, awful. You're like a pale green color. You've lost weight and you look like you haven't slept properly in a month."

Nice to know she was looking like a wreck. Especially when the description came from a man who graced the front covers of sports magazines.

"Do you need to see a doctor? Maybe they could run some tests to check if there is something else wrong."

"I'm fine, Webb. I'm pregnant. I puke, a lot. I don't sleep much because I've been stressed out of my head!"

"Stressed about telling me?" Kade asked, linking his hands across his flat stomach.

Brodie stood up and went to the balustrade. "Partly. But that's done so…feel free to leave."

Kade didn't look like he was going anywhere anytime soon. He just held her hot gaze. "I'm sorry I reacted badly." His smile was self-deprecating and very attractive. "Not my best moment."

"Yeah, accusing me of trying to trap you was a high point," Brodie said, looking toward the beach. "Apology accepted. You can—"

"Go now? Why are you trying to get rid of me?"

"Because I have stuff to do! I need to call my lawyer, see a doctor, plan mine and the baby's future!" Brodie cried.

Kade stood up, walked over to her and touched her cheek with his fingers. "It's not going to be like that, Brodie."

"Like what?" Brodie whispered.

"I know you think you are going to do this alone—because, hell, you like being self-reliant—but I'm in it for the long haul."

"What?" Brodie demanded, thrown off-kilter. What was he talking about?

"I am going to be this baby's father in every way that counts."

Brodie looked at him, aghast. What was happening here? "Wha-at?"

"You're going to have to learn to be part of a team, Brodie, because that's what we are, from this point on." Kade tapped her nose and stood back, his stance casual. But his eyes, dark and serious and oh, so determined, told another story.

"I don't understand."

"I am not going anywhere. We're in this. *Together*."

What? No! She didn't play nicely with others. She had no idea how to work within a team. She was a lone wolf; she didn't function within a pack. And really, what the hell did he think he was doing, acting all reasonable and concerned?

That wasn't going to work for her. She made her own decisions and she didn't like it that with Kade, she wasn't in charge. He might sound laid-back but beneath his charm the man was driven and ambitious and bossy.

But even as she protested his change of heart, she had the warm fuzzies and felt a certain relief she wouldn't be carrying this burden alone.

Even so, she shook her head. "There is no *we*. This baby is my problem, my responsibility."

"This baby is *our* problem, *our* responsibility. Mine as much as yours," Kade replied, not budging an inch. "Quit arguing, honey, because you're not going to win."

Behind her back Brodie gripped the balustrade with both hands. "What does that mean? Are you going to change diapers and do midnight feeds? Are you going to drive around the city trying to get the kid to sleep? Or are you just going to fling some money at me?"

Anger flickered in Kade's eyes. "I'll do whatever I need to do to make your life easier, to be a father. I will support you, and the baby, with money, but more importantly, with my time and my effort. I'm repeating this in an effort to get it to sink into that stubborn head of yours, you are not in this alone."

"I want to be," Brodie stated honestly. It would be so much easier.

His fingers touched her jaw, trailed down her neck. "I know you do, but that's not happening. Not this time."

Panic flooded her system and closed her throat. Wanting to protest, Brodie could only look at him with wide, scared eyes. She needed to push him away, to end the emotion swirling between them. "You just want to get into my pants again."

The only hint of Kade's frustration was the slight tightening of his fingers. She waited for him to retaliate but he just brushed his amused mouth in a hot kiss across her lips.

"So cynical, Brodie." He rubbed the cord in her neck with his thumb and Brodie couldn't miss the determination on his face and in the words that followed. "I want you, Brodie, you know that. But that is a completely separate matter to us raising a child together. One is about want and heat and crazy need, the other is about being your friend, a support structure, about raising this child together as best as we can."

"We can't be both friends and lovers, Kade!"

"We can be anything we damn well want," Kade replied. "But for now, why don't we try to be friends first and figure out how we're going to be parents and not complicate it with sex?"

He confused and bedazzled her, Brodie admitted. She couldn't keep up with him. She felt like she was being maneuvered into a corner, pushed there by the force of his will. "I don't know! I need to think."

Kade smiled, stepped back and placed his hands in the pockets of his khaki shorts. "You can think all you want, Brodie, but it isn't going to change a damn thing. I'm going to be around whether you like it or not." He ducked his head and dropped a kiss on her temple. "You might as well get used to it," he murmured into her ear.

Before Brodie got her wits together to respond, Kade walked across the patio to the outside stairs. He snapped his fingers. Simon lumbered to his feet and they both jogged down the stairs. Brodie looked over the balustrade as they hit the ground below.

"And get some sleep, Stewart! You look like hell," Kade called.

Yeah, just what a girl needed to hear, Brodie thought. Then she yawned and agreed it was a very good suggestion.

Kade glanced down at his phone, the red flashing light indicating he had a message. He looked across the table to his friends and partners and saw they were still reading a condensed version of Logan's contract. He slid his finger across the screen and his breath hitched when he saw Brodie's name.

He hadn't spoken to her for two days but he kept seeing her in his mind's eye, looking down at him from the patio of the cabin—bemused, befuddled, so very tired. He had deliberately left her alone, wanting to give her time to get used to the idea of them co-parenting.

Back in the city. Thought that you might want to know.

Kade smiled at her caustic message. Not exactly gracious but coming from the independent Brodie, who'd rather cut off her right arm than ask for help, it was progress.

He quickly typed a reply.

Feeling rested?

A bit.

Any other symptoms?

Do you really want to know? He grimaced at the green, vomiting emoji tacked onto the end of the message.

Ugh. Will bring dinner. Around 7?

Tired. Going to bed early.

Oh, no. When was she going to learn that if she retreated he would follow? You have to eat. I'm bringing food. Be there.

Suit yourself.

That was Brodie speak for "see you later." Kade tapped the screen and smiled. The trick with Brodie, he was learning, was to out-stubborn her.

"Kade, do you agree?"

"Sure," he murmured, looking straight through Quinn. He'd have to tell his friends at some point but there were reasons why he didn't want to, not yet. He was still wrapping his head around the situation and he wasn't ready for his friends to rag him about it. He still felt raw. The situation was uncertain and, consequently, his temper was quick to the boil.

Besides, it was one of those things he needed to discuss with Brodie... Was she ready for the pregnancy to become public knowledge?

He didn't think either of them was ready for the press. Especially since Brodie was supposed to be finding his dream woman. His next date. She was, after all, his damned matchmaker.

No, he definitely wasn't ready for the news to be splashed across the papers and social media. It was too new and too precious. Too fragile. Kade half turned and put his hand into the pocket of his suit jacket, which was hanging off the back of his chair. Pulling out a container of aspirin, he flipped back the lid and swallowed three, ignoring the bitter powder coating his mouth.

He'd had a low-grade headache since he'd left Brodie and he'd been popping aspirin like an addict. It was a small price to pay for a very large oops.

Kade looked up when he heard a knock on the glass door. Two seconds later his personal assistant leaned into the room. "What's up, Joy?"

"There's someone here to see you and she's not budging," Joy told him after tossing a quick greeting to Quinn and Mac. Joy snapped her fingers. "Someone Stewart."

Kade frowned. Brodie? Was something wrong? She'd just been texting him. He stood up abruptly and his chair skittered backward. Crap! Something must be wrong. Brodie would never come to his office without calling first. He started toward the door and stopped when he saw the slight, stylish figure of Poppy Stewart walking toward them.

"Poppy? Is she okay?" He winced at the panic in his voice.

Poppy frowned. "Why wouldn't she be?" she said when she reached him. Kade placed a hand on his heart and sucked in a deep breath while Poppy graciously, but very firmly, sent Joy on her way. "We need to talk."

"You sure she's okay?"

"When I left she was eating an apple and drinking ginger tea. She has a slew of appointments today and was heading downtown later." Poppy walked into the conference room and Mac and Quinn rose to their feet.

"My, my, my," she crooned, holding out a delicate hand for them to shake, her mouth curved in a still sexy smile. "You boys certainly pack a punch."

Kade rubbed his forehead. God, he wasn't up to dealing with a geriatric flirt. And why the hell wasn't the aspirin working?

"Poppy, why are you here?" he asked, dropping back into his chair.

Quinn pulled out a chair for Poppy and gestured for her to sit. "Can I offer you something to drink? Coffee? Tea?"

"I'm fine, thank you," Poppy replied.

Mac frowned at Kade. "I'm Mac McCaskill and this is Quinn Rayne."

God, he was losing his mind along with his manners. "Sorry, Poppy. Guys, this is Poppy Stewart."

"Stewart?" Quinn asked. "Any relation to Brodie Stewart, the matchmaker?"

"Great-aunt," Kade briefly explained. He caught his friends' eyes and jerked his head in the direction of the door.

Mac just sat down again and Quinn sat on the edge of the conference table. It would take a bomb to move them, Kade realized, so he stood up. "Let's go to my office, Poppy. We'll have some privacy there."

"You need privacy from your best friends?" Poppy asked.

Mac lifted an eyebrow. "Yeah, do you?"

"Right now, yeah!" Kade snapped. He rubbed his

jaw before gripping the bridge of his nose with his finger and thumb.

"You haven't told them," Poppy said and he heard the amusement in her voice. Glad she was finding this funny because he sure as hell wasn't.

"Told us what?" Quinn asked, his eyes alight with curiosity.

Poppy's open hand drifted through the air, silently telling him it was his call whether to answer his friends or not. They had to know sometime. If he told them now, then he'd avoid them nagging him to distraction.

Kade looked toward the open door and crossed the floor, slamming it shut. They all knew the signal: closed door meant what was said in the room stayed in the room. Both Mac and Quinn nodded their agreement.

"Brodie is pregnant," Kade quietly said. He handed Mac a rueful smile. "I'm right behind you in the new-dads line."

Kade was grateful that beyond quietly congratulating him, Mac and Quinn didn't make a big song and dance over his announcement. Instead they just left the room, still looking shocked. All their lives were changing at a rapid pace. Just a few months ago they had been the most eligible bachelors in the city. Now Mac was getting married and he and Kade were both going to be fathers.

Then again, none of them ever eased their way into a situation, Kade thought as Mac shut the door behind him. They always jumped into the deep end and swam hard. "They took it rather well," Poppy said, linking her hands around her knee.

"They were behaving themselves in front of you," Kade explained. "Trust me, when they get me alone, they'll rip into me."

Kade dropped his head and rubbed the back of his neck. White-hot pain shot up his spine and bounced off the back of his skull. Hell, he hadn't had a migraine for years and, he recalled, they always started like this. It had been so long since an attack he'd stopped the habit of carrying medicine with him to take the edge off the pain.

"Are you unhappy about this baby, Kade?"

Kade had to concentrate hard for her words to make sense. "Not unhappy. Surprised, getting used to the idea. Wondering how we're going to make it work."

"You will," Poppy told him, sounding convinced. "And Brodie being pregnant is the reason I am here.

"I am scheduled to go on a cruise in a week or so. Ordinarily I would cancel the cruise and stay home with Brodie. I'm worried about her. But I am one of the tour leaders and they need me."

Kade held up a hand and silently cursed when he saw his vision was starting to double. Dammit, he had about fifteen minutes, a half hour at most, before he fell to the floor. "Do you want her to move in with me?"

"Not necessarily, but I am worried about her, Kade. She's sick and stressed and she's not sleeping, not eating. If no one keeps an eye on her, I worry I'll come back to a skeleton that swallowed a pea."

"How long are you away for?" God, it was getting difficult to concentrate.

"Two months. Are you okay? You look awfully pale."

That would be a negative. "I'll look after her... I'll keep an eye on her," Kade muttered, slurring his words.

"Oh, my God, you really don't look well. Can I call someone for you?"

He wanted to shrug off the pain, to act like nothing

was wrong, but it felt like there were pickaxes penetrating his skull. "Call Mac, Quinn. Tell them…migraine."

"I'm on it." Poppy jumped up so fast the foot of her chair scraped along the floor and the sound sliced through Kade's head as he dropped his head to the desk.

When Brodie arrived at Kade's loft, Quinn opened the door to let her in. Brodie was surprised when he bent down and dropped a friendly kiss on her cheek. "Hey, pretty girl."

She couldn't feel offended. Quinn was so damn good-looking he could charm a fence post out of concrete. "Hey, Quinn." Brodie dropped her bag on the hall table and saw Mac standing by the floor-to-ceiling windows looking out at the incredible views of the city. "Hi, Mac."

"Hi, Brodie." He walked over to her and, equally surprisingly, dropped a kiss on her cheek.

"How is he?" she asked, biting her bottom lip.

"He's over the worst of it and this one was bad." Mac ran a hand through his hair.

"Does he get them often?" Brodie asked.

Quinn shook his head. "No, not anymore. He used to when he first joined the Mavericks but he hasn't had one for years."

"We think it's stress-induced," Mac quietly added. He looked at her stomach and back up to her eyes again and Brodie flushed. "He's got quite a bit to be stressed about at the moment."

"I told him he doesn't have to be! This is my problem. I can deal with it." Brodie felt sick and sad. It wasn't her fault Kade had endured two days of pain, that he'd been restricted to a darkened room, all because she'd told him she didn't need him.

She didn't need him.

"You don't know Kade at all if you think he'd just walk away from you and his child," Mac replied, ignoring her flash of temper. "And it's not only your situation causing his stress. He's dealing with a hell of a lot, work-wise, at the moment."

Brodie folded her arms across her chest and sucked in a calming breath. Mac was right; she didn't really know anything about Kade and she knew even less about what he dealt with on a daily basis.

Brodie looked down at the container of soup in her arms. She'd had a friend in college who suffered from migraines and she knew she battled to eat anything solid for days afterward. Chicken soup had been all her friend could stand. So, Brodie had whipped up a batch and decided to bring it over.

A little get-better-soon gesture from her baby's mommy to her baby's daddy. That was all that this visit was. All it could be. "Is he awake? Would he like something to eat?"

Quinn took the container from her and walked toward the kitchen. "He's still sleeping and likely to be asleep for another hour or two." Quinn exchanged a look with Mac and spoke again. "Hey, can you do us a favor?"

"Maybe," Brodie cautiously answered.

Quinn put down the container and placed his hands on the center island separating the dining area from the kitchen. "Can you hang out here for an hour or two and then wake Kade up and try to get him to eat?"

Mac nodded his agreement. "Our new player arrived in the city earlier this afternoon and the three of us were supposed to take him out to dinner. Quinn and I can still do that if you hang around here and feed Kade."

"Sure."

"We'll call you later and see how he's doing. If you think he's okay, then we'll go back to our own places."

"You've been here for two days?" Brodie asked, surprised.

Mac flushed. "We've taken shifts. He's a friggin' miserable patient and we could do with a break."

Kade had good friends, Brodie realized. Very good friends. There for each other through thick and thin. Brodie ignored her envy and nodded. "Go, I'll be fine."

"We know you will." Quinn walked up to her, placed his big hands on her shoulders. He gave her a slow, sweet, genuine smile. "Congratulations on the baby, Brodie. We can't wait to meet him…or her."

Brodie felt her throat tighten. "Thank you."

Quinn turned away and Mac bent down to give her a small hug. "Yeah, from me, too, Brodie. I don't know how you two are going to make this work but we're rooting for you. And Rory wants to have lunch. She says the two of you are reasonably smart people and you can figure out the pregnancy thing together."

"I'd like that," Brodie murmured.

Quinn pointed at the container. "Make him eat. He'll feel better for it."

Mac clapped Quinn on the shoulder and steered him to the door. "Stop fussing. Brodie can handle it."

"I know but he gets all depressed and mopey after a migraine," Quinn complained.

"Brodie. Will. Handle. It." With a last eye-roll at Brodie, Mac steered Quinn through the doors. He looked back and flashed Brodie a grin. "I swear after raising these two, having a kid is going to be a breeze."

Eight

"Go away, Quinn."

"Sorry, not Quinn." Brodie pushed open the door to Kade's bedroom and walked into the darkness to stand at the end of his bed. Her eyes adjusted and she took in his broad back, the yummy butt covered in a pair of loose boxers, the muscled thighs and calves. He was in great shape—long, lean and muscular. Powerful.

"Brodie?" Kade rolled over and leaned on one elbow. He pushed his hair back from his forehead and squinted at her. "What are you doing here?"

Brodie clasped her hands behind her back. "I brought you some chicken soup and your buds asked me to check on you to see if you're not, well, dead."

"They'd be so lucky," Kade growled, sitting up and resting his elbows on his bent knees.

"How are you feeling?"

"Horrible."

"That good, huh?"

Kade lifted a muscular shoulder. "It's a combination of relief that the pain is gone and mental exhaustion. My head is sore."

"Do you still have headache?"

"Not a migraine…" Kade tried to explain. "It's more like my brain is tired. For a day afterward I feel exhausted, like I have a mental hangover."

"Are you sure you're not pregnant? Add nausea and vomiting and that's how I feel all the time."

"Sorry, babe." Kade patted the mattress next to him. "What are you doing over there? Come here."

She really shouldn't. If she sat down next to him she wouldn't be able to keep her hands to herself and then she'd get naked and he had a headache. And he needed to date other women—women she'd found for him!—and she was supposed to be keeping a mental and emotional distance so there were like, a hundred reasons why she shouldn't sit down, why she shouldn't even be here…

Despite all that, Brodie walked around the bed to sit on its edge. Kade immediately wound an arm around her waist, pulled her backward and spooned her from behind. His hand covered her breast and she sighed. "Kade…"

"Shhh." Kade touched his lips to her neck and thumbed her nipple. It bloomed under his touch and she felt heat rushing down, creating a fireball between her legs.

"I need you," Kade whispered in her ear. "I need to be inside you, touching you, being with you. Say yes, Brodes."

Brodie rolled over to face him and touched his jaw, his lips. She opened her mouth to speak but Kade placed his fingers over her lips. "I don't want to hear that this is a bad idea, that we shouldn't, that this is madness. I know it is and, right now, *I don't care*."

Oh, in all honesty, she didn't, either. Wasn't she allowed to step away from the complications and just enjoy his touch, take pleasure in the way he made her feel? Making love to Kade was sheer bliss and, after the weeks she'd endured, wasn't she entitled to some fun? To escape for a little while? It didn't have to mean anything. She wanted him, needed him—in her, filling her, completing her.

"You have too many clothes on, babe." Kade covered her breast with one hand. She arched into his hand, frustrated at the barriers between him and her skin.

"I'm happy for you to take them off as quickly as you can," Brodie whispered, curling her hand around the back of his neck.

"Then again, I rather like you like this. All flushed and hot and horny."

Brodie whimpered when Kade's hard mouth dropped over hers and his tongue tangled with hers. He used his arm to yank her on top of him and her thighs slid over his hips so she was flush against his erection, the heat of which she felt through her loose cotton trousers. His mouth teased and tormented hers—one minute his kisses were demanding and dominating, then he'd ease away. Lust whipped through her as she angled her head to allow him deeper access. His kisses seemed different from anything they'd shared before…there was more heat, more desire, more…of something indefinable.

Unsettled but still incredibly eager, Brodie gripped his shoulders as he undid the buttons on her shirt and exposed her lace-covered breasts to his intense gaze. Kade used one finger to pull down the lace cup and expose her puckered nipple. Then his tongue licked her and sensations swamped her. She moaned when he flicked open the tiny clasp holding her bra together and revealed her torso to his exploring hand. He pulled aside the pale yellow fabric of her bra and swiped his thumb across her peaked nipple. She arched her back, silently asking for more. Kade lowered his head and took one puckered nipple into his mouth, his tongue sliding over her, hot and wet. Kade heard her silent plea for him to touch her and his hand moved to her hip, pushing underneath the waist of her trousers.

"Lift up," he muttered and Brodie lifted her hips and straightened her legs, allowing him to push the fabric down her thighs.

Kade tapped her bottom. "Move off for a sec."

She rolled away and he whipped off his boxers. He put his hands on her knees and pulled them apart before dragging his finger over her mound, slipping under the fabric to find her wet and wanting.

"I want you so much."

"Then *take* me." Really, did the man need a gilded invitation?

Kade sent her a wicked smile. "Yeah, in a minute."

"How's your head?"

Kade looked down and lifted an eyebrow. "Just fine and eager to say hi."

Brodie laughed and slapped his shoulder. "Your other head!"

"Also fine."

Brodie rubbed her thumb against the two grooves between his eyebrows. "Liar. Do you want to stop?"

Brodie hissed as two fingers slipped into her passage.

"Do I look like I want to stop?"

"Kade!" She reached for him, fumbling in her eagerness to get him inside her. "Please, just…I want you."

"I want you this way first. I want to watch you come, with my fingers inside you and my mouth kissing yours." Kade lifted his head and looked into her eyes. "You look good like this, Brodie. You look good anywhere, anyhow."

She was so close, teetering on the edge. *Kade!*

"You take my breath away when you lose yourself in me, in the way I make you feel. How do I make you feel, Brodie?"

He was expecting her to speak, to think? How could she answer when she felt like she was surfing a white-hot band of pure, crazy sensation?

"Tell me, Brodie."

"Free," Brodie gasped. "Safe. Sexy."

Cherished, Brodie silently added as her climax rocked her. All those wonderful, loved-up, fuzzy emotions she had no business experiencing. Brodie cried out, partly in reckless abandon and partly in pain as her heart swelled and cracked the plaster she'd cast around it.

She was being wild but she didn't care. She'd deal with the consequences, and the pain, later. Right now she just wanted to feel.

She wanted to feel alive. Just for a little while.

Brodie had to open various cupboard doors before she found soup bowls and three drawers before she found a ladle. She placed a bowl of soup in the microwave to heat and while it did its thing, she scratched around until she found place mats and flatware.

Brodie looked up as Kade entered the kitchen and her breath caught in the back of her throat. Kade looked shattered but somehow, just dressed in a pair of straight-legged track pants and a plain red T-shirt, hot. His hair was damp from his shower and his stubble glinted in the bright light of the kitchen.

Kade frowned and walked over to a panel on the wall and dimmed the lights. "Better," he muttered. He walked back to the island and pulled out a bar stool and sat down.

The microwave dinged. Brodie grabbed a dish towel and pulled out the hot bowl of soup. She put it onto the place mat and pushed the mat, a spoon and the bowl in Kade's direction.

He wrinkled his nose. "I appreciate the offer but I don't think I can eat."

"Listen, Quinn—who, surprisingly, is a fusser—will call and I need to tell him you ate or else he is going to come over here and make you eat." Brodie dished some soup for herself. "And frankly, tonight I think he could make you. You look about as tough as over-boiled noodles."

"Thanks."

"At least I didn't say you look like hell." Brodie pointed her spoon at him.

Kade winced. "Sorry, but you did. You are looking better. Still tired, but better."

"I've been living on chicken soup." Brodie sat down and nodded at his bowl. "It's good, try it."

Kade dipped his spoon, lifted it to his mouth and Brodie waited. When he smiled slowly and nodded she knew he approved. "It's my mom's recipe. A cure for all ailments." And, years later, still doing its job.

They ate in comfortable silence until Brodie looked around the loft and sighed. "My dad was a builder. He would've loved this place."

"You sound uncomfortable when you talk about your parents," he said. "Why?"

Because she was, because she felt guilt that they'd died and she didn't. Because she still missed them with every breath she took. Kade waited for her explanation and, despite her tight throat, she told him what she was thinking. "It's just hard," she concluded.

"You're lucky you experienced such love, such acceptance. They sound like they were incredibly good parents."

Brodie pushed away her plate, looking for an excuse not to talk. But she couldn't keep doing that, not if they were going to co-parent. She needed to learn to open up, just a little. "They were. I was the center of their universe, the reason the sun came up for them every morning." She rested her chin in the palm of her hand. "That makes me sound like I was spoiled, but I wasn't, not really. They gave me more experiences than things. They gave me attention and time, and, most importantly, roots and wings. I felt...lost when they died. I still feel lost," Brodie admitted. "And so damn scared."

Kade took one more sip of soup before standing up. He picked up the bowls and carried them to the sink, leaving them there. On his return trip, he stopped at Brodie's chair and held out his hand. "Let's go sit."

Brodie put her hand in his and followed him across the room to the mammoth sofa. Kade sat down and pulled Brodie next to him, placing his hand on her knee to keep her there. They looked at the city lights and Brodie finally allowed her head to drop so her temple rested on Kade's shoulder.

"What scares you, Brodie?"

Brodie heard his quiet question and sighed. "Love scares me. Feeling attached and running the risk of losing the person I am attached to scares me. Being a mommy scares the pants off me."

"Why?"

"I know how quickly life can change. One day I was bright, happy and invincible. The next I'd lost everyone that mattered to me." She had to continue; she couldn't stop now. "I not only lost my parents in a single swoop, but my two best friends, too. I survived the accident with minor physical injuries and major emotional ones."

He didn't mutter meaningless words of sympathy. He just put her onto his lap, his arms holding her against his broad chest.

Him holding her was all she needed.

"Tell me about your childhood," she asked, desperate to change the subject.

Kade stared out the window at the breathtaking views of False Creek and the city. Brodie wondered if he ever got used to it. Kade, reading her mind, gestured to the window. "I do my best thinking here, looking out of this window. It's never the same, always different depending on the time of day, the month, the season. It's a reminder that nothing stays the same. As a kid my life was nothing *but* change."

Brodie half turned so she could watch his face as he talked. This was the first time they'd dropped some of their barriers and it was frightening. This was something she'd done with her friends, with Chels and Jay. She was out of practice.

"After my mom died, my dad packed up our house, sold everything and hit the road. He wanted to see the country. He wanted to paint. He couldn't leave me behind and he wouldn't stay so I went along. I went to many, many different schools. Some for months, some for only weeks. In some places I didn't even get to school. My education was—" Kade hesitated "—sporadic."

Brodie knew if she spoke she'd lose him so she just waited for him to continue talking.

"But while I hated school, I loved to play hockey and I could always make friends on the ice. Especially since I was good and everyone wanted me on their team. But invariably I'd find a team, make some friends, start to feel settled and he'd yank me off to someplace new."

"I'm sorry."

"So in a way we're the same, Brodie."

Brodie frowned, unsure of where he was going with this. "How?"

"You're scared to become emotionally involved because you're scared to lose again. I'm scared for the same reason." Kade dropped his hand to pat her stomach. "We're going to have to find a way to deal with those fears because this little guy—"

"It could be a girl."

Kade's smile was soft and sweet. "This baby is going to need us, what we can give her. Or him. Individually or together."

His words were low and convincing and Brodie finally accepted he wasn't going to change his mind about the baby. He was determined to play his part parenting their child. Okay then, that was something she would have to get used to.

So, how did they deal with their attraction while they learned to navigate the parenting landscape?

"Problem?"

Brodie wiggled her butt against his long length and heard his tortured hiss. "The fact that we are stupidly attracted to each other is a problem."

"It is?"

"I am not falling into a relationship with you just be-cause we are going to be co-parents, Kade."

A small frown pulled his strong eyebrows together. "Were we talking about a relationship?"

"I just... We just..." Dammit, he made her sound like a blithering idiot.

"Relax, Brodie." He touched her lips, her jaw. "I want you, just like I wanted you forty-five minutes ago, last week, six weeks ago. Not because of the baby but be-cause you drain the blood from my brain. It's a totally separate issue from us being parents. We can do it."

"I don't see how."

"That's because you could complicate a three-piece jigsaw puzzle," Kade teased. "So we slept together again..."

"Yeah, we weren't supposed to do that."

The corners of Kade's mouth tipped up in amuse-ment. "On, the plus side, at least we know you won't fall pregnant."

"Ha-ha." Brodie stared at his broad chest. "I still think we should try to be friends. Our lives are compli-cated enough already without dealing with sex."

"Why can't we be friends who make love?"

"Because it never works. What if you meet someone you like, someone you desire more than me? I still have to find you two more dates. What if you fall head over heels in love with one of them?"

Kade's hand on her thigh tightened and then relaxed. "What if the sky fell down in the morning?" he drawled. "Do you always borrow trouble like this?"

Her sky had fallen down and trouble had landed on her door. She just wanted to protect herself from it happening again. Was that so wrong? Talking to him, opening up, was dangerous. If she wasn't careful she could love him. She couldn't—wouldn't—allow herself to do that.

Brodie started to move away, to climb off his lap, to find some physical and emotional distance, but his arms held her close.

"No, don't go, Brodes. Just rest that brain of yours, take some time to regroup. Stop thinking."

It was such a huge temptation to rest a while in his embrace. Surrounded by him she felt like nothing could hurt her, that the world and her life weren't quite as scary as she imagined them to be.

"Just rest, sweetheart. We'll figure it out, I promise." Kade's deep voice sounded almost tender. Brodie curled into him and placed her cheek on his chest, her ear directly over his heart. If she closed her eyes she would just drift off...

Brodie rolled over onto her stomach and looked across the coffee table. It was a beautiful day and the sky was a bright, clear blue. Beyond False Creek the Pacific Ocean looked grumpy and the wind teased the water, creating white horses on its surface. If she ignored the morning sickness, she felt better than she had for days, maybe weeks.

Last night, instead of thinking, planning, shoring up her defenses, instead of arguing, she'd allowed Kade to pull her head back to his chest and loop his arms around her. His hand, drawing lazy circles on her back, had lulled her to sleep. She had a vague memory of him picking her up and placing her on the large couch and wrapping his long body around hers as she slept. He'd kept her restless dreams at bay and the feeling of being protected, cared for, had allowed her to drop into a deep, rejuvenating sleep.

Brodie sat up and pushed her hair out of her eyes. She looked over her shoulder and saw Kade standing at the center island, watching her. Something deep, hot and indefinable sparked between them and Brodie bit her bottom lip. Sexy, rumpled man, she thought. How was she supposed to resist him?

"Come here, Brodie," Kade said, his voice as deep and dark as his gaze, the order in it unmistakable.

She knew what would follow if she stood up. She heard it in his voice, saw it in the desire flashing in his eyes, in the way he gripped the counter, tension rippling through his arms. He wanted her...

Brodie knew she shouldn't, knew this was a mistake but she stood up anyway. On shaky legs, she crossed the space to the kitchen, walked around the island and stopped a foot away from him. Seeing a half-empty glass of orange juice, she picked it up and took a long sip. Excitement and desire caused her hand to shake and orange juice ran down her chin.

Kade wiped the droplets off with his thumb. "I have to kiss you."

Brodie started to speak but Kade shook his head. "No, don't say it's a mistake, that we shouldn't be doing this. Just forget about everything else. This is just about you and me... There are no other complications right now. They'll be back later, but right now...? There's nothing but you...and me."

"I was just going to tell you to hurry up," Brodie whispered, lifting her face. "Hurry up and kiss me, Kade."

Kade leaned forward, cupped the side of her face in his hand and lowered his mouth to hers. Part of her thought that if Kade did nothing else but kiss her for the rest of her life, she could die happy. Another sec-tion of her brain just squawked warnings: they had to be friends only. She still had to be his matchmaker. They shouldn't be doing this. If the media found out they would go nuts. Then Kade took control of her mouth, her brain shut down and she felt energized, revitalized, as if he'd plugged her in to recharge.

"Take me to bed, Kade," she muttered against his lips as her arms looped around his neck and her fingers played with the taut skin there.

Kade groaned. "Yeah, that was my intention. Except that my bed is too far." Kade used his forearm to push everything standing on the center island to the far edge of the block before bending his knees and wrapping one arm around her hips. In one easy, fluid movement he had her sitting on the island, their hands and mouths now perfectly aligned. Brodie placed her palms on Kade's shoulders and tipped her head to give him better access so he could brush his lips against her neck, her jaw, her cheekbones.

"You are so beautiful."

She wasn't, not really, but right now she believed him. Feeling sexy and confident, she dropped her hands and gripped his T-shirt, slowly pulling it up and over his chest, wanting to get her hands on those muscles. Kade used one hand to finish pulling the T-shirt over his head and toss it to the floor. Brodie sucked in her breath. His track pants were low on his hips, displaying his ripped abdomen, those long obliques over his hips. Those sexy muscles made her feel squirmy and stupid and so, so wanton.

Brodie's fingers drifted over his abdomen and hips, the side of her hand brushing his erection. She heard Kade suck in a breath. Liking the fact that she could make him breathe faster, that she could make his eyes glaze over, she pushed her hands inside his pants and pushed them over his hips to fall into a black puddle on the wooden floor.

"Whoops." She smiled against his mouth.

"Since the urge to strip is all I ever think about when you are in the room, I'm not complaining," Kade said, his mouth curling into a delighted smile.

His smile could melt ice cream, make women walk into poles and stop traffic. It heated up every one of Brodie's internal organs and made them smile, too.

He had a hell of a smile, Brodie thought, especially when she felt it on her skin.

Nine

A few days later, Brodie parked her car next to Kade's and ran an appreciative hand over the sleek hood. Had Kade realized this car was something he'd have to give up or, at the very least, that he'd need to buy a new one to transport the baby? There was no room for a car seat and she doubted a stroller would fit in the trunk.

So much was changing, Brodie thought as she headed to the entrance of his apartment building, quickly keying in the code to open the front doors. She and Kade were sort of lovers, kind of friends, about to be parents. The parenting bit was the only thing she was certain of, she thought as she walked into the private elevator that opened into Kade's hallway.

Kade could rocket her from zero to turned-on in two seconds flat. And he was funny and smart… She was crazy about him.

Brodie rested her head against the panel of the elevator, petrified she was building castles in the air. She was pregnant and it was so natural to look to the father of her baby for sex, for comfort. It made complete sense. Who wanted to be a single parent, who wanted to go through this frightening, exhausting, terrifying process alone? But castles built on fantastic sex and thin air and wishes could collapse at a moment's notice. Kade wasn't going to be her happily-ever-after guy. She didn't believe in happily-ever-after. She believed in getting through, doing the best she could, building a safe and secure life. There was only one person she could rely on 100 percent and that was herself.

Brodie hit the emergency stop button and rested her forehead against the elevator door. She had to pull back from him, had to put some distance between them. She was being seduced by what-ifs and how-it-might-be's. She couldn't afford to think of Kade as anything more than the father of her child. He was her temporary lover but he wasn't her partner or her significant other.

He *definitely* would never be her husband.

The last time she'd planned her future she'd had it ripped from her. She'd lost everyone she'd loved in one fell swoop and she refused to take that risk again.

She couldn't taste love, hold love and lose love again. That was too big a risk to take.

She smacked the emergency button and the elevator lurched upward.

No, she'd had her fun…too much fun. It was time to back the hell away and get a handle on this relationship. She needed to dial it back to a cordial friendship. She could do that. And she *would* do that before the story broke in the press. Presently the press saw her as nothing more than his matchmaker but they'd soon sniff out the truth. With her spending nights at his place, they'd been lucky to keep it a secret this long.

Luck, as she knew, always ran out.

Kade walked into his loft, ignored Mac and Rory and Quinn, and walked straight over to Brodie. He picked her up and turned her upside down so her head was facing the floor. She gurgled with laughter and placed her hands on the floor to steady herself.

"Kade, she's pregnant!" Quinn grabbed his arm. "What are you doing?"

"I'm getting blood to her head, something that was obviously missing when she chose my date," Kade replied, easily restoring Brodie to her feet. "She's lucky I didn't hang her over the balcony."

Brodie wiped her hands on the seat of her pants and sent him a cocky smile. She hadn't been remotely scared at being tossed around like a doll, Kade mused. Her eyes were bright and full of mischief. "Really, Stewart?"

Brodie attempted an innocent shrug. "What? She's a biokinetics engineer and a part-time entertainer."

"And a full-time loony. She wants to be a freakin' mermaid." Kade pointed an accusing finger at Brodie.

"What are we talking about?" Mac asked, mystified.

"The latest date Brodie and Wren sent him on. He had lunch with her today," Quinn explained. He turned to Kade. "You do know it's weird that you're going on these dates while Brodie is pregnant with your child?"

No, the thought hadn't occurred to him, he sarcastically, silently replied. Brodie and he had an understanding—basically, they both understood they had no idea what they were doing. "Blame Wren. Besides, the dating is done."

"When did you do date number two?" Mac asked.

"A couple of weeks back. Teacher, triathlete. We had lunch," Kade answered him. "I am now off the dating hook."

"Anyway, getting back to today and this date—" he pointed a finger at Brodie "—revenge will be sweet."

Brodie didn't seem particularly concerned, so Kade left her to talk to his friends and headed for the kitchen. On the plus side, he'd fulfilled his duties to Wren's publicity campaign. The public could vote, speculate and talk about his love life until the damn cows came home but the only woman who interested him, on any level, was standing on his balcony, carrying his child.

He opened the fridge, yanked out a beer, saw Quinn behind him and reached for another. Kade handed Quinn a bottle and closed the fridge door with a nudge of his knee. He cracked open the beer and took a long swallow. He looked across the loft to the balcony where Brodie stood. It was a nice evening, his friends were here and he'd ordered Thai for dinner. He'd had a busy, drama-free day and then he'd joined Quinn and Mac on the ice for a workout. While the news had been unexpected, he was going to be a father and he was starting to become excited at the prospect.

Life *should* be good.

So what was the problem? In a nutshell, it was this half on, half off, up-in-the-air arrangement he had with Brodie. Half friends, sometimes lovers, future parents, both of them wanting, on some level, to run. He was jogging in place but Brodie had her sneakers on and was about to sprint, as hard and as fast as she could.

As soon as she could.

Kade felt he was living the same life he'd lived with his father, not sure how the next move would affect him.

Every day was new territory for him and he felt as unsettled as he had when he was a child.

Quinn's fist smacking into Kade's biceps rocked him back to the here and now. "What the hell was that for?"

"I talk to both you and Mac but neither of you listen! It's like talking to a blow-up doll."

"You should know," Kade grumbled, rubbing his arm.

Quinn's fist shot out again but Kade stepped back and the fist plowed through air. Kade sent Quinn a mocking glance. "Too slow, bro."

Quinn picked up his beer bottle, sipped and after lowering it he spoke again. "You concentrating, dude?"

"Yeah." Kade leaned against the kitchen counter and crossed his legs. "Speak."

"Your dad is having an exhibition in a couple of weeks, downtown."

So? His father was a well-respected artist and frequently held exhibitions in the city. James didn't invite him to any and Kade didn't attend. It worked for both of them. "Not interested."

"The exhibition is called 'Retrospective Regrets.'"

Kade didn't give a crap. His father wasn't part of his life, hadn't been part of his life for a long, long time. And he liked it that way.

"I just thought you might like to tell him he's going to be a grandfather."

He hadn't wanted a son so Kade doubted he'd be interested in a grandchild. But maybe he should give James the benefit of the doubt? Maybe he'd changed. Kade cursed at the hope that flickered.

"I'll think about it."

Quinn knew better than to push. He just shrugged

and lifted his beer bottle in Brodie's direction. "What are you going to do about her? Are you going to marry her, live with her, demand joint custody?"

Kade wished he knew. "I definitely want joint custody, everything else is up in the air." He rested his beer bottle against his forehead and sighed. "It's all craziness."

"Well, I suggest you figure out what you are before the news of your impending fatherhood hits the papers. If you don't know they'll decide for you."

Because the media's focus had been on his dates and the future of the team, so far he and Brodie had managed to dodge that bullet, but Kade wasn't under any illusions they'd keep the baby a secret indefinitely.

Quinn grinned. "On the plus side, my BASE jumping and having to talk myself out of being arrested aren't quite so bad when you measure them against the fact that another Maverick-teer is going to become a father, barely a month after Mac."

Kade would cross that burning bridge when he came to it. And talking about daredevil stunts... "Talking of, are you insane? You could've been killed!"

"Only if my chute didn't open," Quinn cheerfully agreed. "Then I would've made a dent in the concrete. *Splat!*"

Kade sent Brodie an anxious look, grateful she hadn't heard Quinn's cavalier attitude toward death. "Not funny, Rayne." Kade stopped, whirled around and slapped his hand on Quinn's hard chest. He scowled at his best friend. "Brodie lost everyone she loved in one accident. Don't you dare be glib about death, yours or anyone else's, around her! Got it?"

Quinn rubbed the spot on his chest. "Jeez, okay! Got it."

Kade walked away and Quinn scowled at the ceiling. "I'm running out of friends to play with," he muttered.

Later in the week, after a night long on pleasure and short on sleep, Brodie stood at the center island in Kade's kitchen, and scowled at her daily calendar on her tablet screen. Her schedule was utterly insane and she would be rushing from one appointment to another, all with men looking for a happily-ever-after. Didn't they realize the closer and the more perfect the relationship, the more pain they could expect to feel if the relationship went south? The end always hurt the most when the connection felt the best. Argh…she normally never thought about how her clients progressed after she matched them. Damn this situation with Kade for making her so introspective!

Kade, on his way up from the gym, walked past her to the sink and filled a glass with water. He whistled when he caught a glimpse of her schedule. "And I thought I had a hectic day ahead."

"Crazy, isn't it?" Brodie sipped her coffee and scowled at the screen. "I won't take all these men on as clients, some I'll be able to help and some I'll discard because, well, they'll be idiots."

Kade rested the glass on his folded arm. "Why matchmaking, Brodie? Why earn your living from something you don't believe in?"

Why would he think that? "But I do believe in it. I do believe people function best when they are in healthy, stable, supportive relationships. Being alone sucks."

"But you avoid relationships. You are alone," Kade pointed out.

"Yeah, but that's the choice I've made." Brodie

picked up a banana from the fruit bowl and slowly peeled it. "I know it's ironic that I, commitment-phobic as I am, own a matchmaking service."

Kade put his hands behind him and gripped the counter. "Okay, so why do you?"

Brodie looked across the loft to the rainy day outside. She took a bite of the banana, chewed it slowly and then placed it on the side plate next to her half-eaten toast. Should she tell Kade? Was she brave enough to open up a little more? She rarely—okay, never—spoke about Jay. She had trained herself not to think about him. But Kade was the father of her baby and she almost trusted him. Well, as much as she could.

"In the car crash, I didn't only lose my parents, I lost my best friends, as well. Chelsea and Jay. We were all in the car. I survived, and they didn't. We were like you and Mac and Quinn—inseparable." Brodie swiped her finger across the program to close her calendar. "Jay and I always knew that, one day, we'd move on from being best friends. Three weeks before the crash, we finally admitted we loved each other. We started sleeping together, everything was new and bright and wonderful." Her voice cracked and Brodie cleared her throat.

Kade took a step forward but Brodie held up her hand to stop him. If he touched her she would start to cry and she had clients to see. "I lost my world in the space of three minutes. But I was so loved, Kade. So damn much."

"And you don't want that again?"

"I can't *lose* that again. I'll have this child and that'll be enough. This child arrived by sheer fluke and I've accepted that the baby is life's way of forcing me to love again. To love in a different way."

"And will that be enough?"

Brodie lifted one shoulder in a tiny shrug. "It has to be. It's all I'm prepared to risk." Her smile felt a little shaky. "I am going to be the best mother I can be. I am going to be your friend, your lover, for as long as that works or until you meet the woman you can't live without." Brodie rubbed her hands across her eyes. "I hope you find her, Kade. I'd like you to. I think you deserve her."

"And I think you deserve the same."

"I wouldn't be that lucky, not twice. Life doesn't work that way." Brodie pushed her tablet into its case and sighed. "I have to go. Busy day."

"It's barely seven, Brodie, and I need to talk to you about something else."

Brodie frowned at his tone. Being bossed around so early in the morning really didn't work for her. "Okay, what?"

"So gracious." Kade walked across the kitchen to take a mug from a shelf. He jammed it under the spout of his coffee machine and pushed a button. Brodie tapped her fingers against the counter, listening to the sounds of the beans grinding. She was feeling exposed and hot, like her skin was a size too small for her body. That's why she didn't usually talk, she reminded herself. It made her feel sad and funny and...weird.

"I'm going to need to tell the press something about us and soon."

"Why?"

Kade looked at her over the rim of his mug. "We spend a lot of time together and someone is going to realize that. And when you start showing, they'll go into overdrive. Wren suggests we hit them with a press release and cut off the speculation. So what do you want to be called? My girlfriend, my partner, my common-law wife?"

Brodie grimaced as he said the word *wife* and Kade scratched his head. "Okay, so not wife. What?"

This was far too much to deal with so early in the morning. "I don't like titles. I don't believe in them. We are what we are…"

"I'll just tell the press that. It'll work," Kade said, sounding sarcastic.

"I don't know, Kade!" Brodie cried. "Tell them we are friends, that we intend to remain friends, that we are having a baby together! That's all the information they are entitled to. That's all the information we have."

"They'll make it up if we don't give them more. Or they'll dig and dig until they find more," Kade warned.

She couldn't control their actions, Brodie thought. She could only control her own. And right now she had to get to work or else she'd be late for her breakfast appointment. Besides, she really didn't want to talk about this anymore. With Kade or the world. "I'm not ready to say anything yet. And I've got to go."

"Dammit, Brodie! We have to deal with this at some point."

Yeah, but not now.

"Think about it," Kade told her, obviously frustrated. "Are you coming back here tonight?"

Brodie slung her bag over her shoulder and walked toward the front door feeling hemmed in. "Maybe."

That one word was, right now, all she could commit to.

Brodie looked up when Colin tapped on the frame of her door and ambled into her office.

"Hey, Col." Brodie rested her forearms on her desk and sent him a fond smile.

"How are you feeling?"

"I'm well. The morning sickness has passed, as has the tiredness." Brodie bit her bottom lip. "Did you tell Kayla?"

A shadow passed through Colin's eyes as he nodded. Colin and Kayla had been trying to get pregnant for more than five years and were now trying IVF. Hearing Brodie had become pregnant via a one-night stand had probably rocked Kayla.

"She took it rather well, considering. She said to tell you she wants to meet the baby's daddy."

Yeah, about that. Brodie still hadn't told Colin, or anyone else, about Kade.

"Maybe," Brodie hedged.

Colin sighed. "You're going to keep us guessing, aren't you?"

Brodie rubbed her forehead with her fingertips. "It's complicated. We're trying to work through it and until we have a plan, I'd rather just keep his identity quiet." She wrinkled her nose. "I might end up parenting on my own and he won't be a factor."

Not that there was a snowball's chance in hell of that happening. This was, after all, Kade she was talking about.

"Understood," Colin said, before straightening. "So, business…"

Business talk she could do. Mostly because it stopped her thinking about Kade and their future. Business wasn't complicated or demanding and it didn't mess with her head. Or her libido. "What's up?"

"I don't know about you but I am overwhelmed. My schedule is crazy."

Brodie looked at her screen and the thirty unopened emails from prospective clients. Ironically, the publicity generated from being Kade's matchmaker had generated almost too much business. "It's crazy."

"I was approached by a couple out of Los Angeles who want to relocate to Vancouver. They have a matchmaking business in the city." Colin passed her a black-and-pink business card.

"I know the Hendersons," Brodie said, flicking her nail against the card. "I investigated their business model when I was starting this business. They are reputable, smart and sensitive."

"Well, they have just sold their business and they are moving here."

Brodie immediately connected the dots. "Are they going to start up here?"

"They want to semi-retire. They want to work but they don't want the responsibility of running an office or staff."

"Are you thinking about bringing them on board… with you?"

Colin picked up her pen and tapped it against his knee, leaving tiny blue dots on his khaki pants. "And with you, if you are as overwhelmed as I am. It's a win-win situation. We feed them clients, take a commission and we manage how big a bite they take."

Brodie looked at the pile of folders on her desk and realized it might be the answer to her crazy workload. And she'd find it easier to juggle her career and being a new mother if she had some help. "Are they keen?"

"They are keen to talk," Colin replied. "They'll fly out here if we ask them to."

Her phone chirped and Brodie looked down at the screen.

Will be home late. Will you be okay?

God, she'd been okay for the past three months and for nine years before that. She'd managed to feed herself, dress herself, get herself to work, establish a career. Why did Kade and Poppy think she had dropped sixty IQ points just because she was now pregnant?

Arrrgh.

Brodie ignored Kade's message, pushed back her chair and stood up. She gripped the back of the chair.

"Or we could go to them." God, a trip out of the city would be an unexpected blessing, Brodie thought. She could get some distance from Kade, have some time alone to think.

You just don't want to deal with the emotions Kade pulls to the surface.

I just want some time to think! Is that too much to ask?

You've got to stop lying to yourself...

Oh, shut up.

Brodie looked at Colin. "What do you think? You up for a trip?"

"Sure. Are you allowed to fly?"

Brodie tamped down her irritation. "I am only a few months pregnant. The baby is the size of pea so yes, I can fly. Jeez!"

Her phone beeped again. I can cancel dinner if you want me to.

Kade! Really? She tipped her head at Colin and sent him an I-dare-you look. "Let's fly out tonight, see the Hendersons in the morning? I might stay in Cali for the weekend, do some sightseeing, some shopping."

Colin jumped to his feet, nodding enthusiastically. He was always up for an adventure and was, thank goodness, impulsive. "That sounds like an excellent idea. I'll call the Hendersons. Can you book flights?"

She could and she would, she thought, glancing down at the screen of her phone. Because she *definitely* needed to put a border and a couple of cities between her and Kade Webb.

Ten

Kade couldn't remember when he'd been this angry. Angry, disappointed…hurt, dammit. And the fact he was hurt pissed him off even more.

Gone away. Will be back in a few days.

A few days had turned into a week and he still didn't know where the hell Brodie was and, crucially, whether she was all right. She was ducking his calls and not returning his increasingly irate text messages. His… whatever the hell she was…was AWOL and he was not amused. Not amused as in ready to slam his fist into the wall. He'd do it but he recalled, from previous experience, it hurt like a bitch.

Kade stood on the balcony off his master suite and gripped the edge of the balustrade, peering past the trees to the street below, hoping to see Brodie's car. He wanted to make sure she was okay, to make love to her, to put her over his knee and spank her silly for driving him out of his mind with worry.

What if she never came back? What if she'd just packed up and left town, heading for…wherever? What would he do? How would he find her? Would he make the effort to track her down?

Of course he would. Apart from the fact she drove him insane, she was the mother of his child. For that reason alone he'd follow her to the ends of the earth…

Jesus, Brodie, where the hell are you?

Kade heard the subdued chime signaling someone had accessed his private elevator and since Quinn was out of town and Mac was home with Rory, it had to be Brodie. *Thank God.* She was the only other person who had the code.

Kade waited for the elevator doors to open and his heart both stumbled and settled when she stepped into his loft. He did a quick scan, confirmed she was physically in one piece and told himself not to lose his temper.

Yeah, that wasn't going to happen.

Brodie only needed one look to see Kade was pissed and exceptionally so. His eyes were the color of bittersweet chocolate and flat with anger and residual worry. She'd needed time away but she'd been wrong to avoid his calls, to avoid talking to him.

She'd done him a disservice; Kade was a fully functioning adult and he would've understood her need for some time alone to think. But she'd been unable to pick up the phone and tell him that—due to embarrassment and pride. Instead she'd let him worry and, judging by the increasingly irate messages he'd left her, stew. She deserved the verbal slap she was about to get and she braced herself to take it.

She'd created this situation and she wasn't going to whine about the consequences. She'd acted like a child because she'd felt smothered, and she deserved to be treated like a child now that she'd returned. He'd yell and she'd apologize and hopefully it would all be over soon.

"Hey."

Kade frowned and started to walk in her direction. Ah, hell, he was even angrier than she realized. Brodie lifted up her hands in apology. "I'm so—"

Her words were cut off by his hot mouth on hers and she could taste his frustration. His fingers dug into her hips and he yanked her into him, slamming her against his hard frame and his even harder erection. She couldn't help it; she encircled her arms around his neck and poured her own frustrations into the kiss…

I want you but I don't want to rely on you. I like feeling protected and cared for but it scares me spitless. I'm so close to falling in love with you but I can't let myself be that vulnerable again.

Brodie felt Kade tugging her shirt from her jeans and sighed when his warm hands spanned her back. His thigh pushed between hers and suddenly she was straddling his hard leg. Her body responded immediately by rocking against those hard muscles, moaning when the friction caught her in exactly the right place. Kade immediately responded by slipping his hand down the back of her jeans and he growled when her tight pants stopped his progress.

"Get them off."

This was too intense, too urgent, and Brodie knew they should back off, but she didn't want to. She wanted him out of control and reckless, demanding and insistent. He was feeling raw and so was she. It added an edge of excitement she'd never experienced before. It was primitive sex—hot, urgent—and she wanted to ride this maelstrom with him.

If they worked off enough frustration they'd be able to talk calmly and she'd be forgiven sooner. Besides, there was nothing wrong with channeling their anger into something that afforded them a great deal of pleasure...

Kade's fingers working the zipper of her jeans pulled her back into pleasure. He pushed her pants and her thong down to her ankles. Brodie stepped out of her backless wedges and kicked her feet free as Kade placed one hand behind her butt and lifted her up and into him. His tongue invaded her mouth again and she knew this would be hot and fast and crazy.

Bring it on!

Matching his urgency, she pulled his shirt up his back and over his head, forcing him to let her go so she could pull it off his arms. She ran her hands down his torso—she'd missed his body, missed *him*, more than she should. Far more than was healthy.

She hated that but she loved this. Loved his hot, masculine, hair-roughened skin. She placed her mouth on his chest to taste him as her hands dropped to his shorts, pulling his belt open with unsteady hands. She needed to feel him in her grasp, needed to taste him on her tongue, to fill her, to complete her.

She needed him.

She both loved and hated the need he stirred inside her.

Kade pushed her hands aside and quickly stripped. She reached down to touch him but he grabbed her wrists to stop her. He encircled them with one hand; easily restraining her while his other hand gripped her jaw and tipped her face up so her eyes collided with his.

Anger and desire were both still there. "We probably shouldn't do this."

"I know." Brodie licked her lips. "But I want to anyway."

"You sure?" Kade demanded, his voice rough. "Because it's not going to be pretty. I'm going to ride you, hard."

Brodie lifted her chin. "I can take everything you hand out, Webb. I'm not a hothouse flower."

The fingers on her jaw loosened and his touch turned tender. "Dammit, Brodie." He rested his forehead against hers.

It was her turn to touch his jaw, to allow her fingers to walk over his face. "You won't hurt me and I need you. I need you so damn much."

Those amazing eyes hardened, just a fraction. There was hurt beneath the anger and she was sorry for it. "You could've fooled me."

Brodie gave him what she could. "Right now, I need you as much as you need me. Give me that, Kade. The rest we can fight about later."

"And we will fight."

"I know." But that was for later so Brodie stood up on her tiptoes to align her mouth with his.

"How are we going to do this?" she whispered against his lips. "Where are we going to do this? Bedroom? Couch?"

Kade's eyes darted around the room. "Too far. Too civilized."

He spun her around and placed her hands on the hall table. Standing behind her, he put his palm on her stomach and pulled up her butt. Brodie swallowed, ferociously excited. So this was…new.

Kade's hand stroked her spine and her lower back, kneaded her butt before sliding between her cheeks to find the damp, moisture between her legs. She heard him sigh and then he was sliding inside her, the position filling her more deeply than he ever had before.

She felt exposed and dominated, but thrilled to her core, which he happened to be touching. His arms encompassed her, crisscrossing her from chest to thigh, and she felt protected and enveloped as her climax built. He was so deep inside he hardly needed to move and his thrusts turned gentle. Bright white lights sparked in her head as the warm, rushing wave pummeled her.

She screamed; he groaned. He pumped against her, once, twice, and then he exploded inside her, his arms tightening as a shudder ran through his body. Slowly coming back to herself, Brodie realized her fingernails were digging into Kade's forearms. The only thing keeping her from doing a face-plant on the floor was Kade's python-like grip. She sucked in a shallow breath and felt his lips on her neck. She was still half-dressed, her bra and shirt still on.

Whoa, Nelly.

Kade's arms loosened and he pulled her upright, sliding out as he did so. He dropped one arm but kept the other around her waist, anchoring her to his side. Brodie stared at the oil painting above the hall table and wondered if she could ever look at it again without remembering the hot sex they'd had beneath it.

"You okay?" Kade asked, his voice low, rough.

Brodie cleared her throat and nodded. "Yeah."

"I didn't hurt you?"

Brodie looked down at his arms and saw the deep grooves her nails had left in his skin. She traced her fingertip over the marks. "I should be asking you that."

"I'm good." Kade's arm tightened once and his hands flexed on her hips before he let her go. He picked up her jeans and handed them to her. "Go on up. I'll get clean downstairs."

Normally they'd shower together after sex and frequently showering would lead to round two. Brodie sighed. Guess that wasn't going to happen today.

He was still mad. Well, he'd warned her. Brodie nodded and walked toward the stairs, embarrassed he would watch her bare butt the whole way.

But when she turned around at the top of the stairs he'd disappeared to the lower level and his solitary shower.

Wishing she could run away again, Brodie headed into his bedroom and the en suite bathroom. She wouldn't get away with running again.

Brodie found Kade on the balcony, dressed in a faded pair of jeans and a pale blue T-shirt. He sat close to the edge, his bare feet resting on the railings, a beer in his hand. Brodie, dressed in the clothes she'd arrived in, saw there was a diet cola and a glass on the table so she sat down and perched on the cushion.

Kade poured her cola into the ice-filled glass and handed her the cold drink. He sat back and linked his hands behind his head looking like the urban, relaxed businessman he was. Except she also saw the tension in his jaw, the banked anger in his glittering eyes.

"You missed your doctor's appointment and the first ultrasound."

"I called and rescheduled."

"Thanks for letting me know," Kade said, his tone bitter.

Brodie frowned. She'd briefly mentioned the appointment to him and he'd never indicated his intention to go with her. "I didn't know you were planning to go with me."

Kade cut her a look. "Of course I was, Brodie."

Wow...okay. "I thought you'd only take an interest in the baby once it was born."

"I. Take. An. Interest. In. You." Kade spat out the words.

"Oh."

After a couple of minutes, Kade broke the silence. "I was worried about you. I thought something had happened to you, to our baby. I couldn't find you. I didn't know where to start looking."

Brodie closed her eyes at the note of desolation in his voice, the hurt he was trying so hard to hide. Brodie turned her head and looked at his hard profile, the way the evening breeze picked up his hair and blew it over his forehead.

"My dad did that once."

Oh, God, no.

"Did what?" she asked, not really wanting to know the answer because she knew it would make her feel ten times worse than she already did.

"Disappeared. I was about ten and I came home from school and he wasn't around. By eight that night I was worried, by midnight I was terrified. Three days later I was out of food and out of my mind with worry. Ten years old and I had cramps in my stomach from hunger. The morning of the fourth day I decided to skip school and go to the police. I was leaving the house when he pulled into the driveway, looking like he'd rather be anywhere rather than back in whatever town that was, with me."

Brodie gripped the arms of her chair and closed her eyes, silently cursing Kade's waste-of-space parent. She heard Kade stand up and felt the brief kiss on the top of her head. "I was terrified then but that had nothing on what I felt this past week." Kade's voice sounded like it had been roughened with sandpaper. "Everything is up in the air with us and I get that. I don't want to take over your life or control it or you. But if—when—you go, keep in contact, okay?"

Brodie nodded once, sharply, and forced the words past the tears in her throat. "I don't know what you want from me, Kade."

Kade walked around the chair and stood between her and the railing, the dim lights on the balcony casting shadows over his taut face. "I have no idea, either. I'm as confused about where to go, what to do as you are. But the one thing I do know for sure is that running away doesn't help. My father ran from town to town, from creditor to creditor, nothing ever changed. Because wherever you go, there you are."

Kade's fingers raked through his hair. "But maybe you could talk to me before you run. And I need you to come to grips with having me in your life. Because, even if we aren't going to be together, I am still going to be part of your life because—" he pointed to her midsection "—that is my kid, as well. We're in this together. So, on some level, I need you to trust me, to believe I won't let you down."

But he would. Everyone did.

Before she could respond, he continued, "But, Brodie, you only get this one chance. You run again and that's it. That's you telling me you don't want me in your life, in any capacity."

Brodie bit her bottom lip. "And the baby?"

"I will not abandon my child." Kade rubbed the back of his neck. "Lawyers, supervised visits until the baby is old enough and formal arrangements for custody. We'll be handing over the baby in parking lots. We'll be apart and separate, co-parenting but not communicating."

God, that sounded…awful. Dismal. Depressing.

"Don't do that to us, Brodie. Don't make it like that," Kade said, his voice soft. "I'm not asking for anything other than for you to let me in. To share something of yourself, to trust a little, or even a lot."

Kade's hand drifted over her hair and he bent down to kiss her temple. "I'm going to bed. Feel free to join me. Let me know if you decide to leave."

Brodie nodded.

"And Brodie?"

"Yes?"

"Don't ever ignore my calls again, okay?"

Brodie tied the laces on her running shoes, brimming with energy. Her morning sickness was all but gone and she felt energized and healthy and ready to resume exercising. She wasn't going to hurtle around Stanley Park like she normally did but she'd get her heart rate up and her blood flowing. Surely that had to be good for the baby?

Brodie left her apartment and skipped down the stairs, thinking she still missed her early-morning runs with Kade. So much had changed since they'd first met. She was carrying Kade's baby, they were having hot sex, sometimes at his apartment and, like last night, sometimes at hers. After their fight last week, she was doing her best to be more open, to communicate better.

She loved spending time with him and she couldn't help wondering whether he felt the same, if he missed her at all when she wasn't around? Oh, she knew he liked her, he adored making love with her, but was that the sum total of his feelings? Was he feeling more, wanting more?

Because, dammit, *she* was starting to want more.

Brodie nibbled the inside of her lip. She'd promised herself she wouldn't do this again, with any man, but she was sliding further and further down this slippery slope that might be love. With every smile, every conversation with Kade, she felt another one of her walls dissolving. Soon she'd be stripped bare and at the mercy of the vagaries of life and love. It would hurt.

And how would she ever know if Kade truly loved her and not the idea of her as the mother of his child? What if they became too swept up in playing the happy family and when the novelty wore off he decided this wasn't what he'd signed up for and bolted? How would she cope then?

No, teetering on the edge of love or not, she couldn't risk relying on him and being let down. People always thought they wanted one thing and then it turned out they wanted another. Sure, everyone had a right to change their minds, but she'd prefer it wasn't her heart Kade practiced on.

She'd rather be his friend and his part-time lover for as long as that lasted. When it ended, she'd still be his friend. And he'd be hers. She could do that…

Possibly.

Brodie pulled open the front door, ran down the pathway and bumped smack into a bunch of men standing on the curb. Cameras flashed and she lifted a hand to shield her eyes. What the hell?

"How long have you being seeing Kade?"

"When are you due?"

"Is it a boy or a girl?

"When did you and Kade hook up? Before you matched him?"

"Are you getting married?"

She didn't need to be a rocket scientist to realize the press knew Kade was the father of her baby and she wasn't going for a run this morning.

"You owe us a statement, Ms. Stewart."

"She owes you nothing, Johnson." Kade's deep voice broke through the shouting. Brodie looked up and there he was, holding out a hand. His car was idling behind the reporters and it represented safety and quiet, both of which she needed right now. Brodie grabbed his hand and allowed him to pull her through the throng of reporters.

"Aw, come on, Kade. We need something."

"I can give you a swift kick if that would help." Kade opened the passenger door for Brodie and she slipped inside. Kade shut her door but she could still hear the questions, the demands. Then the crowd quieted and Brodie looked out the window to see that Kade, his back to her and blocking the cameras, had quieted the crowd. "You guys can take potshots at me, ask me anything, but Brodie is off-limits."

"How long have you been together?"

"Are you getting married? Are you living together?"

"Was her matchmaking you just a publicity stunt? Did you lead those women on?"

"Has Myra accepted your offer to buy the franchise? We hear that the rookie is going to sue you personally."

Kade didn't say another word but walked around the car to the driver's seat. He opened his door and dropped inside. He slammed the door shut but rolled down his window.

"You said we can ask you anything. Not fair, Webb!"

Kade grinned. "I said you can ask me anything, I never said I would answer." Kade started the car, floored the accelerator and drove off. Brodie turned around in her seat to look at the agitated crowd behind them.

"They do not look happy."

"Screw them." Kade veered the car around the corner.

Brodie grabbed her seat belt and pulled it over her chest, clicking it into place. She looked at the creeping speedometer and bit her lip, tasting fear in the back of her throat. "Slow down, please?"

Kade sent her a quick look, then immediately slowed down and placed his hand on her knee. "Sorry. You okay?"

"Fine," Brodie replied, looking at his annoyed profile. "So, how did they find out? Did Wren do a press release?"

"No." Kade shook his head. "We were trying to delay it as long as possible, to put some distance between you becoming pregnant and arranging those stupid dates for me."

"So how did they find out?"

"Someone recognized us when we went to see the ob-gyn."

Brodie twisted her lips. "Anyone in the waiting room could've leaked the story, could've taken a photograph of us."

"And they did. They sold the story to the tabloids and

the paper that broke the news has had a photographer following us for at least two weeks. We're a double-page spread," Kade told her, driving in the direction of his apartment.

"Dammit." Brodie sighed. "Guess I am now, officially, one of Webb's Women."

"You are Webb's only woman." He glanced down at her stomach. "Unless there's a girl in there, then you'll have to share the spotlight."

He was using a jokey, upbeat tone and she didn't know whether he was being serious or not. He placed his free hand on her tummy but kept his eyes on the road. "Twenty-six weeks, Brodes, and we'll know."

Kade glided to a smooth stop in front of a traffic light and turned his head to look at her.

"God, the press will eat you up and spit you out."

"I am tougher than I look, Webb." The light turned green and Kade accelerated away.

"Just keep saying 'no comment.' Maybe you should move in with me—my place is a lot more secure than yours."

That wasn't going to happen. Brodie noticed Kade's eyes were dark with worry and his jaw was rock-hard with tension. She knew he cared for her, that he loved making love with her, but even after her trip to California and their fight, she hadn't been sure of how much until this moment. He was genuinely worried for her. Did that mean he loved her?

Stop jumping to conclusions. You're getting way ahead of yourself.

If she moved into the loft, then there was no way she'd be able to keep any emotional distance from him. Whenever they were together she found herself leaning into his shoulder, almost grabbing his hand, and she spent far too much time staring at his mouth.

"Nothing is going to happen to me. I'm healthy, the baby is healthy. And I can deal with the press."

Kade tapped his finger against his steering wheel. "Tell me again in two weeks when they are still shouting questions at you every time you step outside," he muttered.

"I'll be fine." Really, how bad could it be?

Eleven

"I feel like I've answered a million questions about me, what about you?"

Brodie clicked Save on her tablet and watched her database update before her eyes. She recognized the flirtation in the man's voice, the barely disguised interest. She glanced down at her bare ring finger and wished she was wearing her fake engagement ring. It had been a brilliant way to deflect unwanted male attention.

Thanks to the media that wasn't going to work anymore.

Ross Kimball was new to Vancouver, a marine biologist, and he knew no one in the city. During her hour-long interview she'd ascertained he was wealthy, judging by his nice suit, expensive watch and designer shoes. He'd only been in the city a month, he knew nothing about ice hockey, which was brilliant since she was tired of being gossip-column fodder and if she heard the words *Kade's baby-mama* bandied about again she'd stab someone with a fork.

For this moment in time she was Brodie again, matchmaker and businesswoman, and not the woman Kade impregnated. Win.

"As soon as I receive your background report and after I receive your first payment, I'll start the process."

Ross smiled. "Great. Would you like another cup of tea? Juice? Coffee?"

Brodie started to refuse but then she saw loneliness flicker in his eyes. What would it hurt to spend ten minutes talking to this guy? And it would be refreshing to talk to someone who did not want to discuss her and Kade and the baby she was expecting. Instead of refusing she nodded and leaned back in her chair. "Okay. I'll have an orange juice."

They spoke of the weather and the city and Ross's impressions of her hometown. "So, how did you become a matchmaker?" Ross asked.

Brodie gave him the standard spiel and when she was finished, added softly, "I hope I find you someone you can connect with."

"Are you…connected with anyone?"

She'd opened the door to these questions so she'd give him a little leeway. "It's complicated."

"It usually is."

"I'm seeing a guy. We're friends. Good friends."

"You're not in love with him?"

How could she answer when she wasn't sure what the answer was? How could she be in love with Kade when what they had was so different from what she had before? Jay had been sunshine and light, easygoing and happy-go-lucky. Kade was powerful, frequently sarcastic and reticent. The two men were galaxies apart. How could she possibly love such wildly differing men?

Was it love or was it just lust?

"What are you thinking about?" Ross asked.

"The difference between love and lust," Brodie replied.

"Tell me."

"Love is an intense affection for each other. It takes times to grow." Like fifteen years. "Lust is based on physical attraction." Lust was wanting to jump Kade every time he walked into the room. "It can transform into love over time. Love is about how interconnected two people are."

She and Kade were having a baby together. How much more interconnected could they be? He knew about Jay and her parents. Her great-aunt regularly called his cell for a chat. His friends had become hers, she was far more comfortable in his loft than she was in her own apartment and he'd taken her car to be serviced. She picked up his laundry.

They were interconnected.

Maybe she loved him. But that thought made her feel intensely guilty because this bubbling mess of feelings she had for Kade was deeper and darker and harder and crazier than she'd ever felt for Jay. She had survived his death. She knew without qualification she could not live in a world that did not have Kade in it.

God, this was crazy! What had happened to her? Why was she doing this? She knew what it felt like to love and lose, and what if she allowed herself to delve into this emotion and all he wanted to be was her friend with brilliant benefits? What if he, tomorrow or the next day or the year after that, met the love of his life and decided to move on from her, from them? How would she stand it? How would she cope seeing him and talking to him and co-parenting with him while knowing he left her to sleep in another woman's bed? That he was holding another woman, loving her, laughing with her?

Brodie was such a fool. This had to stop. She had to pull herself back from the brink, to keep control. Yes, withdrawing from Kade would hurt but it would be nothing compared to what could happen down the line.

She could do this; she had to do this.

"Wow. That was one hell of a trip you took," Ross said, his expression speculative.

"Sorry." Brodie picked up her juice and took a long swallow. "What were we talking about?"

"Your fellow and whether you were in love with him."

"I don't believe in love." The words flew out of Brodie's mouth. Seeing his startled expression, she wished she could take them back. But then, suddenly, it was more important someone listen to what she was *saying*. Because if she could convince him, then maybe she could convince herself.

"At least not for me. I believe in sex. I believe in friendships, in being independent, in standing on my own two feet. I believe in my career, in forging my own path, in keeping an emotional distance."

"He's not the one?"

Brodie made herself meet his eyes, trying to talk herself off the ledge. "I'm having his baby and, admittedly, he's stuck around but I don't expect he'll stay for much longer. Having a baby is a novelty, a whim, and he'll lose interest. He has a low boredom threshold."

Oh, God, nothing was further from the truth, and verbalizing those lies didn't change how she felt about him. They just made her feel nasty and bitchy and guilty, dammit!

Under the table she patted her tummy and silently spoke to her child. "Ignore that, kiddo, your dad is not like that. In fact, the problem is that he is utterly wonderful. I just don't know how to handle him."

Kade stood in front of the six-by-eight-foot oil painting dominating one wall of the gallery and reluctantly admitted his father was a ridiculously talented artist.

He recognized the scene—it was the view from the rickety back porch of a cabin in Pleasant, a town north of Whitehorse. He hadn't seen the snow-covered mountains, the icy beauty of the scene, he just remembered his skates had been too small and he'd had holes in his parka. And the cupboards had held little more than bread and cereal. His father had just spent the last of his money on more oil paints, a canvas and brushes.

Kade looked at the familiar signature in the bottom corner and waited for the flood of resentment and the bite of pain that usually accompanied it. When neither arrived, he took a step back and cocked his head, wondering what had changed. His father was his father and his childhood hadn't been a barrel of laughs, but it was, thank God, long over. Being his father's son had taught him resilience, how to be tough, that nothing came to people who didn't work their asses off. James's success was proof of that. He'd been consumed by his art and had thrown everything he had into it and, judging by the fact that this painting was on sale for seventy-five thousand dollars, sacrificing a relationship with his son had been worth it.

Kade blew out his breath, finding it strange not to feel bitter. He really didn't, not anymore. His father was his father, selfish and obsessive. Nothing was important to his father but his art. That there was no hint of the child who explored the country with him in any of the paintings exhibited was a pretty big clue he wouldn't care that he was about to become a grandfather.

Art was all that mattered.

Kade had felt like that about his career until Brodie dropped back into his life. Suddenly he had to—wanted to—think about someone else. He couldn't work fourteen-or sixteen-hour days anymore. He needed to find a balance between work and home, especially when the baby arrived. Besides, he didn't want to spend so much time at work. He enjoyed Brodie's company and he wanted to spend time with his child. He would not be his father's son.

Kade turned away from the painting, finally at peace with the fact that he would never have a relationship with James. He'd lost his father a long time ago, if he'd ever really had him. Kade could finally put these particular demons to rest.

With a considerably lighter heart Kade left the gallery. As he stepped onto the sidewalk, he felt his cell vibrate. He read the incoming message from Wren and clicked on the link she provided.

A reporter had gotten Brodie to open up—through subterfuge, but still. Worse, he'd gotten her to talk about how she was feeling, something Kade had difficulty doing. Strange that it should hurt so much. She could talk to strangers but not to him?

And then there was what she'd said to the blogger, scumbag that he was. Her words had Kade feeling like a clawed hand was ripping his heart apart. She didn't believe in love, didn't want it in her life and didn't believe Kade could provide it.

Despite everything they'd gone through, she still thought he was playing games, that he would bail. He might no longer think he was his father's son but Brodie certainly did, judging by the fact that she'd publicly stated she was expecting him to leave.

Man, that hurt. Even more painful than the hunger, the fear, the uncertainty he'd experienced as a kid. To have the woman in his life thinking so little of him...it felt as if she'd used his heart as a hockey puck.

Why? Kade stared down at his screen, unable to get his feet to move. Why did he care so damn much?

Because he loved her.

Crap, dammit, hell.

Because, like he'd always been with his father, Kade was desperate for her to love him. Because, again like his father had been, Brodie was Kade's world. And, like James, Kade wasn't hers.

How the hell had he let this happen?

Kade started to walk. He needed to move or else he would scream. He was in love with her, she didn't love him. What did he do now? He could walk away, break it off. In a couple of months he could sic his lawyers on her, demanding custody rights, and they could communicate that way. He didn't have to talk to her again if he didn't want to.

He didn't want to; he felt too raw.

Or he could go to her, give her a chance to explain. See if there was anything they could salvage out of this train wreck of a relationship. No, not a relationship; Brodie didn't believe in those... He should just let the lawyers deal with it, with her, but his feet didn't agree. They just kept walking in the direction of Brodie's office.

They might, if he was really lucky, let him walk right on past her building.

* * *

It was after eight in the evening and Brodie was exhausted. She couldn't wait to go home, maybe sink into the spa bath, preferably naked, with Kade. Pushing her chair back from her desk, she stood up and winced when the button of her black pants pushed into her stomach. She was going to have to buy some bigger clothes. Her tummy was growing at an alarming rate and, unfortunately, she suspected her bottom was following the trend.

Maybe Kade could show her some exercises she could safely do to keep her butt from spreading. Her tummy was on its own.

Brodie opened her lower drawer to pull out her bag and sighed when her computer signaled the arrival of a new email. She'd never been able to ignore a ringing phone or a new message so she clicked the mouse.

What?

It took a moment for her to make sense of the words on the screen. It was from the company she and Colin used to run background reports. It was fairly important their clients were who they said they were. That they weren't broke, had a criminal record...

Because she was swamped with clients this week, she'd done the interview with Kimball before she received the background checks, something she didn't like to do. If she had waited, she would've known Ross Kimball was not who he said he was. He wasn't living at the address he stated; there were no marine biologists working in the area, or in the country, under that name and his contact numbers were bogus.

Brodie pulled out her chair and sat down. She'd been played and played well. Who was Kimball and why had he used such an elaborate ruse to meet her?

It didn't take her long to come up with an answer. Kade. And her relationship with him.

Since the world found out she was carrying Kade's baby—*a new generation of Mavericks!*—she'd been bombarded with requests for interviews and she'd refused every offer. Her standard response was a consistent and, she guessed, infuriating "no comment."

As Kade had said, the press had gone looking for a story and Ross had sneaked in via the back door. He'd played the role well, she thought. She hadn't once suspected he wasn't who he said he was.

So, who did he work for and what had he penned? And how could she find out, preferably before Wren and Kade did?

What had she told the man? They'd discussed the city and how lonely it could be, he'd flirted with her and she'd shut him down…

Shut him down by telling him she didn't believe in love…

"'Brodie Stewart is a walking contradiction, someone who earns a very healthy living matching people in that eternal quest for true love while discounting the notion for herself.'"

Brodie jerked her head up and winced when she saw Kade standing in the doorway to her office, reading from his phone. Well, guess she didn't have to go looking for the article. Kade—via the annoyingly efficient Wren, she presumed—had accessed it on his smartphone. And, judging by his furious expression, he was less than thrilled by its contents.

Brodie leaned her head against the back of her chair. "Who is he?"

"Ross Bennett. A blogger with an enormous following. Quite well-known for his ability to twist the truth,"

Kade replied, looking back down at the screen. Then he started to read, his tone flat and terrifyingly devoid of all emotion.

"In an interview with Ms. Stewart, she candidly admitted she didn't believe in love. 'I believe in sex. I believe in being independent, of standing on my own two feet. I believe in my career, in forging my own path, in keeping an emotional distance.'

"She doesn't seem to have much faith in Kade Webb, either. Webb, according to Ms. Stewart, won't stick around for the long haul. To Kade, having a baby is a novelty and she expects him to lose interest."

Brodie gripped the arms of her chair. Oh, this was bad. This was very bad.

"Luckily for the Mavericks, Bennett is regarded as a trash-talking, sensation-seeking journalist. He is best to be ignored. Wren thought he was sucking the story out of thin air, but I heard your voice in those words. What happened?"

"He posed as a client and he fooled me," Brodie reluctantly admitted.

Kade leaned a shoulder into the wall, his face a blank mask. His eyes were flat and emotionless and his mouth was a hard line. Kade was, she knew, incandescently angry. Maybe this was the final straw; she'd pushed him away so many times…maybe this time she'd pushed him too far. She'd tested his commitment to sticking by her and their child and he'd passed every test. But this was no longer a game, she realized; she'd pushed too hard and too far.

She didn't need him to verbalize his intentions; he

was done. The moment she'd both dreaded and welcomed was here and the pain would follow. She would deal with it and then she would go back to her safe, emotion-free life.

The life she wanted, she reminded herself. The life she felt comfortable in. The lonely, color-free, safe, boring life.

"Did I ever give you reason to think I would fade away?"

"No."

"That I was playing at being a father?"

Brodie shook her head.

"I read that blog while standing outside the gallery exhibiting my father's latest work. It struck me you could've been describing my father—that's the way he was, the way he acted."

God, she hadn't thought of that. Hadn't meant him to think that. He was *nothing* like the man who sired him. "I'm sorry."

"Being sorry doesn't help, neither does how I feel about you." Kade shook his head. "I can't keep doing this, Brodie. I can't fight your fear anymore, you've got to do that yourself. I told you I'll be here for you but you don't want to believe it and I can't force you to."

Kade shoved a hand into his hair. "For you to think that, verbalize it, means you either believe it or you want to believe it. It doesn't matter which. Either way it tells me you are intolerant of intimacy and you deliberately cut yourself off. And this—" Kade showed her the screen "—this is you running. I'm not going to be the sap who runs after you, begging you to give me another chance. I did that with my father, I will not do it again. I've given you enough chances. I'm worth more than that and, frankly, so are you."

Brodie felt the kick in her stomach, in her heart, in her head. "Okay."

"Okay? That's it? That's all you have to say?"

She wouldn't throw herself at his knees and beg him not to leave her. It was better this way; it had to be. "What do you want to do about the baby?"

"The baby? God!" Kade looked like he wanted to put his fist through a wall. "Right now I'm so damn mad at you I can't think! Do you not understand you are throwing away something pretty amazing to hide behind those walls you've built up? I'm scared, too, Brodie. Raising kids, being together, is meant to be scary!"

"There are no guarantees, Kade."

"Of course there aren't! You just take what happiness you can and run with it. You just feel damn grateful for it." Kade rubbed his hands over his face. "I'm talking to a freaking brick wall. Have fun hiding out, Brodie. As I said, I'm done."

Brodie nodded once and bit her bottom lip, everything in her trying to keep the tears at bay. "Okay."

"Okay? That's all you have? For God's sake..." Kade slapped his hand against the door frame as he whipped around. "Talking to a friggin' wall."

Brodie waited until she heard the door to the outer office slam closed before she finally allowed herself to cry. Hunched over and hurting, she watched from a place far away as tears ran off her face and dropped to the carpet below.

Yeah, the pain was here, accompanied by desolation and despair. It was okay, she'd been here before and she'd handled it.

She could do it again.

But right now she just wanted to cry, for herself, for

her child, for the butterflies in her stomach that were dying a slow and excruciating death.

Kade was convinced he held the record for the fastest heartbreak in the history of the world. Within the space of the afternoon he'd realized he loved Brodie and that nothing would ever come of it. His mind wanted to stop loving her but he knew his heart always would.

Kade loosened his tight grip on the stem of his wineglass and stared at False Creek, for the first time not seeing the beauty below him. It had been twilight when he returned home from work tonight, three weeks since he'd walked out of Brodie's office and her life. And while he could remember the exact date and time his life turned dark, he had no idea what time it was now.

Brodie had done what he'd expected, maintained radio silence. They hadn't spoken, messaged, emailed or texted each other and he felt adrift. Before Brodie hurtled her way into his life he'd felt content with his lot, generally happy. He hadn't wanted a relationship and had been content to have an affair here, a one-night stand there. No promises, no hassle.

Brodie had been nothing but a hassle and an all-around pain in his ass, but when she wasn't annoying him, she brought light and laughter to his life. Kade placed his forearm over his eyes and cursed his burning eyes.

He finally loved someone with everything he had and she wanted jack from him. Life was laughing at him.

He wanted to go to Brodie, wanted to beg her to allow him to be part of her life, but he knew that was a road heading straight to a deeper level of hell. He'd be seeing her again in five months or so anyway, and maybe by then he would've stopped thinking about what they could've had.

Growing up with his father had taught Kade that chasing rainbows led to disappointment. You couldn't force someone to love you. Love wasn't something to be demanded; it either was or it…wasn't.

He loved Brodie and while he suspected she could love him, she didn't. She wouldn't allow herself to love him and he wasn't going to beg. He wanted everything and he wouldn't settle for anything less. He couldn't; the resentment would kill him and, worse, it would kill his love for her.

So he'd love her from a distance for the rest of his life. That was the way it had to be so the sooner he got used to feeling like crap, the better.

Kade sat up, rested his forearms on his thighs and dangled the glass between his knees. He could wallow or he could distract himself. He could call Quinn and they could go clubbing. He could go to Mac and Rory's for dinner. He could do some work or a gym session.

What he wasn't going to do was to sit on this couch in the dark and feel sorry for himself. Yet it was another fifteen minutes before he got up and another ten before he crossed the room to flick on some lights.

He just needed time, he told himself. A millennium or two might be long enough to get over her.

Twelve

The summer holidays were almost over and the vast beaches on the west side of Vancouver Island had been, for all intents and purposes, returned to the birds and the crabs that were the year-round residents of the island. Soon the leaves would start to turn, winter would drop the temperature and the storms would roll in.

But for now, Brodie and Poppy walked the empty beach, bare feet digging into the sand, watching the rolling waves kiss the shore. The stiff breeze pushed Brodie's thin hoodie against her round tummy and kicked sand up against her bright blue yoga pants. She loved this place, Brodie realized. Away from Vancouver, away from the city, she could breathe and think.

"When are you going to stop punishing yourself for living?" Poppy asked as she took Brodie's arm.

Brodie pushed a hunk of hair out of her eyes and squinted at Poppy. "I'm not punishing myself."

"Really? Well, the way I see it there is a man on the

mainland who wants to be part of your life, who wants to raise this baby with you, but you are determined to take the hard road and do it all by your little lonesome. Is that not punishing yourself?"

"That's me protecting myself," Brodie retorted.

"From what? Pain?" Poppy asked. "From loneliness?"

Brodie stared out to sea and focused her attention on a ship on the horizon and ignored Poppy's probing questions. She didn't want to think about Kade, though there was little else she thought about these days. She definitely didn't want to talk about him.

But Poppy wasn't intimidated by Brodie's scowling face or her frown. "News flash, you are so damn lonely you don't know what to do with yourself."

"Pops, please."

Poppy dropped her arm and they stood side by side, looking out to sea. Poppy released a long breath. "Do you see that ship?"

She'd only been staring at it for the past half hour. Brodie nodded, glad Poppy had dropped the subject of Kade. "It's a container ship, probably headed for Japan."

Poppy nodded, her expression contemplative. "There's a saying about ships and leaving the harbor... do you know it?"

Brodie shook her head.

"It goes something like this—'a ship in the harbor is safe, but that's not what ships are built for.'"

Brodie wrinkled her nose. How silly she'd been to think Poppy had dropped the subject; Poppy only stopped when she'd brought you around to her way of thinking.

"Ships aren't built for safety but neither are humans.

We should take risks. We *have* to take risks. You and Kade? Well, that's a risk worth taking."

"I'm scared. Of loving him too much, scared it won't last forever. Scared he thinks he loves me but only loves me because of this baby. So scared he might—"

"Die?" Poppy interrupted. "What if you die? What if a freak tsunami washes you off the beach right now? What then? What if you die giving birth? What then?"

"That would suck," Brodie admitted.

"It really would. But would you want Kade to be alone for the rest of his life, to—metaphorically speaking—wear black widower's weeds, too scared to love again, laugh again? To live again?"

Dammit. She knew where Poppy was going with this but she couldn't find anything to say to get out of this quandary. All she could think of was that it was easier for Poppy to say it than for Brodie to do it.

"Well?" Poppy demanded.

"But—"

"There are no buts. Jay would hate to see you like this. Your parents would be so disappointed in you." Poppy grabbed Brodie's chin and forced her to meet faded blue eyes. Poppy's body might be old but her eyes were alive and fierce and determined.

"Do you love him?"

Brodie couldn't lie, wouldn't lie. "Yes."

"These are your choices and you need to think them through. You can wallow and live a miserable half life until you die. You can keep punishing yourself, keep disappointing yourself because you don't have the balls to choose differently."

"God, Poppy."

Poppy ignored Brodie's desperate laugh. "Or you can take your butt back to the city, throw yourself at his feet and apologize for being an ass. Find out if he loves you, if this is a forever thing. Face your fears."

"That's a hard decision to make, even harder to do," Brodie protested.

"Do it anyway," Poppy suggested. "Be brave enough to be happy, Brodie. Don't let your fear win. You are stronger than that, more courageous than you think. Just do it, my darling. Reach out and grab the future you've always wanted."

"But what if I'm too late?" Brodie asked, unsure why she was asking this question because she wasn't going to go to Kade, wasn't going to ask for another chance. That was crazy talk…wasn't it?

Poppy's sweet smile held more than a trace of satisfaction. And triumph. "What if you're not?" She placed a wrinkled hand on Brodie's face. "Don't make me get tough with you, Brodie."

"This isn't you being tough?" Brodie demanded with a sarcastic laugh.

"Honey, I haven't even warmed up yet. I can go on for hours," Poppy stated prosaically. "You might as well just give in now and save us both the time and energy."

Brodie put her arms around Poppy's waist and rested her head on her great-aunt's shoulder. "Well, when you put it like that…"

Brodie used her shaking index finger to key in the code that would take her straight up to Kade's apartment. She hoped he hadn't changed the code. That would be mortifying. She entered the last number and waited for the elevator doors to slide open. When they did she had to force herself to step inside.

She could do this. She had to do this.

If she didn't speak to Kade tonight, she never would.

She would talk herself out of being brave. She'd allow herself to backslide, to rationalize why she would be better off alone.

Talk the truth, even if your voice shakes.

Poppy's words stuck with Brodie and she repeated them to herself as the elevator took her higher, and closer, to the love of her life.

And he was that. Jay, dear Jay, had been marvelous, but her feelings for Kade were deeper, harder and stronger. Maybe that's why she'd been fighting this so hard. Loving Kade wouldn't be easy but he'd be worth it.

She had to tell him, had to see if he felt the same.

As the elevator stopped at the top floor she touched her stomach in that age-old protective gesture women had been using through the centuries.

Wish me luck, baby. Here's hoping we get to be a family.

Brodie stepped into the dark loft, the lights from downtown Vancouver dancing in the floor-to-ceiling windows. The apartment was ridiculously quiet and she bit her lip, feeling like an idiot. She hadn't considered the notion that Kade might not be here. He could be anywhere—with his friends, out of town, on a date. The only thing worse than Kade coming home with a date would be finding Kade upstairs in bed with another woman. With the doors closed, she wouldn't be able to hear a thing.

It had only been three weeks. He wouldn't have moved on so soon, would he? Then again, she'd kept pushing him away, telling him that what they had was only sex. Maybe he was upstairs, doing all those fabulous things he did to her…

Brodie threw her bag onto the couch and stormed toward the staircase. If she'd been bawling her eyes out while he slept his way through the pack of puck bunnies, Brodie might be forced to do something drastic.

What, she wasn't sure, but it would hurt. A lot.

Brodie flung open the door to his bedroom and hurtled over the threshold, stopping when she realized his enormous bed was neatly made and, crucially, empty. Brodie closed her eyes and hauled in a deep breath.

"You're acting like a crazy woman, Stewart," she muttered.

"Can't say that I disagree."

Brodie whirled around and saw Kade standing in the doorway to his en suite bathroom, a towel wrapped around his narrow hips. Man, he was gorgeous. How could she have walked away from that?

He was sexy and hot but he was also a good man. Someone who was loyal and kind and considerate and… hers.

"What are you doing here, Brodie?" Kade asked, his expression forbidding.

"Uh…" Okay, she was being silly but she just had to make sure. "Is there anyone in there with you?"

Kade turned his head to look back into the bathroom. "Busted. Come on out, honey," he called.

Brodie's heart ker-plunked. She placed a hand on her sternum and tried to find something to say.

"God, Brodie, don't be an idiot," Kade snapped. "There's no one here. I was just messing with you."

Brodie scowled. "Don't do that, okay?"

"I think I've got a right," Kade retorted. He pushed his hand through his wet hair. "I can't stand here, almost naked, with you in the room. Why don't you go downstairs and keep walking across the apartment until you hit the elevator. I doubt there's anything you have to say that I want to hear."

"No." Brodie lifted her chin.

"No?"

"No, I'm not going to do that."

Kade shrugged, sent her a sarcastic smile and walked to his closet. Dropping the towel to the floor, Brodie watched him go into the small room, bare-ass naked. Man, he was so messing with her.

"So why are you here? Missing the sex?" Kade asked as he reached for a pair of sweats.

"Yes," Brodie replied, thinking honesty was the best policy. "Of course I am. We are fabulous together and I love making love with you."

Kade pulled on the sweats and turned, gripping the top of the door frame with white fingers. "Is that what you're back for?" He took in her leggings and bohemian shirt. "Fine. But you're a bit overdressed. Strip."

"Stop being a jerk, Kade," Brodie snapped.

"Then again, if it's just sex you're back for, then I am not interested." Kade dropped his arms. He rubbed his hands over his face and when he looked at her again, those beautiful eyes were bleak. And his voice, when he spoke again, sounded desolate. "Just go, Brodie. Please."

She'd done this, Brodie thought, ashamed of herself. She'd hurt him. She'd wounded this powerful, smart man just because she'd been too scared to take a chance. To live. Well, that stopped now, right this minute. She needed to be better than that; her child—their child— and Kade deserved better. But how to tell him? What to say?

Brodie walked past the bed to the open balcony doors and thought about Vancouver Island. Remembering Poppy and their conversation, Brodie pushed her shoulders back and placed her hands behind her, anchoring herself to the door frame.

"When I was about eleven, I was a bridesmaid and I fell in love with the idea of love. I became slightly obsessed with weddings, with the idea of happily-ever-after. Jay was the boy from down the road and even then, I thought he might be the one."

Brodie risked looking at Kade, relieved to see he was interested in what she was saying. His expression was still remote and, to be honest, scarily forbidding, but he hadn't kicked her out. It was progress but she had a long way to go. "I made a scrapbook. What my dress would look like, the color scheme, my bridesmaids' dresses, the whole shebang."

"Is there a point to this?" Kade asked, impatient.

Brodie ignored him. "Strangely, I pretty much nailed what I wanted for a wedding at eleven. When I flipped open the scrapbook shortly before the accident, excited because Jay and I were moving on from being best friends to something more, there was little I wanted changed. But one aspect jumped out at me and it's been bugging me."

"Pray tell."

Still sarcastic, Brodie sighed. "Jay was dark-haired and blue-eyed, short and stocky," Brodie continued. "My eleven-year-old self didn't have him in mind when she was imagining her groom. Jay looked nothing like the tall, blond, sexy man in my scrapbook."

Kade didn't say anything but Brodie noticed his expression had turned from remote to speculative.

"Do you think my younger self knew something I didn't? Even then? Don't you think that's spooky?"

"I don't give a damn about your eleven-year-old self," Kade stated, his tone brisk. "I want to know what you want, right now."

Right, time to jump off this cliff. God, she hoped

he was going to catch her. "You." Her voice cracked
with emotion. "I just want you. Any way I can get you."

"Explain that," Kade demanded, his eyes locked on
hers.

Brodie wished he would come to her, initiate contact. "This has nothing to do with the fact we have
such incredible sexual chemistry, or that you're my
baby's father. Or that you are hot, which, I have to say,
is a bonus..." Brodie smiled but Kade didn't react. He
didn't say a damn thing, just continued to stare at her
with those hot, demanding eyes.

Oh, crap. He was going to make her say it. She
hauled in a breath and gathered her courage. "I love
you. I just want to be with you." Brodie bit her bottom
lip. "I'm so sorry about what I said, did. I was trying to
fall out of love with you. But I need you to know I believe you are nothing like your father, that I know you
will be a spectacular dad."

Kade rubbed his jaw and then the back of his neck.
"Jesus, Brodie."

"I'm sorry. For everything I said because I was so
damn scared." Brodie stared at her red ballet pumps.
She turned her head and looked at Kade. He seemed
gobsmacked and, she had to admit, not very damn
happy at her proclamation. She'd been too late. She'd
lost him.

Brodie forced her rubbery legs to walk toward the
door. She scooped up her bag as she walked past the
bed.

"What do you want from me, Brodie?" Kade inter-
cepted her and placed both his hands on her upper arms.

Brodie shrugged. "Nothing you can't give me, openly
and honestly. I just want you in my life, any way I can
get you. With or without the baby, I love you. It's taken

me a while, but now it's suddenly simple. It's fine that you don't love me. I still want you to be my friend, to co-parent with you, to be our baby's dad."

Kade cupped the side of her face with his big hand and she finally saw the beginning of a smile. "For a bright woman, you can be incredibly dense on occasion."

What did that mean? What was he trying to say?

Kade's thumb drifted over her bottom lip, down her chin. "I can love you. I do love you."

Brodie felt her heart expand, fill with a warm, bright light. Before it could start dancing around her rib cage, she grabbed it in an iron fist. "In what way?"

"In every way that counts. " Kade kissed the corner of her mouth. "And more. A lot more."

She loosened the hold on her heart. "Meaning?"

"Meaning I love you, too. I will always love you. I never expected this to happen to me, not like this. We met again and I feel like I've been riding a hurricane and I've loved every minute. You drive me nuts, you turn me on. I think about you all the damn time." He swallowed some emotion and Brodie blinked back her tears.

"I imagine the family we can have, the fun we'll have," Kade continued, "I dream about the love that will color our lives."

Brodie smiled slowly, her heart dancing. She placed her hands on his pecs and rested her forehead on his chest. "Oh, God, I feel light-headed. I am so relieved." Kade's hand cupped the back of her head. "While I was running away, I realized I'd so rather be scared with you than be without you. I'd rather stand in an electrical storm with you than be safe by myself. You're my it, Kade—the blond, big man my eleven-year-old self recognized so long ago."

"Brodie." Kade's arms tightened around her and easily lifted her so her mouth aligned with his. "Welcome home, baby. Don't run away anymore."

"Thank you for giving me another chance," she murmured against his lips.

"I've missed you." A mischievous smile crossed his face as humor and relief chased the last residue of hurt and disappointment from his eyes. "So does this mean I have to get rid of the girl in the bathroom?"

Brodie tapped on the door to Kade's office and popped her head in. It was the end of the day and her man sat behind his desk, his fingers flying across his keyboard. He looked up and the frown on his face disappeared as his smile reached his eyes. They'd been back together for a month and the butterflies in her stomach were still going mad, occasionally accompanied by a tiny flutter that was all Baby Webb.

"Hey, gorgeous." Kade leaned back in his chair as she closed the door behind her. She walked over to his desk and plopped herself into his lap, lifting her face for a thorough, very sexy kiss. Kade pulled away and placed his hand on her round tummy. "How's my other girl?"

"Your *boy* has started to play ice hockey in my womb," Brodie replied. "We have a doctor's appointment next week."

"I haven't forgotten." Kade looked at his watch. "As much as I love the idea of you surprising me at work, I thought you had a late meeting."

"I did but I canceled." She was about to add she forgot to wear her fake engagement ring but she knew that might prompt Kade to suggest he buy her a real ring.

She knew a proposal was coming but she wanted to do something different...

Hence her visit to his office.

Brodie climbed off his lap and sat on the edge of his desk so she could see his face. "So, Wren called me and told me she's posted the final blog on our endeavor to find your happily-ever-after."

"You're my happily-ever-after." Kade placed a hand on her knee. "I told her to take that nonsense down. It's silly to have it on the site when everyone knows we are together, a couple, in love and that we are having a baby."

"Still—" Brodie tapped her finger on the screen of his laptop "—take a look."

"You've seen it?" Kade asked, sitting up.

"I approved it. I hope you do, too." She licked her lips and watched as he double-clicked the icon on the screen to bring up the Mavericks' website. He went to the relevant page and started to read. Brodie tucked her shaking hands under her thighs and read along with him.

There was a photo of them in the top right-hand corner with the words *Kade's future* as a title.

As a matchmaker, I have matched many couples and it gives me great pleasure to play a small part in helping people find happiness in love. I have, in the process of trying to find Kade's life partner, found the same happiness and nobody was more surprised than I was when I realized Kade was mine.

I never thought that love, permanence and commitment would be a part of my future again but I am honored and thrilled to have found it with Kade.

He and our child are my future, my joy, my heart. So, sorry, ladies of Vancouver, but Kade Webb is officially and permanently off the market.
Yours,
Brodie

Brodie found her courage and said the words she'd been practicing for the past week. "So, my mom's engagement ring is very real and I'd like to wear it. Are you game, Webb?"

Brodie watched as Kade slowly turned and sent her his charming, emotional, full-blown smile. He leaned back in his chair and linked his hands across his stomach. "You proposing, Stewart?"

Brodie lifted one shoulder. "It's a suggestion…"

"I like your suggestion," Kade softly answered her.

Warmth coursed through her, relaxing and rejuvenating her at the same time.

Kade gestured to the screen. "Why this, Brodes? It's a pretty public declaration."

That was the point. Brodie attempted to explain. "I know, it'll be the only time I'll ever do or say something about us on social media, but I needed to. I've lived in the shadows for so long. I've protected myself so well, I wanted to show you exactly how committed I am to you, to us. I wanted you to know I'm still scared but I'm not going to run away." She stared at her shoes. "Maybe it was just me breaking through my cocoon."

Kade stood and tipped up her face. "Thank you." He placed his hands on the desk and dropped a sexy, sweet kiss on her mouth. "I love you so damn much and I can't wait to marry you. Hand the ring over and I'll do the bended-knee thing."

Brodie grinned. "I can't wait to see you on bended knee and I love you back."

Kade smiled against her lips. "First and last time. Now that our future is sorted, let's talk about the important stuff."

"Where we're going to live—your loft—and when we're going to get married? I was thinking the sooner the better."

Kade's eyes glinted. "Actually, I was talking about the *really* important stuff, like how soon I can get you naked—"

The door burst open and they broke off their deep kiss and looked around to see Quinn standing in the doorway.

"Oh, for God's sake, do you two do anything other than grope each other?" he demanded, slapping his hand over his eyes.

"Not really, no." Kade scowled at his friend. "What do you want, jerkoid?"

"Rory's on her way to the hospital, she's in labor. We're going to have our first Maverick baby!"

Kade grabbed his jacket and Brodie's hand. "We're right behind you." At the door he kissed Brodie again and tucked her into his side. "The future looks good, babe."

Brodie sighed and placed a hand on her stomach. "It really does."

And this time, for the first time in far too long, she was convinced of it.

* * * * *

Pick up the first book in the
FROM MAVERICKS TO MARRIED *series,*

TRAPPED WITH THE MAVERICK MILLIONAIRE

and these other sexy, emotional reads from
Joss Wood

TAKING THE BOSS TO BED
YOUR BED OR MINE?
THE HONEYMOON ARRANGEMENT
MORE THAN A FLING?

"So do we enter into a contract, my king?"

"You still think you have a choice, don't you?" he said, cocking one brow at her. "Are you always this optimistic?"

"I always have a choice," she replied.

She sensed rather than heard him as he came and stood behind her. Was it her imagination or did she feel the heat of his breath against her naked skin? A shimmer of awareness crept over her body.

"Then you are indeed fortunate," he said close to the shell of her ear.

His voice held a whisper of a thousand words left unsaid. Ottavia closed her eyes and concentrated on remaining still. On simply absorbing his nearness and trying to separate out the individual reactions her body clamored with.

"A king does not have many choices," he said, exposing a surprising insight into his mind.

* * *

Contract Wedding, Expectant Bride
is part of the **Courtesan Brides duet:**
Her pleasure is at his command!

CONTRACT WEDDING, EXPECTANT BRIDE

BY
YVONNE LINDSAY

First Published in Great Britain 2016
By Mills & Boon, an imprint of HarperCollins*Publishers*
1 London Bridge Street, London, SE1 9GF

© 2016 Dolce Vita Trust

ISBN: 978-0-263-91873-1

51-0816

Our policy is to use papers that are natural, renewable and recyclable products and made from wood grown in sustainable forests. The logging and manufacturing processes conform to the legal environmental regulations of the country of origin.

Printed and bound in Spain
by CPI, Barcelona

A typical Piscean, *USA TODAY* bestselling author
Yvonne Lindsay has always preferred her imagination
to the real world. Married to her blind-date hero and
with two adult children, she spends her days crafting the
stories of her heart and in her spare time she can be
found with her nose in a book reliving the power of love,
or knitting socks and daydreaming. Contact her via her
website, www.yvonnelindsay.com.

To my Writers in the Wild buddies,
and to Soraya Lane, with grateful thanks
for all your support and, at times
(yes, I'm looking at you, Soraya!),
goading and bullying, all of which get
me to "The End" with a happy sigh.

One

He was here.

She knew it by the way the energy inside the tranquil island castle shifted and switched up a gear. Ottavia smoothed her gown over her curves for the fifteenth time that afternoon and told herself again that she wasn't nervous. Not really. In her profession as a courtesan, she was accustomed to dealing with powerful men. Dealing with a king couldn't truly be that different…could it?

The exquisite French Charles X ormolu clock on the mantelpiece continued to tick quietly, marking the seconds as they dragged by. But thankfully, she didn't have to wait long. The ornate wooden doors leading into the high-ceilinged room swung open. Her stomach clenched in anticipation. A frisson of nerves shimmered down her spine. But, instead of the royal visage she'd expected to see, one of the king's advisers—Sonja Novak—stood there instead.

The woman was, as usual, impeccably dressed in a Chanel suit and her iron gray hair was swept into an impossibly neat chignon. Her classically beautiful features were schooled into a bland expression that, as far as Ottavia could tell, was about as close as the senior member of King Rocco's staff ever came to a smile.

"His Majesty will see you now."

"I will see him here," Ottavia replied as firmly as she could.

She should have known it would earn a particularly scathing look.

"Ms. Romolo, the King of Erminia summons you into *his* presence. *Not* the other way around."

"Then His Majesty will be disappointed, won't he?"

Dredging every last vestige of courage, Ottavia turned her back on the woman and directed her gaze out the window. She counted slowly, regulating her breathing and slowing her rapid heartbeat with each number—one, two, three… She was at seven before she heard the huff of outrage, closely followed by the brisk click of heels on the parquet floor. Then, blessed silence.

Ottavia allowed a small, triumphant smile to curve her lips. He would come to her. She knew it as certainly as she knew the carefully composed face that greeted her in the mirror each morning. She'd seen the expression in his eyes at their first meeting and recognized it immediately. Granted, she hadn't been looking her best. Who did when they'd been held captive for several days without so much as a change of clothing? But, even dressed in the same traveling outfit she'd worn for almost a week, her face without makeup, she'd seen that look. He wanted her. And she had years of experience manipulating that want in the men she encountered.

Besides, he owed her. Not only had his sister kidnapped Ottavia, Princess Mila had had the cheek to steal Ottavia's clothing and borrow her identity, pretending to actually *be* Ottavia as she took on the engagement with the courtesan's current client. In the meantime, Ottavia had been held captive for several days until she'd been able to escape. Granted, she'd been held captive in a luxury suite in one of Erminia's best hotels, but that didn't excuse anyone from their part in what had happened. Then, when she'd rushed to the king to warn him what his sister was up to—in an attempt to muzzle her and keep her from speaking to the press, he'd *also* ordered her to be held captive. Not that it had helped. The story had gotten out anyway, even though Ottavia had done nothing to spread it. But the scandal had blown over eventually. And her clothing had finally been returned to her two weeks ago. So now only one obstacle remained—dealing with the king.

Ottavia rolled her shoulders in an attempt to loosen some of the tension that gripped her body but it was no use. It rankled to be at someone else's mercy. She was a woman used to being in charge of her own life, one who made her own decisions. Helplessness did not sit comfortably on her softly rounded shoulders at all.

Ottavia was so engrossed in her thoughts, so bent on stoking the fire of indignation that burned angrily inside her, that she almost didn't hear the doors behind her open again. She turned, instantly aware of the palpable presence of power that now filled the room. Despite her hard-won composure, she couldn't help the visceral reaction that rocketed through her body at the sight of her king standing before her.

Taller than her by at least six inches, she was forced to look up into his unusual sherry-colored eyes. His body was still, but those eyes—they were alive. Not for the first time, she was reminded of a sleek jungle cat stalking its prey, waiting to pounce. The idea should have terrified her—instead, it sent an unexpected shimmer of heat rippling through her body.

But he wasn't immune either, she noted with satisfaction. She saw the way his gaze was pulled to the column of her throat above the high neckline of her dress, then lower to where her beaded nipples made their presence known through the fine silk of her gown. Her lips curved in the slightest of smiles and she drew in a deep breath, one that made her breasts swell and rise gently.

Ottavia swooped into a graceful curtsy and bowed her head—she was more aware than most that you caught far more flies with honey—and remained beneath her king, waiting for his command to rise.

"Your deference is too little too late, Ms. Romolo," he intoned, and his deep voice hummed through her body. "Rise."

As she did so she looked up at him from beneath her long lashes, noted the firm set to his lips, the tiny lines that bracketed his mouth and the tension in his jaw. He was displeased. It was a risk she'd thought worth taking. Ottavia rose to her full height, squared her shoulders and held her tongue.

The woman stood in front of the window and he had to admire her strategy. Silhouetted by the filtered late afternoon light—every lush curve and gentle swell of her body limned with a golden glow—she was an eye-catching sight. But she had tangled with the wrong person if she thought positioning would give her any psychological leverage. He hadn't ruled Erminia for the past fifteen years without learning an almost inhuman level of self-control. His duty to his country demanded no less.

Rocco stepped closer to her until there was a scant foot between them. To the courtesan's credit, she didn't so much as flicker an eyelash even though he knew damn well he was an intimidating presence—he'd spent his life working on making people believe it. And, no matter how angered or amused he might have been by her audacity in attempting to invoice him for her time spent as his captive, he certainly had no plans to show it.

He thrust a sheet of paper toward her.

"What is the meaning of this?" he growled.

"I believe even you must be familiar with the term invoice?" she said.

Her voice was low-pitched and perfectly modulated, rolling over him like a velvet touch, heightening his awareness of her on a physical level that took him by surprise. Was this how she plied her trade? he wondered. Seducing a man with her voice before using the other wiles she doubtlessly wielded with expertise? His lips curled in defiance. She would soon learn he was no simple mark easily swayed by a beautiful woman.

"You are my prisoner." He rent the invoice in two and let the pieces drop to the floor at his feet. "You have no right to *bill* me for your time here. As my captive, you have no rights at all."

She raised one perfectly plucked arch of an eyebrow in response.

"I beg to differ, Your Majesty. The way I see it, your family owes me a great deal."

He had to admire her gall. There weren't many who dared challenge him.

"We do? Enlighten me," he demanded.

"There is the matter of my not being able to fulfill my contract because first your sister, and subsequently you, have kept me against my will. Like most of your subjects, I have financial responsibilities. I find myself unable to meet them when I am not paid for my time."

Rocco let his gaze drift over the woman. It certainly was no hardship to do so. Her neck was long and graceful, tapering gently to sweetly feminine shoulders exposed by the cutaway sleeve line of the deceptively simple gown she wore. The ruby hue of the fitted dress complemented the softly tanned glow of her skin. Was she this color all over, he wondered, or did her skin pale in those enticing hidden areas?

She did not seem to appreciate having her words ignored. "You have treated me unfairly and you continue to do so," she said. "Release me."

There was passion beneath her words and a spark of fire in her eyes making them burn bright. He found he quite enjoyed needling a reaction out of her.

"Release you?" He watched her carefully as he paused and considered her request, and saw the flash of hope that sprang into her gaze. "I think not. I'm not finished with you yet."

"Not finished?" she all but spluttered. "You never even started."

"Ah yes, and there is the problem, Ms. Romolo. You have invoiced me for your time here. I imagine that has been calculated at your usual rate?"

She inclined her head with consummate grace and elegance.

"Then you would agree, wouldn't you," he continued smoothly, "that I am owed a discount for *lack* of services rendered."

He stepped back and watched the unguarded flurry of emotion that caught her enchanting features. She composed herself quickly and drew in a shaky breath.

"Does Your Majesty wish to avail himself of my services?" she asked.

If she had asked him five minutes ago, he would have given her an emphatic no in response. This woman had caused him no end of trouble. If she had not accepted a contract to serve as temporary courtesan to King Thierry of Sylvain, both Rocco's kingdom and Thierry's could have been spared an endless amount of trouble.

Thierry had been, for several years prior, betrothed to

Rocco's sister, Mila, in an arranged marriage. Discovering her betrothed's plans to avail himself of a courtesan had driven Mila to the reckless step of trading places with Ms. Romolo, so she could ensure her husband-to-be would take no lover other than herself. Her plan had worked—at first. But when he'd discovered her deception, Thierry had been incensed—and when the news had, somehow, leaked to the press, making them into a media spectacle, Thierry had called off the engagement entirely. It had taken a disastrous event to reunite Mila and Thierry…but finally they had reconciled and wed, and were now blissfully happy. It had all worked out in the end.

That didn't make him any happier with Ottavia Romolo, though, without whom all of this could have been avoided. So no, he had never truly considered availing himself of any of her considerable charms. He'd been too busy wishing that she'd take herself to another country entirely and let them deal with the chaos she brought in her wake.

But now, with his senses tingling and his mind intrigued, he found himself considering a far more affirmative response.

"I haven't decided yet," he answered.

"Nor have I offered," she countered.

Oh, she was good—valiantly holding on to her pride and dignity even while the threads of control of this situation escaped those long slender fingers. Heat burned low in his groin at the challenge she presented—and the temptation. His response to her both irritated and stimulated him. Much like the woman herself.

"You are mistaken if you think you have a choice, Ms. Romolo."

She lifted her chin defiantly. "I always have a choice. I am glad you have destroyed my initial invoice," she continued with a smile.

Rocco was surprised. Of all the things she could have said, he hadn't expected that.

"I'm pleased to hear it," he said. "But why?"

"Because, Sire, my price has gone up."

Two

Silence stretched between them. Ottavia boldly stared straight into her king's eyes, hoping that her anxiety would not show—that he wouldn't sense that beneath the fall of the luxurious fabric of her gown her legs had turned to jelly.

His brows pulled together in a straight line, his sherry-colored eyes glowed like polished amber. Not the bright color so often associated with the fossilized gemstone, but a deeper hue. One that spoke of layers of complexity that she instinctively knew were synonymous with the powerful man standing before her. And he *was* powerful. As easily as he'd ordered her held here in this beautiful small palace—isolated on a stunning island in the middle of a lake—he could have her cast into a windowless prison for the rest of her days.

She realized she was holding her breath when tiny dark spots began to dance before her eyes. She allowed herself a shallow breath, then another but, as if she was mesmerized by his stare, her gaze remained locked with his. The spots receded slowly but her clearing vision did nothing to calm the wild hammering of her heart or the fear that plucked at her soul. Had she gone too far? She'd always fought to maintain the upper hand in all her relationships and every one had served its purpose in helping her achieve her final goal. While charm was usually her weapon of choice she had a feeling that King Rocco would run roughshod over such a tactic. He was not a man known for playing nice.

It galled her that he had so much power over her. Hadn't she sworn that no man would ever make her decisions for her or control her life again? And yet, in this, she was effectively helpless. *Work to your strengths*, she reminded herself, and allowed her stance to soften. She allowed her lips to part, just slightly, and moistened them with the tip of her tongue. He'd noticed, she realized with a flare of satisfaction. His eyes had flickered to her mouth; his nostrils had flared ever so slightly on an indrawn breath.

She'd cast her bait, but had she hooked him?

"You had better be worth it," he growled.

His voice was deep and slightly rough. As if he was fighting his own internal battle. Ottavia allowed herself a smile, lowering her eyelids slightly.

"So do we enter into a contract, my king?"

She lingered over the last two words, using every skill at her disposal to make them sound like a caress—a promise. She knew she'd failed when he threw his head back on a hearty laugh that transformed the seriousness of his face into something far more appealing. Something that pulled at her with a magnetic strength she'd never experienced before. Eventually he calmed.

"You still think you can control how this turns out, don't you?" he said, cocking one brow at her. "Are you always this optimistic?"

"I am *always* in control of myself and my choices," she replied.

Even as she said the words she knew they hadn't always been true. Certainly not when she'd been fourteen and her mother's latest lover had begun to show an unhealthy interest in her burgeoning figure. Even less when her mother had discovered that interest and Ottavia had overheard her mother haggling with her lover over how much he would be prepared to pay to have her.

She fought back a shudder. Those days were behind her. She'd taken control of her life that day. Made a conscious choice and resolved to never be at anyone's mercy ever again.

Ottavia forced her thoughts into the present and recalculated her strategy. Perhaps King Rocco needed a little more enticement. She took a step back before turning and slowly walking closer to the windows that overlooked the gardens and the lake. If she hadn't been so acutely attuned to the man she'd turned her back on she wouldn't have heard the sharp intake of breath as he noticed the long sweep of her back, laid bare by the open cut of her gown. It was as if she could feel the heat of his gaze follow the line of her spine until it dipped into the deep V of fabric that covered the swell of her buttocks.

She sensed rather than heard him approach behind her. Was it her imagination or did she feel the heat of his breath against her naked skin?

"Then you are indeed fortunate," he said close to the shell of her ear.

His voice held a whisper of a thousand words left unsaid. Ottavia closed her eyes and concentrated on remaining still. On simply absorbing his nearness without analyzing the individual reactions clamoring throughout her body.

"Fortunate?" she asked, her voice surprisingly husky.

"A king does not have many choices," he said to her surprise.

"I would have thought that you had it all, Sire."

The air behind her shifted—the heat that had smoldered against her suddenly gone—and she knew he'd stepped away. Because with those few words he'd said too much, perhaps? Slowly, she turned around. He stood on the other side of the room, his hands loosely clasped behind him as he stared at a portrait of his late father on the wall.

"I have a proposal for you, Ms. Romolo," he said without looking at her. "It would behoove you to agree."

"Just like that? Without knowing the terms?" she asked. "Without negotiating? I think not."

"Do you negotiate everything?"

"I am a businesswoman."

He spun to face her. "Is that what you call your...trade? A business?"

"What else would you call it?" she challenged.

The corner of his mouth quirked upward. Ottavia fought the urge to bristle. He was testing her. That much was obvious. If she was to get what she believed she was owed by him, she needed to hold on to every last thread of self-control that she possessed.

"Come here, Ms. Romolo." He crooked a finger at her.

She would do as he'd commanded, but only because she wanted to, she told herself as she glided forward with all the elegance and poise she'd learned in the past fifteen years.

"Sire?" She bowed her head as she drew before him.

A low chuckle escaped him and she felt her own lips twitch in response.

"Subservience does not suit you." With the point of one finger he tipped her chin up so she looked him in the eye again.

Her lips parted on a gasp as she recognized the sudden flare of hunger in his gaze. A gasp that he captured as he lowered his mouth to hers and took her lips in a kiss that stole every rational thought from her mind. Caught by surprise, she gave herself over to his touch, to his taste.

To the plundering of his tongue as it delved into the moist recesses of her mouth. A sound, a growl from deep in his throat as she touched her tongue to his, sent unaccustomed desire unfurling through her body. Her blood heated, her insides clenched on a spear of need that completely took her breath away.

And then, just like that, it was over. She teetered slightly on her heels before gathering sufficient wits to steady herself. A swell of anger bubbled at the back of her mind. Outrage swiftly quelled the yearning that hummed through her veins as she realized he thought he had the right to simply take from her without permission. Disappointment followed hard on the heels of her anger. Here was another man who saw her as something to be used at his whim, and discarded.

She had to regain the upper hand once more, so she swallowed her indignation and smiled at the man standing opposite her.

"Sampling the merchandise?" she asked tartly.

Against his better judgment Rocco calmly smiled in response. No easy feat when a large percentage of his blood supply had headed due south in response to that kiss. He was beginning to see why the courtesan was in such high demand. She was addictive. Only one kiss and he wanted more. It had been so long since he'd indulged in something purely for his own pleasure. The needs of his country came first, always. But the country could hardly be harmed by him taking this opportunity to sate his desires. Maybe some good, satisfying, no-strings sex would help him clear his mind.

"You say your fee has gone up," he started. "Perhaps you undervalued yourself to begin with?"

He could see his remark had startled her when she made no comment. Rocco pressed his advantage.

"I will avail myself of your services and in return I will

pay that paltry invoice you sent to me—and then some."
He hesitated and tilted his head. Looking at her as if assessing a fine piece of art before continuing. "Name your price," he snapped.

Ottavia named a sum that was astronomical compared to the invoice she'd sent him.

"You place a very high value upon your services, Ms. Romolo," he said, torn between exasperation and amusement. She thought she could scare him away with her demands? Well, she had another think coming.

"To the contrary. I place a very high value on myself," she replied.

But he'd caught the faint tremor in her voice. She knew she'd overstepped the mark with her ridiculous price.

"I will pay it."

He watched as she reached one hand to play with a tendril of hair. Round and round her index finger she wound it, the almost childish gesture looking unaccountably adorable on such a sophisticated, elegant woman. She stopped suddenly, letting her hand drop to her side as if she'd just realized what she was doing and straightened her shoulders—a businesswoman once more. And yet, for that brief moment she'd been playing unconsciously with her hair, he had the feeling he'd seen the real woman behind the courtesan's facade. Like everything else about her, it captivated him.

"Do we have an agreement?" he pressed.

"We have not discussed a term of length."

"For that sum I should expect our contract to be open-ended," he said, his exasperation clear.

"I'm sure you realize that would be counterproductive to my business," she replied with a slight smile.

Once again, unexpected mirth mixed with irritation. She looked like a sensual goddess—one who promised no end of hedonistic delight—and yet she had a mind and acuity as sharp as any negotiator he'd ever come across. She was, in fact, unlike any woman he'd ever met before. It was as if she didn't really care whether he wanted her or not—as if she'd be equally happy to walk away—and he found the concept captivating. Challenging.

There was nothing he liked better than a challenge.

"A month, then," he said.

Even as he said it, he realized that spending a month with her, as appealing as it sounded, might be unrealistic. He couldn't stay hidden in this retreat for too long—he had duties elsewhere requiring his attention…such as his hunt for a bride. But with his sister's recent, and very happy, marriage to his country's primary antagonist, surely he could allow himself a bit of a break, if he stayed in contact with the capitol city through email and phone.

"A month," she repeated. "Very well. If you would allow me access to my cell phone and my computer, I will draw up the appropriate documentation and provide your people with my account details—" she cast a disdainful glance at the torn-up invoice on the floor "—again."

"You do that," he replied. "And I will see you, in my private chambers for a late dinner, at nine thirty this evening."

He headed for the doors and paused before opening them. "And, Ms. Romolo?"

"Sire?"

"Don't bother dressing for the occasion."

Satisfied he'd managed to gain the upper hand and have the last word with the exasperating creature, Rocco let himself out the receiving room and headed down the corridor. Sonja Novak materialized by his side as he strode toward his office.

"Shall I arrange for the woman's departure?" she asked as she fell in step with him.

"No."

"No?"

"She will be staying here. With me. For the next month, or until I tire of her—whichever comes first."

Somehow, he thought it would not be the latter.

"B-but—" Sonja started to protest.

Rocco halted in his tracks and fought back the urge to sigh heavily. Was there a woman left in Erminia who listened to him anymore? It seemed that everywhere he went women contradicted him. First his sister, then the courtesan and now his most trusted adviser. "I am still King of Erminia, am I not?"

"Of course you are."

"Then I believe I am entitled to decide who will stay here as my guest. I know you have been at my right hand since my father died, and at his before that. But do not forget your position."

She inclined her head. "I apologize, of course."

"And yet I sense that you continue to think I'm making a mistake."

"Keeping a courtesan is probably not the best decision when you're trying to woo a bride."

This time Rocco did sigh. "I am aware of that." And once his bride was chosen, he fully intended to dedicate himself solely to her, with no outside affairs. But with that future awaiting him—a lifetime of uncertain happiness with a bride bound to him by duty rather than love—could he really be blamed for taking this chance to indulge himself while he was still free? "Now, is there anything else that urgently requires my attention?"

"Nothing that can't wait until tomorrow," Sonja admitted.

"By the way. Ms. Romolo is no longer my prisoner. Please ensure her electronic devices are returned to her and that she has access to the internet."

"Is that wise?"

He gave her a look that spoke volumes as to his frustration that she should continue to question his authority. In response, Sonja bowed her iron gray head again and murmured her acquiescence.

"Thank you," Rocco replied through clenched teeth and continued to his suite of rooms on an upper floor in the castle.

He strode through to his bedroom. The formal suit he'd worn for traveling home from Sylvain today felt like little more than a straitjacket. He ripped his red silk tie, woven with the Erminian heraldic coat of arms of a rearing white stallion, from beneath the starched white collar of his shirt and let it drop onto a chaise by the window. No doubt his valet—who he'd left in the palace in the capitol, preferring to see to his own needs here at the lake—would have had a fit if he could see the lack of respect Rocco had for his clothing. But, as each layer fell from his body, he felt a little more free, a little less like a king.

Naked, he grabbed a pair of running shorts and a T-shirt from his bureau and yanked them on together with socks and a well-worn pair of running shoes. If he didn't get some exercise soon, he'd go mad, or at the very least, lose the temper he was famous for keeping such a tight rein on.

Today had been frustrating but he'd handled it—as he always did. But the next few hours were for him and him alone—well, as alone as one could be with a security detail shadowing your every step. Rocco pounded down the back stairs of the castle, ignoring the team as they trailed him, and set out on the castle driveway pumping his legs as hard as he could.

Ten kilometers later he was wrung through with sweat but only just beginning to breathe hard. He cut back his pace to a more leisurely jog and let his thoughts fill with the joy that had been incandescent on his sister's face at her marriage to King Thierry just a day ago.

Rocco could still barely believe it had all gone ahead,

especially after Thierry had called off the wedding. Without the unification of their countries, war along their border had seemed imminent—fed, no doubt, by the subversive movement that wanted Rocco removed from his throne and their pretender crowned in his place.

It was only months before that Rocco had even learned of this supposed pretender, who claimed to be an illegitimate child of Rocco's father, the late king. The pretender's name and identity was a closely held secret, but his movement had gained an uncomfortable number of followers, agitating for change even if it came at the cost of open war.

Erminia had tread a very fine line to avoid hostilities—especially with Andrej Novak, his head of the military and Sonja's son, strongly advising they substantially increase the presence of their armed forces on the border. The situation had worsened after the scandal had broken of Mila's actions, kidnapping Ms. Romolo and taking her place. And when Mila had flown to Sylvain personally to meet with Thierry and plead for another chance, only to be turned away, Rocco had expected armed conflict to begin within a matter of days. But then Mila was kidnapped while returning home to Erminia, and everything changed.

Rocco's heart lurched in a way that had nothing to do with his exercise at the memory of those terrifying days when his sister had been missing, held captive in an abandoned fortress by men demanding that Rocco renounce the crown in exchange for Mila's safe return. Thankfully, King Thierry and a covert operations unit managed to safely extract her, though with their focus on the princess, the kidnappers were able to flee, unidentified.

The thought of those kidnappers—and their political allies—along with the pressure they kept raising on Rocco to try to convince him to turn over his throne sent a bolt of anger through him that caused him to pick up his pace a little again. Behind him, he heard a collective groan from his security detail and he couldn't help but smile. His team was fit and strong and fast, but he made it his goal to be equally so, and if he pushed them just a little bit more each time, then so much the better.

He needed every boost to his spirits he could get now that the political maneuvering of his enemies had created a new problem for him. Marry, or lose the throne. The very idea was so outmoded it was ridiculous. Of course he'd always planned to marry. He'd even, many years ago, been on the verge of becoming officially engaged. But Elsa, the young woman he'd met while in university, had shied away from his proposal. A commoner, she'd loathed constantly being under the microscope of media and the world at large when she accompanied him to state functions.

At least that had been her excuse. With the twenty-twenty vision of hindsight, Rocco could see that perhaps she simply hadn't loved him enough. In which case, it was just as well their relationship had gone no further.

Which brought him squarely back to the predicament he now faced. In a year he would be thirty-five. According to an ancient law, only recently uncovered and exposed by his opponents in the country's parliament, to remain monarch he needed to be married and have produced legally recognized offspring by the time of his thirty-fifth birthday. If not, he could be ejected from the throne—leaving it open for the pretender.

Rocco had been forced to do a great deal of soul-searching in the months since the threat had become so very real. Would he give up the throne voluntarily? Perhaps, if the new ruler could be relied upon to be a fair and reasonable man—one devoted to his people and the betterment of his country. But with Mila's kidnapping, it had become abundantly clear that the pretender to Rocco's birthright was not a benevolent man.

No, he had a duty to his people to defend his position

and to see to it that the threat against them all was neutral-
ized with the least harm done. And if that meant marrying a woman he barely knew, would possibly never love?
Well, so be it. To that end, he'd asked his advisers to prepare a dossier of women suitable to assume the role of his
consort. European princesses and women of noble birth
abounded, as did the rumors of their behavior and sexual
proclivity that, unfortunately, had narrowed his options.
His principles meant too much to him for him to be able
to accept a bride with a lower standard of behavior. Now,
there was apparently a short list of only three.

Rocco slowed to a walk on the graveled driveway of
the castle, his hands on his hips, his breathing heavy. His
thoughts now looked ahead. Tonight, he'd planned to study
the profiles he'd been provided with in more detail—to
see if there was some spark of interest from him for the
women presented.

A flash of color and a shadow of movement at an upstairs palace window caught his eye, reminding him that
tonight he had an even more challenging event ahead of
him. Despite the kilometers he'd run, despite the fact that
weariness should be pulling at him, he felt invigorated, re-
freshed. Eager to get to the task at hand—if Ottavia Romolo
could be called anything so mundane or simple as a task.

He'd take tonight. He'd luxuriate in her body, her allure.
Tomorrow would be soon enough to face reality.

Three

Ottavia tore her eyes from the vision of male strength and vigor below on the driveway. Her fingers trembled as she let go of the curtain and shifted out of view. How was it possible that he was even more attractive to her dressed in activewear than he had been in his formal suit only an hour or so ago? He'd never looked less regal, or more physically appealing. There was an unconscious raw energy swirling around him, quite different from the power he'd so deliberately wielded when they'd talked earlier.

Ha, talked. That almost made their conversation sound as if it had been civilized when the undercurrents that had run between them had been almost primal. Ottavia sighed, unused to this sensation that twisted and turned inside her. Unused to feeling this level of attraction for any man. In fact, she'd always actively avoided it.

Yes, she knew most people assumed that because she was a courtesan she was a body for hire and that sexual desire was part of the package, but that was never true.

Not on her side. And while she knew many of her clients were physically drawn to her, sex was *never* a part of her role in her clients' lives—she had very strict rules about that. She never took a client on without making those rules supremely clear. Whenever a man disagreed, she simply walked away. Sexual intimacy with her was not something she would permit anyone to buy ever again.

Those who agreed to her terms had the benefit of her company and experience for the duration of their contract—knowing that her role was to make their lives as comfortable and happy as she possibly could.

She'd be the ear that listened to them at the end of an arduous day. The consoling voice when they suffered. The consummate hostess with the utmost discretion. But not their lover, no matter what enticements they offered to change her mind.

Honestly, she'd never even been tempted. She made an unofficial policy of avoiding contracts with men who she found attractive. It was simpler—cleaner—not to blur that line, to be able to focus on her companion's needs without getting distracted by her own desires. Even when she'd negotiated her contract with King Thierry of Sylvain, who was unquestionably a handsome and appealing man, she had remained unaroused. She couldn't feel any true attraction to him when the correspondence they had shared prior to their planned rendezvous had made it clear that his priority was to learn from her how to build a strong marriage with his future bride.

That helped her to keep her physical desires away from her work. Always, there was the reminder that she was an impermanent feature in her clients' lives. She was there to amuse, or entertain, or soothe, or instruct…for a while. But never was she there to stay. So she was always tuned in to her clients, aware of whatever steps she needed to take to

be the perfect companion, to match their needs and requirements. But never, never had she felt like this.

It was as though her skin was too tight for her body, as
if every nerve buzzed with anticipation.

A sharp rap sounded at the door to her room, making
her jump. She fought to compose herself and felt a flash of
annoyance as Sonja Novak let herself into the room without
waiting for Ottavia's call of consent. Sonja was followed
by a footman, dressed in the staff's standard uniform of a
navy suit and tie. Ottavia's eyes swiftly took in the items
the footman carried.

Her laptop and her phone. Relief flooded her. Finally,
she would have access to the outside world.

"Your devices," Sonja said coldly as she gestured to the
footman to put them on the delicate writing desk. "King
Rocco has directed that you be given access to the castle
Wi-Fi and the printer on this floor. The password to the
internet has already been installed on your computer and
you have been added to the castle network. You will find
a printer in the business suite at the end of the corridor."

"Thank you," Ottavia said graciously, even though she'd
have much rather commented along the lines of "about
time," instead.

"I sincerely hope His Majesty's trust in you is not misplaced," Sonja remarked as the footman exited the room.

"Misplaced? Why should it be?"

"You're hardly what I would call trustworthy, are you?
Always selling yourself to the highest bidder? How can we
be certain you won't abuse your...position here?"

A flame of anger licked to life inside Ottavia, but she
kept it banked down. It wouldn't do to show this woman
how much her remark insulted. But then, maybe that had
been Sonja Novak's intention all along?

"We?" Ottavia repeated. Did others join the woman in
her concerns? Sonja declined to answer. Ottavia met the

other woman's hard glare with a gentle smile. "If I could have some privacy now, please…?"

For the second time that day, Ottavia turned her back on her. She knew it was a dangerous move. In battle, one never turned one's back to the enemy, but she had no wish to engage in any further conversation. The entire time Ottavia had been held here, the king's adviser had made it more than clear that she felt Ottavia should never have sullied the glorified air of the castle.

"Ms. Romolo, you may think that now you are no longer a prisoner here you have the upper hand over me, but you are mistaken. Don't push me, or you will regret it. And do not, under any circumstances, betray King Rocco's trust in you."

"You can let yourself out," Ottavia responded.

It was only once the door snicked quietly closed behind her that Ottavia allowed herself to relax. She huffed out a breath of air and eagerly reached for her phone. There'd be messages she needed to attend to. She thumbed the power button but was frustrated by a completely blank screen. Flat, obviously. Never mind, in her suitcase were her chargers.

She retrieved the chargers and plugged in both her phone and her laptop. Her heart sank when she saw how many voice mails were stored on her phone. She listened to each one, her heart aching. Her cheeks were wet with tears by the last. Ottavia sighed and put her phone down on the table with a shaking hand. Should she call Adriana now?

Her heart said yes even while her mind cautioned no. Evenings were always the worst; a call now could leave Adriana's caregiver with a wealth of stress for the night. No, the morning would be better.

Steeling herself against her heart's plea, Ottavia placed her phone on her bedside table and turned instead to her laptop. As she opened it, Ottavia wondered if her computer had been examined during the time they'd held it. No doubt. Her phone, too. Well, she had nothing to hide, she thought with a surge of frustration for the position she had been forced into.

Forced into for now, yes, but not to stay. The reminder echoed through her mind. Yes, King Rocco had held her captive here for some time, but she was here now of her own volition. Her own choice. And she had a job to do.

A small smile curved her lips as she booted up the laptop and opened a contract template, swiftly keying in the necessary data, highlighting some sections, deleting others. When she was satisfied she had everything within the contract that she needed, she sent the document to print. Her lips formed a grim line when she saw the palace printer installed in her printer queue, its presence confirming that, yes, they had been into her computer. At least she kept no sensitive data on here relating to her previous client base.

Ottavia let herself out of her room to search for the business suite. Even as she opened the door and stepped out into the richly carpeted corridor she felt as if she was doing something wrong—as if she was still a prisoner, but now on the verge of escape. There was an irony in that, she realized. A deep irony. The contract would ensure there was no escape for her for a while at least, and strangely, that didn't bother her as much as it should.

Perhaps it had something to do with the contents of the contract—if Rocco didn't agree then she would be on her way north, home. Her contract, her choices, her safeguards. Would her sovereign agree? A piece of her hoped not, knowing that she'd have a much easier time regaining her hard-won composure if she was away from the king and the unwelcome and irresistible attraction she felt for him. But then another part of her—a part she didn't want to examine too closely—wanted to see just how far that attraction would take them both…

The business suite Sonja Novak had mentioned was exactly where she'd said it would be. Even though it had clearly irritated the woman to give Ottavia the freedom of the castle, or at least this floor, she'd done what she'd been instructed to do. Freedom was a relative thing, however. Ottavia didn't doubt for a second that she was under surveillance. The discreetly placed cameras around the room and at intervals on the corridor made that abundantly clear.

The knowledge made her take her time—sauntering across the room and inspecting the equipment there, before going to the printer and lifting the sheets neatly stacked on the tray. She idly flicked through the printed pages, even though she knew exactly what they said, then separated them into the two sets and secured each with clips from a dish on a nearby desk. Then, with a nod of satisfaction she returned to her room.

It was still early evening and she had plenty of time before her nine thirty rendezvous with the king. What should she wear? What was it he'd said? *Don't bother dressing for the occasion?* She smiled. She knew what he expected and she would deliver exactly what he'd asked for. After all, wasn't that what she did best? Deliver on men's expectations?

A slightly bitter taste filled her mouth. Their expectations, yes, but always, *always*, on her terms, and her king may find that getting what he asked for was another thing entirely.

Rocco turned as he heard the knock on his door. Nine thirty. Perfect timing.

"Enter!"

The door swung wide to admit his courtesan. A thrill of anticipation raced through him, making him feel even more invigorated than he had after his run. The sensation rapidly turned to shock as he let his eyes drift over the woman standing in the doorway. Gone was the sensuous drift of silk over skin. Gone was the perfectly arranged swath of hair falling over her shoulders. Gone was the makeup that had accentuated her fascinating gray-green eyes and the slope of her sculpted cheekbones. Even her lips were denuded of any tint of color.

As the surprise faded, humor pulled from deep inside him. So, she'd taken his words literally and hadn't dressed for the occasion. The last thing he'd expected was for her to turn up in, however, was yoga pants and a faded and stretched T-shirt with a scruffy pair of sneakers on her feet. Even her hair was pulled back in a ponytail so tight that it gave him a headache just looking at it.

And yet, she'd failed to obscure her natural beauty and grace or the way the well-washed fabric of the oversize shirt slipped off one shoulder, exposing the sinfully delectable curve of her shoulder and a hint of the shadow of her collarbone. What was it about her that could cause something as simple as the play of light and shadow on her skin to send his senses into overdrive? He relished finding out.

"Your Majesty," she greeted him, dipping into a curtsy.

It should look incongruous, dressed as she was, and yet her movements were so smooth, so flowing, she still managed to convey a lithe, sensual elegance.

"Ms. Romolo, please let's not carry on this farce that you respect me or my position."

She rose and lifted her chin as she met his gaze. "But I do respect your position, Sire."

The deliberate omission, making it clear that she did not respect *him*, stood like an elephant in the room between them. Rocco was not one to ignore a gauntlet laid down so blatantly.

"But not me."

"In my experience, respect is earned. On a personal level, outside of your role as my king, I hardly know you and, to be totally honest, my experiences with you to date have not exactly been positive."

So, she wasn't afraid to beard the lion in his own den. He had to admire her courage—there weren't many so bold in his household—even if the words themselves did little to calm the alternate exasperation and desire that battled for dominance every time he was within a meter of her.

"I always do what is best for my people. That is not always what is best for the individual."

Her eyelids swept down, obscuring her gaze. "And for yourself, Sire? Do you ever do what is best for you?"

He didn't answer as a timer went off in another room.

"That will be our dinner."

She looked around, apparently expecting members of his staff to come out and serve them. When no one appeared, her gaze shifted back to him—a question clear in her eyes.

"Here in my personal chambers, I prefer to live privately—without staff. I've prepared the meal for us," he said by way of explanation.

"You cook?"

Astonishment colored her words and her expression—a fact in which Rocco took deep satisfaction. For once, it seemed, he had the capacity to shock and surprise her.

"Cooking relaxes me. I don't do it often."

"And you are in need of relaxation?"

"It's been a hectic few weeks."

Ottavia nodded. "It must have been terrifying for you when your sister was kidnapped."

"You heard about that?"

"I had no access to television or newspapers, but while your staff is very loyal to you, they also love your sister. I gleaned what I could from their conversation."

Heads should roll over her revelation. The privacy and security of the royal family was paramount, now more than ever. But could he really blame the people who had practically raised him and Mila for being visibly concerned for his sister's safety?

"Clearly my staff needs a reminder about the nondisclosure statements in their contracts," he said, but his tone was more rueful than grim.

"Speaking of contracts—?"

"Not now." He gestured to the binder she clutched in one hand. "Leave that here. First, food."

Without waiting to see if she followed, he walked across the sitting room and through an arch to the compact but well-appointed kitchen, where he'd prepared the seafood marinara that was his favorite dish. He carried the platter out through the open French doors onto a balcony that overlooked the topiary garden and goldfish ponds. In daylight, even from here on the third floor, he could occasionally catch glimpses of bright orange as the fish swam among the water lily pads. But right now, with a purple tinged sunset kissing the horizon, the grounds below were a tapestry of shadows.

He set the dish on the ready-laid table and reached for the sparkling wine settled in the sweating ice bucket. The cork shot off with a satisfying pop and he was reminded of the court sommelier's instruction that sparkling wine should always be opened making no more than the sound of a woman's sigh. And, yes, just like that, desire flooded him again—making him all too aware of the figure that hovered in the doorway. Did she sigh? he wondered. Or did she moan while in the throes of passion? He'd find out soon enough.

"Take a seat," he instructed, gesturing to the chair opposite.

"Thank you," she replied.

She remained silent while he dished up for them both. A fact that both surprised and pleased him. He appreciated that she, too, enjoyed peaceful quiet and didn't feel the need to fill the silence with endless, needless chatter.

"Bon appétit," he said and lifted a monogrammed crystal flute in her direction. "To our first dinner together."

She mirrored his action and their glasses clinked, the sound a promise on the air between them.

"And to you being a halfway decent cook," she murmured before taking a sip of the wine.

She closed her eyes as she swallowed, her lips parting on a soft sigh of appreciation. Rocco fought back a groan. He had his answer, and it was even more enticing than he'd expected. Her eyes flicked open, catching him staring at her, and he saw her pupils dilate in response to his scrutiny.

Ever so deliberately, she took another sip of the sparkling wine before putting her glass down on the table.

"Very nice," she commented and picked up her napkin to dab softly at her lips.

"From my own vineyard," he said, attempting a nonchalance he was far from feeling. Ottavia Romolo made him feel young, made him want to be foolish, made him want to feel things he had kept a tight rein on for far, far too long.

"Did you blend the wine yourself?"

"No, my vintner had full control over this vintage," he acceded.

"But you have blended your own, haven't you?"

Had she researched him? Even if she had, he couldn't imagine where she could have found that detail. "Yes," he replied. "I have. It's not commonly known."

"But it's something you enjoy, isn't it?" she pressed.

"How could you tell?"

She smiled and he felt it as though it was a caress.

"The tone of your voice, the look in your eyes. You have a lot of tells, Sire."

He didn't like the thought of that. "Then I must school

myself to be more careful. It wouldn't do for everyone to know what I'm thinking or how I feel."

"I can imagine that would get you into all sorts of trouble."

She'd said it with a straight face, but he sensed the humor behind her words. She was gently poking fun at him, encouraging him to poke fun at himself, making him relax almost in spite of himself. He could begin to see why she was successful at her role. She listened, she observed—and just now, when she spoke, it was both worth listening to and, strangely, exactly what he wanted to hear at the same time.

Suddenly he regretted serving their meal before studying their contract. He wanted it signed and the deal done so he could explore his attraction to her further. Attraction? Hell, he just wanted to explore *her*. Wanted to lose himself in the tresses of her hair, to sink into the welcoming curves of her body, to slake the hunger that had nothing to do with food and everything to do with physical appetite.

He watched as she sampled the meal he'd created, politely feigning obliviousness to the turmoil in his mind. Everything about this woman made him want to forget his responsibilities and to live in the moment. To breathe her in until nothing else existed but the two of them. The ember of an idea that had begun to simmer at the back of his mind earlier today began to flare a little brighter.

To be a balanced monarch one needed to lead a balanced life—and there was one part of his life that had been lacking ever since his relationship with Elsa had ended. He'd had liaisons, sure, but no relationships. No one to off-load to at the end of a difficult day. No one to share hopes and dreams for the future. He wouldn't have that with Ottavia Romolo under her contract as his courtesan, he reminded himself. But perhaps that contract could be amended— expanded into something that would give him everything he craved.

"This is quite delicious," she said, interrupting his thoughts.

He watched as she speared a succulent prawn on the end of her fork and swirled up a ribbon of pasta. He swallowed against the sudden obstruction in his throat.

"You sound surprised," he commented.

"A king who cooks, and cooks well? Who wouldn't be?"

Cooking was an outlet for him. One he indulged in less often than he'd like to. A bit like everything else that gave him pleasure.

"Do you cook?" he countered.

"A little."

"Perhaps you will prepare a meal for me one day."

"Perhaps," she acknowledged with a slight bow.

His eyes were instantly drawn to the slender line of her neck, exposed by the high ponytail that currently strangled her hair. His fingertips itched to stroke her, just there beneath her earlobe. To discover if she'd shiver with delight beneath his touch. He clamped his hand tight around his fork and reached with the other for another sip of his wine. It made no difference. The urge to touch her remained. Thank goodness he was a strong man, one who'd learned to keep a tight rein on impulse and to project control at all times. But once, just once, it would be nice to be able to simply let go.

Maybe, once they'd signed her damned contract, he would.

Four

Ottavia watched him carefully as they completed their meal. While, outwardly at least, her king appeared no different than any other man, she had the sense that beneath the facade lay another man entirely. Oh, sure, she knew that, logically, beneath the elegant trappings of his finely woven cotton shirt and expertly cut trousers was a magnificent male body. You couldn't watch the way he moved and not realize that. Besides, she'd seen him come back from his run today. Seen the way his sweat-soaked T-shirt had clung to every muscle across his shoulders and his chest, seen the powerful bulge of strength in his arms. And then there'd been the fit of his shorts as he bent and stretched out those well-developed thighs.

At that memory, she reached for her wine and took a long sip, letting the cool bubbling liquid soothe the heat and dryness that had suddenly become apparent in her throat. Yes, she told herself. He was a truly prime specimen of all that was beautiful in the male form. But that power could be as dangerous as it was attractive. She wondered again how he'd react to the terms of her contract. Part of her still wished he would refuse to sign and send her on her way. But another part, the woman she kept a tight rein on—the one who found King Rocco of Erminia a tantalizing prospect dangled before her—hoped he'd accept them, or even try to renegotiate.

A thread of longing tightened deep inside her, making her inner muscles clench in anticipation. She fought the sensation, telling herself it was as ridiculous as it was unexpected. She, the queen of personal constraint, did not allow herself to be so affected by any man, least of all this one.

Perhaps it was some variant on Stockholm syndrome, she told herself, allowing a ripple of amusement to tease her mouth into a smile. There, that was better. If she could laugh at herself, laugh at her situation, then she could most definitely overcome any physical yearning that threatened to derail what was, essentially, her job. Which brought her back to the contract.

It made her nervous to spend time with him without the parameters between them fully outlined. She placed her fork down on her plate and shifted anxiously in her seat. King Rocco was quick to notice.

"Something wrong?"

"Nothing," she answered a little too swiftly. "At least not with your cooking."

"Then, what is it?"

"I…" She hesitated and weighed her words carefully before deciding she had nothing to lose except the money he'd pay her. "I find myself in a situation that I am unaccustomed to, to be honest."

"What, dinner with me?"

"Essentially, yes."

"I'm just a man."

She laughed softly. "You really think so?"

"Okay, so I'm a king. But that's *what* I am, not *who* I am."

His words gave her pause. Made her wonder, how many people actually knew him for who he was? Did anyone?

"Who you are is not important to me," she said, but even as the words fell from her lips, she knew them for a lie. She needed to regain the upper hand in this situation, and quickly. "Except, perhaps, as a client. Which brings me to our contract. Now you've eaten perhaps we can get down to business."

"If you insist," he answered before wiping his mouth with his napkin and dropping the cloth on the table.

His chair scraped along the tiled floor as he stood up and came around to her side of the table to help her from her chair.

"Thank you," she acknowledged.

"Take a seat inside, I'll bring the wine."

"Wine?"

"Negotiations are so much better when done over a drink, don't you think?"

He smiled at her, but she saw that his humor didn't quite reach his eyes.

"Who said I'll be negotiating?" she replied, then turned her back on him, walked into the sitting room and picked up her file.

The king was not far behind her.

"I always negotiate," he said, handing her refilled flute to her.

"Everything?"

"Ah, yes. You have me there. When necessary, I decree."

Nerves tightened around her stomach, making her regret that last forkful of marinara. Her hand trembled as she opened the binder and took out one copy of her contract.

"This is my contract. The extent of my services is listed in the schedule at the rear."

"Your…services. Right."

He leaned forward and tugged the papers from her fingers. At the brush of his hand against hers, another tremor rippled through her, making the papers shake. His eyes sharpened and he gave her a long considering look before casually crossing one leg over the other and taking a sip of champagne.

"You seem nervous," he stated. "Why is that?"

She needed to own this tension between them. Accept it and move on. "It's not every day I do business with a member of the royal family let alone the head of our nation."

"But you have had many influential clients, have you not?"

"I do not discuss my past clientele. Ever."

"Commendable. I'm sure your discretion is vital to your success and your continued employment."

"That's one way of putting it," she said, uncomfortable with the track he was taking despite her efforts to keep things on a straight course. "Please, if you would read the contract and sign it, then we can commence."

"By all means, I look forward to that."

She forced herself to relax against the plush sofa and slowly sipped her wine as he flicked through the introductory paragraphs of her contract. His dark brows pulled together as he concentrated on each clause. She couldn't stand this any longer. She got up and moved about the room, looking around with interest at the personal items he had on display. Ones that reflected the man himself. There was a strong suggestion of how important his family was to him, with small collections of photos, both formal and informal, clustered here and there. She also noticed a large bookcase was packed with books. Thrillers mostly, with the occasional book on politics or social policy.

She was surprised he'd chosen for them to meet in a room that was so very much his. Ottavia respected the need for him to be guarded about the personal side of his life. In the current age of media frenzy every time a public persona put a foot wrong, there was immediate backlash. And this king in particular could not afford any backlash right now. She wasn't an idiot. She knew that there were fractures in his parliament, and she'd heard the rumors that there were some who did not appreciate him as their ruler. If anyone had to keep himself squeaky-clean it was the man on the other side of the room. Which begged the question—why had he demanded she remain here at the castle?

She started in surprise as she heard the slap of papers on the coffee table in front of him. King Rocco stood abruptly and sought her out.

"*This* is your contract for me?" he said, his voice the epitome of steely calm.

But Ottavia sensed the carefully controlled fury beneath his words. Her contract was not what he'd anticipated. Not at all. She made no apology for that. Instead, she merely inclined her head in affirmation.

"There is something missing," her king pressed.

"Missing? No, I don't think so. That's my standard contract."

He scoffed, clearly doubting her word—but at least he didn't flat out call her a liar. "What about intimacy?" His question was blunt and to the point.

"Intimacy, Sire? I expect our conversations and our time together will be extremely intimate, and you can rest assured that no matter what is said, it will remain between us and us alone."

"Don't play games with me," he growled, coming toward her with a light in his eyes that sent a shiver down her spine.

She fought the urge to flee, instead standing her ground and responding as levelly as she could.

"I do not play games, although we could make games a part of clause 6.2 if you so desire. I'm told I make a fair tennis partner and I've been known to win a hand or two at poker."

His hands curled around her upper arms. His grip was not so hard as to mark her skin, but there was no way she could easily pull free. Beneath his palms she felt fire in his touch. Fire that matched the heat in his gaze and the heightened color on his cheeks.

"I'm not talking about tennis and you know that."

"Then I am at a loss," she said, still striving to keep her voice level even as her heart raced in her chest and her breath began to come in short, sharp inhalations.

King Rocco bent his face to hers. "Sex, my courtesan. Hot, lusty, physical, sweaty, satisfying sex."

Ottavia locked her knees so that her legs might stop their trembling. Yet despite all her efforts, her body caught aflame with each syllable he enunciated so carefully and slowly.

"Um, that's not in the contract. In fact, I'm sure you read the part where it explicitly mentions that sex is *not* permitted."

"A mistake, surely? Especially when it's quite clear that your body was made for pleasure. Yours…and mine."

His face was closer to hers now—his breath a puff of air against her as he bent and inhaled her scent at the curve of her neck. She couldn't hold back the tremor that rocked her. Braced herself for the touch of his mouth against her skin. Every nerve in her body stretched taut and she felt the rush of desire and need pool low and deep in her belly.

Ottavia drew in a short breath, attempting to pull her thoughts together, to formulate an appropriate response— to hold firm to her rules. She lived by rules. They kept her safe. Kept her sane. But safety and sanity were hard to cling to when breathing in the scent of the cologne he wore—an enticing blend of sandalwood, lemon and some spice she couldn't quite discern. The very thought should be abhorrent to her and yet her body told her otherwise.

"Ottavia?" he prompted, his lips now so close to her skin she could feel the heat of them.

She held herself rigid, determined not to lose ground by pulling away but equally determined not to give in to the lure of what his touch promised. If she gave in, she'd be giving too much of herself. With him nothing would be simple and she very much doubted that she'd be able to walk away at the end of their specified time together with any part of her psyche intact. And she had to be strong. She had to be whole. For Adriana if not for herself.

"There will be no sex," she managed to say through trembling lips. "There never is."

She rocked as he abruptly let her go.

"What do you mean there never is? You are a courtesan, are you not? What is that if not a mistress and all that entails?"

Frustration and puzzlement warred for supremacy on his handsome visage—frustration winning in the end. Ottavia took a sip of her drink and dragged her ragged thoughts back together.

"As set out in the schedule attached to the contract, you can see that I have a double degree in economics and fine arts. I am well versed in protocol and etiquette and I am a consummate hostess. I can discuss financial matters, whether they relate to worldwide economies or personal households. I can advise on art, literature and discuss the merits of the great poets and philosophers to whatever lengths you desire. I can host your guests and ensure that they want for nothing during their time under your roof. I can provide company, solace, humor and I give a mean foot rub."

She paused and drew another breath. "I do not have sex."

"That's preposterous! Everyone has sex."

"Perhaps that is true of most people. Not me."

King Rocco shoved a hand through his hair. "You mean you've never had sex with any of your clients, ever?"

"That's exactly what I mean."

"And these other men…? Your previous clients? They *agreed* to that?"

"They did."

"And they were happy with that?" A frown now creased his brow.

"They were."

"I find that very hard to believe."

Ottavia tried not to smile at the exasperation in his tone but it was clear that she'd failed when the frown on his forehead deepened.

"What's so funny? Are you playing a trick on me?" he demanded imperiously.

"No tricks, Your Majesty. Yes, there have been men who have requested sex as part of their contract. My answer has always been no. They've either accepted my terms, or called off the arrangement. There is no other option, Sire."

He huffed a sigh of irritation. "Enough with the formal address. When we're alone, you're to call me Rocco, do you understand?"

"But, Sire, you seem unwilling to sign the contract. Without that, why would we ever be alone?"

"We will be alone because I accept your terms, Ms. Romolo."

"Y-you do?"

"I do. On one condition."

A sinking feeling assailed her. "And that is?"

"That the contract be open to, shall we say, amendment, provided that both parties are willing."

It sounded reasonable enough the way he said it. But reasonable did not explain the grim determination in the lines of his face or the single-minded purpose that reflected in his eyes. If anything had become clear to her in her dealings with her king it was that the man was nothing if not determined.

Still, his phrasing gave her the ultimate control in the end, didn't it? *Both* parties had to be willing to make amendments, and there was no way she was going to change her stance on this. She would not be coerced. She would not be forced ever again.

"Fine," she said firmly and reached to collect the contract from where he'd dropped it, together with her binder that still sat on the coffee table. "I'll make the appropriate changes and resubmit the documents to you in the morning."

"No." King Rocco moved to stand beside her and took the papers from her hand. "You have a pen?"

She nodded, then removed the pen she kept inside her folder and silently handed it to him.

He took it from her and gave her another of those unwavering looks. "We will make the addendum here and now."

Rocco sat back down and riffled through the contract pages, pausing only to initial each page before reaching the final one and adding a new clause in bold, heavy strokes of the pen and initialing that, also. Then, he struck his signature at the bottom of the page before reaching for the second copy of the contract and repeating the exercise.

The whole time he did so, Ottavia remained rooted to the spot. She wondered if he hadn't somehow laid a clever trap for her in gaining her acceptance of the new clause. But, as she'd rationalized to herself, all she had to do was refuse to alter her terms.

How tricky could that be?

Once he'd finished, he stood up and offered her his seat. The contracts spread out on the table before her, but all she could focus on was how the residual heat of his body on the leather chair permeated the fabric of her yoga pants and seared the back of her thighs.

"Ms. Romolo? Is there a problem?" he prompted from behind the chair.

She steeled herself to pick up the pen. It didn't seem to matter what he touched, he left a lingering impression of himself behind. She quickly flicked through the contract pages, adding her initials to his and quickly scanning the newly added clause. It seemed innocuous enough and made it quite clear that the agreement of both parties, in writing, would be sought and recorded before any amendments were made with such amendments to include sexual intimacy and other duties that may arise from time to time.

Ottavia looked up. "Other duties? Would you like to specify what you mean by that?"

He shrugged. "Who knows what may come up? We can agree upon them when they arise."

Despite having the distinct impression he was holding something back, Ottavia bent her head and reread his addition. Basically, it still came down to the both of them being in agreement. All she had to do was disagree and she had her out. Pushing aside the anxious niggle that hovered in the back of her mind, she initialed next to his handwriting and added her signature.

There. It was done.

Five

"We can commence in the morning," she said, rising from the seat and reaching out for a handshake to signal the end of the proceedings.

But Rocco did not take her hand. Instead, very slowly, his face creased into a wide smile. A tug of attraction pulled mercilessly at her. What on earth had she let herself in for? It didn't take long to find out.

"We commence here and now." He took her things from her and let them fall onto the seat she'd just vacated. "And I prefer to seal this deal with a kiss, don't you?"

"B-but, the contract states—!"

"Nothing whatsoever about kissing," he finished for her.

She wanted to protest, but the words simply would not come out. Instead she felt her body soften to allow him to pull her into his arms, and when he lowered his lips to hers, so sweetly and so gently, she knew she'd been well and truly caught in a trap so cleverly engineered that she would have her wits and her will sorely tested in the coming weeks.

His lips were firm and hot against hers and, try as she might, she couldn't ignore the teasing tug of his teeth against her full lower lip or the gentle swipe of the tip of his tongue as she fought, and failed, to deny him access. Her hands swept up to his chest, but instead of forming some leverage between them, her fingers curled in the cotton of his shirt as she sought to become even closer with him.

This was madness, she told herself. She didn't engage with her clients on this level—had promised herself she never would. Was she really no different than what her mother had said—worth no more than she'd been the day her mother had bartered her daughter's body for her lover's money and interest?

The thought speared through her with unerring and excoriating accuracy. She was not that person! Ottavia wrenched her mouth from Rocco's, her heart pounding in her chest and her breathing difficult.

"Please," she begged, "let me go."

In an instant she was free.

"Ottavia?"

"J-just give me a minute to catch my breath."

"What is it? Are you all right? You were there with me, every step of the way until—"

"Until I wasn't," she finished for him, dragged every last speck of self-control back together. "I told you that sex was not part of the contract."

"It was just a kiss," he said softly.

Just a kiss? The man was crazy if he thought he, or what he did, was *just* anything.

"It was outside the parameters of what we agreed," she insisted.

"How so? Is a kiss not companionable?"

"Don't bandy semantics with me, Your Majesty," she snapped back, irritated beyond belief—at herself even more so than at him.

Damn him, but she'd actually begun to enjoy their embrace. She'd almost forgotten her promise to herself. He was dangerous, far more dangerous than she'd ever imagined.

"Rocco, remember?"

"Fine, Rocco, then. Either way, it doesn't matter what I call you. Now, since our business tonight is complete, I will thank you for dinner and take my leave."

"Oh, you're not going anywhere."

Ottavia fought not to curl her hands into fists of annoyance. "Why not?"

"While we dined, your possessions were moved to my rooms here. For the duration of our contract, you will be staying with me."

The coil tightened into a knot. "You moved my things? Before we'd even signed the contract? Before you even knew what was in it? That was insufferably presumptuous of you."

"Perhaps, but I'm known as a man who goes for what he wants, especially when it serves the greater good."

"And how does having me here do that?" she demanded, before realizing the folly of giving him the opportunity to explain. He was far too persuasive. She cut him off before he could speak. "No, I won't have it. This is not part of—"

"Your contract? I think you'll find that it is. As part of your compensation I am to provide you with accommodations, am I not?"

"I had perfectly acceptable accommodations, before."

"It's up to me to decide what is suitable for you, and those rooms are not of the standard I would want for my courtesan."

A note of possession hummed through his last two words. Ottavia fought against the sense of helplessness they provoked and couldn't bring herself to respond.

"How much more salubrious could you get than my own private rooms?" Rocco said, spreading his arms wide.

Every muscle in her body, at once taut and tensed for argument, sagged in defeat. He had her beaten; there were no two ways about it. Fine then, she'd stay in his chambers if that was what he so desired. It was more intimate than she preferred to be with her clients, but that's where the intimacy would begin and end. She inclined her head.

"Fine, please tell me where my room is. I'm tired and I would like to go to bed now."

"Ottavia, don't sound so downtrodden. It's not all bad."

"Whatever Your Majesty says," she said with a small burst of exasperation.

If she'd thought to annoy him by using his title, she was sadly mistaken.

"Come with me," Rocco said and gestured for her to follow.

Ottavia was surprised at how many rooms his chambers comprised. Not only was there the kitchen and living room she'd already been in, but there was a formal dining room along with a well-equipped gym. He led her down a gallery lined with windows overlooking the gardens. About halfway along, Rocco stopped and threw open a door to a massive bedroom. She couldn't help the appreciative sigh that rose from within her.

"I'm to sleep here? It's beautiful," she said, stepping inside.

Rocco nodded and followed her in. "You'll find your things in that dressing room," he said, gesturing to one set of double paneled doors. "Your toiletries should already be in the bathroom through there."

"Your staff is very efficient," Ottavia said after opening the first doors he'd indicated and sighting her garments hanging neatly. A quick check of the ornate bureau showed her lingerie and sleepwear equally tidily arrayed.

"I work with only the best," he replied.

His voice was nonchalant but he pinned her with his

leonine stare, and despite herself, Ottavia felt a magnetic pull toward him.

"Well, I'm very glad you won't be required to compromise your standards with me," she said as lightly as she could.

He chuckled, the sound reaching across the distance between them to wrap itself around her nerve endings and squeeze a little.

"I'll leave you to it. I have some business to attend to."

Before she could say another word, he was gone—the heavy bedroom door closing silently behind him. Weariness tinged with a hefty dose of relief flooded through her body. Being with Rocco was exhausting. She would need her wits about her tomorrow, and the next day and the next.

Rocco strode to his study, his entire body humming with barely suppressed energy. This business with the courtesan was proving to be far more invigorating than he'd ever imagined. He pushed open the door to his private office and stopped in his tracks. Sonja Novak stood by the window. She turned to face him, disapproval painted in stark lines across her face.

"I didn't expect to see you here. It's late," he said, entering the room and taking his seat at the desk.

"You have installed that woman in your apartment?"

"I have," he answered, challenging her to make a protest.

She didn't roll her eyes but he knew she disapproved. In fact, it radiated off her in waves. Instead of speaking, however, she pointed to a dossier on his desk.

"The newly updated list of prospective brides for you."

"Updated? Again?"

"One of the final three has just expressed her desire to become a Carmelite nun, which leaves you with two princesses to choose from," she said, her voice clipped and to the point.

Rocco fought the urge to roll his eyes in frustration. "I'll deal with them in the morning."

"In a hurry to return to your courtesan?" The question was delivered in a matter-of-fact tone, but behind it he sensed her deep disapproval.

He refused to have this conversation with her again. "When it comes to my private hours, it is no one's business but my own as to whom I spend my time with," Rocco growled and snatched up the revised dossier.

Two prospective princess brides left—the only two who met his requirements. What did that say about the state of the world? he wondered. He lifted their photos out of the folder and, in turn, studied the women carefully. You couldn't tell much from a photograph, he decided. Certainly not anything important like, did they make your blood heat and your heart race when you drew near to them? Did their scent intoxicate you, canceling out all other distractions and allowing you to focus solely on them?

He shook his head.

"Are you rejecting the princesses based on their photos? Without even having met them?" Sonja's voice reminded him he was not alone.

"No, just thinking of all my options." He put the photos back in the dossier and snapped it closed. "By all means, arrange for each of the women to visit me here. I can't be expected to decide on my life's partner based on photos and what amounts to nothing more than a résumé."

"Does it really matter which one you choose? Surely you can father a child with either one of these women."

There was something in Sonja's tone of voice that disturbed him.

"You think that is all this is about? Creating an heir?"

"Well, isn't it? Forgive me for being the practical one here but you *are* running out of time. May I have your permission to be completely frank?"

She'd never asked his permission before and was well-known in court circles for her acerbic and freely given opinions. If she felt the need to get permission first, then she must be about to say something that she thought would infuriate him. He was almost tempted to send her away and avoid the issue. But avoidance wasn't his way. As king, it was his duty to listen to those who would ask him the hard questions, push him to make the hard decisions, and those were both things Sonja had always unhesitatingly done. The fact that more often than not she was proved right was one of the reasons she remained on his staff. He nodded.

"Your reluctance to marry—are you considering giving up?"

"What?"

"This quest to find a bride in case you are unable to overturn the succession law in parliament…don't you think it might be too little too late? Perhaps…" She took in a deep breath and looked him square in the eye before continuing, "Perhaps you should consider the needs of your people above your desire to remain king. Wouldn't they benefit from a stable government rather than one torn over the issue of its rightful monarch?"

"Are you suggesting I abdicate in favor of some unknown person who *pretends* to his right to my throne?"

He held on to his temper, but only by the merest thread.

"Call me the devil's advocate if you will, but perhaps the throne truly *is* his right by birth?"

"We don't know that because he hasn't seen fit to grace us with his details," Rocco snapped in return.

No, the man remained behind a cowardly cloud of intrigue and subterfuge. What Rocco wouldn't give to get his hands on information that would lead to uncloaking his secretive, and dangerous, rival.

"But what if it is his right?" she pressed.

"You sound as if you support this unknown usurper."

"My loyalty to your father and his children has never been in question," she said proudly. "I'm merely presenting another viewpoint. After all, you may still be successful in parliament, yes? If the law overturns, marriage may not be necessary, after all. Now, if there's nothing else, I think I will retire for the night."

He gave her a curt nod and watched in silence as she let herself out of his office. Once she was gone he replayed her words. Why did he feel that he didn't have her wholehearted support? It worried him. He needed to know that those in his inner circle were loyal to him, especially someone like Sonja who wielded considerable power of her own and represented him on several government committees.

Her question about him giving up had made bile rise in his throat. As far as he was concerned, it wasn't an option. It was not the way he'd been brought up and it certainly wasn't what felt instinctively right for himself or for his people. He was their rightful leader and until a better man came forward publicly to challenge him, he would continue to believe he was the best man to ensure an even hand at the helm. If someone had managed to undermine Sonja Novak's fealty to her king he would find out who that person was. And then, perhaps he'd also find out exactly who was behind this crazy scheme that was starting to tear apart his nation at the seams.

Rocco turned to his computer and logged in to his email, finding several matters that required his immediate attention. Sighing, he switched his attention to the things he could do something about and worked in silence for the next couple of hours.

It was well past midnight when he was done, and his eyes burned in their sockets as he made his way back to his rooms. It had been a demanding day on several levels and he was physically and mentally exhausted. Sometimes, like now, he wondered how different his life would have been had he been born into a regular family—an ordinary existence. It must be the tiredness talking, he reminded himself as he let himself into his suite and stood silent for a moment, drinking in the peace of this, his sanctuary in his busy world.

In the distance he heard the sonorous chime of one of the grandfather clocks that graced the hallways. In only four hours he'd need to be up and running, back on full duty again. But between then and now he would sleep, recharge and ready himself to start all over again. Because that's what he did. Started over, and over. Always with his eye on the main prize.

He dropped the dossier he'd brought back upstairs with him onto the coffee table. Then he walked down the corridor to his bedroom and let himself in. He didn't bother with any lights, but went through to the bathroom and had a quick shower before preparing for bed.

He'd never felt the mantle of his leadership sit so heavily on his shoulders as he had these past months. It wouldn't be so bad to be married, he reasoned—to be able to share his responsibilities with someone who'd ease his load, emotionally if not physically. Would one of the two women remaining on his short list be that person?

He certainly hoped so. Both were well educated and trained in royal protocol. But did they have a fire in their bellies? Did they feel passion? Would they fight with him, indulge in battles of wits the way the courtesan had today?

At the thought of Ottavia, all the weights and cares that pressed down on him seemed to lift, at least for a moment. The woman captivated him. Not only was she quite possibly the most enticing and beautiful creature he'd ever had the pleasure of laying eyes on, she was almost hypnotic with her special brand of charm and intelligence.

His body stirred with interest, but he knew that interest must remain unfulfilled for now thanks to the terms of that ridiculous contract she'd drawn up. He smiled at his reflection in the mirror. He was nothing if not resourceful and he wasn't blind. He'd both seen and felt her reaction. She wasn't as immune to him as she wanted to be.

One thing Ottavia Romolo would learn was that he was intensely goal oriented—that he kept going until he reached his target. Some said he was stubborn, and perhaps that was true. Personally, he preferred to call it focused, and he always followed through until completion. It was what he did best and that wouldn't change now.

Rocco let his towel drop to the bathroom floor and flipped the light switch before going back through to his room. He lifted the sheets and slid into the silky soft Egyptian cotton. Ottavia lay, fast asleep, on the other side of the bed, her breathing smooth and even. Believing herself safe, secure—and she was.

Just, perhaps, not from herself.

Six

Ottavia woke the next morning with the distinct impression she was not alone. But a quick glance around the sumptuously decorated bedroom showed she was the only person there. Still, the sensation lingered and she sat up in the massive bed, where she'd enjoyed what probably had been her best night's sleep in a long time, and looked around.

She gasped as she realized the other side of the bed showed indications of recent occupancy. The sheets were mussed and there was no mistaking the indentation on the feather pillow. Nor was there any mistaking the old-fashioned pale pink rose on that pillow, complete with a handwritten note.

The rose released a faint burst of fragrance as she picked it up and held it to her nose. It was just a hint of scent, so subtle as to almost not be there at all. And the color—the outer petals were a creamy white, the center a soft blush pink—was incredibly beautiful. She turned the bud in her hand and noticed one outer petal was imperfect—damaged by insects or weather. She touched a fingertip to the crumpled edge. The imperfection didn't detract from the beauty of the flower; instead it added character. She liked the fact that it had been left that way.

Like herself, she thought, the bloom had weathered adversity before it reached this stage of beauty. But it was ridiculous to think he had chosen the flower for that reason. It wasn't as if he knew what made her damaged.

She looked at the indentation in the pillow again and swept up the note he'd obviously left for her.

You are as beautiful when you sleep as you are awake.

That was it. No signature, but she recognized the bold slash of pen across the paper from his handwriting on their contract. Had Rocco slept here beside her all night? Had he watched her? All evidence showed he had. And she hadn't so much as noticed? She shook her head. Indulging in the sleeping tablet she'd taken before slipping in between the sheets last night had been a rare moment of weakness and something she couldn't afford to repeat. She had to keep her wits about her—even, it seemed, at rest.

With the drug in her system, she'd been completely helpless last night. What if he'd decided to renege on the terms of the contract and forced her to be intimate with him? She cast the idea from her mind almost as quickly as it had come. She didn't know him well, but she sensed that he'd never force any woman. He was nothing like— No, she wouldn't even begin to entertain the thought.

She dropped the rose on the bedside table and slid from the mattress, her bare feet making no sound on the thick carpet as she made her way quickly to the paneled doors she hadn't bothered to explore the previous night.

She pushed them open, her eyes narrowing as she took in the rows of suits and shirts, arranged by color and season by the look of them. Every built-in drawer was filled with menswear, and the obviously handmade shoes on the rails beneath the suits looked like a perfect fit for the man who was king of Erminia.

Ottavia backed out of the dressing room. So, he'd installed her in his room—and in his bed, no less. Annoyance swelled. He no doubt thought he'd won some invisible battle by manipulating her this way. She'd clearly underestimated him and that was a mistake she would not make again.

It was abundantly clear he wanted her, sexually. She'd felt the impressive evidence of his desire when they'd kissed yesterday. An unaccustomed flush of heat swept over her. His desire had definitely never been in question, but hers? That had surprised her. She'd never had any problem separating mind and body from her role. In fact, she had carefully maneuvered her client list to ensure the situation had never arisen.

She was good at her job. While she could not claim she deeply enjoyed her work, she found it acceptable. It ensured she was well paid, which was the most important thing. Not for her own sake, but for Adriana's, to keep her sister at the facility where she was well-cared-for and protected in a country that had an appalling record of care for those born with special needs. It had been difficult at first, making ends meet while supporting the cost of her care, but Ottavia had persevered.

She thought again of the contract she'd signed with Rocco last night. The sum she'd chosen had been designed to put him off, not to tantalize him. But he'd agreed and that money, managed carefully with what she had managed to invest over the years, could probably keep her for the rest of her life without the need to be a courtesan ever again.

Of course, her existence would be simpler, less exotic and elaborate—and hadn't she craved that all along? The chance to lead an uncomplicated life? She'd be thirty at her next birthday. Not old by any standards, but her beauty would begin to lack the freshness of youth and with it her shelf life would very likely diminish, she thought cynically. Not unlike the bloom Rocco had left for her this morning, one day she too would be spent.

The melodic chime of a clock in the sitting room reminded her that the day was passing. After a quick shower she dressed in one of the sleeveless tunics she favored, teamed with a pair of wide-legged trousers in a deep amethyst tone. She brushed her hair out, leaving it to fall loose around her shoulders, and applied her makeup with an artistic hand—lining her eyes more heavily than usual and applying a solid slash of magenta pink to her lips. Finally satisfied with the bold impression she'd make, she left the suite of rooms and went in search of her king.

She didn't have to go far, as he was coming down the hallway toward her. Garbed in another perfectly pressed suit, paired with a dove-gray shirt this time and with a tie emblazoned with the ubiquitous Erminian crest, he could pass as any businessman in the capitol city. But no one could deny the power that exuded from him, or the air of entitlement that sat so snugly across his shoulders. He was a king born and bred. In one hand he carried an embossed folder.

"Have you eaten?" he demanded as he drew nearer.

"Good morning to you, too, Sire."

"Rocco. And you didn't answer my question."

"No, I haven't eaten yet," she commented.

"Good, come with me."

Was this how he expected to treat her? To toss commands at her as if she was little better than a performing seal?

"Please," she said calmly, not moving an inch even though he'd already begun to walk away.

Rocco stopped and turned toward her. "I beg your pardon?"

"If you'd like me to come with you, then you need to ask nicely. I'm sure that one of your many tutors or nursery maids taught you the benefit of good manners, even if your parents did not."

He arched one dark brow in response. "You think to malign my family?"

"Is your rudeness something of your own making? If so, then I do apologize for any aspersions I have cast upon your family. I'm sure their example was exemplary and that you simply chose not to follow it."

He stepped toward her, coming to a halt with less than a hand's breadth between them. "I am your king. It is your duty to obey me."

"Are we going to squabble about everything, Sire?" She sighed softly.

"Only if you don't do as you're told," he said with a stern frown.

But Ottavia didn't mistake the look of humor that flickered and warmed in his eyes.

"And the name is Rocco," he added. "If you can remember that, then perhaps I can remember to say please once in a while."

Her lips twitched in response. "Then, Rocco, I would be delighted to accompany you."

"Thank you."

They traversed the hallway and he guided her into a small private elevator that took them to the ground floor. He led her onto a wide terrace.

"They'll bring your breakfast soon," he said as he held a chair out for her. "While we wait, I would like to seek your opinion."

"My opinion?"

"You sound surprised."

"Well, I am. You have not struck me as the kind of man for whom other people's opinions matter."

"Ahh," he answered. "And I suppose my...*rudeness*... led you to that conclusion?"

"Not to mention your holding me captive on the suspicion that I *might* cause trouble for you."

"I was protecting my sister," he replied in a voice that made it quite clear that protecting what was his was paramount in his life.

Ottavia felt a shaft of envy. It was not an emotion she admitted to often but, for once in her life, she craved to be the protected rather than the protector. She wondered if Rocco's sister had ever realized what a champion she had in her brother.

Rocco continued. "I would be an autocratic leader if I didn't seek the opinion of others from time to time."

"True." She paused as a neatly dressed maid brought a heavy tray laden with cups and saucers, a milk jug and sugar bowl, and an ornately engraved silver coffeepot. "Thank you, Marie," she said to the young woman. "I'll pour for us."

The girl bobbed a curtsy. "I'll be back in a moment with your croissants, ma'am."

"You know her name?" Rocco asked, a curious expression on his face.

"Of course."

"Hmm, you surprise me."

"How so?" she asked, pouring two cups of black coffee and her hand hovering over the sugar bowl. "Sugar?"

"No, no milk, either. Thank you," he finished with exaggerated politeness before picking up the cup and taking a sip.

"There, that didn't hurt, did it?" Ottavia smiled in response as she added both milk and sugar to her coffee and stirred.

"I would have thought you wouldn't bother with small details like learning the names of my staff—especially since you were a prisoner here."

"I had to find something to do to pass the time. Besides, I have always thought that good service should not go unappreciated," Ottavia said lightly. "Now, what was it you wanted to ask me?"

Rocco tapped his forefinger on the folder he set down on the table. "I'm curious to see what you think of these women. It appears that in the whole of Europe there are only two princesses left who are considered suitable for the position of my wife."

"Do you know either of them personally?" Ottavia asked, all the while pushing aside the unexpected streak of jealousy that pulsed through her at the thought of Rocco marrying some unknown woman.

Stop being ridiculous, she told herself sternly. *You have no attachment to him whatsoever, nor do you want one.*

Rocco eyed her over his coffee cup for a moment before replying. "I don't. But that isn't important. I need to find a wife. Preferably one who is fertile."

"And must she have strong teeth and a biddable nature as well, Sire?"

Rocco uttered a sound that resembled nothing less than a growl. "It is not a joking matter. I need a wife and an heir."

He hesitated a moment, as if weighing up how much he should tell her.

"Rocco, you don't have to tell me any more if you don't want to but please rest assured of my complete and utter confidentiality."

He nodded sharply in acknowledgment. "There is a law, which has been mostly ignored for the past several hundred years, that relates to succession of the crown."

Ottavia waited patiently as Rocco explained the law. Then she sat back in her chair and studied him carefully.

"Goodness," she commented.

"Is that all you can say?"

Questions whirled around in her mind but she held on to them as Marie returned with a basket of warm croissants and small pots of jam and marmalade.

"There you are, ma'am. Enjoy your breakfast." She curtsied to Rocco and then to Ottavia again before withdrawing.

"Eat before those get cold," Rocco urged her. "Please."

Ottavia laughed out loud. "There, see? You *can* do it."

He smiled at her and she basked in the open and natural friendliness of it.

She selected a croissant and tore it open, inhaling the scent of the freshly baked pastry before spreading it with a sliver of butter and a little marmalade.

"Did you want some?" she offered, suddenly uncomfortable under his steady gaze.

"No, I've eaten already."

"You don't know what you're missing out on," she replied pushing aside her self-consciousness and biting into the moist and flaky roll with delight.

Rocco watched her and fought with the urge to lick his lips. Did she attack everything with the same level of passion and gusto? He certainly hoped so. For a woman who could appear to be the epitome of grace and beauty, she also exuded an earthy sensuality at times.

He tapped the folder again. "Back to the matter of my bride. These are the short list. I'd appreciate your thoughts."

"Mine?" Her finely plucked brows flew up in arches of surprise. "Whatever for?"

"You extolled your virtues last night, as a woman of education and discernment. I'd like you to put those skills to use."

She replaced her croissant on the china plate before her and took another sip of coffee. "Surely you have a multitude of advisers who would be far better suited to aiding you in your choice of a bride than myself," she said as she carefully set her cup back down.

"Undoubtedly, but here you are, and I find myself interested in your opinion."

He picked up the folder and handed it to her.

"You want me to read these now?"

"No time like the present."

The crisp click of sharp heels sounded across the paving of the terrace. Rocco looked up in irritation. He'd specifically asked not to be disturbed, but of course Sonja wouldn't think that edict applied to her.

"Sonja," he acknowledged, looking up at her.

The older woman's gaze swept the table, her eyes alighting on the folder that Ottavia now held. "You have an urgent call. It's the prime minister."

Rocco rose. "I'll be right back, Ms. Romolo. Wait for me here. Please."

Ottavia smiled in response. "Since you asked so nicely, of course I'll wait for you."

He found himself smiling back, an act that earned a look of surprise from his adviser.

"You have left your documents on the table," Sonja pointed out as he walked away with her.

"I know."

"Your private documents," she reiterated. "Aren't you concerned she will attempt to read their contents?"

"I certainly hope she will, for I have already asked her to do so."

"Have you completely lost your senses?"

"Not the last time I looked. I've asked Ms. Romolo for her opinion on my potential brides."

"I can't imagine why you would value her thoughts," Sonja remarked in surprise before pulling herself back together. "Anyway, that is of little significance. Whatever your courtesan thinks, you will marry one of the women in that folder. You have no other choice now."

Rocco's steps halted abruptly and his blood ran cold. "No other choice? The vote is in?"

"It is." Sonja opened the door nearest to them and gestured for him to enter.

Rocco eyed the bright steady light on the phone on the desk as if it was the eye of a serpent that was coiled and ready to strike. And wasn't that indeed the case? Wasn't there a viper in his midst, causing all this unrest?

"Thank you, Sonja, you may wait outside."

She bowed her head and closed the door behind her. Perhaps he'd imagined it, but had he seen a faint glimpse of triumph on her face? Perhaps he was just becoming oversensitive about the issue in what was an extremely trying time. Maybe he was seeing things where they didn't exist. But, he couldn't help remembering her words from the previous night and wondering how many of the rest of his staff felt he should stand down, too.

He shook his head. He couldn't afford to think about that now. More pressing was taking the official call from his prime minister confirming the outcome of the vote to nullify the succession law. He reached for the phone.

When the call had ended, Rocco sank back against his chair and closed his eyes. He'd honestly believed that his efforts to overturn the law would succeed. After all, hadn't the law been devised at a time when a man was old at thirty-five years, not like modern times when a man was entering his prime at that age? He certainly didn't feel old and decrepit, with the need to signify an heir as the end of his reign approached. There were plenty of other European heads of state who had fathered children, legitimate and otherwise, well after the age of thirty-five.

No matter his internal arguments, it didn't change the facts. He had to marry and the news made the contents of the dossier he had left with Ottavia all the more important. On paper, either woman would do. In fact, in ancient times, he or his advisers would have simply made a choice and married the maiden without ever having met her. The very thought of it made his mind and body revolt.

And yet, wasn't that precisely what he'd expected his sister to do after their father had brokered her marriage when she was still no more than a child? Rocco began to experience a new appreciation for what he'd put Mila through for the past several years, not to mention gain a stronger grasp of her reasons for masquerading as her fiancé's courtesan in an attempt to make him fall in love with her. Her quest had been successful, but not without its bumps in the road.

He wondered what Mila would think of the situation he now found himself in. He knew she was a great advocate of marrying for love. If she'd been anywhere but on her honeymoon he'd have asked her opinion, and no doubt surprised her with the request because when had he ever sought her judgment on any issue? The next time they saw one another he would begin to make amends.

But right now, he had a call to make.

"Andrej?" he said when a man answered on the first ring.

"Your Majesty," the head of his armed forces replied.

"I want you to redouble your efforts to find out exactly who is behind this attack on my position. Someone has weaseled their way into the minds of more than half my parliament."

"The vote did not go as you hoped?"

"If the abstentions had been yeas we would have won, but whoever is feeding this drivel to our politicians has created enough doubt that they now question everything."

"I will do as you wish."

"Thank you, Andrej. It's good to know who my allies are."

Rocco's words were heartfelt. He'd known Andrej Novak

his whole life. Two years older than him and the son of Sonja Novak and her late husband, they'd spent a lot of time together growing up. Rocco trusted him implicitly.

"Will that be all?" Andrej asked.

Across the line Rocco heard the faint repetitive click that signaled Andrej had another incoming call.

"Yes, for now. But please keep me apprised of what you find as soon as anything comes to light."

"Understood, Sire."

He looked out the window across the terrace to where Ottavia sat, idly flicking through the contents of the folder. He still didn't know what to make of her...or of the effect she had on him. Hadn't he voluntarily asked nicely more than once today? He felt his lips curl into an ironic smile.

Even now, looking at her across this short distance, he felt the mesmeric pull of her personality. Sensed the siren song of her allure. How did any man spend time with her and not want to make love with her? Not want to feast upon the bounty of her sensuous curves, or coax cries of passion from her lush lips and see those fascinating gray-green eyes cloud with need?

There was nothing else he could do right now. He was wasting time here when he could be with her, gently whittling down her resistance. The thought immediately struck him as manipulative, but he pushed the thought aside. A man didn't get what he wanted by waiting patiently. And he had little time at hand with the pressing urgency of his marriage to think about. He would not be like his father and keep a mistress. Once he was engaged he planned to be wholly faithful to his bride. But in the meantime...

Rocco got to his feet and headed for the door. Sonja still waited outside his office and slid her cell phone discreetly into her pocket as he came out the door.

"What are you going to do now?" she asked.

"Now? I'm going to choose a bride. Did you do as I asked regarding bringing the women here?"

"I did. They are both expected here later in the week."

"Good. Thank you."

Sonja looked startled. "I beg your pardon?"

"I said, thank you."

Her eyes widened a moment before she composed her features once more and inclined her head in acknowledgment. "Would you like me to organize the reception? It can be scheduled for a week from now. Obviously you will need to invite a number of members of parliament and their respective partners. The numbers should quickly reach two hundred."

"Compile the guest list and send out the invitations as quickly as possible. The rest, I will leave to Sandra," he said, mentioning the event coordinator on his staff. "I know Mila's wedding was supposed to be her last function before her maternity leave, but Ms. Romolo can assist and you can confirm attendees with her."

"Is that wise?" his adviser blurted.

"She is experienced in entertaining. I think it would be beneficial for us to utilize that experience."

He heard Sonja mutter something under her breath.

"If you have something to say, do me the courtesy of saying it to my face."

"I'm sure she is experienced in a lot of things, however I would not have considered a royal reception to be among her—" Sonja paused, clearly searching for the right word. "Talents. Besides, I don't think you should be giving her so much responsibility. What will people say?"

"Why should that be a problem? She has acted as hostess for several high-profile businessmen in Erminia in recent years."

"Hostess." Sonja gave an inelegant snort.

Rocco gave her a hard look and she composed herself again.

"My apologies, Sire."

"If there are no further matters requiring my attention, I think you should take the rest of the day off. You've been under a great deal of pressure while we waited for the vote and it's beginning to show."

"Nothing I can't handle," she protested.

"Sonja, take the day. Please."

They stared at one another for a full thirty seconds before she averted her gaze. "Very well, but I do not like the idea of you being left alone with the machinations of that courtesan. I believe you will regret having that woman here. Her presence does not augur well for your future."

"You have warned me, as I would expect you to do, and your words are duly noted. Now go, make the most of the summer sun, do something you enjoy."

Sonja sniffed in response, turned and stalked away, her annoyance visible in every line of her body. Rocco watched her leave, playing over her words in his mind. Could it be that she was right? That he was risking his future? He'd never had any reason to doubt Sonja's advice in the past, so why was he turning away from it now?

Another morning, another rose on her pillow. Again, he'd slept beside her. Again, she'd slept so deeply she hadn't noticed, though this time she had not used a sleeping pill. Strange, then, that she'd slept so well all the same. Against her better judgment, Ottavia smiled and dragged the rose across her lips. Its texture was cool and silky smooth. This was crazy, she thought. She should not allow herself to be... *wooed*, for want of a better word, by a man who clearly just wanted to bed her. Still, he had made no move on her and, aside from those kisses that had undeniably heated her blood, he hadn't touched her again.

She got up from the bed and added the bloom to the one he'd given her yesterday. She would need a bigger vase if he kept this up on a daily basis, she thought as she went through to the bathroom to prepare for the day. She had a great deal of work ahead of her. It had surprised her to be told she would be assisting his event coordinator in planning the reception for the two princesses and their entourages next week. Sandra, the event planner, was expecting her first baby and, while she could handle the organization side of things, she would not be able to spend the hours necessary on her feet to attend the function and see it ran smoothly on the night. With Ottavia's experience as a hostess for her clients, Rocco had said she would be the best backup for the situation, which had come as quite a shock.

She had done a lot of interesting things in her career, but she'd never had to stand by the side of a man while he was shopping for a wife. Of course, it was rarely an issue. Most of her clients had been widowers, unwilling or simply unready to dive into dating again, yet wanting to feel a connection to someone in a safe, controllable way.

In her usual business engagements, she would never consider a client who was openly pursuing another woman, just as she would never accept a contract from a man who was currently married. Even if her assignments were not sexually intimate, they were still *emotionally* intimate, in a way that a married man should not be with anyone but his wife.

But for the king, she was willing to make an exception, if only because his plans for his wedding seemed more like a business merger than an attempt to build a loving relationship. He was not betraying his future bride by spending time with Ottavia. If anything, she was doing the future queen a favor by training him to treat the women in his life with somewhat improved manners.

Once she was dressed Ottavia went downstairs for her video call with the event planner. There were menus to plan and decorations to discuss and sleeping arrangements to coordinate for the guests who were expected to begin arriving over the next few days. Sonja Novak had given her a copy of the invitation list, reluctantly and with an admonition that its contents were to remain completely confidential. On seeing the names of those attending, both royal and political, Ottavia was not at all surprised.

The morning passed swiftly and she was surprised when she was interrupted by Marie, the maid, coming to her in the small office she'd been allocated.

"His Majesty would like you to join him for lunch, ma'am," she said with a small bob of a curtsy.

"Thank you, Marie. Where can I find him?"

"On the main terrace, ma'am. It's his favorite place to eat when he's here."

Ottavia packed away her notes and locked them in the drawer of her desk before checking her appearance in the small mirror behind the door. A flush of anticipation had bloomed in her cheeks and her eyes were unnaturally bright. Perhaps she was coming down with something, she mused, then poked her tongue out at herself and shook her head. No, she couldn't lie. He excited her—everything about him excited her—and it galled her to admit it. But the physical signs were unmistakable. All she could do was hope that it wasn't as obvious to him, lacking her training in interpreting body language. If he suspected the depth of her attraction to him, she had no doubt that he'd find some way to use it to his advantage—and that was something she couldn't allow. She was the kind of woman who always maintained the upper hand. Always.

She made her way to the main terrace and walked toward the umbrella-shaded table where he sat. Her eyes roamed his body, taking in the crisp white shirt, the impeccably knotted tie at his throat, the way his head bent as he studied a sheaf of papers in his hand. She knew she made no noise as she walked along the paved surface, but something alerted him to her presence. She saw the instant he stilled, then watched as he lifted his head and looked directly at her.

A punch of awareness hit her square in the solar plexus and beneath the silk tunic and leggings she'd donned this morning her skin felt tight and sensitive—as if with his gaze he'd touched her. A featherlight touch, designed to tease, to test. Ottavia shoved the thought from her mind with ruthless determination. It was as if he could seduce her with a look. No man should have that much power over anyone, least of all her.

Rocco rose to his feet as his courtesan approached and he reached for her hand, sweeping it to his lips and pressing a kiss on her knuckles.

"I'm glad you could join me," he said.

Despite the brightness of the day her pupils were dilated and her lips were parted slightly as if she was trying to draw breath any way she could. He smiled. It satisfied him greatly to know he affected her—and in a positive way, he noted.

"How are the plans progressing for the reception?" he asked, holding out a chair for her as she settled at the table.

"I think I have it all in hand. I have to admit, I was surprised you asked me to take care of it for you. What if I make a dreadful mess of it all?"

He sat opposite her and picked up his water glass, eyeing her over the crystal rim. "You don't strike me as the kind of person who makes dreadful messes."

"Okay, fine, I won't. I have far too much personal pride for that," she admitted.

"Tell me more about yourself," he asked. "With your education you could have taken on many various careers. Why did you choose to become a courtesan?"

She sat still a moment. He'd caught her off guard with

his question, obviously. Finally, she gave him a smile. He was beginning to recognize this one. It was one she used to charm and distract, so that she could appear to answer the question and yet reveal nothing at all.

"I enjoy the lifestyle," she answered simply. "I like wearing nice clothes, living in luxurious surroundings, being driven around in expensive, fast cars. I make no excuse for that."

"Living in the manner to which you are accustomed?" he probed.

"Something like that."

There it was again. That fake smile, this time paired with an answer that was no answer at all. He narrowed his eyes at her. She left a great deal unsaid. He could accept that. They were only just beginning to get to know one another. Staff brought out their salads, soon followed by small medallions of venison with a sautéed vegetable medley. After they'd eaten, Rocco leaned back in his chair and studied her. Perhaps she'd be more forthcoming if she knew more about him.

"This is my favorite place in the world, did you know that?" he said, staring out toward the lake and watching a small family of ducks as they swam across the water.

"I do now," Ottavia answered him, and he could hear a different kind of smile in her voice. A genuine one. "What is it about here that is so special to you?"

Ah yes, she was happier being the questioner than the questioned.

"I think it's because it's the place where my parents were happiest," he said, surprising himself with his answer.

It was totally honest and straight from the heart. Unguarded. And, for once in his life, it didn't bother him to tell a virtual stranger something so personal about him.

"Do you have many happy memories of growing up?" she asked.

"Enough. What about you? Were your parents happy together?"

She looked surprised by the question and he could see her carefully formulating an answer in her mind. He knew, instinctively, that whatever came from her mouth would be what she thought he wanted to hear. It wouldn't be the truth—so he didn't want to hear it at all.

"Don't answer that if you don't want to," he said, rising from his chair. "Shall we walk for a while, instead?"

"That would be lovely," she said, pushing back her chair.

He'd been on the mark then, he gathered as he shook out his napkin and tipped the contents of the bread basket into it and pulled up the corners in a knot.

"What are you doing? Surely if you need a snack for later on you can simply ring for one?" she teased.

"You'll see," he answered and reached for her hand.

Holding it in a warm, loose clasp he led her down the wide steps that led onto the expansive lawn. He felt a light tug as she stopped, midstep.

"These roses," she said, pointing to the many plants in large concrete urns spaced along the terrace. "Are they the ones you bring me in the morning?"

"You like them?"

"Yes, I do. They're beautiful."

He nodded. "Their name is Pierre de Ronsard. They were my mother's favorite. She planted many of these bushes herself. When she was here, it was one of the few times when she could be real and indulge in the things that brought her personal pleasure, like gardening, without having to worry about other people's opinions."

"I can see why it brought you so much joy to be here with her then," Ottavia commented as they began to walk again.

"We could be a family here," he answered simply, then debated his next words. What did it matter, he told himself. It wasn't like it wasn't public knowledge. "Until they fell out of love with one another, anyway."

"I know what you mean," she responded, real understanding in her voice. She was being honest now, open—and he appreciated it more than he could say. "My parents fell out of love with one another when I was about ten," she continued. "It was a confusing time. I was born in the United States and after the breakup my mother brought me back to Erminia. They weren't married and it all happened very fast."

"Your father was from the US?"

"No, he was Erminian, also. I never saw or heard from him again once we came here."

"I'm sorry."

"Don't be. It was all a long time ago."

They walked along the lawn and toward the lake. The ducks Rocco had spied earlier spotted them immediately and began to swim toward them.

"Oh, look at them," Ottavia exclaimed in delight. "Can we feed them?"

Rocco lifted up the napkin. "Your wish is my command," he said unraveling the knot and passing her a few slices of bread.

He watched as she tore it to pieces and threw it to the ducks who squawked and splashed and acted like they hadn't eaten in a month. She was a beautiful woman when she was composed and acting her part, but when she was like this—natural and laughing and simply enjoying the moment—she was even more so. It made him want to know her better, to understand more intimately the enigma of what lay behind those eyes of hers—eyes that reminded him so much of the lake he loved.

But like the stretch of water in front them, she was equally deep and full of secrets. And he looked forward to discovering exactly what they were.

Seven

Ottavia waited in the grand salon for the guests to arrive. The afternoon had been punctuated by the sounds of helicopters, boats and cars arriving at the castle and the atmosphere had changed from one of tranquility to one that buzzed with energy. Anticipation hung in the air along with a sense that people were watching and waiting for a scandal or a disaster. A shiver ran down her spine. She didn't like this feeling and would have preferred not to be here this evening and, instead, to remain behind the scenes, but Rocco had insisted.

She smoothed her hands down her gown in a reassuring motion. She'd chosen this dress from among the gowns she'd had in her luggage for its ability to conceal rather than reveal—this event was for the princesses and she did not want to draw attention to herself tonight. Even so, while the forest green jersey covered her from neck to ankle, the cut had been designed to maximize her feminine charms, so she'd done her best to downplay that fact by wearing minimal jewelry and using only the lightest hand with her cosmetics.

Everything was in place. She'd liaised then checked and double-checked with the kitchens and the staff and the evening would run like clockwork. If only she could be as sure that the guests would behave equally as impeccably. There had been an uproar yesterday when the guest list had been leaked somehow to the national newspaper. A great many noses had apparently been prematurely put out of joint at not being included at what was believed to be an important royal event.

There was nothing she could do about what had happened, she reminded herself. The only thing she could do was keep an eye on tonight and hope that those who were here conducted themselves with the decorum that befitted their stations. If they didn't, there was little she could do about it aside from ensuring that troublemakers were discreetly removed and sent safely on their way.

Ottavia mentally ticked off her list. She'd done everything she could. She'd even personally seen to the placement of the flowers for the grand salon and on the tables on the terrace outside, and she'd overseen the stocking of each of the two bars—one indoors and one out—and given strict instructions to the waitstaff on the circulation of the trays of hors d'oeuvres that the kitchen staff had painstakingly created.

Considering the evening had been organized at such short notice, Ottavia was pleasantly surprised with how smoothly it had all come together and how quickly the guest confirmations had been returned. *Still*, she thought with a private smile, *it's not like anyone was likely to refuse an invitation from their king.*

"Share your thoughts?" Rocco asked as he came up beside her. He was resplendent in a white tie and tuxedo that enhanced his dark hair and his olive skin, making his eyes glow like well-aged whiskey.

Ottavia reached up and brushed an imaginary speck of dust from his lapel. "Oh, it's nothing worth sharing," she commented lightly.

Rocco caught her hand in his and looked deeply into her eyes. "You are exquisite this evening," he said, his voice deep and thoughtful as if he was only just looking at her for the first time.

A flush of heat bloomed in her cheeks. She was used to compliments—they meant nothing to her—but this felt intensely personal. As if they were the only two people in the luxuriously appointed room that shone with chandeliers and gold leaf as though it had been drawn straight out of a fairy tale.

"Thank you, Your Majesty," she said, dropping her eyes. "You look exquisite, also."

Ottavia fought to keep her tone light, almost teasing, but knew she'd failed when her breath caught at the end, betraying her own reaction to him—to his nearness, to his touch. He'd heard it, too. When she looked back up, she saw that his lips had curved into a sensuous smile that sent an ache of longing deep into her core.

"I've been thinking about your prospective brides," she said in an attempt to deflect his attention from her and back to where it ought to be this evening.

"Is that so?"

"Yes, they both appear to be equally accomplished but I wondered—what do they have in common with you?"

"With me? Why should that matter?"

Ottavia chewed lightly at her lip, choosing her words carefully. "Well, I've studied the princesses' files and on paper they appear to be perfect candidates, however, I would have assumed a man like yourself would prefer a partner—someone to stand by you—rather than a shadow to simply follow in your wake."

"You would assume that, would you?"

She sighed in impatience. "You did ask for my opinion."

"And I'm sure you have more of it to impart."

"I do. With your permission?"

He inclined his head.

"Erminia is unstable at present, and the law requires that you choose a bride to stabilize your reign. It concerns me that your people will judge any woman you marry at this time as merely being a means to an end. That end being you remaining in the position of monarch."

Rocco lifted one hand to stroke his jaw. "So you believe that my people may be less accepting of anyone I marry now?"

"I believe they will be less accepting if they believe you only wed because you had no choice and that you clearly do not, or cannot, love your queen. Your people need to see a united marriage—not one simply of convenience."

"Love on demand?" he commented with a cynical lift of one brow.

"At least an obvious mutual respect and attraction that can lead to lasting love."

"That sounds very romantic, but impractical."

"That may be, but you can be pretty sure it's what people want to see. Think about those fairy-tale happy-ending royal marriages the tabloids ignore after the initial pomp and ceremony. Think about the stability of those nations and then compare them to the countries where the media thrive on speculation on any unhappiness and scandal within their leaders' private lives. Sire, if your people can see hope, see love, they will also see a brighter future."

Rocco appeared to weigh her words carefully before giving her a decisive nod. "I will think about what you've said and bear that in mind when I make my decision."

The ornate double doors to the salon swung open and liveried footmen stood at either side.

"Come, it is time for the guests to arrive," he said, taking her arm and leading her to the doorway.

Ottavia walked with him, acutely aware of his touch on her arm and his presence at her side. If she wasn't careful, this powerful man beside her would slide through a chink in the armor she so carefully protected herself with. *Remember your promise to yourself,* she silently chastised. *Your choices, your life lived the way you want it. Trust no one but yourself.*

She arranged her features into a welcoming and professional visage as the first of several guests were announced. She wasn't oblivious to the appreciative assessments by many of the influential men who came through the door, nor was she unaware of the equally disparaging and occasionally outright curious stares of the women who accompanied them. Through it all she maintained her air of quiet self-possession.

As the salon filled, Ottavia found herself watching Rocco carefully as he engaged in conversation with Princess Bettina. The other woman's body language spoke volumes as to her awareness of her position in life. The youngest daughter of a northern European ruler, she appeared to be confident and self-assured. Ottavia mentally reviewed the woman's accomplishments—a patroness of several charities, known for her prowess on horseback to the point of serving as a representative of her nation in the Olympics—she would make an interesting companion for Rocco. Her fair complexion and silver-blond hair provided the perfect foil to Rocco's darkness—as if they were night and day.

But would she challenge him when he needed to be challenged? Ottavia wondered. And would she comfort him even when he refused to admit he needed comfort? Did they have the chemistry that would make for a successful connection? Would her body light with an internal fire every time a glance from him met with hers? Looking at the woman and the cool, clear expression on her classically beautiful features, Ottavia doubted it.

"Excuse me."

A female voice interrupted her thoughts. Ottavia turned with a smile on her face, which faltered just a little when she recognized the woman standing by her as Princess Sara.

"Certainly, can I assist you with anything, Your Royal Highness?"

"What exactly is your position here?" the woman asked haughtily, her green eyes speculative beneath arched auburn brows.

"I'm King Rocco's guest this evening," Ottavia explained, deliberately keeping her description as simple as possible.

The other woman smiled, her expression reminding Ottavia of one of the foxes that ran in the forests nearby.

"His guest." She nodded slowly. "I see."

Ottavia was acutely aware that the woman probably saw a great deal more than that.

"Was there anything else you needed, ma'am?" she asked, injecting her voice with the deference due to the princess solely because of her position.

The woman smiled again. "I think we'll be able to get along, don't you?"

"Get along?"

Princess Sara nodded in Rocco's direction. "*Yes*, you and I, when the king and I are married." She gave Ottavia an assessing look. "I think you will be just the distraction he needs."

"I'm sorry, ma'am." Ottavia tried to hold on to her temper. "I'm not sure what you are talking about."

"Oh, come now, don't be coy. I'm aware of what my

responsibility will be toward him when we marry, just as I'm equally aware of your reputation and your…" She ran her eyes over Ottavia from head to toe, continuing, "…obvious talents. I would have no objection to my husband's needs being satisfied elsewhere once I produce the requisite heir and a spare. He looks quite…lusty, doesn't he? I don't imagine the reproduction side of things will take too long and then you can have him back."

Ottavia dared not speak. This woman was undoubtedly beautiful and accomplished, but where was her heart? If their positions were reversed Ottavia would want nothing to do with any woman Rocco had purportedly bedded. Nor could she ever imagine being willing to share his attention and affections with another woman. She wouldn't be able to trust herself not to want to scratch their eyes out. The realization struck her with shocking honesty. She'd never been possessive in her life, certainly never about a man. How had Rocco managed to get under her careful guard so quickly, and so thoroughly? She needed some space, some air to breathe. Somewhere she could analyze these unsettling thoughts and reassemble her mental armor.

"If you'll excuse me," she managed to enunciate through lips that felt numb.

"Certainly," Princess Sara responded with a regal nod of her head before turning away.

Ottavia strode to the terrace and away from the twinkling fairy lights and the hum of conversation. At the far edge she wrapped her fingers over the top of the stone balustrade and gripped it tight. No, she told herself. She did not feel like this about her clients. And yet, the idea of Rocco's body entwined with either one of the princesses' sent a piercing spike of jealousy through her body.

She didn't care about him, she told herself. She couldn't. It wasn't as if they were lovers or even partners. She was his courtesan and their relationship was confined to the dictates of the contract she herself had drawn up. She did not feel attraction. She would not be victim to her physical demands.

Hadn't she made that vow to herself? Promises forged in pain and tears and helplessness?

For her, personal power was everything. She knew how to play on people's superficiality, on their needs. She valued the people who hired her only for what they could bring her. Yes, that made her appear mercenary, but she didn't care. Security was everything. For her and for Adriana.

She felt a pang in her chest. She'd video-called Adriana earlier this afternoon—her baby sister was the only person in the world that she loved unconditionally and with all her heart. Adriana had begged her to come and see her. Each one of her tears had been a blow to Ottavia's psyche. Adriana barely understood the concept of time, but she did understand how many crosses marked off the days until they would be together again, and as far as the fourteen-year-old was concerned there were far too many.

It was for her that Ottavia did this. It was for Adriana, and others like her, that she wielded her feminine mastery over men so she could ensure a safe haven for as long as the teen drew breath. Born with Down syndrome, her intellectual disability was at the profound end of the scale. Add to that the complication of an inoperable congenital heart defect and it took a great deal of care and time and money to ensure Adriana's life, for as long as she lived, both nurtured her and was comfortable.

Ottavia's only regret was that her work commitments took up so much of her time. Her clients expected her to be available to them around the clock, which left her with few opportunities to spend quality time with Adriana. But it was her work that made everything else possible—that paid the bills for the facility and that built a retirement nest egg that was nearly complete. Once she'd saved enough to support the two of them for the foreseeable future, Ottavia would retire, buy a home for her and Adriana to share and leave this false, glittering world of high society behind forever.

Ottavia squared her shoulders and turned back toward the light and sound of the party. It was for Adriana that she did this, she reminded herself again. For Adriana and herself, and the future she wanted them to have together.

She took a deep breath and slowly walked back to the assembly, smiling and talking as she worked her way back through the crowd. Her eyes constantly checked that the staff circulated evenly through the guests with the trays of canapés and that none of the guests became too intoxicated.

When it was fully dark, everyone was ushered outdoors for the fireworks display over the lake. Ottavia hung back, observing the gathering, rather than inserting herself as a part of it. She became aware of the presence of a man in the shadows when he began to walk toward her. There was something about him that was vaguely familiar to her and at first she thought it was Rocco, but as he drew nearer, she realized she'd never met this man before.

"Ms. Romolo," he said, stopping at her side.

"You have the advantage of me, sir," Ottavia answered with a slight smile.

The hairs on the back of her neck prickled and she felt her heart begin to race, but it had nothing to do with attraction. This man certainly exuded power, but of a more lethal kind, she decided as she waited for his introduction.

"General Andrej Novak, at your service," he said with a slight bow.

Rocco's head of the armed forces. Ottavia had heard of the man—who hadn't after Princess Mila's kidnapping? The man had been wounded while trying to protect the princess. It was sheer chance that the kidnappers left him for dead and that he was able to fly the abandoned helicopter—the princess's transport, which had been hijacked by the kidnappers—back to safety. But she'd never realized what a lethal presence he projected. She fought to control the shiver of apprehension that stealthily crept down her spine.

"Are you enjoying yourself tonight, General?"

He appeared to consider her words for a moment or two before answering. "Nights such as this are always better with a beautiful woman at one's side."

His words should have sounded like a compliment, yet they made Ottavia's skin crawl, especially when accompanied by the salacious look in his eye.

"I am curious," he continued. "When does your contract with our esteemed leader come to an end?"

"I believe that is between King Rocco and myself," she said smoothly.

A sudden boom in the air made her flinch in surprise as the first of the cavalcade of fireworks burst through the clear night sky. The general moved a little closer, putting an arm around her back.

"I ask only because I find myself in need of a companion such as yourself. A woman who can be relied upon to be discreet, yet satisfying. I'm told you come highly recommended."

Again that ripple of unease trickled through her.

"I'm not sure I understand what you mean," she said coldly.

He bent his head closely to hers and whispered the names of some of her lesser known and intensely private clients. Information she'd believed to be confidential. She instantly drew back, her features freezing into a mask of shock.

"That's privileged information!" she blurted out.

"And I am nothing if not privileged," he said, his voice a low, insidious growl. "Remember that, Ms. Romolo. I have access to your entire life."

Before she could summon a response, he was gone again, melting into the shadows the same way he'd appeared. The words he'd used were innocuous enough, but the emphasis he'd placed on the words *privileged* and then her *entire life* had sent a spike of unease through her. Her mind was quick to expand on all manner of possibilities—none of them reassuring. Ottavia had learned not to ignore her instincts and there was definitely something about this man that had her radar flicking on to high alert.

Right now, she felt threatened, anxious, vulnerable—no doubt exactly as he'd intended when he'd issued his veiled threat. And it had definitely been a threat. An icy cold sense of foreboding filled her and she flinched as another resounding boom filled the air, followed by gasps of awe from the revelers on the terrace as cascades of color filled the night sky.

Ottavia made her way inside and to the bar. "Scotch," she demanded, "neat."

The bartender hastened to fill her request and a glass appeared before her. She lifted the tumbler to her lips and poured the fiery liquid into her mouth. As it scorched its way down her throat she closed her eyes for a moment. Drew on every last ounce of internal strength that she possessed. Her instincts urged her to leave this place. But she'd signed a contract. She couldn't simply walk away.

She opened her eyes and murmured a quick thank you to the bartender before heading back out onto the terrace. The crowd was still absorbed in the spectacle of light and color in the sky. She looked around and breathed a small sigh of relief. General Novak wasn't anywhere to be seen. Some of the tension that had gripped her eased off when she spotted Rocco.

Ottavia tried to ignore the odd sensation that assailed her as she watched him. His head was bent to Princess Sara's, his lips curved in a smile at something she said, and the other woman's hand sat possessively on his forearm. Ottavia swallowed against the sudden bitterness on her tongue.

He was a means to an end, she reminded herself firmly. That was all. The means to freedom, to be precise. She would fulfil her duties here and then disappear, just as she'd always planned to do one day. Fade into obscurity and live a normal life. And then she wouldn't have to worry about men like General Andrej Novak ever again.

Eight

Rocco looked around the grand salon, his eyes searching for the one person he wanted to see, but Ottavia was nowhere to be found. Irritation made him frown as he moved toward the ballroom and peered through the throng of dancers who circled the floor. No, she wasn't here, either.

She had to be here somewhere, he thought, as he politely sidestepped his guests. It was past midnight and he'd had quite enough of playing host and jumping through the necessary hoops required of him tonight. He wanted nothing more than to withdraw to his chambers and escape the crowd of people who considered themselves a part of his inner circle but with whom he continued to feel like nothing more than a stranger.

Even Andrej, it seemed, had deserted him tonight. Normally he could count upon his childhood friend to be at his side, but it seemed he had made an early withdrawal from the event.

At least the princesses appeared to be enjoying themselves, Rocco thought as he glanced across the room, spying first one auburn-haired beauty and then the fairer head of the other. Both women were striking and certainly accomplished, but he'd felt no spark with either of them and all evening he'd been forced to ask himself if he could go through with marriage to a stranger, purely to provide an heir in the requisite time.

He had to, he reminded himself, and tried to imagine a life, a future, with either one. But every time he did, the only woman he could see beside him had luxurious hair dark as night and secretive eyes of gray-green. So where the hell was she hiding?

Rocco ducked out into a hallway before coming to a rapid halt by the servant's staircase. He heard voices. Ottavia's and one much, much younger. He peered carefully around the corner and saw two heads bent together. He recognized the elegant coiffure of his courtesan, but the twin braids of a little girl of about four or five years old beside her surprised him. He hadn't seen the child before but she appeared to be on very good terms with Ottavia, in whose lap she currently nestled.

"Is this a private party, or can anyone join in?" Rocco asked, making his presence known.

The little girl looked up and an expression of awe mixed with an equal dose of panic crossed her face.

"Your Majesty," Ottavia said smoothly as she looked up. "Please join us rather than looming there like some evil dragon."

The little girl giggled and burrowed against Ottavia's chest.

"You think I'm a dragon?" Rocco asked, surprised but lowering himself onto a step just below where they were perched.

"A big growly fire-breathing dragon," Ottavia said dramatically.

The little girl giggled again and peeped shyly at her king. Rocco winked.

"I'm not really a dragon," he said in a loud whisper. "But don't tell everyone else that."

"I won't," the child replied.

"This is Gina, she's Marie's daughter and she should be in bed asleep. But apparently she had a bad dream and came searching for her Mamma. She was crying when I found her but I told her she was a very brave girl."

"Was no one else looking after her? She wandered the castle on her own?" Rocco said. He realized immediately that his questions had sounded rather gruff when Gina hid her face in Ottavia's chest again. "Well, that would make her very brave indeed," Rocco said, toning his voice down again.

"Apparently her grandma, who was minding her, wouldn't wake up. I sent someone to check on the grandma. Thankfully, she is simply a deep sleeper. She will be down shortly to collect our intrepid adventurer," Ottavia said smoothly. "Were you looking for me?"

Rocco looked at her with the child in her lap. She looked so natural and comfortable. Apparently not caring that her expensive gown was tearstained on one side, or that the little girl was now playing with a tendril of hair that had slipped from Ottavia's hairdo. His fingers itched to do the same.

"Yes, I was."

"Is there anything wrong?" Ottavia asked.

"Oh, miss, I'm so sorry!" An older woman scurried down the stairs toward them, her footsteps faltering as she recognized the man seated at the bottom of the stairs. "Your Majesty! Please forgive us," she exclaimed, dipping into a deep curtsy.

"Gina, go to your grandmother," Ottavia said, giving

the little girl a kiss on her brow and setting her on her feet. "And, Juliet, there is nothing to forgive. Is there, Sire?"

"No, of course not," Rocco answered.

The older woman took the little girl by the hand and after bobbing another curtsy started back up the stairs. Rocco gave Ottavia his hand and helped her to rise to her feet.

"It seems you are a woman of many talents," he said as she smoothed her gown over her lush curves before reaching to pin the tendril of hair back into its confines.

"Because I didn't run screaming from a frightened child?" she replied, her voice touching on sarcasm.

"I doubt there are many here tonight who would have done the same."

"Your guests will be missing you," she said, ignoring his comment. "You should return."

He took her hand and threaded it into the crook of his arm. "Yes, let's."

"That's not what I meant," she said, attempting to tug free. "We are not a couple, Sire."

"Rocco, remember."

"Not when someone may overhear us and get the wrong impression."

"The wrong impression? Of what?"

Ottavia appeared lost for words for a moment. "Well, you wouldn't want to put off your prospective brides."

He began to lead her back to the ballroom. "Oh, I don't think that will be a problem."

"You don't? Then you've decided on one of the ladies?"

Was it his imagination or did she sound a little disappointed? He certainly hoped so. The idea that had being simmering in his mind now grew and took a firmer shape.

"I was considering that perhaps it's time we make another addendum to our contract."

"Another addendum?"

"Yes, to specify those other duties you questioned."

A frown pulled between her brows. "If you're suggesting we continue our arrangement, such as it is, after you are married, then I'm afraid you are destined for disappointment. I never work with married men."

"You do not support adultery?"

She shook her head vehemently. "Rather than make further amendment to our contract, perhaps you should release me now. It wouldn't be right for me to remain here once you are officially engaged to someone else."

They neared the ballroom doors and Rocco drew to a halt. "But, if you leave, then I won't be able to do this—"

He pulled Ottavia into his arms, her body neatly fitting against his. He bent to kiss her, nibbling softly at her full lower lip before sucking it gently into his mouth and stroking it with his tongue before deepening the kiss.

It was foolish of him—reckless. Some of the most important people in his country had come to this event to meet the princess who would become his bride, and it would be a shocking scandal if he was caught kissing someone else. But he couldn't resist. The thought of her walking away from him drove him nearly mad. He would not allow anyone to put distance between them—not even her.

She stiffened in his arms for just a moment, but then she relaxed, became pliant. Her hands slid up to his chest, her fingers gripping the lapels of his jacket as she opened her mouth, her tongue dancing lightly with his. A surge of heat and need ran through him and he pulled her closer, letting her feel the effect of their embrace, making sure there was no question about who it was that he desired.

The muffled sounds of the ballroom on the other side of the doors suddenly became louder and Rocco tore his mouth from hers, looking up and recognizing the man who had come through them.

"Ah, Andrej," he said smoothly, but without letting Ottavia go. "I thought you had retired for the evening."

"Retired already? No. I was—" He hesitated a moment, his gaze flicking to Ottavia and then back again. "Otherwise occupied."

If Rocco hadn't known that Ottavia had been busy with young Gina, Andrej's inference just now would have made him leap to the conclusion that she'd been with Andrej instead. His friend's gaze swept across his courtesan again and Rocco saw a glint of something there. Was it amusement? Or maybe it was something else? Avarice perhaps? Rocco told himself not to be so fanciful. Andrej was known for maintaining his own bevy of beauties. Rocco was merely feeling territorial about the woman at his side, and the sooner he made that official, the better.

"Your Majesty," Andrej replied. "The Princess Bettina has been seeking you out. I told her I'd find you. Shall I tell her that you are otherwise occupied?"

"No, I will go to her," Rocco answered with a sigh of irritation. "Ottavia, would you excuse me?"

"Of course," she answered. "I'll go and attend to some running repairs."

"Perhaps you should, also," Andrej said, with a pointed look at Rocco's mouth.

Rocco used a handkerchief to swipe his lips, smiling ruefully as he wiped away the last traces of Ottavia's lipstick. "Thank you. Now, perhaps you would escort me to the princess."

"Unless you'd prefer I keep an eye on the courtesan?" Andrej replied, again with that same slow smile as he turned and watched Ottavia head toward a ladies' room.

Rocco fought back a surge of irritation at Andrej's leering attitude toward Ottavia. "No, Ottavia is quite capable of finding her own way back."

"I'm sure she can. She struck me as very..." He hesitated as if searching for the right word. "Resourceful," he finished with another one of those smiles.

"You've met with her?"

"I have, she's very beautiful. I can see why you'd allow yourself to be distracted."

Again that possessive rush clouded Rocco's mind. He controlled the urge to tell Andrej to keep his thoughts to himself. True, the two men had always been competitive with one another, but there was absolutely nothing offensive about what Andrej had said. In fact, he hadn't been the only man here tonight to pass comment on Ottavia's beauty or her desirability. And yet, no one else's remarks had brought out this swell of anger or suspicion. Rocco gave himself a mental shake. This was ridiculous. His reactions were purely a by-product of the pressure that was currently upon him to satisfy that absurd law.

"Take me to Princess Bettina," he commanded and allowed Andrej to precede him through the door.

Five minutes later Andrej had excused himself. Princess Bettina was saying what a wonderful evening she was having, but Rocco listened with only half an ear while he continued to watch for Ottavia's return. It was crazy, this urge that drove him to seek her out all the time. It seemed the more he saw of her, the more he wanted to be with her—and he begrudged every moment she spent circulating through the room once she finally came back.

"I see your Ms. Romolo has returned," Princess Bettina commented.

Rocco turned his full attention back to the princess only to see her smile calmly in response.

"She is who you have been watching out for, isn't she?"

He was discomforted to realize he'd been so obvious. But, he wondered, did it bother her at all?

"Oh, don't worry," the princess continued. "I understand. A man like yourself has needs. At least you have good taste. She has done a wonderful job arranging this evening."

"Thank you, I shall pass on your compliment."

"You do that. Now, if you'll excuse me?"

He gave the princess a small bow and watched as she wended her way through the crowd and rejoined her lady-in-waiting near the bar. The exchange puzzled him. He'd had one similar with Princess Sara earlier this evening. Was neither woman at all fazed by the fact that a woman—one others assumed was his mistress—had been at their party tonight? He hadn't consciously realized he was testing them and it had come as a surprise to discover their complete acceptance of Ottavia frustrated him.

It was as if both princesses expected him to have a lover—not just now but even after his marriage. Did that mean they expected infidelity from their husbands as a matter of course? Or that they expected to take their own paramour, or paramours, as well?

The very thought repulsed him. He was not the kind of man who shared. He'd seen firsthand how destructive things could become when a couple no longer loved one another and sought their pleasures elsewhere. When he married, it would be to one woman, forever. But the idea of forever with either Princess Bettina or Princess Sara seemed like an excruciatingly long time.

After the end of his relationship with Elsa, he'd found it difficult to trust another woman with his heart. And as busy as he was with his duties to his country, it had been easy to bury himself in work. Sex had become something he had discreetly indulged in, in order to assuage his physical needs, but he'd kept his emotional needs sequestered in another part of his mind where they were rarely examined. Even so, he'd always imagined—hoped, even—that one day he would love again.

Now, however, faced with a lifetime of marriage to either of these princesses, he felt his whole body revolt at the idea. It made him examine more closely what he expected in a marriage. If the truth was to be told, he wanted a love as profound as that which his sister and her husband now shared.

Rocco already knew he was a good ruler—he would be a great one with the right woman at his side. But who was that woman? He very much doubted that either Bettina or Sara filled that bill.

The crowd had begun to thin and he could see Ottavia easily as she mingled here and there. He remembered how she'd looked back on the stairs with little Gina in her arms. How right and natural it had been to see her like that, even in her finery. Would either candidate bride have given the same care and attention to an upset child as Ottavia had? Would they even expect to give it to one of their own?

At the thought of his own children Rocco felt an indescribable swell of protectiveness rise through him. His children would know they were loved and cared for—by their parents and their people. But there was only one way to ensure that. The idea that had bloomed earlier grew in substance, becoming more appealing by the minute.

His eyes fixed on Ottavia and she looked up from what she was doing and caught him staring. A flush of color stained her cheeks and her lips pulled into a small smile, just for him.

Did he dare? Could he take his courtesan and make her his queen?

Nine

Sonja Novak entered Rocco's office door and drew to a halt in front of his desk. He raised one brow in query.

"Both the princesses are leaving and I understand you have made no effort to ask either of them to marry you."

"That's true," Rocco said, leaning back in his leather-covered office chair. "It is probably because I don't wish to marry either of them."

Sonja's finely plucked brows shot high on her forehead. "Your sense of humor is misplaced, Rocco."

"I am not making a joke. Marriage is a serious business. If I felt I could make a successful union with either of those women, don't you think I would do it for my country?"

"Then what are you going to do? Time is not your ally in this. Or perhaps you have given up?"

"I have an alternative idea that I wish to discuss with you. Take a seat."

"I'm all ears," Sonja said, smoothly settling her trim figure into a visitor chair.

Rocco studied the woman. In the early days after his ascension to the throne, he had turned to her frequently, relying on her cool, calm advice and her extensive knowledge of Erminia and the people within its borders. As he'd grown older he'd begun to trust his own judgment. So much so that in the past ten years or so, Sonja's role had been more to provide information rather than advice. Still, it would be interesting to see what she thought of the scheme that had grown in strength in his mind since the reception a week ago.

"Obviously I have to marry, but there is no dictate on exactly *who* I must marry."

Sonja nodded slowly in agreement but didn't rush to comment.

Rocco continued. "I had always hoped that I could choose a bride who was Erminian. One who understands our nation, our people. One who I can rely on to stand by my side without conflict. One to whom I feel a strong attraction both physically and mentally."

He could see Sonja's mind was working flat out behind that apparently serene expression—noted the exact moment when it dawned on her where he might be heading with this conversation. She paled and he saw her hands grip the arms of her chair as if she had to physically hold herself there, or fall from it in shock.

"You are not talking about marrying that Romolo woman," she said with loathing in every syllable.

"I am. It makes perfect sense. She's here. I don't have to waste time courting her. We can marry privately in the castle chapel."

"You can't possibly marry her!" Sonja expostulated. "She's a pros—"

"She is a *courtesan*. There is a difference. I wouldn't be the first monarch to marry his mistress," Rocco reasoned. "Besides, weren't you the one to tell me that all that was required was for me to marry and produce a legitimate issue?"

"You can't be serious. The woman makes her living selling herself to men. Even Andrej—" Sonja's voice abruptly cut off.

"Even Andrej, what?" Rocco asked, feeling an uncomfortable twist in his gut.

"It's nothing. Really. It doesn't matter because you will not marry her."

She may have thought it nothing but Rocco was suddenly reminded of the look in Andrej's eye when he had been with him and Ottavia at the reception. Sonja continued.

"What of fidelity? What of her reputation for being able to get whatever it is she wants from any man?"

"You should not make such assumptions about her character. Besides, even if I marry a princess, I have no more guarantee of fidelity. My parents, theirs before them—"

"They are not in question here," Sonja protested. "You are. Your people will not respect a woman like that. You simply can't ask that of them. No one will stand beside you if you go ahead with it. It reeks of desperation. In fact, it's impossible to even contemplate. If you are prepared to lower yourself to these extremes to hold on to the throne then I think perhaps it's past time you considered abdicating."

Rocco looked at her in surprise. He'd expected resistance but not expressed quite this vehemently. This was not the first time she'd suggested he should stand down. What the hell was going on? Had she, too, turned to the other side? He gave her an imperious stare.

"Thank you for your opinion. Please extend my thanks to the princesses for coming here to the castle and for their time. But I won't be marrying either of them."

"What are you going to do now?"

"I thought I might take a turn on the lake with Ms.

Romolo. Let the boat crew know and have them see to it that my boat is readied for me."

Sonja all but spluttered, "You're going boating at a time like this? You really don't care about what your people think, do you?"

"I care, Sonja. It's because I care that I don't want to make a hasty and empty marriage to a woman who means nothing to me. Besides, it's a lovely day. We all need to take time out occasionally. Even you."

Sonja's lips firmed into a narrow line of disapproval that matched the expression on her brow. "This kind of behavior is exactly why some wish to see you deposed. Mark my words. You reap what you sow."

Rocco's temper rose. He didn't often show anger but when he did, most people had the wisdom to keep their mouths shut and make themselves scarce.

"Are you saying I'm a careless monarch?"

"Take from my words what you will. I have work to do, even if you seem to think you do not."

With that, and without waiting to be excused, she rose sharply and stalked out of his office. He stood and watched her go. Today Sonja had more than overstepped the line and possibly even shown her hand as no longer being among his supporters. To have her flat-out scold him to his face wasn't something he'd expected. Sure, she'd always been outspoken, but never had she been so fierce. Straightening his shoulders he began to walk back out to the terrace. Sonja's behavior troubled him. He'd trusted her for so long that it was second nature. The idea that she would stand so boldly against him was shocking and disturbing.

Was this truly an indication of how his people would feel if he presented them with Ottavia as his queen consort?

The thought was a sobering one, but he didn't want to

begin second-guessing his decisions now. He would prevail, one way or another. He had to. It was far, far too important to simply let go.

Ottavia sat outside on the balcony of Rocco's private suite and stared unseeingly out across the lake. She didn't understand him and that confused her. He was unlike other men she'd met before. Every night since they'd signed their contract, they'd slept together. But not like any other man and woman. No, they'd simply lain side by side. His strong, steady breathing a constant presence, the heat of his naked body a perpetual reminder—even in sleep—that she was not alone. It was oddly comforting, even if it was unsettling at the same time.

Aside from those tantalizing kisses they'd shared, he hadn't requested or attempted to coerce any more from her. It hadn't stopped her awareness of him. Not at all. If anything, being in such close proximity with Rocco had only heightened it. It had left her bewildered and oddly wanting. Not a state of mind she'd ever had to contend with before and not one that she enjoyed, either.

A sudden hand on her shoulder made her jump. The heat of Rocco's fingers seeped through the fabric of her blouse and into her flesh, sending an unexpected thrill of anticipation through her body.

"Did your meeting this morning go well?" she inquired, fighting to keep her voice level as she looked up into his perfectly formed features.

She noticed he'd changed from the suit he'd worn earlier into more casual trousers and an open-necked shirt. Even so, there were lines of strain around his face that were at odds with his informal attire.

"No, it did not. I'm in need of some distraction. Would you like to come out on the lake with me?"

She hid her surprise. She'd heard the princesses were

scheduled to leave the castle later today. An announcement of which one he'd chosen as his bride had to be imminent, and yet he expected her to go out on the lake with him? Perhaps he didn't mean just her.

"That sounds lovely. Will the princesses be joining us?"

"No, they will not," he said rather emphatically.

"Oh. Well, do I need to change?"

His gaze swept her body, taking in the cropped capri pants and sleeveless silk blouse she wore. Despite steeling herself she felt every nerve respond as if his look was a physical touch.

"You are perfect as you are. It's still a little too cold for swimming, but it will be relaxing, nonetheless, to simply be out on the water. Before we go, however, I would like you to read this."

He handed Ottavia some printed sheets of paper. She scanned them quickly, gasping in shock as she began to understand what they contained.

"Rocco, you can't be serious. You don't want to marry me!" she exclaimed.

He returned her gaze, his eyes somber. "Why not? We already have a contract together. This is merely an extension of it. Fine-tuning, if you will."

"Marriage is a bit more than fine-tuning. It's a serious business."

"And I have never been more serious in my life."

Ottavia stared at him. He really wasn't kidding. "Are you certain you have thought this through?"

"Absolutely. Look, you don't have to decide this minute. Think on it. Think of what I can offer you."

"That makes it sound so mercenary."

"It is a contract, Ottavia. No more, no less than the one we have already brokered. If the concept is so unappealing to you then simply don't sign it. But also consider, if you will, the advantages of such a union. We are attracted to one another, are we not? We respect one another. We could make this a *true* marriage in every sense. Wasn't it you who only recently suggested I make a marriage based on obvious mutual respect and attraction that can lead to lasting love? I believe we can achieve that together, don't you?"

He cleverly used her own words against her and made it all sound so simple, but Ottavia knew nothing could be further from the truth. He'd made his expectations clear in the document. He wanted a full marriage and an heir as soon as physically possible. The contract also demanded complete fidelity. That condition had been highlighted in bold print and was nonnegotiable. Everything about the contract made her nervous. She'd never planned to marry. Had never before met the man who could possibly change her mind.

Until now, perhaps.

She shook her head. No. It was unthinkable. She had no royal training, no background. Absolutely nothing to offer him like the visiting princesses did. And she most certainly had shadows in her life that would not bear exposure to all and sundry. Would he accept Adriana once he knew about her? Would he allow her to be a part of their lives?

"Why me?" she blurted out. "Why not Princess Bettina or Princess Sara? They are far more suitable than me."

He gazed out at the lake for a moment before turning his attention back to her.

"I could not imagine a future with either of them. Their unquestioning acceptance of your presence here made me realize I expect—no, I demand—more from marriage than either of them were obviously willing to give."

Did that mean he imagined a future with her?

Ottavia let his words sink in. At least there had been no false declarations of love, although, if he meant what he'd said when he quoted her own words back at her, he seemed to believe he could come to love her. It was far more than she'd ever expected and the idea was terrifying. She drew in a deep breath and calmly put the new contract on the table.

"I see. Obviously I will need to think about this."

"Understandable, but I ask that you not leave me waiting too long."

Of course—the succession law. The need for Rocco to provide an heir was a pressing one. He had so much at stake. But, then, so did she. Not only would she be marrying, against everything she'd ever thought she'd do, she'd be having a child, or children. She'd always sworn she would never bear a child. Feeling the way she did, could she do it? Could she become physically intimate with Rocco with a view to bringing a child into their lives?

Rocco held his hand out to her.

"Come, you will be able to think better once we have been out on the water."

She took another deep breath before laying her smaller hand in his. The disparity in their builds and his ultimate power over her, both real and imagined, was never more apparent than in that moment. And it reminded her that if he so wished, he could have forced her compliance in his bed these past few weeks. But he hadn't. The knowledge was as unsettling as it was a relief, and the juxtaposition of her thoughts kept her on edge.

Hand in hand they descended through the castle, then walked across the lawn. She spied the boat shed nestled in among some trees on the edge of the lake. As they drew nearer, Ottavia heard the low thrum of a powerful jet engine from inside. She felt a small frisson of trepidation.

"You have life vests on the boat?" she blurted out as they entered the boat shed and she took in the sight of the sleek lines of the powerboat sitting proud on the water. "I'm not a particularly confident swimmer should something go wrong."

"We do, don't worry. Besides, you have me to look after you."

She firmed her lips and nodded as, after a brief conversation with the boatman, he boarded then turned to offer her his hand once more. The boat rocked slightly when she came aboard, and she stumbled against him as her feet found the deck. Her breath whooshed out in a rush as she put her hands out, her palms flat against the hard planes of his chest.

"I'm sorry," she said, moving away quickly and finding a seat.

"Don't be," he teased. "Having you throw yourself at me, well, it's possibly the brightest spark in my day so far."

She couldn't help it, she laughed out loud at the ridiculous expression on his handsome face. "You're breaking my heart, here."

"Somehow I don't think your heart is all that engaged," he said with a sharp look in her direction.

Ottavia composed her face into a smile to hide that his comment had struck a well-protected nerve. She did not allow her heart to be engaged. Ever.

"I'm sorry," he continued. "I didn't mean for that to sound cruel."

She looked up in surprise. "It wasn't," she assured him, but she wondered just how much he'd seen. Just how much she'd revealed.

Rocco opened a small compartment on the side of the boat and pulled out two slim line life preservers.

"Here, let me," he said, putting one over her shoulders and fastening the belt at her waist.

"There doesn't appear to be a lot to this," Ottavia said, plucking at the horseshoe-shaped casing he'd put around her neck.

"They're a low-profile type of vest that doesn't restrict

your movements. They're designed to inflate automatically if you fall into the water."

"Right," Ottavia acknowledged slowly.

She held her breath at his nearness as he double-checked the fastenings and fit of her life jacket. He was so close she could see the sunburst of gold that rimmed the pupils of his eyes before his irises darkened into the deepest amber. She couldn't help it, she had to breathe in the scent of him. Crisp and fresh yet with an underlying hint of spice and the forbidden that Ottavia instinctively knew did not come from any bottle.

"How do I look?" she said with an insouciance she was far from feeling when he stepped back.

She regretted her words the moment they were out of her mouth as he sharpened his perusal of her.

"Enthralling," he said after what felt like an eon. "But anxious. Are you not comfortable on the water? We can forget about it and do something else this morning."

"No, really, it's fine. I—" She hesitated a moment before saying the words that had startled her as they came to mind. "I trust you."

His features softened but if anything his gaze intensified. Ottavia found herself captive beneath his stare, her eyes drifting from his and lower, to the line of his lips. A loud squawk from a duck coming in to land on the lake broke the spell that had frozen time, and Rocco gave her a brief nod.

"Let's go," he said, before turning to the controls of the boat.

Ottavia focused on relaxing every muscle in her body as he expertly cast off the ropes from the stern to the boatman who still waited on the indoor dock, and began to power out into the lake. He kept the speed to a minimum, cruising sedately along and pointing out buildings and land formations of interest before he pulled the engine back to idle and allowed them to drift for a while.

"It's so peaceful out here," Ottavia commented. "I can see why you love it."

"Would you like to have a turn at the wheel?" he asked.

Ottavia thought about it for a moment. Sometimes fears were best met head-on. Dredging up her courage, she answered. "Okay, but I warn you I have never done anything like this before. I hardly ever even drive a car."

"You don't like to drive?"

"I rarely have to."

She noted the brief set to his jaw at her words and silently castigated herself for reminding him that other men usually paid for the privilege to see her driven wherever she needed to go. But what else did he expect, she rationalized—he knew her profession. And so would anyone else who questioned her suitability to join him in marriage. She couldn't consider accepting him, could she?

Rocco moved behind her as she came to stand by the wheel, his arms coming around her on either side.

"Is this how you teach all your boatmen?" Ottavia teased.

"No," he murmured. She felt his hands at her hair, sweeping a swath away from the side of her neck. The cool brush of air preceded the press of his lips against her skin and she shivered in response. "Only the ones I want to marry."

His voice was so deep and gentle that it strummed softly against her defenses, weakening them when she most needed them to be strong. It would be all too easy to accept his proposal, but there was still so much she needed to consider.

A beating sound filled the air and she looked up in the sky as first one, then another helicopter lifted off to hover over the castle and the lake briefly before turning and flying away. Princesses Sara and Bettina had departed. They would be alone now at the castle. No guests to entertain over breakfast, lunch and dinner. No more princesses vying for Rocco's attention. She would have him all to herself.

"Let's begin your first lesson," Rocco said, nuzzling the side of her neck again.

Somehow she managed to ignore her racing pulse and concentrate on his words of instruction, whispered close to her ear and filled with innuendo that made her imagination run wild. How did he have this effect on her? Why did she let him?

"Let's try for a little more speed," Rocco said and put one hand on the throttle and pushed it forward.

Ottavia felt her hair whip around her face, and his face, too, most likely.

"My hair—" she started to say over the roar of the engine as they shot across the smooth, clear water.

"Smells divine," he answered, pushing the throttle a little further. "Do a slow turn to your right," he instructed and laid his other hand over one of hers on the steering wheel.

Together they made the boat sweep in a wide arc and despite her anxiety about the water and his nearness, Ottavia began to enjoy herself. She laughed out loud as they shot forward again in a straight line. Intoxicating exhilaration pulsed through her. Behind her, Rocco was steady and the heat of his body imprinted through the sheerness of her blouse. While it was her hands on the steering wheel, he was still most definitely in command of the boat. And her, too, she realized. To her surprise, she didn't mind one bit. She couldn't remember the last time she'd felt so carefree or had had such fun. Or had felt so safe.

She puzzled over the sensation and the fact that it was Rocco who made her feel this way when for so long she'd relied only on herself. Part of her power over men had always been that they had needed her. Not the other way around. But over the past few days she'd found herself impatiently waiting to see Rocco in between his engagements with other guests at the castle. Listening for his step or finding pleasure in hearing the timbre of his voice as he drew near. Strangely enough, he made her feel happy, almost content. She couldn't recall anyone ever having that effect on her and she'd never realized just what a special gift it was. She, who had prided herself on never needing any man, was coming to rely upon him in ways she'd never anticipated.

She didn't want to need a man. Her mother had been that person. One who'd gauged every facet of her life by her ability to hold on to a man. So when her looks had begun to fade and her lover's eyes had turned to her daughter...

Ottavia's fingers tightened unconsciously on the steering wheel as she slammed the lid on her wandering thoughts. She'd overcome that time in her life and would never be that vulnerable ever again. She was forgetting her role here as courtesan—was allowing herself to be seduced instead by the splendor of her surroundings and the charm of her client. A client who wanted to marry her, to provide her with stability and affection—and maybe even love? Did she dare open herself up to that? "It's so beautiful, I never realized those cliffs at that end of the lake were so high," she said.

They continued to cruise along the lake, picking up speed as they neared the cliffs. It wasn't until she noticed Rocco begin to ease back the throttle that she felt a shift in his body language. Gone was the relaxed demeanor of before.

"What is it? What's wrong?" she asked, turning her head back to look at him.

"Go and sit down," he said, lifting his arm so she could

slide out from the controls and take a seat on the other side of the boat. "There seems to be something wrong with the throttle."

A knot of fear tightened in her stomach as she did as he'd said. From her perch, she watched him jiggle the throttle lever, but there was no discernible change in their speed. The other end of the lake zoomed up ahead of them.

"Hold on!" Rocco ordered as he attempted to sweep the boat into another arc. "Dammit!"

"What is it? What's wrong now?" She tried to sound calm, but she could hear the way fear streaked her voice.

"The steering's not responding properly, either." He looked up and stared her straight in the eye. "If this doesn't work, we're going to have to jump."

He quickly unlooped his belt from his trousers and tried to lash the steering wheel hard to one side, but the boat seemed to have taken on a life of its own. Rocco reached for Ottavia's arm and pulled her up. Together they staggered to the transom at the end of the boat.

"I don't think I can do this," Ottavia cried out.

"You have to. We're headed straight for the cliffs. If you don't jump we could both die."

"You go first," she pleaded.

"I'm not leaving you," Rocco insisted.

He braced himself, scooped her into his arms and hefted her over the side. Ottavia screamed as she hit the lake. The water was cold, shocking her into holding her breath as she briefly sank beneath the surface. Her life jacket automatically inflated, drawing her up to the top again. Water was up her nose and she couldn't see, all she could hear was the sudden roar of the boat's motor and then the most awful sound as it rode full tilt into the cliff face. She flailed about and tried desperately to see where Rocco was. Had he jumped, too, or had he still been aboard when the boat had crashed?

Debris filled the water around her, some of it raining down from the air and she began to scream his name.

"It's all right, I've got you!" Rocco appeared in the water beside her and wrapped one arm around her. "Hold on to me, I'll kick us toward the shore."

Ottavia did as he said, too stunned to do little more than be a deadweight for him to tow.

"You should be able to put your feet down now," Rocco directed as they neared the shallows of a small beach on the edge of the lake.

Her legs could barely support her but she somehow managed to find the strength to move under her own steam and staggered up onto the beach.

"Wh-what h-happened?" she asked as tremors of shock and cold shook her body.

"I don't know but I'm certainly going to find out," Rocco growled. "That wasn't just a simple malfunction."

She looked up at him. His jaw was a determined line and there was a glint of something almost feral in his eyes. Once more she was reminded of a jungle cat. Of strength and power straining to be unleashed. It was then she noticed the trickle of blood coming down the side of his face.

"You're bleeding!" she cried out and reached to see where his injury was. Ottavia pushed back his wet hair and discovered a small cut on Rocco's brow, just on his hairline. "It's not a big cut but it's bleeding pretty hard. I don't have anything to stem the flow, unless you can tear a strip off my blouse?"

"I have something better."

He reached into his trouser pocket and pulled out a soaking wet, folded handkerchief. He squeezed out the excess of water and handed it to her. Ottavia took it and pressed it against the wound.

"Does that hurt?" she asked. "I don't want to press too hard."

In response he put his hand over hers. "It's okay. Are you all right? You didn't hurt yourself when I threw you overboard?"

"No, no, I'm fine. Shaken, obviously. Wet. Cold." She gave him a shaky smile. "But fine. You saved my life."

Rocco opened his mouth, about to say something when they heard the sound of approaching boats.

"It seems we have been rescued," Rocco commented sardonically.

Ottavia wanted to say something, to thank him for what he'd done, but they were quickly surrounded by his staff, including a medic who took Rocco out to one of the boats without her. She was taken aboard a second vessel and before she knew it she was wrapped in thick towels and returned to the castle.

Once there, she was checked by a doctor and declared well enough not to require further medical attention. One of the older maids, Juliet, was appointed to accompany Ottavia to Rocco's suite and helped her out of her wet clothes and into a shower. It seemed as if the scent of lake water still clung to her, along with the stink of fear. She rinsed off again and again, eventually stepping out of the shower stall and straight into a warmed toweling bathrobe Juliet held for her.

She felt she ought to protest at such treatment, but the older woman merely shushed her and, using another warmed towel, began to dry Ottavia's hair. Juliet then sat her down at the bathroom vanity and gently combed out her tresses, exclaiming every now and then at how long and thick her hair was. When she was done, she extracted a hair dryer from one of the drawers and proceeded to finish drying Ottavia's hair off.

Without styling products and a straightener, Ottavia's hair became a wild mass of thick waves. Inwardly she groaned at the work that would be ahead of her to tame it back into its usual sleek fall, but right now she was far too tired to care.

"Good," Juliet said when Ottavia's hair was dry enough to earn her satisfaction. "Into bed with you and I'll have a tray brought up for your lunch."

"Bed? No, I'm fine, really."

"Just a short rest then," the woman coaxed.

"Okay." Ottavia sighed in defeat. She really didn't have the energy to argue.

She hadn't been in bed long before Juliet bustled back into the room with a tray. She lifted the covers off the plates to reveal poached salmon dressed with a fragrant caper butter sauce and a small green salad on one plate, and a slice of a particularly decadent-looking white chocolate and raspberry shortcake on another.

"You will eat it all," the maid said firmly.

Ottavia raised her brows at the other woman. "Who appointed you my keeper?"

"His Majesty," the woman said, wiping an imaginary speck of dust off the bedcovers. "He personally said to ensure you were looked after. Now eat."

"Is he…is he all right? His head was bleeding when I saw him last." To her surprise Ottavia's voice wobbled a little.

Juliet's stern expression softened. "He is fine. He came in to change while you were showering. He said to tell you he will be in his office and will be tied up in meetings for the rest of the day."

Ottavia could well imagine it. No doubt he'd be supervising the investigation into what went wrong out there himself.

"Well, it's good that he's okay."

"Indeed. Eat your lunch then rest. His Majesty requested you remain safely here in his chambers."

It was the word *safely* that persuaded her to do as she

was told. He had quite enough on his plate without worrying about her. Instead, he should focus on whether the trouble with the boat was deliberate or not. And, if it was deliberate, had it been aimed at him or at her? Ottavia picked desultorily at her food. Despite the aroma and the presentation she found she had next to no appetite. When Juliet came back for the tray she tsked in annoyance.

"His Majesty won't be pleased."

"Please, don't trouble him by telling him."

It was the last thing he needed to concern himself with. After the other woman left, Ottavia pushed up from the bed and sought some clothing. She would remain here as Rocco had requested, but she didn't have to stay in bed. Once dressed she went to the main sitting room and tried to find something to occupy her attention, flicking through magazines and then television channels until she gave up on both and allowed herself to simply sit. And to think.

She'd never considered her mortality before. Never stopped to wonder what might happen if, in the blink of an eye, her life ended. While she'd recorded instructions and left them with her lawyer as to what should happen if she predeceased Adriana, she'd never actually imagined it happening.

The reality was she could have died today. She and Rocco both. The thought sat uncomfortably—a tight knot nestled beneath her diaphragm. She got up and began to pace the room.

She thought she had control but today had proven it was an ephemeral thing at best. There was so much still that she hadn't done—so much she hadn't experienced. Ottavia had always imagined she'd have the rest of her life to decide when she would do the things she'd always wanted to try. She'd never watched a sunrise from the top of a mountain, or skinny-dipped in the sea. There'd been no time for travel, except at the whim of her clients, and there were so many countries and cultures she wished to explore, including revisiting the United States—the country of her birth.

Nor had she experienced the kind of love a man and woman could share. Logically, she knew it was possible. That not all men were like the man who'd attacked her fifteen years ago. But she'd never imagined for a minute that she'd want to know real love—real intimacy—for herself.

But now? In the aftermath of so nearly losing her life? It made her realize that she'd very possibly been wrong. Fear was one thing, but one had to learn to conquer it. She'd already won so many private battles, but this was one she'd always been too fearful to attempt to fight. Maybe it was time that changed. Maybe it was time to face all her demons. To be bold. To grasp life with both hands while she still could.

Ten

Rocco let himself into the suite and made his way through to his bedroom. He was exhausted. After the drama of the morning, followed by the rest of the afternoon in meetings, he wanted nothing more than to crawl into his bed and sleep for the next twelve hours.

An investigation was underway, under Andrej Novak's supervision, with inspectors crawling over the debris that had been pulled from the lake already. Not that there'd been much to find. That end of the lake was deep and there was talk that they'd have to bring in one of the navy's under-water robots to find and hopefully recover whatever was left of the boat's hull and engine. But Rocco had his suspicions about what had happened.

His fleets—whether they be air, water or road based— were always immaculately maintained. One system mal-function, well, yes—he could possibly accept that that could happen. But two major faults occurring at the same time? It had to be deliberate, which made it an equally deliberate attempt on his life and that of his courtesan. The knowledge left him with the same sick, helpless feeling of anger as he'd experienced when his sister had been kidnapped only a few short weeks ago.

It was one thing to attack him, but to attempt to take out an innocent at the same time? A growl slipped from his throat and he clenched his hands into tight fists. When he found out who was behind this, they would pay dearly, he vowed silently.

A sound caught his attention and he stiffened, listening carefully, his body poised for another threat. He was surprised to see his courtesan walk toward him from the balcony outside his bedroom—he'd expected her to be fast asleep at this late hour. She was dressed in a floor-length diaphanous white robe, her hair a tangle of wild dark curls that made his fingers flex with the need to feel their texture and dive into their glory. He fisted his hands in his pockets and drew in a steadying breath.

"Ottavia, how are you?"

"More to the point, how are you?" she asked, flicking on one of the bedside lamps before coming nearer and lifting a hand to his brow where a stark white dressing covered the five tiny stitches the doctor had insisted upon.

"Tired, angry, frustrated," he answered in all honesty. He caught her hand in his and pressed a kiss into her palm. "I hope you are suffering no aftereffects?"

"I am quite fine," she said, gently pulling free from his clasp but not before he saw the light flush on her cheeks.

She could try as hard as she liked, but she wasn't immune to him.

"Can I pour you a drink?" she asked, moving toward the ornately carved wooden sideboard that stood against one wall of the bedroom.

"Thank you, I could definitely do with one."

He watched her graceful movements as she selected two

crystal glasses, tumbled ice in each and then poured two generous measures of his finest whiskey.

"Do they know what happened?" she asked, handing him his glass.

"Not yet, but they will," he said firmly.

He took a long draft and relished the flavor on his tongue before swallowing.

Ottavia put a hand on his arm. "It wasn't an accident, was it? Someone tried to kill you today."

"They tried," he acknowledged and forced himself to tamp down the anger that continued to boil beneath the surface. "But they did not, and will not, succeed."

"I never really thought about dying before today," she said in a voice that reflected the shock she so valiantly hid behind her elegant composure. "I thought I had it all worked out. My future, what came next—I never stopped to think, what if there is no future?"

"For as long as I draw breath, I will make sure you always have a future, Ottavia. You have my solemn promise."

"That is more than a courtesan deserves."

She took a sip of her whiskey and the ice clinked against the side of the glass as her hand trembled ever so slightly. He hated to see her like this and hated knowing the attack against him was responsible for putting the cracks in the fabric of her existence.

"It is what every one of my subjects deserves, no matter their profession."

He took the glass from her and put it on the table with his own before grasping her hand and raising it to his face. He brought her fingertips to his lips and pressed a kiss against them. "There, I have sealed my pledge to you. Nothing can break it now."

"A kiss, on my fingers?"

"You're right," he murmured, letting her go. "I think

that is probably not quite enough. I should release you from your contract. Allow you to leave. To go somewhere safer."

A look of determination came into her eyes. "I was thinking along different lines."

He raised an eyebrow in question. "You were?"

"I was thinking, specifically, of the new contract you offered me."

Rocco's breath caught in his lungs. "In what way…*specifically*?"

He watched as Ottavia turned and gathered up papers from the bed. She handed them to him. He looked at her for a moment before turning his attention to the contracts—to her neatly inscribed initials on each page and to her signature at the bottom. In silence, she handed him a pen. Without a second thought he initialed and signed the documents, then let them fall to the floor as he reached for her.

She came willingly to him, raising her arms and sweeping her hands to the back of his head before pulling his face down toward hers. Her lips took his in a caress that sent his senses soaring to dizzying heights. There was no subtlety about her demand that he open his mouth, the same way there was no denying the way his body reacted. Every cell jumped to attention, focused on the woman in his arms—on the tug of her teeth on his lips, the stroke of her tongue.

When she pulled away he was breathing heavily, his heart pounding in his chest.

"I want to make love with you, Sire. Will you allow me?"

There was a roaring sound in his ears. He nodded, or at least he thought he did. Right now he felt a little as though he'd stepped into an alternate universe. One where dreams possibly did come true.

"Let me undress you," she whispered and her hands tugged at the buttons of his shirt, but he lifted his own to grab hers—to still them in their task.

"Ottavia, wait."

"Rocco, please. Let me."

"No."

"You don't want me?"

"Want you? Of course I want you," he ground out. "But answer me this. Was your decision made out of a sense of duty or recompense for what happened today?"

She hesitated and moved away from him. He instantly regretted ruining the moment, but in the next second she undid the robe she wore and let it slide off her shoulders, revealing her body clad in only a sheer white nightgown. His mouth dried as his eyes feasted on her. Through the gauzy fabric he could that see the dark areolae of her nipples had tightened into peaked buds. And, lower, the neatly shaped triangle of hair at her mound. She moved and her full breasts swayed a little with the motion, her nipples momentarily clearer then enticingly hidden behind the folds of the nightgown.

"If I tell you that I do not give myself to you out of some misguided sense of duty but simply as a woman who wants a man, what would you say?"

"I would say that it was the shock speaking. That you might regret your actions come morning."

"I am beginning to understand why you are so beloved by your people. You really do place the needs of your subjects first," she said with a smile before reaching for one of his hands and holding it, palm down, against one breast. "Feel me," she urged him. "Does this feel like shock to you?"

Beneath his palm he felt the firmness of her breast, the peak of her nipple a hard nub. He moved his hand so that he could swipe his thumb over that taut peak and felt her shudder, heard her sharply indrawn breath as she captured her lower lip between her teeth.

"No, this doesn't feel like shock," he answered her, his voice a gravel-filled growl.

She took his other hand, and cupped it at the apex of her thighs. "And here? Does this feel like shock?"

He was stunned by the heat that emanated from her. She pressed the heel of his palm more firmly against her and a soft moan slipped from her throat.

"No," he answered again. This time his voice was even raspier than before.

"Then allow me to make love to you, my king."

"You are certain?"

"Yes."

He looked up and met her gaze, met the fire that burned in her eyes, saw the flush of need that stained her cheeks.

"Undress me then," he commanded.

She made quick work of the buttons of his shirt, peppering his skin with small strokes of her fingertips, light licks of her tongue. He'd never allowed himself to be this passive before in his life—never allowed anyone else to hold the upper hand. But it felt right with Ottavia and somehow, instinctively, he felt he had to allow her to take the lead. By the time she'd rid him of his clothing it felt equally right to let her push him back on the bed and to allow her to climb over him.

Her thighs straddled his and her small hands stroked his body. Everywhere she touched, and even everywhere she didn't, felt alive in a way he hadn't experienced before. She took her time, exploring his body as if the male form was new territory to her and the fall of her hair across his skin added new levels of torment and titillation. Each featherlight caress of the dark curls made his nerves sing with need. Even the drift of the fabric of her nightgown was a torment. He bunched his hands in the material that pooled on her legs. It was as soft and warm as the skin of her inner thighs.

He had waited so patiently for this moment. Now that it was here it felt doubly precious, especially given the experience they had shared this morning and the agreement they had signed. She was alive and here, in his arms, in his bed, in his future. Willingly. It was, he realized, what he'd wanted from the moment he'd set eyes on her, and he was a man who always got what he wanted. The reality, however, showed every sign of surpassing his expectations.

This—every touch, every kiss—felt like a gift because it came from her. Without coercion, without a silent agenda. It was two people with a need for one another. A need that drummed through his veins with every beat of his heart.

His hands slipped under her gown, his palms burning as they grazed the curve of her hips. Through the buzz of desire that clouded his brain he identified that Ottavia stilled in her movements for just a few seconds. Her body in that brief moment was taut, as if she anticipated something unpleasant. But then she relaxed, her body easing again as he kept his touch light, his movements gentle.

She was a conundrum. A woman who oozed sensuality and confidence and yet her touch, her reactions, were those of a woman eager but uncertain in the bedroom. She bent and pressed a kiss to one of his nipples, her teeth teasing his skin, her breath hot and moist. Desire coiled tight inside him and he fought the urge to spin her onto her back. To shove her nightgown up higher until he could see all of her and then plunge into that part of her body that beckoned to him with a call that spoke to the primal need he normally kept buried deep inside.

His body shook with restraint as her hands, her mouth, drifted closer to his aching shaft, and when she captured him, stroked him, kissed him, thought and reason abandoned his mind and he could only give himself over to sensation.

Ottavia shifted, pulling her nightgown off in a swift movement that finally laid her body fully bare to his gaze. She was so beautiful she made his eyes ache. Her skin held a light tan, her breasts were full, her nipples dark and tightened into points that begged for him to touch, to tease, to taste. He skimmed his hands up her rib cage, cupping her breasts with a reverence he'd never felt before.

She shuddered and closed her eyes, leaning into the palms of his hands. A groan of need came from her and when she opened her eyes again she looked directly into his and he felt as if he was looking deep into her soul. The knowledge hit him like a bolt of lightning. His proud and beautiful courtesan was offering herself to him. All of herself. It was almost enough to send him over the edge, but he clung to his control with everything he had inside him.

She shifted again, this time lifting her hips and positioning her body over his. Rocco held his shaft, positioned it at her entrance and expelled a harsh breath. He wished he could speak, tell her what she was doing to him, but he recognized her need for silence right now in the look in her eyes as, with her gaze locked with his, she slowly lowered her body.

Rocco surged, meeting her halfway, filling her, feeling her body expand and accept him. She was exquisitely tight and it took the remnants of his control not to withdraw and rush upward again.

"You feel…" Her voice trailed away, lost for words.

"I feel *you*," he replied, his voice thick with restraint.

She smiled and moved, her hips undulating, driving him to the brink of madness.

"This is too much. I feel too much," she sobbed.

"Not yet," he ground out through gritted teeth. "It gets so much better."

He reached for her. His fingertip tingled as it brushed the hair at the apex of her thighs, as he caressed her, feeling for the bead of nerve endings he knew would allow her to fly free of the restrictions that still held her earthbound.

She gasped as he brushed her clitoris, crying out as he

pressed and swirled the sensitive bud until her entire body shuddered and clenched. Her internal muscles became almost unbearably tight around him, squeezing in an orgasmic rhythm that was his undoing. He couldn't hold back a second longer. His answering cry was raw, unfettered, as his climax ripped through him, his hips bucking as instinct overcame reason.

Ottavia lay sprawled over Rocco's chest, listening to the steady beat of his heart. She'd always sworn she'd never allow another man to touch her, but she hadn't counted on a man like the one who now slept beneath her.

Lovemaking such as this had been beyond her imagining. Realistically she knew her body had always been capable of pleasure such as this, but she had never trusted another soul with herself the way she trusted Rocco.

She'd come a long way from the terrified fourteen-year-old girl who'd woken up to find her mother's lover's hand across her mouth and his body pinning her against her mattress. She'd come a longer way from the excruciating pain of him forcing his body onto hers—tearing into her, destroying her innocence—and even further from the shock, the next day, of her own mother's betrayal when she'd overheard her negotiating a price to drop the charges for what he'd done rather than allowing the authorities to pursue him.

What she'd experienced now was nothing like the invasion of self she'd endured back then. There had not been a second where she'd felt powerless or frightened. The only similarity she could think of now was that she felt vulnerable. Not because she was afraid of Rocco, as she'd been of the man who'd raped a defenseless girl, but because she finally understood that Rocco was the man who had finally claimed her heart.

She'd protected herself for so long. Guarded her spirit

and her body with equal ferocity. And, when she'd given herself just now, she'd given *all* of herself.

Deciding to make love with Rocco had been the most difficult choice in her life to date, but she'd known without doubt that she couldn't go on the rest of her life without doing so. After the incident this morning, she had to experience all that life had to offer her—especially when it was hers for the taking with a man like him.

Rocco was different from any other man she'd ever met. Of course, he'd been born to a life of power and privilege, and he wielded that power as easily as most men breathed, but there was so much more to him. He cared—genuinely cared—about his people. For a man like him, one so used to command, to allow her to control virtually every aspect of what had transpired between them tonight, it defied everything she'd ever expected.

Emotion rocked her. She, the woman men wanted but could never truly have, had finally fallen in love.

Eleven

It was too much. She carefully lifted her weight from Rocco's slumbering form and slid from the bed. Picking up her discarded robe and pulling it on, she went into the bathroom.

She stood in front of the mirror, studying her face, searching for some monumental change in her appearance that possibly matched the immense shift in her mind and heart. How cruelly ironic that she should fall in love now with a man who had contracted her for marriage as easily and matter-of-factly as he'd contracted her as his courtesan.

Ottavia began to pace the bathroom floor. How had she allowed herself to get into this state, to fall in love? How had the commanding man, blissfully asleep in the other room, managed to work his way under her defenses and into her heart? It mattered little now, she decided. It was done. She'd given herself, and it had been her decision and hers alone. He hadn't been the first man to try to inveigle his way past her barriers, but he would most definitely be the only one to succeed. She knew without a doubt that she could never give of herself to another, what she had freely given to him.

Even so, the idea of returning to the bed with him was more than she could contemplate right now. Wired and wide-awake, she wondered if a soak in the bath might help calm her overwrought mind. She turned to the massive oval bathtub, turned on the taps and drizzled in a liberal dose of fragrant foaming oil. Soon the rich scent of roses filled the room. Once the bath was full she stepped into it, closed her eyes and inhaled deeply the scent. Ottavia began to feel herself relax.

It was done. She'd made her decision to lie with her king and it had been truly the most magnificent experience of her life. There'd only been that one moment, when he'd first held her hips, that she'd begun to experience the briefest of flashbacks, but his grip had been loose, not painful—his hands warm and gentle, not clammy and grasping.

She was so deep in her thoughts, she didn't hear the bathroom door open, didn't feel the lap of water as Rocco slipped in beside her in the massive bath. But she did feel his strong arms slide around her body and lift her onto his lap.

"I woke to find you gone. I didn't like it," he murmured against the top of her head.

"I wasn't far."

"Thank goodness. Ottavia, I have something I need to ask you."

"Ask away," she said, leaning back against him and accepting that, with him, she truly had nothing to fear.

He was a noble man. An honorable one. She could never have agreed to marry him otherwise. And he'd given her pleasure on a scale that had almost blown her mind. No wonder people became slaves to sexual pleasure if it felt like that. Arousal suffused her body, making her feel languid and more aware of Rocco's body behind hers.

"It isn't an easy question. But I wondered…"

She shifted and turned so that she faced him, her eyes searching his face. All she could see was indecision in his gaze. It shocked her. She'd never seen him anything but confident.

"Rocco, what did you wonder?"

Even as she asked the question she felt a frisson of unease trickle through the back of her thoughts.

"Are you, I mean, were you a virgin?"

Shock plunged through her. Had she been so fumbling, so inept in her lovemaking, that he'd suspected he was her first true lover? She wouldn't lie to him, she couldn't. Not to the man who held her heart even if he didn't know it. She drew on all of her experience and pulled her lips into a smile and forced a laugh.

"Not for many years," she said as lightly as she could manage.

Relief filled his eyes. "That's good. I would have hated for your first time to be less than perfect for you."

Tears sprang to her eyes and she looked away, but obviously not quickly enough. Rocco's hand shot out and gently grasped her chin, turning her back to face him.

"Tears, Ottavia? Why?"

"I—" She frantically reached in the recesses of her mind for something appropriate to say, but instead all she could feel was the overwhelming care that emanated from him.

That he would say such a thing, even think it, cut straight to her heart. Her first, and only time up until tonight, had certainly been the polar opposite of perfect and hearing those simple caring words from Rocco made her wish that somehow she'd fought harder, longer, anything to have prevented what happened—to have saved herself for this night and this man. Logically, she'd accepted a long time ago that the assault had not been her fault, but logic was hard to hold on to in a victim's mind.

She leaned forward and kissed Rocco sweetly on his lips. "You are a good man, Rocco."

He pulled her closer to him, kissed her in return, his hands sweeping around her back and sliding up and down her spine in a caress that lit a new fire deep inside her. A fire that cleansed and burned away old fears, old memories, old hurts. She kissed him back, her arms wrapping around his shoulders, her fingers tangling in the hair at the nape of his neck.

His arousal was a tangible thing beneath her and she moved against him, her body slick with rose oil and water. She ached to feel him fill her again as he had before, to send her soaring back to the dizzying heights of pleasure and satisfaction that he'd brought her to before. Rocco's hands slid around to the front of her body, first cupping her breasts—his fingers pulling gently at her nipples—before he pulled his mouth from hers and bent his head to first one peak and then the next.

Sensation spiraled through her, tugging at her core with an invisible thread that wound tighter and tighter, binding her to him in ways she'd never imagined possible. And then she felt his fingers at that central point of pleasure, felt them circle and press and circle and press. Bit by bit she began to ride a new wave, higher, faster, until a starburst of delight radiated from where he touched and spread to her extremities. She slumped against him, boneless with pleasure. Beneath her she felt his muscles coil and bunch and with a sweeping movement he had lifted her in his arms and was stepping from the bath. He set her on the marble top of the vanity and she gasped as the cold marble contrasted with her wet, slick, overheated skin.

"What—?" she began, then stopped as he spread her legs wide and positioned himself between them.

His erection stood hard and proud between them. She reached for him, wrapping her fingers around his length and stroking him firmly, marveling at the texture of his skin and the steely hardness that lay beneath it.

"Are you ready for me?" he asked, his voice deep and low, his amber eyes burning with a hunger that she knew deep down inside she could satisfy.

For so many years she'd thought she was a woman in control. She'd had no idea what control meant until now. It was there in every line of the man before her. In the veins that stood out on his neck, in the rigid posture of his body, the taut muscles of his stomach and arms. He waited, for her.

"Yes," she whispered, guiding him toward her, the coldness of the vanity forgotten in the heat of his gaze and the sheer need reflected there. "I want you now."

Her breath hitched as he entered her, her eyes sliding closed on the jolt of pleasure that shook her. She braced her arms behind her.

"Open your eyes, Ottavia," Rocco commanded.

She did as he said and once again, her eyes locked with his. He slid in a little farther, sending more zaps of sensation along her nerve endings, before withdrawing just a little. He repeated the move, over and over, until she was on the verge of begging him to go all the way. The sheer intimacy of looking into one another's eyes, their bodies joined as one, rocked her, and she caught her lower lip between her teeth—desperate to hold back the sound that built within from escaping.

"Look at us," he instructed. "Look at where we are joined."

Again, she did as he'd instructed and the moan she'd been so desperately holding back escaped from her. Rocco picked up his pace, his grip on her thighs tightened, his face and chest suffused with color. The wave inside her built and built as with each stroke he drove deeper, more completely inside her.

"Touch yourself," Rocco ground out, reaching one arm around her waist to support her. "Touch yourself as I touched you."

Her fingers were tentative at first, her touch light, but she quickly found a satisfying rhythm that worked with his movements and within minutes she was hurtling toward completion once again. The second her inner muscles spasmed she felt him release, felt the massive tremors that passed through his body and into hers. It was more than she'd ever anticipated could happen between a man and a woman. More personal, more spectacular—quite simply, more.

When Rocco pulled out of her she made a small sound of protest but that was all she was capable of. She was spent, lethargic with satisfaction. Rocco grabbed a towel and gently cleaned her before he wiped them both dry. Then he swept her up into his arms and walked back into the bedroom, turning off lights as he went. He placed her gently on the bed. She rolled onto her side and he slid in behind her, one arm around her waist, his broad strong hand resting on her belly.

"Now, we sleep," he commanded.

And for once, she didn't wait for him to say please.

It was dark and all she could feel was a heavy oppressive weight pinning her down. She tried to move, but couldn't. There was hot breath on her face. A grasping cruel hand on her breast. She tried to scream but a meaty palm covered her mouth, pressing down so hard she could barely breath.

Then pain, searing burning pain.

"Ottavia! Wake up, it's all right, it's only a dream."

Light flooded the room as Ottavia sat bolt upright, her heart racing and her body bathed in perspiration. Her breathing ragged. Rocco loomed over her and she instinctively shied from him. He moved away swiftly, but reached out a hand to touch her cheek and to wipe away a tear.

Only a dream, he'd said. It had been a nightmare then and it was a nightmare now. It had been years since she'd had one as bad as this. Normally she managed to pull herself awake, but this time she'd been locked in the past. Reliving every moment. She shuddered again.

"Are you all right?" Rocco asked carefully, still keeping his distance. "Can I get you something?"

Ottavia shook her head. Nothing could change what had happened. Not running away, not counseling, not taking charge of her life. She'd had days, months, where she'd wondered if she'd ever be all right again. But she was nothing if not a survivor. She'd get through this, and the clawing miserable aftermath of reliving her nightmare, as she had so often before. Breath by breath, day by day.

"Do you want to talk about it?" Rocco pressed.

"Not really," she answered. "I get bad dreams sometimes. Doesn't everyone?"

She shrugged as if it wasn't of any consequence but she could see that she hadn't fooled him.

"You were terrified."

"Like I said, bad dream. What time is it?"

"Four a.m."

She nodded. "I won't get back to sleep now. If you don't mind, I'll just get up and go read in the sitting room."

"I'll make you some tea," he answered swinging his legs over the edge of the bed.

She knew she should try to convince him to go back to sleep, but a part of her craved the company. "Thank you. That would be nice."

Ottavia picked her nightgown up from the bedroom floor and went through to the sitting room, while Rocco pulled on a pair of trousers. She watched as he went into the kitchen and filled the kettle and set it to boil. She was so used to coping—well, living through—these episodes on her own that it felt foreign to have company.

Even in the early days, after she'd run away from her mother and had eventually been put into a foster home, she'd simply coped as best she could whenever something triggered a flashback. Feeling Rocco's powerful and solid presence so nearby was an unexpected support. There had only ever been one other such supportive person in her life. Her first client. The man, in fact, who had trained her.

She'd been working as a chambermaid in a hotel and he'd returned to his room early one day and caught her reading one of his books. Rather than reprimand her, he'd invited her to discuss what she'd gleaned from its pages. When he'd offered her a job working for him as his companion, she'd initially refused—thinking he expected far more than she was willing to give. After her attack she'd been wary of all men, but he'd eventually earned her trust by gently mentoring her and encouraging her to expand her education and lift her horizons.

And now a king brewed her a pot of tea. Her mentor would have been proud.

"Better?" he asked, concern still evident in the lines on his brow and the expression in his warm eyes as he brought out a tray set with a teapot and two mugs.

"Yes, thank you."

He sat beside her and poured, then offered Ottavia a steaming mug.

"Want to talk about it?" he asked.

She hesitated then silently castigated herself. Hadn't she just spent the night sharing the deepest intimacy possible with this man? Hadn't he woken with her, stayed by her, made her tea—all without question? Moreover, she had promised to be this man's wife, the mother of his children.

He deserved to know. Somehow, she had to find the words to tell him.

She shivered, the malevolence of her nightmare still clinging to her mind. She didn't know if she could handle putting her experience into words.

Rocco interrupted her thoughts. "It'll be all right, Ottavia. You're quite safe with me. You don't have to say anything if you don't want to."

It wasn't fair. After the pleasure they'd shared they should at least be allowed to enjoy the closeness of honesty now, shouldn't they? Anger toward her attacker formed a dark and vicious cloud in the back of her mind. He'd already stolen so much from her. She would not allow him to taint this, as well.

"It's fine. *I'm* fine," she said firmly.

Rocco held his mug with one hand and reached out with the other to gently massage her neck. "Are you okay with this touch?" he asked, watching her carefully.

She didn't know how to handle this side of him. She was far happier dealing with the absolute ruler, the haughty, authoritative man who commanded and whom people obeyed. Not this man who now treated her with such gentleness and care. Emotion threatened to overwhelm her and she fought back the bloom of tenderness that rose in her chest. Control—she had to maintain control at all times. Unable to speak, she simply nodded.

His fingers were strong as they worked the remnants of tension away.

"If you ever tire of being king of Erminia, you could always get work as a masseur," Ottavia commented wryly.

"I'll bear that in mind," he said with a chuckle.

Twelve

It was good to hear her sound more like herself, Rocco thought as he felt her muscles begin to soften.

He thought of how frightened she'd been when he'd woken her. No, he thought, frightened was too weak a word for the horror and revulsion that had lingered on her face in the seconds after her eyes had opened. He'd wanted to press her for answers, to find out exactly what it was that had painted the stark lines of terror on her face, but instinct had warned him to tread carefully.

He might be her king, but she had made it abundantly clear she was not his to command unilaterally. It didn't stop him wanting to know what lingered in her past, though. Something had happened between them last night that had forged an inexplicable bond. A bond he did not want broken.

He looked at a clock on the wall. It was getting close to five. Almost time for him to start his day. For the first time in his life he resented his responsibilities. All he wanted was to be with her. To spend more time getting to understand this complex woman who was slowly but surely finding her way into his heart.

"Rocco?"

"Hmm?"

"You should know why…"

"Ottavia, if you're ready to share it with me, I would be honored to listen." He cupped her face gently. "But only if it won't hurt you to speak of it."

"No, you need to know," she answered.

She kept her eyes forward, her body rigid again as if what she was about to share was so painful she needed to brace herself before even speaking of it. He took one of her hands and folded it in his, giving her his quiet assurance. Then, he quietly waited.

"When I was fourteen, I was attacked," she eventually began, her voice faltering as she fought to find the words— as if saying it out loud made it all too real for her again.

Rocco fought the urge to rise to his feet—to smash something with a curled fist as rage boiled inside him. Attacked? Did she mean—

"He was a friend of my mother's. A very…close friend. Apparently his attraction for her was on the wane and he was casting around for something—someone—younger."

She hesitated and Rocco tightened his fingers around hers. "You don't have to tell me what happened if it's too much."

"No, I need to—for me. For us." She drew in another deep breath. "It was late. I'd already gone to bed, fallen asleep. When I left my mother and her lover were listening to music and dancing in the salon of our house. He'd been watching me all night. Every time he'd pour my mother another glass of wine, he'd make eye contact with me and wink. It made me extremely uncomfortable so I made my excuses and went to bed.

"I had locked my bedroom door, as I always did, but I didn't know he had the keys to the whole house. I woke to his hand over my mouth, his voice in my ear telling me not to bother screaming because no one would help me. No one would even believe that I hadn't been asking for it. He told me that he'd seen the way I looked at him all night, all the enticing glances I'd given him. He squeezed my breasts, hurting me. I was too shocked, too scared to do anything. When he pushed up my nightgown I struggled, tried to scream. He punched me on the side of the head. It rendered me semiconscious—and then…" She took in another deep breath. "Then he raped me."

Rocco made a sound that came out somewhere between a roar and a growl. "I wish you had never had to endure such brutality. What happened after that? Did you tell your mother?"

"I w-wasn't going to because he told me she'd never believe me, but in the morning, as I tried to wash my nightgown, my sheets, my mother found me and demanded to know what had happened. I broke down and told her. I kept saying I was sorry. I felt so defiled, so dirty. Had it been my fault? Had I been coming on to him as he'd said? After all, hadn't we made eye contact several times that night?"

Rocco waved one hand in a dismissive movement. "Never! How could it be your fault? You were an innocent."

"I know that now."

"Did your mother report him to the authorities?"

"She started to. I heard them arguing in her room, afterward. She was bargaining with him."

Rocco's blood ran cold. "Bargaining?"

"She wanted payment from him for taking my virginity. She said she wouldn't press charges if he paid up. I got the impression that if he paid enough…she'd let him have access to me again."

She said the words so simply but he felt their weight

as if it was crushing him. That she'd had to go through that—having the very person who should have been her advocate abuse her trust and attempt to use her that way—horrified him.

"I didn't stick around to wait and see what agreement they came to. I went to my room, grabbed my schoolbag, threw in some clothes and left. I never went back."

Rocco stood, unable to sit still a moment longer. If he didn't move he'd smash something and probably terrify Ottavia in the bargain. Ottavia watched him pace but he doubted she really saw him. She was locked in the memory of her childhood.

"I did what I had to do to survive. I wasn't on the streets more than a couple of nights before child services found me. I refused to tell them who I was, where I was from. They found out, of course—my mother had reported me missing by then. She—she told them that I'd hit on her boyfriend and when he turned me down I'd run away like the brat I'd always been. She was extremely convincing, apparently. They believed her. They tried to return me to her but I made a huge fuss—even threatened to kill myself. Eventually they placed me with a foster family."

"What happened to your mother?" he demanded frostily, wanting no more than to track the woman down and see her get her just deserts—and that boyfriend of hers, too.

"She's gone now." Ottavia's voice was distant but he could hear the betrayal and loss that still clung to her memories. "It doesn't matter anymore."

"It matters," he ground out through a clenched jaw.

Rocco had never felt so helpless in all his life. He was used to meeting things head-on—to solving problems, even if it took every single ounce of ingenuity in his possession. But even he could not turn back time. Could not wipe clean the awful slate of Ottavia's past.

He cleared his throat of the obstruction that had formed there. "What happened then?"

"The foster home was okay. They mostly left me alone. I went to school, but after all I'd been through I struggled with my classes at first, and had to repeat the year. When I turned eighteen, I aged out of foster care. I had a year left of school, but no home and no income so I had to find work. I got a job in a hotel as a chambermaid."

He thought back to her friendliness with his staff. To her compassion and understanding to everyone from the maids who changed his sheets daily through to the head of his household staff. No wonder she related to them so easily. She'd lived their life, done their chores. Lived in their shoes. She should never have had to do that on her own.

"Through my work I met a man."

Rocco bristled instantly. "What kind of man?"

"An older gentleman. He offered me work. Not as his mistress, but as his companion." She let out a small laugh. "I guess you could say I was his Galatea. He saw to my education in so many ways, excluding the bedroom of course. I made it clear from the start that my body was not for anyone else. But he sent me to university, counseled me through getting my degree, supporting all my efforts to better myself. After he died I decided that I could continue doing what he'd taught me. Providing companionship, hostess duties, advice when required. I'd met several of his friends over the course of our relationship—wealthy men who knew what I had to offer—and it was easy to engage new clients. I've been in charge of my own destiny since."

Rocco's emotions threatened to overwhelm him. She'd overcome so much. And yet still a part of him ached for the teenager who'd had her virtue so cruelly torn from her. Her trust abused. Another thought dawned on him.

"Had you been with any other man since…?" His voice

trailed off. He couldn't bring himself to speak of the ugliness that had been forced upon her.

"No."

"Then I—"

"Yes."

Rocco drew in a long breath and let it go again as he processed what she'd just said.

"Rocco, I never believed I would ever want to make love with a man, especially not a man who could wield as much power over me as you do."

"Power you ignore, I might add," he injected ruefully.

"Of course I do." She laughed but her laughter was short-lived. "I thought I was healed of that time in my life. I've had counseling. I've made my own decisions. Chosen to be around the people I felt safe with."

"And you feel safe with me?"

She looked as if she was carefully considering his question and then his heart skipped a beat as a beautiful smile spread across her lips.

"I do, especially now. Until we made love, I don't think I'd ever truly felt less a victim and more a survivor."

He walked to the window and stared out into the dark. Sunrise would not be far off. As he stared at the changing sky he promised himself that one day he would find out who it was that had attacked her and if her attacker was unlucky enough to still be alive, he would make certain that the man paid dearly for his violence.

The sound of someone knocking at the main door to his chambers made him utter a string of curses. Was it too much to ask that they be left alone? With great reluctance, Rocco went to open the door. Sonja Novak—who else? he thought with a grimace.

"The media has gotten wind of the incident yesterday," she said brushing past him to enter the room.

"It was only to be expected," Rocco replied.

"Not of the failure of the boat," she said in clipped tones. Sonja lifted the paper in her hands and read from it. "'While the country remains in turmoil King Rocco flirts on his private lake with well-known courtesan, Ottavia Romolo. Is this really appropriate behavior for our head of state?'" She snapped the paper down onto the chaise in disgust to expose the enlarged photo of Rocco standing behind Ottavia at the helm of the boat. It was clear that he was kissing the side of her neck. "You do not help your cause, Sire."

His eyes narrowed. "Where did that picture come from?"

"Does it matter anymore?" Sonja pursed her lips in disapproval. "It can only have been taken by someone on the estate."

Ottavia lifted the paper. "This looks like an aerial shot."

Rocco rubbed his face. "The only helicopters that came over this airspace were my own, ferrying the princesses to the airport."

Which meant the photo had been taken by someone close to him. Someone he trusted. Rocco felt the slow boil of anger turn into something hot and furious inside him. Whoever did this would regret their treachery. In the meantime, he had fires to put out in the capitol. He had to show his people he was still very much in control of his country.

"Find out who was responsible for this and deal with it. They do not belong on my staff," he said.

"And in the meantime?" Sonja asked.

"I will return to the capitol and do what I can to extinguish this particular fire."

"You may not find that so simple. There are rumors—"

"There are always rumors. I deal only in facts. Arrange for my helicopter to be readied. I will fly myself."

Sonja smiled in response. "Certainly, and Ms. Romolo? Will she be joining you?"

Ottavia said rose to her feet. "I'd like to come with you,

if you want me to, that is. Perhaps it would help if we could make a formal announcement regarding our enga—"

"No, we'll talk about that when you get back. You will stay here," he said more curtly than he meant to.

Ottavia looked surprised. She recovered quickly but he sensed she was hurt beneath it. "Of course. Whatever you say."

"I shall alert the flight crew and advise the capitol palace staff to expect you," Sonja said smoothly and she let herself out.

Rocco looked at Ottavia.

"The timing of this is—"

"Unfortunate," Ottavia inserted smoothly. "But I understand you need to go. Now go, get ready."

In the bedroom, Ottavia curled up on the bed and watched as he entered his dressing room and selected a suit and tie. The lamp's light drew his eye to the shadowy curve of breast, revealed by the gossamer-thin material, and the sight of her punched longing deep in his gut. He wanted nothing more than to join her in that bed and show her just how much she meant to him, but he daren't give in to the compulsion. His duty to his people came first. When he returned he would make it up to her. In his pocket, his cell phone buzzed discreetly and he answered the incoming call.

"The helicopter is ready for you, Sire," Sonja informed him.

After thanking her, he hung up.

"I will be back as soon as possible. On my return, we need to talk," he said firmly.

Not trusting himself to be able to pull away if he kissed her, he strode out of the bedroom.

Thirteen

Fifteen minutes later, Ottavia watched through the window as Rocco's helicopter lifted from the helipad and circled the palace once before flying toward the capitol. Weariness dragged at her body. The night they'd spent together, on top of the nightmare and then telling Rocco of her past had all taken a toll. And then there was the confusion she felt over his behavior after Sonja had interrupted them. He'd been so distant, so abrupt. He'd barely looked at her.

Maybe she was reading too much into his behavior. After all, he'd just received more bad news, he would hardly have been jumping for joy. But deep down she felt that something had changed between them.

Her stomach growled. She supposed she ought to eat something but the idea of eating right now held no appeal. Ottavia took her time dressing before heading down one floor to the library where she'd spent much of her time since she was captive here. Settling herself on the cushions of one of the broad window seats, she started to read a novel she'd picked up a few weeks ago, but within minutes she was asleep. She woke several hours later to the unmistakable footsteps of Sonja Novak approaching her across the parquet floor.

"Can I help you?" she asked, rising to her feet.

"The king has called and asked if you could undertake a special project for him."

"He has?"

"Yes, there is a dinner this evening here at the castle. The king has given instructions that you are to act as hostess. General Novak will be assisting you."

Ottavia's stomach pitched. "General Novak?"

Sonja nodded. "In His Majesty's absence, Andrej is the ideal choice. He is familiar with General Vollaro, the Sylvano leader of their armed forces. The general and his wife, Rosina, have been invited here in a public gesture of goodwill between our two nations. King Rocco specifically requested you be there to entertain Rosina Vollaro. She's shy and inclined to drink too much when her husband's attention is occupied elsewhere."

"So I'm to babysit this woman while the men discuss business?"

Sonja raised a brow at Ottavia's tone. "I know you are more accustomed to mixing with *men* in a social context but I'm sure, with your many talents and vast experience, you can adjust."

As compliments went that one was about as backhanded as they came, Ottavia thought.

"What time must I be ready?"

"General Novak will meet you downstairs in the small salon at seven sharp. Do not keep him waiting. And, please, dress conservatively." Sonja looked her up and down in distaste. "If you are capable of such a thing."

She was gone as quickly as she'd arrived and her visit left Ottavia feeling distinctly unsettled. General Novak. A

shudder of distaste rippled through her. If it had been anyone but Rocco making this request of her she would have
refused. Still, she reminded herself, it was probably a good
example of the types of tasks she'd be expected to perform
once she and Rocco were married. Acting as his hostess
tonight was the least she could do for him.

The only shadow she could see looming was having to
spend time with Andrej Novak. But it was a small enough
thing, wasn't it, she tried to convince herself. A few hours at
most. And Rocco trusted the man implicitly, so she had no
reason not to afford him her courtesy, even if she couldn't
quite give him her trust. And yet, as she readied herself
later that day, she couldn't help but feel a sense of trepidation over what the evening would bring.

She'd been right to be concerned. Andrej Novak had
a real problem with keeping his hands to himself and
Ottavia struggled to keep a civil smile on her face as they
greeted the Sylvano guests on their arrival. As the couple
was shown into the small salon, Ottavia took the opportunity to step forward from the general's restraining arm
on hers to welcome the newcomers and to invite them to
indulge in an aperitif on the terrace.

After initial introductions, Rosina Vollaro and her husband drifted outside to enjoy their drinks in the evening
sun. Ottavia was about to join them when Novak sidled
up behind her.

"Don't think I'm not on to you," he whispered in her ear.

"I beg your pardon?" Ottavia replied, taking a step away
but finding her movement blocked by his body.

"Playing hard to get is attractive from time to time, but
let's face it. We both know what you're just lining me up
for when Rocco ditches you."

This time she managed to create some space between

them. She injected as much ice into her voice as she could when she replied.

"I'm here at His Majesty's request. Do not speak to me in this manner."

"Or what? You'll tell him?" The general laughed and it wasn't a pleasant sound.

"If necessary," she answered haughtily.

"You forget," he sneered. "You are merely a transient being in his world. Here today, gone tomorrow."

But that was where he was wrong. She wasn't transient at all. She was to be Rocco's bride, but that news was not hers to share, not without Rocco's authorization.

"Our guests—" she started, but Andrej Novak interrupted her.

"Are busily admiring the roses outside."

She cast a glance out the door—saw their guests standing by the profuse blooms of the potted Pierre de Ronsard rosebushes, reminding her that Rocco had left her a perfect bloom each morning until today.

"Don't think you can hold yourself above me, courtesan." He said the last word with disgust. "Our king already tires of you."

"That's not true!" she exclaimed.

"On his way to the helipad, he told me you were soiled goods."

A rush of icy shock drenched her, making her skin crawl. Surely Rocco hadn't told this creature her deepest, darkest secret.

Novak continued, a self-satisfied expression on his face. "He keeps no secrets from me. We…*share* everything."

His emphasis on the word *share* hadn't escaped her notice.

"I am no part of that," she said vehemently.

He laughed again.

"He didn't have to leave the castle today. You know that,

don't you? It's just that he couldn't bear to be with you a moment longer after you spilled the truth about your sordid little life to him."

"That's not true!" she blurted out.

"Isn't it?" He took a sip of his drink and then nodded in the direction of the terrace. "Go, you're here to work. Now work."

Ottavia didn't know how she managed to get through the evening but somehow she did it. She couldn't believe that Rocco had divulged her past to this vile man. Or to anyone, for that matter. She thought back to this morning. Tried to analyze his demeanor. Sure, he'd been withdrawn after she'd told her story and, yes, he'd seemed angry, as well. She'd assumed his reaction was due to shock, and perhaps that he'd even been angry on her behalf, but maybe there really had been something more. After all, he hadn't wanted her to accompany him—had even cut her off when she had been about to mention their engagement. And he'd left without even kissing her. Did that mean the general was right?

She felt brittle, as if the merest touch would be her undoing and she'd fracture into tiny pieces. She desperately needed space. The moment their guests left, Ottavia fled for Rocco's chambers, closing the door behind her and dragging in one breath after another.

She started when a knock came at the door and someone tried the handle.

"Who is it?" she called, even though her gut told her exactly who was on the other side.

"We need to talk," Novak replied, his voice hard as steel. "Let me in."

"No, I'm tired."

"That's a shame. I have a message for you from your king and I'm not about to deliver it through a wooden door."

Reluctantly Ottavia opened the door. "Tell me then,"

she said, holding the door and ready to shove it closed the moment he'd delivered his message.

To her horror, Novak pushed the door open and stepped inside. He gave her a smile that made her stomach clench.

"Please, give me the message and leave."

"I don't think so." He came closer and bent forward, inhaling the air near her. "Your scent, it's quite intoxicating."

Ottavia closed her eyes briefly and held her ground. "What did His Majesty want to tell me?" she said through gritted teeth.

"Oh, that he isn't returning tonight," Novak said flippantly before reaching out to twirl a tendril of her hair around one finger. "I guess that means you'll have to make do with me, yes?"

"No!"

Ottavia lurched away, felt the painful tug of her scalp as her hair caught in his fingers before releasing.

"He said I could have you."

"He wouldn't!" she said desperately.

"Oh, you think not? Hmm, I wonder…" Novak circled her like a hungry wolf. "Does he know about Adriana?"

Ottavia's eyes flew wide open. "What about her?"

A smug expression filled Novak's face. "I see he doesn't. It would be a shame, don't you think, for her to be removed from her private institution and placed in a government-run one."

"That will never happen. I pay for her to be where she is."

"And should your funds suddenly dry up? What then?"

"You don't have that power," she refuted.

"Don't I? It's a terrible thing when a person's bank details are hacked." He paused to let his words sink in. She knew that her investments were safe. They were handled by a former client who had remained a close friend. The general was overestimating his power and influence if he thought he could wipe out her assets without anyone interfering. But even though she knew that logically, she couldn't fight the instinctive fear at the thought of Adriana in harm's way.

"Remember what I told you, dear Ottavia. I see everything. I know everything there is to know about you—and Adriana. I can ensure she remains safe. All you have to do is one small thing."

She didn't want to ask what it was. She wouldn't give him the satisfaction. When she didn't answer he reached for her and pulled her close to him, his hand tangling in her hair and pulling her head back.

"Not curious as to what it is, courtesan?"

She'd always been proud of what she did but the way he said courtesan made her feel sick to her stomach.

He sneered lasciviously. "I see I'll have to tell you."

And he did—in awful, explicit detail. She'd originally thought Andrej Novak had to have some level of decency in him. After all, he was Rocco's childhood friend. And hadn't he taken a bullet to protect the princess from harm less than a month ago? Or perhaps he hid his harsh and sadistic side behind a mask of duty to his king. Bile rose in her throat and she forced herself to swallow it down.

"I won't do it. My contract is with King Rocco."

"You will, or your precious Adriana will suffer. How old is she again? Oh, yes—fourteen—the same age as you when—"

"No! You can't!" she cried in horror.

What he was suggesting was an abomination. She'd spent years doing whatever she could to protect Adriana. She'd give her life before she'd let anyone harm her. But Novak wasn't asking for Ottavia's life. He wanted *her*. She'd endured worse, she told herself, and survived. But Adriana wouldn't. Did she really believe he'd be able to get access to Adriana, especially if Ottavia rallied all her resources to protect her. No…probably not. But she couldn't be sure. Her resistance crumbled.

"Fine," she spat. "Let me go."

"Let you go?"

"I need to prepare."

"Is that what you call it? Perhaps you could start by pouring me a drink."

"Let me change first," Ottavia insisted.

"This should be interesting. By all means," he answered with a flourish of his hand. "Change, although I don't see the necessity myself. You'll be naked and willing beneath me soon enough."

Willing? Never, she swore under her breath as she retreated swiftly to the main bedroom. She grabbed a nightgown and robe, hastened to the bathroom and locked the door behind her. Did she dare remain here? Refuse to come out? No, she couldn't. It was Adriana's safety that was at risk.

She peeled out of the gown she'd worn this evening, the same forest green one she'd worn the night of the reception for the princesses, and slipped into her nightwear. When she managed to force her mind away from the ordeal she was about to endure, it circled back to her horror at the idea that Rocco had told the general of her confession this morning. Had the tension she'd felt in his body as she'd told her story been repugnance toward her? Was it true that he no longer wanted her? If so, she would have preferred he'd ended their contract there and then, than hand her off as if she had no further value.

Ottavia blinked back the tears that burned in her eyes. She'd been a fool. All her life she'd told herself she would never trust a man, never fall in love—and what had she done? The exact opposite. Well, she'd learned her lesson.

She stared at her things on the countertop, her eyes

alighting on the vial of sleeping pills she carried with her everywhere but so rarely used. An idea sprang to mind.

How many would it take to render Novak senseless? she wondered. They were fast-acting but he was a big man, strong and heavily muscled. Not unlike Rocco in build, or in looks, she realized, but thicker set. One tablet would barely skim the surface, but she knew that if mixed with alcohol their effect would be heightened. Her fingers were untwisting the lid off the vial even as the idea expanded in her mind. In a second two white pills lay in her palm. Now, all she needed to do was somehow get him to take them.

She would play seductress, coax him into having another drink, or two. And then, she would wait.

The man had the constitution of an ox, Ottavia thought in disgust as Novak stumbled with her in his arms while they danced awkwardly around the sitting room. She'd managed to crush the pills into his first drink, which should have knocked him out cold by now.

"Enough of this dancing," he said thickly. "Let's get down to business."

"If you so wish," she murmured in return, but even so her stomach turned. She couldn't go through with this. Making love with Rocco had been a different thing altogether to what Novak had proposed doing with—no, she thought vehemently, *to* her because she would never, ever be a willing party to this.

His feet dragged as he maneuvered her down the hall to Rocco's bedroom where he pushed her down onto the bed. He swiftly disrobed, throwing his clothing carelessly to the floor. His erection was thick and heavy and she felt her entire body shrink with loathing and fear as he stroked himself. She averted her eyes.

"What's the matter, courtesan?" he asked harshly. "Don't you like what you see?"

He lurched forward, clumsily landing on top of her, his body pinning her even as his hands ripped her nightgown from neck to hem, exposing her. He reached for her breasts—hungrily pinching and squeezing.

"You're going to like what we're going to do next," he slurred.

Ottavia swallowed the scream that rose in her throat. What was the point in crying out? No one would hear her, anyway. Somehow she'd survive this, she told herself, fighting back the fear that threatened to paralyze her. Suddenly she felt a spark of hope. Novak's eyes began to roll back in his head and his eyelids finally started to slide closed. Once he was unconscious, all she'd have to do was push him off her and she'd be free.

In a sudden rush of breath, he was unconscious. But his full body weight collapsed upon her and held her captive. She could barely breathe and struggled to get loose from underneath him, all to no avail.

A sound at the door penetrated the silence of the room and Ottavia's eyes riveted on the wooden panel as it slowly swung open.

"Rocco!"

Fourteen

Rocco took in the situation at a glance and was instantly sickened by the sight that greeted him. Behind him, he felt Sonja Novak push past and enter the room.

"I was afraid of this. I should have warned you, Sire," she started. "Ever since the reception, she's been flirting with Andrej. I'm so sorry you had to find out this way."

Rocco strode across the room and with an almighty heave pulled Andrej's naked form off Ottavia who, white-faced, scrambled to pull her ruined nightgown around her. Rocco couldn't tear his eyes from her, couldn't stop the overwhelming sense that he'd been taken for a fool. Anger rose, hot and swift.

Ottavia struggled to her feet. "It's a lie. She set me up. Her and—" A look of loathing crossed her features as she looked at the naked man unconscious at her feet. "That man. He told me you didn't want me anymore, after what I told you this morning. That you'd *given* me to him. How could you?"

Anguish streaked her face.

"She's the one who's lying. Look at Andrej!" Sonja pushed past him and knelt at her son's side. "He's unconscious. What have you done?" she shrieked at Ottavia. "I'm calling security and a doctor," she continued, pulling her ever-present cell phone from a pocket and dialing.

"Rocco, you have to believe me. He tried to force me—" Her voice trailed off into a sob.

"Oh, that's very convincing," Sonja said, straightening from the floor and grabbing a throw to put over her son's prone and naked body. "You're quite the actress, aren't you? And I suppose you told Andrej the sob story about your past that you fed to His Majesty, also? *Your* version of it, at least."

Rocco stiffened and looked from Ottavia to Sonja and back again. "What are you talking about?"

"I didn't tell him anything except that his interest wasn't welcome," Ottavia cried out. "And who told *you* about my past?" She turned to stare accusingly at Rocco, and he felt his aggravation burn even hotter. *She* was the one who'd betrayed *him*—not the other way around.

Sonja looked Rocco straight in the eye. "She's the one who lies, Sire. I have proof."

"Proof?" Nausea rose from the pit of his belly. He turned and headed for the door. "I'll be in my office. Bring me your proof."

"And Ms. Romolo?" Sonja asked.

"Have security stay with her here."

He did not look back as he headed down the carpeted hallway. Two security guards raced past him as he strode along. He turned and watched them enter his chambers and felt a pang of remorse as he heard Ottavia's voice rise in obvious distress. Hardening his heart, he resolutely continued to the end of the hall and took the stairs to the lower level where he kept his office.

Once there he sank into the leather chair behind his desk and rested his head in his hands. To think he'd rushed back here tonight simply so he wouldn't have to wait another moment to be with her. And all along she'd been playing him for a fool.

Twenty minutes later, Sonja Novak was at his door.

"I'm sorry you had to witness that," she said, coming into his office.

"Andrej—is he all right?"

"He will be fine. The doctor thinks the combination of his painkillers for his shoulder and the wine he had at dinner tonight may have overcome him. Unless of course that woman drugged him. They've drawn blood for testing and he is being monitored."

Painkillers. For the injury he'd sustained protecting Rocco's sister. "See to it that he gets the best care."

"Of course." Sonja nodded.

Rocco got up and paced to the window. He stared outside into the darkened gardens and beyond to the lake.

"You say this has been going on between them for a while?"

"Unfortunately, yes. Andrej tried to dissuade her but I suppose even he is not completely immune to a determined woman."

"You said you have proof that she cannot be trusted."

Sonja sighed audibly. "I do."

"Then tell me."

"The recent leaks to the media—I believe she is responsible. I ordered her laptop to be confiscated again and our IT security specialist found several deleted documents— one was an email from her to the national newspaper from two days before the reception for the princesses."

"And?" he prompted when she hesitated.

"The guest list for the reception was attached."

Rocco's hands clenched into fists of frustration. "Did you find anything else?"

"The photos of the two of you on the boat that day—"

"She could hardly have taken those photos herself," Rocco protested, still wanting to believe there had been some kind of mistake. Yet how could there be? Sonja and Andrej—he'd known them his entire life. Believing Ottavia would mean accepting that the Novaks were lying to him, and that couldn't possibly be true.

"No, but she certainly knows how to wield her seductive powers and her beauty to coerce someone into it. You do know one of your helicopter pilots resigned, effective immediately, on the same day? Suddenly, it seems, he has sufficient funds to establish his own charter business."

Rocco spun around to face Sonja. "But she can't possibly have been behind the sabotage of the boat," he said.

"Couldn't she?"

The seeds she planted were poison in his mind but he couldn't refute them. The information she'd presented just now was damning. Ice ran in his veins.

"If that is all, I would like to be alone."

"There's more."

How much more could there be? He'd been duped most thoroughly. A fool, led by his desire, just like his father had been and his father before him.

"She has a child."

"A child!"

"A girl, apparently. Clearly motherhood does not rank high among Ms. Romolo's attributes—her daughter has been institutionalized since birth."

So it had all been lies. Everything she'd shared with him, Rocco thought with a weary swipe across his eye. If none of it was real, then how was it able to hurt him so much? It shouldn't be so painful to give up the idea of a woman who'd only been a facade, after all.

"Have security bring her here and then when I am finished with her please see to it that she is escorted away from the palace."

"Do you want charges brought against her?"

"No, I just never want to see her again after tonight."

Five minutes later, Ottavia stood before him. While her cheeks were still streaked with the evidence of her tears and her hair was a tangled mess, at least she was dressed.

"Close the door and give us privacy," Rocco ordered the security team.

She didn't even wait until the door was closed before speaking. "Please tell me you're willing to hear me out," she begged.

"Hear more of your lies?" He gave a cynical laugh. "I don't think so."

"Rocco—"

"You will address me as Your Majesty!" he bit back.

He crossed his arms and stared at her, trying desperately to project indifference. She'd been unmasked as a fraud, a liar—someone who had actively conspired against him. So why did he still want to reach out to her, soothe away the false distress covering her features?

She took a step toward him, one hand outstretched.

"Stop!" he said. "You may not touch me. You've done your worst and you've been caught out. I want you out of my castle and out of my life."

"No, you can't mean it. Don't you see? I was set up. Sonja, Andrej, they must have conspired together."

"Really? Even now you continue to lie to me? You expect me to believe you over the two people who have supported me since childhood? And not just me, my father, as well. And at what point were you going to tell me about the child, or did you just hope I would never find out that you had one stashed away?"

"My sister? What does she have to do with any of this?"

Sister? But Sonja had said the girl was her daughter. Perhaps Ottavia was lying—but it was a peculiar lie, one that would be easy to expose. And her confusion seemed genuine.

For a moment, he started to doubt. Could Sonja have been mistaken? Was there some other explanation for all of this? Surely it was only logical to listen to both sides of the story…

No. He pushed the doubts away. That wasn't logic speaking, it was his foolish heart that wanted desperately to believe that Ottavia could not have betrayed him. He would not listen to it. Could not risk being seduced into trusting her ever again.

"You will leave tonight and a flight will be arranged for you to return to your home in the morning," he announced, walking to the door to let the security guards back in.

"You've got it all wrong," Ottavia pleaded behind him. "Please, don't send me away—let me explain. I love you!"

"No more lies, Ottavia. I have had enough."

Ottavia stared at him in disbelief. How had it come to this in the space of little more than twelve hours? Why wouldn't he believe her? Had she misjudged him so badly? She'd found him autocratic from the start but she believed there was more to him than that. Underneath the imperiousness, she thought she'd found honor, decency, even tenderness and protectiveness toward her. She thought she'd found someone who could love her. She couldn't believe she'd been so incredibly wrong.

She pulled every last thread of dignity she had left and injected a harsh note in her voice. "Our contract is over then?"

"The contract was void from the moment you lay with Andrej," he said bluntly.

Ottavia absorbed his words as if they were blows, each

one worse than the pain Andrej Novak had inflicted on her with his brutal hands. She'd given herself to Rocco, all of herself, in a way she'd never believed she would have the strength or courage to do with any man. And now he'd thrown it back in her face as if it was worthless. As if she, too, was worthless.

Tears of grief threatened to blind her but she would not give him the satisfaction of seeing them fall. A guard stepped forward to take her arm.

"That won't be necessary."

Her words were sharp, a mask for the pain that was tearing her apart inside. She'd trusted him, loved him, and it had come to this. She'd been an absolute fool.

The rest of the night passed in a blur. She was returned to Rocco's chambers where she packed her things, removing every last trace of her existence from his life except for her copies of their contracts, rent in two, which she deliberately let drop to the floor.

There'd be no more roses in the morning, no more verbal sparring at breakfast, no more walks at the lakeside. No more passion. She would never trust another man with her heart again.

In the days and weeks that followed, she struggled to hold herself together. It was all she could do to gather her thoughts for her visits with Adriana, dodging the assembled media who continued to congregate outside her building.

She couldn't seem to pull herself together. It was even making her physically ill, causing her to vomit what little breakfast she could manage to eat each morning. Finally, fed up with herself, she went to the doctor.

Ottavia arrived back at her apartment after her appointment not remembering a thing of the cab journey that had brought her home. At least she wasn't sick, she told herself over and over, but in so many ways an illness would have been easier to deal with than the news she'd just been given.

Pregnant.

As much as she wished she could avoid it, she had to tell Rocco. It took some time and a lot of finagling with several of her old contacts but finally she had a number through which she might be able to reach him. It was no surprise when Sonja Novak answered the telephone.

"It's Ottavia Romolo, I wish to speak to His Majesty," she said as assertively as she could.

"You have a nerve." The woman's voice dripped icicles.

Ottavia swallowed her pride. "Please, it's vitally important."

"King Rocco has no desire to speak with you, and I'm quite sure his instructions toward you were clear that he wished for no further contact," Sonja responded. "Goodbye, Ms. Romolo. Do not bother the palace again."

"Wait!" Ottavia blurted out. "Just wait a second…I'm pregnant."

Sonja Novak was the last person she'd wanted to tell, but she needed to reach Rocco and if it meant going through his rottweiler then that's what she'd do.

"Did I hear you correctly?" the woman said.

"I'm pregnant," Ottavia affirmed.

"And this should be of interest to King Rocco, why exactly?"

Ottavia closed her eyes and silently willed the other woman to believe her. "Because the baby is his and he needs to be informed."

Sonja's voice was terse when she eventually spoke. "Give me your number."

Ottavia rattled off her telephone number and listened as the other woman repeated it back. "I will pass on your message to His Majesty. It will be up to him whether or not he calls you."

And with a click the call was severed. It took two days, forty-eight agonizing and excruciating hours, before Ottavia's phone rang again. She checked the caller display. Private number. Hope flared.

"Hello, this is Ottavia Romolo speaking," she answered, injecting a confidence she was far from feeling as she took the call.

"So you claim to be pregnant?"

His voice filled her ears, but not the tone with which she was most familiar. The one that had shared his childhood memories as they'd walked beside the lake, or the one that had murmured to her in the darkness when they'd made love. No, this one was devoid of all gentleness or warmth. This was the voice of a distant monarch, not a lover, not a friend.

"I have no reason to lie to you, Rocco," she said softly. Her hand gripped the handset of the phone so tight the plastic creaked.

"Why should I believe the child is mine?"

"I did not sleep with Andrej. You are the only man I've had sex with in over a decade. It cannot be anyone else's. Why won't you believe me?"

"Because you lied to me about everything else. You should know that I'm well aware that you shared information about our guest list with the media, and coordinated the sale of photos of us on the lake."

"I did none of those things!"

"The proof was in your own computer. Do not attempt to contact me again."

The sharp click of a receiver followed by a disconnected beeping in her ear signaled his end to their conversation. Slowly Ottavia replaced the handset of her phone and sank to her knees. She hadn't stood a chance. Thanks to the manipulation of Sonja Novak and her devil spawn, he didn't believe her. He wouldn't listen. Ottavia's heart shattered into a thousand pieces.

Fifteen

Days later, her life almost resembled normal again when she got a call one evening that changed everything.

"Ms. Romolo?" the caller asked the moment she picked up the handset.

"Yes, who is this?" she responded.

The woman identified herself. "I'm a nurse at the Queen Sophie Memorial Hospital. You are listed as next of kin for a patient we have just admitted."

"Patient?"

"Yes, a Miss Adriana Romolo?"

Ottavia felt a hand grip her heart and give it a squeeze. When she'd video-called Adriana last night she'd seemed a little out of sorts and her caregiver had mentioned afterward that Adriana had a cold and was running a slight fever. Given her medical conditions, any illness had to be monitored carefully, but her caregiver was a qualified nurse. The situation must be serious if Adriana had been taken to the hospital.

The caller continued. "She's been diagnosed with pneumonia. We would like you to come as soon as you can."

Ottavia got the details from the nurse then quickly gathered her things and called a cab to take her to the hospital. Traffic was heavy through the city center and she sat perched at the edge of her seat for the entire journey as if doing so could make the cab drive faster. The second they pulled up outside the main entrance, she flung a fistful of notes at the driver and scrambled from the vehicle. She found her way to the nurses' station where she identified herself.

The nurse introduced herself. "Hi, I'm the one who called. Come with me," she said and gestured for Ottavia to follow her.

They were nearing a room when an alarm sounded, its insistent beep drawing staff from all corners of the ward.

"Wait here!" the nurse instructed.

But Ottavia couldn't wait. This had to be Adriana's room. She slipped in behind a white-coated doctor and watched in horror as she heard him instruct the nurse to drop the back of the bed. Lines and monitors were systematically checked, and a team started CPR on the small frame lying on the hospital mattress. They worked on her for what seemed like hours. Ottavia's eyes remained riveted to the machine, willing it to jump into life, but all it reflected back was a flat line and that awful monotone.

No heartbeat—no matter what they did, there was no heartbeat.

She'd known that Adriana's heart was weak—her long-term prognosis had never been good. Losing Adriana prematurely was always something she'd known would happen in the future. She just never expected the future would be now.

Numbly she heard the doctor call time of death and, one by one, the staff began to peel away. Somehow she coped through the condolences and the medical explanations that were offered. Somehow she held herself together—right up until they left her alone in the room with her baby sister.

She drew up beside the bed, lifted a hand to smooth away the dark tumble of hair that framed Adriana's round face. Tears poured from her and Ottavia made no effort to hold them back.

From the moment she had known of her sister's existence she'd done all that was within her power to keep her safe, to provide a decent life for her. When she was only eighteen she'd taken a then three-year-old Adriana from the government institution where their mother had abandoned her. A Down syndrome child, especially one with high needs like Adriana's, was not the kind of accessory a woman like their mother had wanted hanging around and, regrettably, their country provided minimal care for such children.

Ottavia had spent every cent she could toward her upkeep. Maximizing her earning potential had always been foremost in her mind because without it, Adriana would have had next to no happiness or comfort in her life at all. The plan had always been for Ottavia to save until she could retire and then get a place for the two of them together. She had the money now—the king had had the money from her initial contract with him deposited into her account as a final insult. And she was more than ready to retire. But it wouldn't be the same without Adriana.

"I love you," Ottavia said to the still form on the bed in a voice that was thick with tears. "I will *always* love you, my darling girl."

She bent and pressed a kiss to her sister's smooth forehead and then walked out of the room. There were papers to sign, a funeral to organize, a life to rebuild on her own. She rested the palm of her hand against her lower belly. Not entirely alone, she reminded herself and the thought gave her strength.

The next few days passed in a blur. Adriana's graveside service was attended by only a handful of people, but those that were there had at least known and cared for her. Afterward, Ottavia hosted a small supper at her apartment.

"What will you do now?" asked one of the therapists from the institution where Adriana had lived.

"Now? I think I will return to the United States for a while."

"So far away?"

"I need to regroup my thoughts and decide what I want to do with the rest of my life." Ottavia admitted. There was nothing left for her in Erminia and the knowledge made her heartsick. Was there anything for her in the United States? It was doubtful, but at least there she wasn't known and she could walk through the streets as just one insignificant character among tens of thousands of others. And maybe, in time, she would heal.

Rocco paced the floor of his office in the capitol city. It had been four months since the debacle with Ottavia Romolo and last night his parliament had, after a close vote, requested his abdication. The people were ready to support the pretender on the throne...even though they still did not seem to know who he might be. But Rocco had just uncovered a key piece of the puzzle, and now was the time to act, before he ended up dethroned.

He thought back to the night he'd sent Ottavia away, at the intricately woven lies that had been presented to him. And he'd believed every one of them. He couldn't afford to dwell on that—not now that he had concrete proof of who had been behind it all. The knock that came at the door was followed immediately by its opening. There was only one person on his staff who had the audacity to do that.

"Sonja," he said, before even turning around.

"I have come for your decision," she said uncompromisingly.

"Decision?"

"Parliament's request to you last night to give an answer regarding your abdication. I suggest you make your announcement at lunchtime. I have arranged for the media to assemble in the palace receiving hall and I have prepared your speech."

He gave her a smile. She had no idea that she'd stepped into the noose. "Always so efficient. However, there will be no abdication, Sonja."

Twin points of high color stained her flawlessly made-up cheeks and her eyes burned bright with ferocity.

"No matter what you do now you'll never meet the terms of the old law. You *must* abdicate in favor of your older brother."

Must? The smile that had been on his face disappeared as he prepared to confront the viper in his nest that had hidden in the disguise of the person he'd trusted most. If he'd thought Ottavia's perceived betrayal was a bitter pill to swallow, this was so much worse. His entire family had trusted Sonja, and for what? So she could attempt to put her own son on the throne?

"You are mistaken. I have no older brother. You have to put aside your dreams for your son. Andrej can never be king," he said emphatically.

"He is your father's oldest child," Sonja spat back at him. "He deserves to be on the throne."

There'd been rumors—many of them—that his father and Sonja had once been lovers, but like so many rumors Rocco had dismissed them. Without proof they were nothing more than a nuisance. Even now, despite Sonja's words, he didn't know if Andrej was truly his brother or if Andrej and Sonja merely wished to believe it to be so. In all honesty, he didn't care. His father had been a philanderer.

Rocco wouldn't be surprised if there were several illegitimate offspring scattered throughout the country. What mattered was that Andrej was a man no one should trust as their king.

He had evidence now that the boat had been tampered with that day on the lake and, with the evidence from the money trail for funds used for bribes and to arm the men who had been responsible for abducting his sister several months ago, there was concrete proof that Andrej had been behind it all. Moreover, when the scandal broke of Ottavia's supposed affair with Andrej, several members of his staff had come forward to say that Andrej had threatened or blackmailed them into bed, and that if Ottavia—toward whom they still bore incredible loyalty—had been caught with Andrej, then he had probably done the same to her.

The picture was complete now. Andrej might or might not be the late king's son, but he was definitely a liar, an abductor, a blackmailer, a sexual predator and—if his plan with the boat had succeeded—potentially a killer.

"The whole country is unstable now," Sonja continued. "You think you can avert civil war? You can't. You call yourself the supreme leader of your nation but what do you know of military tactics? Andrej is the only one who can bring this country back to its former glory."

"After he created the instability we now face?"

"The instability I *helped* him create." She smiled smugly. "I knew about the succession law all along—I knew it would create the opportunity for *my son* to be crowned the rightful king. I would have been a far better queen than your weak-willed mother who wanted nothing more than to play with her flowers and hide from her subjects. But your father wouldn't listen. So I made sure that one day my child would reign. It wasn't so hard to wait, although persuading Elsa she didn't want to be your queen was a little harder than I expected. But enough of this—you have no choice now, you must step down."

The news about Elsa came as a shock, but the impact was dulled under the body blow of finding out just how twisted his formerly trusted advisor truly was.

"I am still king and I will fight you with every resource at my disposal," he warned.

And those resources were quite a bit more extensive than Sonja herself probably realized. She thought she had succeeded in turning everyone influential against him, but when Rocco had called for a secret session of the parliament and presented the chamber with evidence of all that the Novaks had done, the members had been horrified and shocked. Or at least, they had pretended to be. Perhaps some of them had known of the steps Andrej and Sonja had taken beyond the boundaries of the law…but now that the evidence was clear against them, no one was willing to be seen as on the Novaks' side. They had agreed with Rocco's decision to have them both arrested. He'd sent a security team to capture Andrej, but had insisted on confronting Sonja himself.

He pressed a button on his desk and four members of his security team entered his office immediately.

"Relieve Mrs. Novak of her electronic devices and take her to the detention center. Hold her there until further notice."

"You can't do this," she spluttered, already resisting the arms that now held her. "My son is the true leader of Erminia."

"Take her," Rocco said, filled with disgust for allowing himself to be so manipulated. For not seeing more clearly that she had been operating under her own agenda for several years now.

Sonja's protests could be heard as his team took her down the corridor. She would be held until she could be officially tried. Oh, they would verify her claim as well—Rocco had ordered the DNA test for Andrej. But whether her son was biologically royal or not, he was still subject to prosecution for the many Erminian laws he'd broken—or ordered others to break. And so was Sonja.

The head of his personal security entered the room.

"Sire, our men met with some resistance, but General Novak has also been secured. He has also been confined at the detention center along with several of his men."

"And the DNA testing?"

"Samples have been taken. The general didn't protest. He is quite confident of being proved correct in his claim."

As if the claim was the only thing that mattered! Didn't the man realize how much damage he'd done, how much trouble he was now facing? The mother and son were far too much alike, both certain that the ends justified the means... even if those ends included something as reprehensible as the disgrace and sexual assault of an innocent woman. But no, he couldn't let himself think of Ottavia now. Not when his focus needed to be on guiding his people through this crisis.

In the end it only took a week to disprove Sonja and Andrej Novak's claim. Sonja, of course, disputed the reports, saying they were rigged, but Rocco had taken the precaution of having the samples taken and analyzed by a laboratory in Switzerland, so there was no question of bias. With no royal blood to provide him any degree of protection from the law, Andrej was charged with an extensive list of crimes. He would be in jail for a very long time—which was a good thing for him, in the end. When King Thierry had returned from his honeymoon and found out that the man was responsible for Princess Mila—now Queen Mila's—abduction, he'd been ready to tear Andrej Novak apart with his bare hands.

The roll-on effect was immense as his people worked

behind the scenes to flush out the Novaks' supporters as quickly and as quietly as possible. No one was willing to publically support them once their crimes were unveiled, but there were plenty of people who'd invested heavily in the political instability the Novaks had courted, and they were not easily quelled. But, finally, the last of the Novaks' supporters was arrested and held awaiting trial. Riding on the wave of public support, a nationwide referendum was held regarding the succession law and, to Rocco's relief, it was overwhelmingly overturned.

He'd repaired his country—he'd held on to his throne. Maybe now he could begin to repair some of the damage to his heart.

Sixteen

He pressed the buzzer several times but there was no response from the apartment upstairs. Rocco turned and strolled down the sidewalk. People milled around him and traffic swooshed by on the wet road, oblivious to his turmoil. He'd thought it would be so easy. He'd decided what he needed and he'd come to get it—her. The crusading knight on his shining white charger. But, despite what his observers had told him, she wasn't there.

She couldn't be deliberately avoiding him. Rocco knew his visit to New York had been kept completely under wraps so there was no way she'd have had any idea that it was him requesting access to her. He must simply have timed his visit badly. His driver held the door open to the town car parked at the curb but Rocco shook his head. "I'm going to walk for a bit," he said to his security team who expressed their alarm immediately. But Rocco held firm. He wanted to be somewhere where he could watch the entrance to Ottavia's building. Where he could see if she returned. Where she couldn't spot him and decide not to return home until he was gone. Down the street was Union Square Park. "I'll head over there."

His team surrounded him at the crosswalk, protecting him even while attempting to look as though he was just another New Yorker bustling about on a Saturday morning rugged up against the autumn air. Rocco accepted it as necessary—after all, he'd been surrounded by one team or another all his life. But he found himself wishing he could be a regular guy. One not unlike the man across the street, waiting with an eager smile on his face and a bunch of freshly purchased blooms from the nearby market in his hand.

A dark-haired woman ran along the sidewalk toward the other man, wrapping her arms around his waist and lifting her face to his with a welcoming smile. Rocco felt a stab of loss pierce him until he realized she wasn't the woman he sought. He still had a chance. For every minute he knew that Ottavia hadn't moved on—to another man, another relationship, another contract—he still stood a chance. He crossed with the crowd and entered the park. A squirrel dashed across the lawn and up a tree next to him, dragging his attention from his scrutiny of the crowds that milled around the farmer's produce market. Beneath the tall trees it was far cooler than on the busy sidewalk. He took a seat on a bench that faced toward Ottavia's street and pulled his collar up against the cold, early winter air.

It was busy at the market and the stalls were thronged with people. Rocco cast his gaze around, searching for the familiar shape and graceful movement of Ottavia's form, the sweep of her long dark hair or the bright-colored clothing she had always preferred. But there was nothing. Had this been a wild-goose chase?

He was not a man used to second-guessing his decisions. The investigators he'd retained had assured him that the address he now watched was hers and that she'd lived there since leaving Erminia after the death of her sister. He'd been horrified to learn the truth about Adriana. But his investigators had uncovered more about his beautiful courtesan than he'd ever expected to learn.

It had come as a shock to learn that she'd channeled so much of her earnings into a trust to ensure that the facility where her sister had lived would continue to run to assist other disabled children for many years into the future. He shouldn't have been surprised to discover that his courtesan was not only discreet, but she was a philanthropist, as well. She was every bit as wonderful as he'd thought her to be on the night she'd agreed to marry him.

God, he'd been such a fool. He should have believed her. He should have *known* she was telling him the truth. Rocco dropped his head and stared down at the ground between his feet. He was desperate to see her. To tell her what an idiot he'd been. To find out for himself if there was a chance she'd allow him to prove his love for her. The shame he felt at abandoning her when she had been the one telling him the truth consumed him. He could only hope she'd listen to what he had to say. A cold voice at the back of mind prodded him. Why would she listen to him after the way he'd treated her, especially when she'd called to tell him about the baby?

A child. *His* child, growing inside the woman he loved. And he'd sent her away.

"Sire?"

"What is it," he replied to his guard.

"I believe she has returned."

Rocco lifted his head and looked across the street; he saw the flash of the ruby red of her coat topped by the glorious fall of her long, dark hair. She waited at the crosswalk and carried several shopping bags. He didn't realize he was on his feet and heading toward her until he heard the sound of footsteps behind him.

"Fall back," he commanded over his shoulder, at the same time keeping his eyes on Ottavia—not willing to let her out of his sight for a moment now that she was here.

Two more steps and he was behind her.

"Ottavia."

His voice cracked as he spoke her name and she wheeled around to face him. Recognition was followed swiftly by pain and shock. Each chased across her features and he watched in horror as all color drained from her face. She swayed on her feet and he reached forward to put out an arm to support her, but she rallied in an instant.

"Don't you dare touch me," she said in a voice that could have stripped paint.

His hand fell uselessly to his side. It was at that moment that he noticed the bulge of her tummy, of the evidence of the babe she carried. A powerful wave of pride and protectiveness overcame him. He hadn't realized that facing the evidence of the life created by them would affect him so profoundly. At that moment, he knew he would move heaven and earth to provide for and safeguard his child—and Ottavia, too, if she'd let him.

"You shouldn't be carrying those heavy bags," he said and reached for them.

"I can manage," she said tightly.

"But you don't have to," he said and gently pulled them from her hands and passed them back to one of his guards.

Ottavia rolled her eyes. "And what now? I suppose you think you're going to walk me home?"

"If you'll let me."

He stared into her eyes, willing her to say yes. The lights changed and everyone around them began to cross the street. With a huff of frustration Ottavia wheeled away from him and started to walk across the street. Rocco hastened to her side, his hand at her elbow.

"I'm not helpless, you know," she bit out in response to his touch and tugged her arm away.

"I know," he answered simply. "I'd like to talk."

They reached the lobby of her building and she halted.

"The time for talking has long gone. There is nothing left to say between us."

Beneath her cool, impersonal words he caught a hint of the piercing pain he'd caused her.

"Please?"

It was the one thing left in his arsenal and thank goodness it worked.

"Fine," she said to him with a glare toward the security detail. "But not them. Just you."

"You heard the lady," Rocco said to his men and took back the grocery bags.

"We will wait for you here, Sire," the leader of the team said, although he didn't look too happy about it.

"He won't be long," Ottavia said before spinning around and heading inside the lobby.

The elevator was small and slow but Rocco relished having the opportunity to study her in the confined space. Her color had returned, to his great relief, and he began to notice the other changes in her that pregnancy had wrought. While she'd never been one of those thin, gaunt-faced women who paraded the fashion runways, the sensual sweep of her cheekbones and the curve of her jaw had never had quite this maternal softness about them as they did now.

His eyes dropped again to her swollen belly and he felt a shocking pull of shame that he'd missed so much of what she'd been through so far in her pregnancy. He'd abandoned her right when she needed him most—and when she most deserved his care and attention. Instead, he'd sent her away. Away to face the death of her sister. Away from the country he knew she loved. Away to prepare to face parenthood on her own. He'd never fully forgive himself…but she was a far kinder person than him. Dare he hope that she might forgive him?

The elevator shuddered to a halt and the doors slowly opened onto the top floor. While the building was old and the hallway narrow, it was fitted with well-chosen fixtures that spoke of a bygone era. The sound of their footsteps on the black marble floor echoed against maple panels lining the walls. Ottavia led Rocco to a door and inserted her key. She pushed open the door and gestured for him to follow her inside. He looked around as he crossed the threshold. The apartment was small and yet it was simply but beautifully furnished and had high ceilings and deep windows facing toward Union Square West.

"You have made a lovely home."

"Don't bother with small talk, Your Majesty. Get to the point of what you want to say and then leave."

He put the groceries down on a covered dining table and turned to face her.

"I thought we'd agreed you would call me Rocco."

"And as I recall, you reminded me of your station at our last meeting and emphatically instructed me otherwise," she said bitterly.

This wasn't going quite how he'd hoped.

"Please, Ottavia, can we forget about that night for just a moment? I really would like to talk."

She sighed and shrugged her coat off her shoulders and threw it over the back of a chair before she walked over to a well-stuffed sofa and sat down.

"So talk."

"You're not exactly making this easy for me."

She arched one brow and he ducked his head in acknowledgment of the cynicism he saw reflected in her eyes. He didn't deserve easy. He'd come prepared to grovel and it was about time he started.

"Get to the point. Why are you here?" she sounded tired

and he noticed the shadows under her eyes. Guilt smote his heart that he should be the cause of it all.

"I want to ask you for another chance."

"With a liar? A woman of no morals? Wow, you really must be scraping the bottom of the barrel in your hunt for a suitable wife who can deliver the requisite baby on time. Or wait—is it that you've run out of time and you're prepared to make do with me, after all?"

Her words flayed him, as he deserved, but as they sunk in he realized that she didn't know that he no longer needed a wife to remain on the Erminian throne.

"There have been changes in Erminia. A lot has happened since you left."

"And I should care about that, why exactly?"

"Because it means I know you were telling me the truth. And because I'm also aware of how badly I treated you. I want to make amends, if you'll let me."

"Amends?" Her eyebrow shot up again. "Do I look like I need you to make amends? As you can see, I am quite self-sufficient. I have no need of your amends, Sire."

Ottavia forced herself to harden her heart to the stricken look that crossed Rocco's face. Right now it was all she could do to hold herself together. But seeing him again—*here*—was almost more than she could take. She had encased her broken heart behind a frozen wall of silence. The words she wished she could speak would forever remain silent. She would not be used. Not by him or by anyone else like him, ever again.

Hadn't she sworn before to protect herself and her heart at all times? And yet, with him, she'd cast aside every vow she'd made to keep herself safe—all because she'd believed she could trust him. She would not make that mistake again.

She dragged in a breath. "You may be a king, but as far

as I am concerned you are no different from any other man. You speak of amends but you only seek to use me, to satisfy your own needs without a care for my own."

"I came here because I know I made a terrible mistake and because I know how badly I hurt you—how completely I betrayed your trust in me. I want to heal that hurt. I want to take you home."

"To do what? To birth your child and watch from afar as other people raise it in your image? I don't think so. As you can see I have a home and I am not beholden to anyone. I live my life, on my terms, just the way I want."

"And does it make no difference to you to discover that I no longer need to marry? That the threat against my position on the throne has been averted and that the old succession law has been thrown out and erased completely while the people who conspired against me have been thrown in jail?"

Ottavia listened in silence as he explained what had happened with Sonja Novak and her son. As he spoke the general's name an all too familiar sense of revulsion filled her anew at what he'd almost done to her.

She was unable to speak initially. Her mind was too busy assimilating everything he'd told her, turning it all around in her mind. She drew in a breath, then another and forced herself to look at him—to take in the lines of strain that bracketed his beautiful mouth, to see the tension in his golden gaze.

"I have only ever had sex with two men in my life. You, and the man who raped me."

She saw the flare of rage in his expression, saw how he struggled to tamp it down.

"I believe you. The man who attacked you is paying now for his brutality in a maximum security prison."

Ottavia blinked in surprise. "You did that?"

"I had to. I would have killed him if I could, but apparently we have laws against that. More's the pity."

His words left her confused but she pushed her bewilderment aside. It didn't matter now. Nothing did.

"Do you know what it meant to me to give myself to you that first time?" she said quietly. "I didn't just give you my body. I gave you every part of me."

"It was a priceless gift. I understand that now."

His voice was deep and filled with emotion. But she couldn't allow herself to be swayed by that. She had to press on.

"And then you threw it back at me. Despite what we'd shared, despite what I'd told you afterward, you *chose* not to believe me. Have you any idea how that felt?"

"And I'm sorry, Ottavia. So incredibly sorry."

"And then you rejected our baby."

For her, that had been the biggest betrayal of all. She stood and wrapped her arms around her tummy, protecting the growing life inside her. The son he'd so cavalierly rejected.

"I have been an ass, I know that. I beg your forgiveness, Ottavia. Please, I will never take another's word over yours again."

She stared at him, every cell in her body urging her to absolve him of the wrongs he'd wrought. To forget the pain she'd endured, the loneliness she'd felt since he'd had her escorted away from the one place in her life where she'd felt a true sense of belonging. From him. But the words wouldn't quite get past the lump of pain that was nestled deep in her heart.

"Can I ask you at least if I can have some access to the baby? Can he or she at least be permitted to know their birthright?"

"He," she corrected him. "Your child is a son."

Rocco's face was a myriad of pain and joy melded into one. "And will you allow him to know me?"

She started to shake her head but then changed her mind and gave a small nod. She'd known all too well what it was like to grow up without a father's love.

It would be unnecessarily cruel to deny her son the chance to know his father—and there had been enough cruelty already. She loved them both—her son and her king. But did Rocco love her? He hadn't said as much. He'd come here filled with remorse and promises to make amends, but she didn't want those kinds of promises. She didn't want to be bound to a man purely because she bore his child.

Faced with her silence, Rocco stood.

"Thank you. I should leave now," he said brokenly. "I treated you abominably and there is no recourse for that. I am so sorry for what I have done to you, but I will never be sorry for having known you or for the gift of your trust that you gave me even though I used it so poorly. I see that what I have said changes nothing and, in fact, as you quite rightly pointed out, there is nothing I can offer you."

Ottavia swallowed against the knot in her throat, blinked hard against the burn in her eyes as Rocco began to walk toward her front door. His hand was on the latch. If she said nothing now they would become strangers who shared a child. What they'd had, what they might have had, would all be gone forever. This was it—her last chance to tell him how she felt, her last chance to ask him if he felt the same for her. The words were thick and heavy on her tongue.

"Wait!"

Rocco turned to face her. Already there was a deep emptiness in his eyes—as if hope had been extinguished forever.

"There is one thing you can offer me," she said walking toward him.

She stopped when she was no more than a foot away.

"And that is?" he asked, his voice devoid of warmth.

"You could offer me your heart."

"It's already yours, Ottavia. It has been since the moment I saw you on the back stairs with little Gina in your arms and I realized that everything about you was what I wanted in my life."

The tears that had threatened before began to roll down her cheeks at his words. He loved her? He truly loved her? She struggled to find some presence of mind to reply in the rush of longing that bloomed in her mind.

"Then I think it's only fair to tell you that I love you, too. It would be foolish, don't you think, for us to live in different countries?"

Life surged back into his eyes and his lips pulled into a smile. "I agree, my courtesan. Where do you propose that we live?"

She smiled through her tears. "Where you are happiest, of course, my king."

"That would be wherever you are, my love. But it might make things simpler if we were to stay in Erminia, don't you think?"

"Yes, I think that would work quite well."

"And will you marry me, Ottavia? Will you become my queen and help me rule Erminia and return it to greatness?"

A surge of elation burst inside her. He loved her. He didn't have to marry her and yet he offered her his heart and his future, anyway. *Their* future—theirs and their children's.

"You didn't say please," she responded with a teasing smile of her own.

"Please?" He smiled in return.

"Nothing would give me more pleasure. Yes, I will marry you. I will be your queen, your wife, your lover and the mother of your children."

Rocco reached for her and pulled her into his arms. The

gentle bulk of her pregnancy made their embrace a little awkward but nothing had ever fit so right, she thought, as she lifted her face to his and, with her kiss, pledged her love and fidelity to the only man who'd ever deserved it. And she knew, deep in her heart, that they'd weather the future together and that they'd all live happily ever after.

* * * * *

MILLS & BOON®

Desire

PASSIONATE AND DRAMATIC LOVE STORIES

0816/51

MILLS & BOON®

The Regency Collection – Part 1

Let these roguish rakes sweep you off to the Regency period in part 1 of our collection!

Order yours at **www.millsandboon.co.uk/regency1**

MILLS & BOON®

The Regency Collection – Part 2

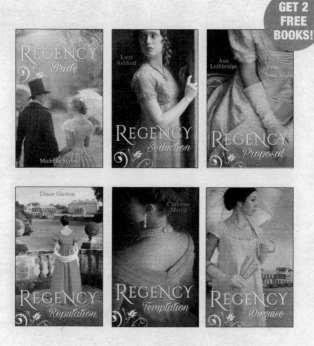

Join the London ton for a Regency
season in part 2 of our collection!

Order yours at **www.millsandboon.co.uk/regency2**